THE
MUSICIAN

THE
MUSICIAN

The Sequel to *The Actor*

DOUGLAS GARDHAM

[signature]

⚫iUniverse®

THE MUSICIAN

iUniverse books may be ordered through booksellers or by contacting:

iUniverse
1663 Liberty Drive
Bloomington, IN 47403
www.iuniverse.com
1-800-Authors (1-800-288-4677)

ISBN: 978-1-5320-4633-9 (sc)
ISBN: 978-1-5320-4634-6 (hc)
ISBN: 978-1-5320-4632-2 (e)

Library of Congress Control Number: 2018906447

Print information available on the last page.

iUniverse rev. date: 07/21/2018

To Patricia Lynne and James Philip—no matter how bright the sun shines or how hard the storm blows, you will always be my beloved sister and brother.

PROLOGUE

Neither a lofty degree of intelligence nor imagination
nor both together go to the making of genius.
Love, love, love, that is the soul of genius.

—Mozart

Thursday, February 7, 1985

As he returned, his mike was in his hand, its round metal weave pressed against his lips. He was singing the last line of the song. His hair hung in front of his eyes.

"Realize, sweet babe, we ain't never gonna part!"

Led Zeppelin was hard to play and even harder to play right, but the Release had found a way to nail it. Ethan loved the last line of the song they closed their show with. It made him think of Christa, though they always seemed to be apart.

It was Thursday, the last of their three nights at Bogart's. If he hadn't seen the name Bogart's lit up on the marquee that faced Bank Street, Ethan wouldn't have remembered they were in Ottawa—or, for that matter, any other place. There'd simply been too much going on in his world. The Release was near the end of a short span of gigs throughout southwestern Ontario, after which they would head back to Toronto and another couple of shows. Ethan wondered how much further they could go. The band wasn't the only thing he had in the works.

He'd just flown back from Los Angeles, a trip he'd taken without the band's knowledge. Upon learning where he'd been, Syd had shouted, "Are we a band?" from the doorway of her motel room. Furious, she'd threatened to leave again. She'd changed her mind about leaving once before, following their show a month earlier in Windsor, Ontario, after catching Ethan rehearsing lines at the house. Ethan thought she might have been serious if she'd had an alternative, but he knew she didn't.

His trip had affected the band in other ways. Syd was higher strung than usual, likely because he'd not been present to arbitrate the band's never-ending bickering, which went hand in hand with living with one another all the time. Ethan had wanted the band to live together in one house—for creative reasons—to live and write their emotions in song. But his intensifying personal schedule did not allow him to be in with the band and elsewhere at the same time.

They left the small stage and ran down the club's aged hallway, which led to the small back room that served as their makeshift dressing room. Worn-out carpet covered the cement floor, and torn posters of acts that had played there in the past lined the scuffed walls. Ethan shouted, "I fuckin' love that song! I wish I'd written it."

"You could have!" Syd shouted back. "Standing on the shoulders of fucking giants!" Ethan looked back at her as she added, "You killed it!"

He wanted a beer in the worst way. Nights like these were unforgettable. He was on fire; the Release was on fire. Fuck, the whole world was on fire.

Greg, their drummer, followed them into the room bent forward, his long brown hair hanging down, covering his face. His left hand, closed except for the long-nailed baby finger sticking out, came away from his face. In his right hand, as if paired with his drumsticks, was a small chrome cylinder.

"That crowd is fucked up!" Greg yelled, dropping his now open left hand to his side. His hands were large, and his skinny, sinewy arms made them appear even larger.

Ethan hated what had been happening to his friend since high school but felt helpless to do anything about it.

"It's you who's fucked up, my friend!" Ethan replied, close to the truth but choosing to ignore it. He raised his hand for a high five.

"Leave it alone, Eth," Syd said, surprising him with a stance he hadn't heard her take before. "He was awesome tonight. He's hangin' tough."

Gus, who looked as if he'd just come out of the shower as sweat beaded in his black beard, was behind Greg, carrying two bottles of Budweiser in each hand.

"Give me one of those," Ethan said, grabbing one of the bottles. He popped the cap off on the edge of an ancient oak desk against the wall, handed the bottle to Syd, grabbed another, and repeated the same trick.

"To the Release!" Ethan shouted, unable to restrain himself. "May the world ready itself for the music it is about to receive."

They raised their bottles. The glass necks clinked together.

"It's our time," Gus said in the lull between gulps of beer.

"You've got that fucking right!" Greg cried, his words a little slow but not slurred, enunciating *fucking* as though just saying the word made him feel better. "The Release is coming—lock your doors, and hide your women!"

"Really?" Syd grimaced.

Nothing beat the exquisiteness of performing well and receiving an audience's appreciative response. It put them all on top of the world. The four of them seemed to absorb the energy of those watching and listening. Time had no place when they were this together.

"There's close to five hundred people here tonight," Gus said, his hand stroking his black beard as if he were trying to squeeze the water out of it. "It's fucking packed."

"We're jammin'," Greg said, smiling. He thrust his fist holding his drumsticks into the air. "Nothing can stop us!"

Ethan took another gulp of his Budweiser. Nothing hit the spot like a beer after a show, but one wasn't going to be enough. Tomorrow was a day off; they could afford to party tonight. Greg was already there.

"We need more fucking beer," Syd announced, looking at Ethan. Her dark eyes seemed to have lost the glint he'd seen seconds before. She still had on the heels that diminished her petiteness.

He leaned his head back and drained his bottle. "Right on, sister."

"Then get that ass moving!" she shouted, opening the door.

"Right behind you," Greg added, nodding at Gus. He raised the red-white-and-blue-labeled bottle as if toasting them. "But don't wait up."

Ethan closed the door and followed Syd down the narrow hallway they'd just run down at the back of the building, which connected with a hallway on the north side that led up to the main hall. As they approached the corner, Ethan saw two guys in zipper jackets standing in front of them. He hadn't noticed them earlier. They were positioned on opposite sides of one of the exit doors. They nodded as Syd passed with Ethan close behind. He couldn't help feeling the two were up to something. *Drugs*, he thought, quick to anger, as that was likely the reason Greg had stayed behind with Gus.

As he passed the two, his anger changed to apprehension. He'd walked down that hallway several times during their stay without a thought to safety, but it felt different now. Syd was only a few steps ahead, but their vulnerability seemed suddenly in his face.

Syd turned the corner, closer to the loudness of the club. The hallway ahead of them was empty. Maybe he should say something to break the moment and his tension. Then, in an instant, he felt the heavy door. *Why now?* They were just going for beers. But the feeling of the door didn't fade, as if it were daring him, as it had before, to open it.

He stopped. "Syd?"

A hand was on his right elbow before he could say more. A split second later, a monstrous grip covered his face. He tried to pull his arm free but was too late. The attackers' hands were quick and overpowering. Ethan didn't have a chance and knew it. As he fought, another hand, stronger than his own, locked around his left elbow. Without thinking, he thrust his right foot backward, connecting with a leg that seemed to fold on impact.

"Fuck," a gruff voice said behind him.

Before he could pull his leg back, hands seized his ankle.

Ethan's face came close to the pair of overhead fluorescent tubes that lit the hallway as he was lifted and pulled backward. Pain lit up his knee as it bent awkwardly sideways. The hand that squeezed his face muted his scream.

"Syd!" he yelled as a hard hand mashed some kind of damp fabric over his face. Even if she heard him, there was little she could do. He bit into the cloth covering his mouth, hoping for flesh, writhing with everything he had, but he was helpless against the brute strength of his attackers. He was simply overpowered. He inhaled the sweet, pungent smell of decay that covered his face. He tried to hold his breath, but the exertion of fighting back left him gasping, and he gulped in air and whatever the cloth was soaked with. His head was swimming. He tried to scream again, but the sound amounted to little more than a muffled grunt.

This couldn't be real.

The light from the overhead fluorescents faded, as did everything else.

The club music played on.

PART 1

PRELUDE

What lies behind us and what lies before us are
tiny matters compared to what lies within us.
                                        —*Ralph Waldo Emerson*

Music expresses that which cannot be said and
on which it is impossible to be silent.
                                        —*Victor Hugo*

CHAPTER 1

Monday, May 21, 1984

The window blinds split the sunshine into separate bars of light on the brown blanket at the end of his bed. They helped brighten the room and his mood. Every day revealed a little more of what had happened. He had no recollection of where he'd been for five months, and he was constantly checking for what was real. It was difficult because he had no way of really telling the difference, except he could remember real things.

"Where's Kenzie?" his mother asked, passing the empty bed his roommate had vacated.

"Left this morning," Ethan replied.

"Did you know?"

"Not until this morning."

Kenzie shared the room with him. Ethan didn't think much would change. Kenzie never spoke. Ethan had never heard him say a word.

"Are you okay with it?" his mother asked.

"It's not much different and just as quiet."

He wasn't about to miss the person who occasionally stared at him but otherwise paid him no attention.

"I suppose," his mother replied, setting her purse on the chair by the window. "So what did you mean by what you said to Dr. Katharine?"

Usually pleased to see his mother, he couldn't explain why he felt a distance had grown between them in the last week or so. Something was missing. She looked older. The gray bags under her eyes seemed puffier; her eyes, always watery, were often brimming with tears when she looked into his.

He smiled as she leaned over his bed and kissed him on the forehead.

"Welcome back" was the first thing she'd said when she came through

1

the doorway of his room after his return. That had been weeks ago now. It was often what she said when giving him a kiss on the cheek, when emotion allowed her only a whisper. She had taken an apartment near Merivale Road following his admission to the Royal Ottawa Hospital in December. She was there now for her afternoon visit.

"I don't know," he said, searching her eyes for a clue as to what she was referring to. "Why?"

"Well, it was enough to make her question your progress," his mother said. Concern lined her forehead, which he remembered being smooth. She continued in a low, serious tone. "She mentioned having you assessed again."

"Really?" he replied as much to himself as to his mother. "And what's the harm in doing that?"

Ethan rubbed his forehead with his fingertips and brushed his light brown hair back. It was longer than he remembered and a little darker. Everything seemed to worry his mother now. Her anxiety made him nervous. Then he remembered.

"It was something about needing a doctor, I think."

His mother's eyes opened wider. "Why'd you say that to the doctor?"

A faint smile crossed his lips. There was something pleasurable in the memory, but he could recall nothing of the actual circumstances. Dr. Katharine had been at his bedside when he'd opened his eyes, and the words "I don't need a break; I need a doctor" had come out of his mouth.

"What was that?" she'd asked, wanting him to repeat himself, scrutinizing him as if she could discern what he was thinking through his open eyes. He had no recollection of anything prior to opening his eyes and seeing her. Wherever his mind had taken him had vanished.

"Yeah, I was kinda dozing. Half asleep."

He didn't know—or care—why he had said what he had to Dr. Katharine.

His eyes returned to the sun's rays on the blanket at the foot of his hospital bed.

"How are you feeling today, sweetie?" his mother asked, passing through the sunlight coming through the blinds, causing the lines Ethan was looking at to disappear momentarily. It was her usual course of conversation, which had become as tiresome as the hospital and its tedious routines. He didn't want to be there anymore—didn't need to be. He wanted to get back to real life.

"Good," he replied, giving his usual answer, slipping his legs off the bed.

He didn't like lying in bed, but it was often where he ended up out of sheer boredom. "Up for a walk?"

"I was hoping you'd ask," she answered, looking toward her purse on the chair. His asking her to go for a walk had become routine too. He relished being outside when the sun was out.

Ethan stood up, stepped forward, and gave her a hug.

"My patience is dwindling," he said as they left the room. He didn't like to think of the room as his, as it implied he was there to stay. They headed down the all-too-familiar hallway. The gray tile floor, the fluorescents that lit the opaque ceiling panels, and the colorless walls dulled his feelings and senses. The hospital no longer served him as a place of healing. It was captivity. He needed the freedom to move on.

Access to the third-floor elevator was a few doors down from the room. They descended to the lobby.

"How was your morning?" his mother asked as they passed through the front entrance doors into the sunshine outside. They angled right to the open area they'd strolled through once a day for the last week.

"Good but sad," Ethan replied as his mother put her hand on the inside of his bent elbow. "I dreamed of Mila again."

"Oh, Ethan," his mother replied, squeezing his arm.

He knew she didn't know what to say. Mila had been a recurring dream since his return. Each time, he would see her from behind. The long brown hair that covered her slender neck and spread across her shoulders always gave her away. In the dream, she would turn, and her brown eyes would take him away to a time before everything had been destroyed.

"Did you see Dr. Katharine this morning?" his mother asked.

Dr. Katharine was close to his recovery and saw him every couple of days. She was the reason he was still there.

"Yes," he said, sticking his right hand in the pocket of his Levi's while keeping his left arm bent so as not to lose his mother's hand on it. "She came by before lunch."

"What did she say?"

"That I'm close," Ethan replied, watching a fat robin hop through the greening grass in front of them.

"Close?" his mother asked. Her voice rose, but her face looked deflated. Her eyes looked lighter, more gray than blue. She had regained her son, but the uncertainty of his mental health seemed to permeate her demeanor, making the skin on her face droop, her arms hang limply, and her shoulders hunch. It saddened him that his well-being was likely the cause of her physical decline.

"Close to being ready to leave," he answered, attempting a smile. He hated the empty feeling his dreams of Mila left him with.

"How's Dad?" he asked, changing the subject. His father was back in Toronto on business matters. He'd be back at the end of the week.

"You know your father," his mother said before pressing her lips together. It was a common expression whenever his father's business came up. "He just can't stay away. But to his credit, he all but gave it up while you were recovering."

"Yeah, Dad'll never change," Ethan said, shaking his head.

His mother smiled and looked on ahead.

Ethan thought of Dr. Katharine as they continued along the sidewalk in silence. The sun was warm on his face. It felt good. He had mixed feelings about Dr. Katharine. His emotions were charged whenever she entered his room. He had an undeniable attraction to her, as if there were more to their relationship, but he didn't know why. Their familiarity seemed to go beyond that of a doctor-patient relationship. What he saw as love despite the twelve-year difference in their ages was not reciprocated. He had come to realize her interest was solely medical; he was an intriguing case—a patient with unusual needs, progressing through a complicated psychosis.

"Did Dr. Katharine give you any indication of how much longer you'd have to stay?" his mother asked, interrupting his thoughts of the doctor.

"Not really," he answered, turning to face the south side of the hospital and its many windows, "but it's got to be soon. I don't know how much longer I can stand it." His frustration came out in his tone.

His mother sighed and squeezed his arm. "You do seem better."

"I know, but you say that every day." He put his hand on hers and smiled. "I don't think that's enough."

They walked a little farther, reveling in the warm spring sunshine. His mother seemed to enjoy the weather as much as he did. Ethan looked at the buildings; he wanted to keep walking away from the constant scrutiny of the hospital's eyes. He didn't know what he would do. There were too many bad memories to stay in Ottawa, and engineering held no interest for him. But that was all second to getting out of this funny farm and assimilating back into what was real.

The cement sidewalk they walked along transitioned to asphalt. They followed its curved route out behind the hospital to an open area edged by a stream that eventually fed into the Ottawa River. Along the route, every couple hundred feet, were wood benches. It was nice to sit and enjoy the outside away from the hospital environs. His mother stopped in front of an empty bench near the water's edge.

"Let's sit for a while," she suggested, letting her hand slide from his arm. "It's too nice a day to waste indoors."

She sat down. Ethan remained standing.

For a moment, he had a sense of déjà vu, feeling he'd been there before, but try as he might, he couldn't connect the feeling with anything tangible. The sense of recollection faded and left him both aggravated and perplexed. Something was there that he couldn't quite latch on to. It was like recognizing a face but not knowing the person's name. He sat down beside his mother on the hard, freshly painted green planks between the cement supports at each end. Though short on comfort, the benches were sturdy.

"I noticed you're doing some reading," his mother said, crossing her legs and putting one hand on top of the other in her lap. "Browning something or other. Is it a new book?"

He'd found *Browning Station* on the windowsill in the room. He'd ignored it at first, having no desire to read or do anything other than sleep after his return. But boredom soon had driven him to do something more than stare at the four walls of the room or his silent roommate. It didn't take long to get caught up in the story of a man who appeared to be well adjusted yet was able to commit atrocious acts of horror. What troubled Ethan as he read the book was how a person could imagine and put down on paper such evil and not in some way have experienced it.

"I think it's pretty new," he replied. He'd put it down the night before after reading a particularly graphic scene: a victim had succumbed to the main character's idea of retribution in the biblical eye-for-an-eye sense. "Apparently, I picked it up one day from the nurses' station and brought it to my room. I read it for hours on end, but I don't remember any of it. Parts are quite disturbing."

Ethan stared at the water flowing by in front of them. It wasn't deep but was too wide to jump across. He was reminded of another time and place— alone, standing on a bridge behind a rusted railing. He could almost smell the cool fall air that had blown across his face. The water had moved fast below the bridge and his feet. He could feel his fear and then hear her voice: "Ethan, it's okay."

He saw her. Mila was at the bar beside her friend Sean. It made him happy. She winked.

"What's it about?" his mother's voice said, interrupting. He was standing up, his feet inches from the water.

"What?" he asked, turning.

"The book—what's it about?"

He'd gone away again. His mind shifted quickly.

"What's it about?" He repeated his mother's question to give himself time to think. "It's a story of how a psychopath fits transparently into society without drawing any attention to himself."

He turned back to the water, as if searching for meaning in its flow. He was glad to have his mother there, even if she wasn't the company he most desired. He didn't move.

"Ethan," his mother said, her voice quiet. He knew her methods; she wanted to be sure he was listening. "Are you ready?"

"Ready?" he asked, knowing what she meant but unwilling to admit it. Like a child, he didn't want to answer. "I don't know what I'm going to do."

Anger simmered inside him as he spoke. That god-awful question of what he was going to do—his mother had a thousand different ways of asking it. The water seemed to flow past like life, hardly giving him a chance to figure it out. Mila was dead. Would he ever be able to get his life back together again without her love? Life without her seemed almost unnecessary at times.

"You'll do what you have to do," his mother replied, getting up and moving closer. She rubbed her hand across the tension between his shoulders.

"I suppose," he agreed, hating the simplicity of the answer, which didn't mean anything. He continued to stare at the passing water. "I can't stay here. I think I'll go back to Toronto."

His mother stepped back. "You can stay with us," she said. "Only if you want to, of course. We know you can take care of yourself."

"Thanks. We'll see." He stiffened, feeling patronized, and then turned from the water. "Let's head back. It's getting chilly."

The real truth was he couldn't stay still for long. There were too many thoughts moving through his head. A dark brooding that he feared would take him away again usually followed memories of Mila.

As they headed back along the asphalt pathway, Ethan wanted to talk about Mila—what she meant to him, how her absence grew in his stomach—but it all seemed too much effort. Something inside him was broken, preventing him from touching and feeling the world. There seemed no way around it.

The agony was oftentimes unbearable. It would diminish but never go away. As they approached the entrance, his mother spoke first.

"Think you'll finish it?" she asked as he opened the glass door in front of her.

"What?" he answered, still struggling to find a way to explain his feelings for Mila.

"The book, whatever it's called—Brown something."

Her question brought back the book.

"*Browning Station,*" he said to correct her. "I think so."

They walked through the foyer. Patients in robes were sitting with visitors in the fake-leather chairs near the large front windows. Sunshine and company pulled many from their rooms. Ethan walked alongside his mother toward the elevators.

"Really?" his mother replied. She seemed preoccupied. He wondered whether she worried about his recovery all the time.

As they passed the front desk, he thought of William Avery, the main character in *Browning Station*. He'd read about the existence of psychopaths in society—brilliant people with evil, incongruous personalities who blended into everyday society like chameleons. Those they interacted with daily accepted their eccentricities.

As Ethan thought about the book, he caught sight of a person at the front desk. He stopped, drawn to what he saw for reasons he couldn't explain. He stared at the back of a woman's head. Her brunette hair was pulled back in a ponytail. The woman appeared to be in a heated exchange with a clerk at the admissions desk. While he stood there watching, the woman stopped, as if suddenly aware of the commotion she was creating. She turned toward Ethan. There was an immediate reaction of something akin to recognition in her eyes. Her lips seemed to take the prompt and curved into what appeared to be a pained smile. A warm comfort he hadn't felt since his return came over Ethan. The woman at once seemed to regain a sense of where she was and turned back to her dialogue with the person behind the desk.

"Who's that?" his mother asked, looking in the direction of the woman Ethan had stopped to look at.

"I don't know," Ethan replied, unhappy with his own answer. There was something familiar about her, but he didn't know what it was.

The elevator doors opened as they approached, as if awaiting their return. His mother stepped in. Ethan followed but not before glancing back in the direction of the front desk for the woman he'd just made eye contact with.

She was gone.

CHAPTER 2

Monday, May 21, 1984

When they arrived back at the room, Ethan was hungry. He wished they'd stayed downstairs and grabbed something in the cafeteria. He'd had his fill of the hospital's menu; he never wanted to see another bowl of lime Jell-O. His medication was waiting in a miniature paper cup on the corner of the brown table that cantilevered over his bed.

They weren't in the room five minutes before Jackie, who occupied the room across the hall, came in. Wearing a tight neon-pink T-shirt and even tighter bell-bottom jeans, she brought her big smile into the room. While most patients wore pajamas, Jackie preferred street clothes and full makeup most days. Ethan couldn't help but notice she was braless.

She was holding open a men's magazine.

"Oh, Ethan," she gushed, "you just won't believe the photos this month."

A woman's naked body stretched across the pages she held out. To some, Jackie's open sexuality might have been funny, if not titillating, but Ethan had seen enough already to know it wasn't. *Sad* was how he had described it to his mother, like a colorful toucan on display at the zoo for everyone to gawk at. Jackie set the open magazine down on Ethan's bed in the way someone might have shown a photograph of a pride of lions in *National Geographic*. Usually oblivious to the world around her, Jackie then moved to show the photograph to his mother, who was now sitting in the chair by the window.

"Ah, Jackie," Ethan said, seeing his mother grimace. Ethan knew his mother had witnessed far more inappropriate behavior in the last number of months, but that didn't mean she was used to it. "Mom's a little tired."

"I'm sorry to hear that, Mrs. Jones," Jackie said, her smile flattening. "You should rest on Ethan's bed."

Jackie started to move his table.

"It's okay, Jackie," Ethan replied, holding the table, knowing how hysterical Jackie could get if her feelings were upset. "Mom likes the chair."

Jackie looked at Ethan with the quizzical gaze he'd come to recognize as petulance. She smiled hard and nodded.

Ethan had taken a liking to a few of his fellow patients following his reawakening. Jackie was one such person. She had a heart of gold, but he was never sure what she might do. Twice before, she'd been to his room while his mother was visiting. The first time, she'd been about to lift the front of her sweatshirt. Ethan had stopped her but hurt her feelings in doing so. It had taken two nurses and an injection to calm her. He knew some of her story. Never-ending sexual abuse from a single-digit age and multiple arrests had landed her in the Royal.

"Are you staying for dinner?" she asked his mother, closing the magazine.

"Not tonight, Jacqueline," his mother replied, preferring to use her full name when speaking to her.

"Oh, there it is," Jackie said, fluttering multicolored fingernails at the window beside his mother. She turned and walked to the window. "My book." She smiled, picking *The Catcher in the Rye* off the sill. "I've been looking all over for this."

Ethan hadn't even realized it was there.

"Thanks, Ethan—you're a honey," she said, blowing him a kiss.

"Glad to be of service," he answered.

Jackie left with her magazine and book in hand, closing the door behind her.

"I must say, Ethan," his mother said, "there's never a dull moment here."

Ethan smiled, but the smile wasn't a happy one. The place that had been his home for the better part of six months was not a place of comfort. Many of his fellow patients were entertaining, but he knew too much now. The funniness had lost its luster. Sanity might have had its challenges, but dealing with those who had lost theirs had taken its toll on his mind-set. Ignorance might have been bliss, but insanity sure wasn't.

Ethan picked up *Browning Station*, which sat on the bedside table. The plastic covering the dust jacket was scuffed, dulling the book's cover.

"You know," he said more to himself than to his mother, "I will finish this. It'll keep my mind off things."

CHAPTER 3

Thursday, May 24, 1984

"It's difficult to explain, Ethan," Dr. Katharine said.

They were in an office on the first floor of the hospital. The doctors used it to speak privately with patients. Ethan had requested the meeting.

"You came out of a delusion your mind created. As with a coma, part of your brain was conscious and functional with your surroundings, while somewhere else, it was healing damage. It's difficult to understand, as you have no memory of what happened. It's like a dream. When we wake up, we remember little, if anything. We don't know what triggered your brain to release you, but it does make an interesting study for insight into the brain's workings."

Ethan heard part of Dr. Katharine's explanation but became lost in her blue eyes. He liked being in her company and looking at her. She made him feel normal and not like a patient being observed, yet he sensed something more, a closer relationship. But she gave him no indication of such a thing. Age lines extending from the corners of her eyes and mouth showed the years between them. Her smile was warm, not coy, but comforting. He understood her occasional wink as reassurance and nothing more.

"You don't need to be here anymore, Ethan," she said, raising her head from the file she'd been writing in. "I'd like to see you in a month or so and keep you on Orap for at least the immediate future. But keeping you here is no longer benefiting you."

"Really?" Ethan stared into the eyes that looked back at him through white horn-rimmed glasses. A twinge of memory nudged him. Her smile accentuated the C-shaped dimples at the corners of her mouth. He'd been there before. The feelings were there, but the place was gone.

"Ethan Jones," Dr. Katharine said, her firm voice jarring him from further reflection, "are you ready to rejoin the world outside?"

Ethan didn't say anything. He was remembering when he'd first met Dr. Katharine. Anger brewed with flashes of Mila and commotion. Images of a bloody room, a body on a bed, and the back of a person surfaced. The rage to strike out was nearly tangible, yet he stayed still. His face tightened as he clenched his teeth and balled his hands into fists. His heart beat faster. He could leave—but Mila couldn't, no matter how much he believed. Mila was gone; death was final. She could come back, but he knew that when she did, she wasn't real anymore. That had been Dr. Katharine's concern from the beginning—that he couldn't distinguish the difference.

That thing.

For an instant, he saw Robbie. He was bent over with a mouth full of blood, only he couldn't tell it was Robbie. He could only feel it was. He saw only the silhouette of a dark image standing over—

"Ethan?" The image vanished as Dr. Katharine spoke again.

Ethan looked at her. The sterile confines of the hospital filled his mind.

"Are you ready to leave?"

"Yes," he replied quickly and loudly, regaining his place in the office and the desk between him and the doctor. He smiled. "I am ready to move on." Then, without waiting for the doctor to reply, he leaned forward, looked hard at Dr. Katharine, and repeated, "Yes, I'm ready."

Quiet followed. Dr. Katharine spoke next.

"Then it's done." She scribbled something on the paper in front of her. "Here's your release." She handed him the paper. "You're something of an enigma, Ethan Jones. I've not encountered anyone quite like you in my professional life. But your stay here is over. It's time for you to take control again."

Dr. Katharine smiled. Her expression made him both melt and feel strong; its depth was much more than two weeks in the making.

"Thank you, Dr. Katharine," Ethan said, standing up. He shook her hand. "Don't take this the wrong way, but I'm happy to be leaving you."

Ethan left the office and headed back to his room to prepare for his next move.

CHAPTER 4

Friday, May 25, 1984

Strange, the hospital and the room—the place he'd called home for the last few weeks—were actually where he'd been living for almost six months. He'd gone into limbo while the world had gone on. He'd returned from the living dead.

He was packing the suitcase his mother had brought in, when his father entered the room.

"I doubt you'll miss this place much." His father laughed, approaching Ethan with his hand extended. His father's dark hair looked grayer like his mother's, but it was still neat and professionally trimmed. Parted on the right side, it looked thinner than Ethan remembered. His father shook his hand in his hard, nearly crushing grip. "I know I won't."

Ethan smiled. He'd miss a few of the characters the world called crazy but little else. They'd had a little party the night before to bid him farewell. Policy was to make the actual leaving quick and quiet to avoid upsetting the routine of the other patients. That suited Ethan just fine.

"Yeah," he said despite his misgivings of what awaited him on the outside. "It's time. I can't be here anymore."

He could only imagine what his parents had been through over the past number of months, including the uncertainty of whether their son would ever return from the confines of his delusions. Even seeing their son, existing in his other world, must have been heart-wrenching.

He thought of his mother and their conversation about being ready to leave. After his meeting with Dr. Katharine, his mother had asked if it was okay for his father to come alone to pick him up. She'd gone home to get the house ready for his return. Ethan thought the real reason was so she could be there to welcome him home and pretend for a little while the whole thing had never happened.

"Are you taking this?" his father asked, holding up a book he'd pulled off the windowsill.

"If it's *Browning Station*, yes," Ethan replied, squinting to see the cover. Like his longer hair, his eyesight had deteriorated during the time he'd spent in his head.

"I never read fiction anymore," his father said, staring at the cover. "I don't have time."

"I can't seem to stop," Ethan said, folding his yellow golf shirt into his suitcase. He looked up, expecting to see a blue blazer hanging in the closet, but in the instant it took to raise his head, the thought vanished. Instead, he stared at his father holding up the book. He hesitated, as if he wanted to say something but didn't know what. He picked up his green sweatshirt to fold.

"What's it about?" his father asked, setting the book on the bed beside Ethan.

Ethan gave the same answer he'd told his mother only days before.

At times, the story seemed so real that it felt as if it were happening to him. Dr. Katharine, on more than one occasion, had mentioned his fascination with the book. He had no recollection of the story outside of feelings that defied explanation. The character William Avery intrigued him. What he managed to get away with right in front his family and friends was remarkable. Avery's understanding of human behavior was extraordinary. His purpose was to right the wrongs of society regardless of the violence required by his methods.

"A real family man," Ethan's father said sardonically. "It's always the quiet ones. They're always observing."

Ethan continued to pack his suitcase, pulling out his T-shirts and a new pair of jeans his mother had purchased. Each of his T-shirts represented something. One displayed Winston Churchill's "Never give up"; another showed Van Halen's *1984* album cover beside George Orwell's *1984* book cover. Upon seeing the Reebok logo on one shirt, something shifted in his mind. His head started to hurt. Beads of sweat broke out across his forehead. He dropped the T-shirt onto the bed and leaned forward, grabbing the steel headboard with his right hand. It was a shirt he'd worn with Mila. He'd forgotten he still had it. For a moment, he thought he would pass out.

"You okay?" his father asked.

"I think so," Ethan replied, staring at the gray-white linens on the hospital bed. He picked up the Reebok T-shirt and dropped it into the wastebasket beside the bedside table. He had the memory; he didn't want reminders. "A little nauseated is all. My stomach has to catch up with my head, you know."

"Actually, I don't," his father said, looking at Ethan and smiling. "I can't imagine what you're going through, despite all the books Dr. Katharine has recommended or given your mother and me."

Ethan kept packing, uncomfortable now, knowing his father was watching. He doubted he would ever get used to the careful way people would observe him when knowing where he'd been. Yet here he was saying goodbye to much of what he couldn't remember. Tomorrow, the room would serve someone else who was somewhere else, just as he had been.

Leaving had been on his mind for days. He'd slept little the night before. How would he cope with rejoining the real world? How would he fit in? Would something set him off and take him away again, maybe forever? He tried not to think about all that could happen once he left the protected boundaries of the hospital. Doctors and nurses upheld these boundaries; he and his fellow patients lived within them. Those who didn't see them as boundaries needed to be there. But once the boundaries were realized, they became unbearable. His last nurse, Janice, didn't agree with the boundaries. She cared too much. She didn't stay. It took a special kind of person to accept the frailties of humanity and not take them on.

"I do feel pretty good," Ethan said, thinking out loud, "except when I think of certain things."

As he spoke, Mila's image surfaced. When he thought of her, he felt a sad tenderness, usually followed by an edge of rage that burned in his gut and moved upward. He wondered if he'd ever be able to think of her without anger following close behind. The evil done to her went forever deep inside him. He might have been able to train his mind to skirt around it, but he doubted it would ever go away.

Shift your focus, Ethan. He heard Dr. Katharine's words in his mind as if she were standing right beside him. He turned his head slightly—*the shift has to be physical*—and then breathed deeply and looked away.

"Dad?" he asked, trying to think of words that wouldn't excite his father in his request.

His father looked up.

"Can we go to the cemetery?"

It seemed strange he hadn't asked before, but before, the question would have prompted more questions—questions he didn't have the energy to answer or even know how to answer. He didn't want to think about it. He just wanted to go.

As soon as the words left his mouth, he wished he had phrased the request as a statement, not a question.

His father's hesitation was immediate. Ethan watched as logic took over his father's movements; he straightened his posture, and his head turned slightly to the left, as if his body were trying to smother the intuitive answer he might give his son. His father suddenly looked older; the bags under his eyes seemed puffier. He squinted, tightened his lips, and blinked, as if love and logic—the latter so important in the male dialogue—were colliding in his head.

"Do you think that's a good idea?" his father asked, his hand moving to rub his forehead. Ethan couldn't help but wonder how the conflict of what his father might want to say and what reason dictated he should never went away. Being right was a human obsession.

"Do you have a better one?" Ethan asked, an edge of anger in his voice. "Facing your fears—isn't that what makes us stronger?"

"You're always ready with an answer, aren't you?" his father replied, speaking to Ethan's words rather than the point in question.

"I've had a lot of time to think about it recently," Ethan replied, trying to smile, though his patience was thin. The anger was there, waiting to erupt—maybe. "What do you say?"

"What would Dr. Katharine say?" his father asked, still appearing to search for the right answer.

"I'm not asking Dr. Katharine."

His father continued to vacillate. His hand moved from his forehead to his hip. Ethan didn't want to admit that his father's concern was the likelihood of such a visit triggering a reaction that might set his son's recovery back weeks or, worse, forever.

"Why not?" his father said finally, rubbing his hands together. His lips pressed into a smile, appearing to question his own words. Being the same height, they looked each other in the eye. "If you want to go, we'll go."

"Great," Ethan said, lacking some of the enthusiasm he'd just exhibited in the exchange with his father. He was as conflicted as his father seemed about the idea of visiting Mila's grave, but he had youth and inexperience on his side.

CHAPTER 5

Friday, May 25, 1984

They had finished packing his father's new brown Honda Accord station wagon by the early afternoon. Dr. Katharine's caring words were in his head: *Give it time, Ethan.* He was as ready as he was going to get.

He'd been outside every day over the past week, walking the hospital grounds both with his mother and on his own. The fresh air helped clear his head. It enlivened him with energy that the hospital squeezed out of him. Carrying his suitcase to the car had the same effect those daily walks had had. He felt good.

But something still nagged at him. He was not as excited as he'd anticipated he would be upon leaving his temporary place of residence. He wanted to go—needed to go—but now that he was going, unexpected misgivings were creeping in. He was stepping into a new unknown. He was going home, where he hadn't lived for eight months. It might have been the right thing to do, but still, it felt intimidating. Dr. Katharine had said it herself: she'd have been worried if he weren't a little nervous. He was facing change, and change was hard always. How hard would it be to adjust to life with his folks again? He was anxious to see his sister, whom he'd seen only once since coming back. He didn't think of her much. But the change had to come. Prolonging it wouldn't make it easier. It was time, nagging uncertainty or not.

"Wanna grab a bite to eat before we go?" his father asked, closing the large back door of the station wagon.

"I'm not that hungry," Ethan said, wanting to get on with their trip. He hadn't been hungry since getting the news from Dr. Katharine that he could leave. "But a coffee'd be good."

"Coffee it is."

Ethan climbed into the car, looking at the front entrance of the hospital.

Disappointment wasn't helping his appetite. Other than a couple of goodbye waves from the nurses on duty and a hug from Jackie, he'd left according to protocol. The floor was operating as it did on any other day. Strangely, the place he'd so badly wanted to leave now had melancholy tugging at his heart. He fastened his seat belt. He couldn't remember the last time he'd been in a car. He'd never been in his father's new Accord. With leather seats and polished wood-grain panels across the dashboard and door, the car exuded his father's exaggerated style.

"I don't suppose you're up to driving," his father said, putting the key into the ignition switch.

"Later maybe," Ethan replied. "I have to get used to the confinement of the box before I start driving it."

"Ethan," his father replied, his tone disdainful, "this is not a box."

Ethan smiled, uninterested in debating the merits of his father's new car.

They had just started away from the curb when something hit the side of the car beside Ethan. He jumped and sucked in air audibly. His head banged the headrest.

"Shit!" he said, turning to look out the side window. "What the fuck?"

A man in a white T-shirt and jeans was standing beside the car, holding some sort of cardboard tube. He was motioning for Ethan to roll down the window. Ethan didn't move until he recognized the dark eyes of a bearded Randolph Baseman.

"Dad, it's Randolph," Ethan said, all but shouting in relief, lowering his window.

"Randolph? Who's Randolph?"

Ethan felt his father lean over against him to see who was there.

"Oh, you mean—"

"Hey, Mr. Jones! How ya doin'?" Randolph said through the open window. His father had become acquainted with Randolph during Ethan's time away.

His father said hello and said he'd grab the coffees to give Ethan a few minutes with his friend.

"This is fucking awesome!" Randolph said, putting a hand on the sill of the passenger door.

Randolph smiled widely, which was his usual expression with Ethan. Ethan pushed open the door and climbed out. They shook hands and locked thumbs.

"You're escaping without saying goodbye?"

"Apparently not," Ethan replied, closing the door, "'cause you caught me. What the hell are you doing here?"

17

"Heard you were heading out and thought I'd pay the Actor a visit before he skedaddled."

He'd become friends with Randolph after coming back. No one called him the Actor but Randolph. Janice, his nurse, had used the nickname a few times before her departure, but that was all.

"You got lucky," Ethan said, leaning against the side of the car. "We're on our way out."

Randolph had admitted himself to the hospital and had left a couple of weeks before. He no longer wanted or needed to be there. He had problems, he'd told Ethan one night, but he needed to face them. Hiding in the hospital wasn't resolving anything. He was taking from those who, as he'd witnessed firsthand, really needed help. His energy was better spent doing what he loved than worrying about the countless other things his mind picked up. There was a balance; anxiety was only part of it, not the sum.

"Glad I caught you then," Randolph answered. He was smiling and banging the cardboard tube against his thigh. "I'm getting my life and my art together." He held up the tube. "The art was never the problem."

"Your comics," Ethan said, figuring out what was in the tube.

"Graphic art, my boy," Randolph said, directing the tube at Ethan's chest as if it were a sword. "Have I taught you nothing of culture? Your words cut deep."

"Whadaya got there?" Ethan asked as he watched Randolph pop off the metal lid and shake the cylinder like a bottle of Heinz ketchup. Randolph let the pages of a brand-new comic unravel in his hand.

"I'm published, man. Got the first copy yesterday."

Randolph held it in his open palm. His face lit up like that of a proud father holding his firstborn. In a way, Ethan thought, he was a father.

"I had to bring it by. Hoped I wouldn't be too late."

Ethan looked at the cover. The face of a madman dressed in a tuxedo stared back at him.

"That's fucking cool, Randolph," Ethan said, almost breathless. Something in the colored image connected with him. The cover was disturbing to look at but impossible not to. Randolph had hit a chord. "I know him, and I don't know why."

Randolph smiled. "I'm relieved. You inspired him. You and that book."

"William Avery," Ethan said without hesitating. He'd read some more of *Browning Station* when he woke up that morning.

"Yeah," Randolph said excitedly. "Your afternoon performances made him real."

Randolph paused and took back the new comic. He carefully rolled it up and inserted it back into the cardboard tube.

"We were treated to some pretty amazing performances," Randolph added, grinning. "Forget television. Everybody watched, even the doctors. Christa loved watching you."

Christa?

The name stopped the conversation for Ethan. He'd heard her name only once or twice, but it triggered something deeper. His heart beat faster, yet the name made him sad.

"Sure, Randy," he said. As soon as the words left his mouth, he could tell something was different.

"You fucking called me Randy all the time."

"When did you get back from Japan?" Ethan asked.

"Just this morning," Randolph replied. "How'd you know? Do I look that tired?"

"I'm heading out for lunch," Ethan replied, but something wasn't right. "Join me? You can drive. It's your taxi."

Ethan noticed Randy's hesitation. He didn't just look tired; he looked exhausted.

"Well?"

"Ethan?"

Something shifted. The whole scene in front of him moved as if one life-size diorama were replacing another—like a living version of Disney World's Carousel of Progress.

"What?" he answered, his eyes locking on Randolph's.

"You okay?"

"Yeah, why?" Ethan answered, knowing something had happened. He'd gone and come back in an instant.

"You were different there," Randolph said, staring him in the eye while turning his head like a dog trying to understand its master. "You can't fake a faker, Ethan." Randolph squinted his left eye and added, "Most of the time, I know what's real and what isn't."

Ethan pushed out a laugh, not comfortable with his friend's insinuation. "That's what got me here," he said, pointing at the hospital over Randolph's shoulder. "Then they get in a quandary when they can't figure it out either."

They both laughed, knowing better than most what went on inside.

Ethan thought about what had happened between him and Randolph. *It's just nerves,* he said to himself. Facing the outside world again was a lot to take in. He was bound to encounter a few anxious moments. Randolph must have triggered something. "Nerves and anxiety," Dr. Katharine had explained, "wreak havoc on how the mind perceives and reacts." Going home and experiencing life on the outside would push him way out of his comfort zone in the hospital. "You're as prepared as you're going to get, Ethan," she'd added, patting his shoulder and smiling. "Sooner or later, you have to play it for real."

"Should have known you'd still be talking," his father said as he approached them beside his car. He was carrying three lidded Styrofoam cups of coffee.

"Did you expect any less?" Ethan replied. He said it as if it were a statement, not a question. Randolph's departure had been tough on Ethan, who'd missed talking with someone who was really present. Randolph had visited once since leaving. Released patients usually had no desire to return—especially sane ones. Reminders came often enough in the middle of the night, when the only escape was waking up.

"No, but we probably should get a move on."

His father handed a coffee to each of them and then walked around to the driver's side of the car to get in. Then, as if choreographed, Ethan watched a tall dark-haired woman approach Randolph from behind.

"Here you are," the woman said, stopping beside Randolph and grabbing his arm. "You're never where I expect you to be."

"Sorry, Rachel," Randolph said, putting his arm around the woman. "I found him out here—about to leave without saying goodbye. Rachel Duri, meet the Actor, Ethan Jones."

Ethan smiled and extended his hand. Rachel transferred the book she was carrying to her left hand and shook his hand. She was a big-boned woman with a large, soft hand. Her grip was light but had a "Hello; I'm here" firmness. Her brown skin was flawless; her round, smiling face was smooth. Crimson fingernails matched her lipstick. The dark eyes that looked back at him were edged in a purple eye shadow that made the whites of her eyes even brighter.

"Glad to meet you, Rachel," Ethan said, smiling.

"Likewise. Are you really an actor?"

Ethan kept smiling and shook his head.

Randolph interjected. "Sorry." He winced and turned to Rachel. "Ethan's the phenom I told you about who came back to the real world while I was here. He acted out the book." Randolph held up the tube in his hand.

"I don't know that *phenom* is the right word," Ethan said with a sigh, "but the Actor came from that other world, or so I'm told."

"You're leaving?" Rachel asked.

"Yes," Ethan said, trying to see what book was in her hand. "Randolph attacked the car as we were pulling away."

"That's wonderful!" Rachel exclaimed, seeming genuinely pleased for him. "I wish you well."

"Thank you. What are you reading?"

Rachel held up the book. "I picked it up in the shop inside."

"*Browning Station.*" Ethan smiled.

"I heard about the book on the radio the other night. Randolph's obsessed with it. Sounds creepy."

"Creepy and disturbing," Ethan said. "I've been reading it during my stay—both now and apparently before."

"You must know it well," Rachel said.

"Somewhere in here," he said, pointing to his head, "not that I can remember. It's like I'm reading a new book now."

"It's getting popular," Randolph said. "I've seen it in a few places."

Ethan raised his arm to check the time on his gold Seiko, as was his habit. It felt good to wear it again. The hospital had removed it—policy and procedures. Like a wisp of smoke, a thought came and went unacknowledged. It was almost one o'clock.

"I'd better say goodbye," Ethan said, lowering his arm, "before Dad gets too antsy. We've a long drive ahead of us."

He opened the passenger door. "Very nice to meet you, Rachel, though I don't know what you see in this guy." He laughed.

Rachel smiled. "At times, I don't know either." She cocked her left eyebrow and looked at Randolph.

"Don't forget I'm holding the car keys," Randolph said with a straight face. "Your place is a long way from here."

"Yeah, but it's my car," Rachel retorted. "I'll only walk once."

The hint of a smile curved her red lips. She placed the back of the hand holding *Browning Station* on her hip. She looked to be kidding around, but Ethan sensed she was no pushover.

"Good luck with the comic," Ethan said, and he climbed into the car.

"I'll see you, man," Randolph replied, and he stepped back, holding Rachel's hand.

As they pulled away, Ethan thought Randolph looked happy. He wondered whether he'd ever see him again. He hoped so.

CHAPTER 6

Friday, May 25, 1984

In less than five minutes, they were on the 417, heading west out of downtown Ottawa, fifteen minutes from the cemetery.

"Still want to go?" his father asked after the silence following their departure from the hospital. The traffic was building but surprisingly light for a Friday afternoon.

"Yes," Ethan answered, still concerned about whether it was the right thing to do but trying his best not to think of potential consequences. His chat with Randolph had done little to reassure him, but having his hospital friend show up to see him off had been worth it. His little spell had been unmistakable despite his denying it. Randolph had triggered something. That he'd returned was reassuring, but why had he gone and come back so quickly? More for himself than his father, he added, "I have to."

How his father knew where Mila was buried he didn't know. He didn't ask either, as mustering the courage just to make the visit was hard enough. He didn't want to think of what had happened; he wanted to think only of his good times with Mila: Cokes at the Kitchen, walks along the canal, or times alone in her dorm room. The doctors, especially Dr. Katharine, struggled to understand how he could recall such detail about the times before his going-away period but nothing during it. In a month, he and Mila had built what he hoped now was a lifetime of memories. He kept the memories on a shelf in his head to retrieve like books and enjoy as if Mila were sitting right beside him. He could feel the silky lightness of her brown hair across his fingers and trace her soft lips with his fingertips and then kiss them. He recalled the way her breasts pressed against his chest when they embraced, and she would snuggle into his arms. But those memories were usually followed by the emptiness of her absence, which, no matter how hard he tried, he couldn't fill. The nothingness remained tight in his stomach after nightmares woke him in the night—nightmares in which he was helpless to save her, suffering the horror again and again until dawn's light rose to release him. Visiting her grave would be the closest he'd come to her since the murder almost six months ago. He was glad his father knew how to get there.

Ethan looked down at his new Levi's and rubbed his hands on his thighs, drying hands that weren't wet. The jeans fit perfectly. His mother could still pick his size—a mother's intuition maybe, he supposed. The red short-sleeved polo shirt with the little embroidered player over his left breast fit as if it had been made-to-measure. Clothes that fit made him feel good. Even as a kid, he'd felt the fit was more important than the color or style—outside of the extremes of pink or polka dots. His mother had bought the clothes with special instructions that he not wear them until he left. If he didn't like them, she'd exchange them until he did. His smile when he'd come out of the room's bathroom wearing them had confirmed she'd again succeeded.

His father took the first exit ramp west of Kanata. After turning northward, they drove a couple of miles and turned left at the end of the road. In a matter of minutes, a field of headstones appeared on his right, shaded by large maple trees. His father slowed down as they approached the entrance.

Ethan didn't see any other cars.

"You know where her grave is?" Ethan asked. It sounded strange to hear himself say such a thing. He was reluctant to go on yet didn't want to be anywhere else.

"I do," his father said. "I've been here a couple of times."

"You have?" Ethan replied, surprised. "You never said anything."

"Never came up. Your mother didn't want to talk about it. Dr. Katharine said you had to come to it on your own terms."

"You talked to her about it?" Ethan asked, amazed that he hadn't known.

"Yes, I discussed it." His father paused for a moment and then went on. "Ethan, there's no instruction manual here."

Nodding as the Accord slowed, Ethan sensed his father's frailty.

They moved along the paved roadway onto the fresh gravel of the entrance. As with most cemeteries Ethan had seen in passing, the grass was green and well kept. The graves were in lines perpendicular to the laneway they drove along. Many of the headstones had flower arrangements in various states of decay on or around them.

"It's pretty dead around here," Ethan remarked, not thinking of what he was saying until he heard himself say it out loud. It seemed to lighten his mood.

"It's that kind of a place, Son."

They both snickered in a moment of shared levity.

The gravel popped beneath the tires of the Accord as they edged forward. His father brought the car to a stop.

"Do you want to be alone?" his father asked.

Ethan could feel his anxiety growing. "Yes."

"It's over there." His father pointed through the windshield to the right.

"Thanks." The word came out as if from someone else's mouth.

Ethan pushed open his door. The gravel crunched beneath his new deck shoes—part of his mother's purchase—as his feet touched the ground. Gripping the edge of the doorframe, he pulled himself out and stood up; his legs were more stable than he expected. Without closing the door, he walked in the direction his father had pointed toward the many headstones, each unique and different. Most were rectangular, in shades of pink, purple, black, and gray, each precise and polished. They were perfect in their craftsmanship, marking the imperfect lives whose names they bore. It wasn't hard to identify her gravestone. The top was polished gray-black granite engraved with theatrical drama masks. As he drew close, he read, "The Lord is my shepherd." The name engraved below it was Susan Alexandra Reed. Unexpected relief flowed over him; it wasn't Mila's. He wasn't ready yet. He looked back at his father, who shook his head, signaling to move farther right.

The next grave had bold engraving displaying the name Joachim Ray Hillier. A small pinkish stone was beside that. He kept moving. "Gone fishing with the angels" was engraved in another headstone. He admired those who looked at death with a sense of humor. He couldn't.

Stepping forward, he glanced at a small headstone he'd almost walked by. "Only angels are taken before their time" was arched across the top. The name Michelle Camilla Monahan was chiseled into the stone. Try as he might, he couldn't look away. His stomach tightened. His face grew hot as he read the name again. Pressure rose inside his chest. His breath shortened. His stomach erupted. Nausea was on him like a wave he hadn't seen coming. He dropped to one knee. His hand went to the headstone. The granite was cool but rough against his palm and fingers. He paid little attention. His stomach clenched as its contents spewed onto the green grass in front of him, releasing the anguish that threatened to take him down. He was powerless to fight it. When the spasm ended, he raised his head and looked at the polished pink granite. *Michelle Camilla Monahan.* He couldn't remember knowing that Mila was short for Camilla or that Michelle was her first name.

Vomit plowed its way out of his mouth again. This time, it came harder, thrusting him forward and causing him to plant his hands in the mowed grass to catch himself from falling into his own sickness. Though prickly, the grass was much softer than the hard granite his hand had slid off. He thought it odd to notice the texture of the grass. It made him more aware of the death of his love buried beneath him.

His eyes closed.

He was in a room he hadn't been in for a long time. Metal scraped metal. He knew the sound and what it was—a key pushed into the door's lock. The door opened, missing the person standing in the dark behind it. He watched the young woman close the door and reach for the light switch. The arms of the one standing behind the door rose, bringing the clear plastic bag up over the woman's head. In the split second it took the light to come on, the bag was over her face and pulled tightly around her slender neck. Ethan watched like a spectator. It was all he could do.

Mila was pulled backward into her attacker. Rage flashed through Ethan, yet he was helpless to do anything, forced by some curse to watch the brutality of his love's attack. He screamed. The pull of tendons in his neck was tight, but he heard only silence.

He watched Mila kick wildly while her attacker held on. Her strength was remarkable but no match for her attacker's power. The monster held her above the floor, unable to stop her flailing legs. The plastic was taut around her neck. He agonized upon seeing her legs slow as her oxygen depleted, hoping for her miracle escape. With everything he had, he screamed for her not to give up. But his scream remained silent.

In a last futile effort, she grabbed at the plastic, but she could find no leverage. Her legs thrashed again, this time managing to trip up her attacker. They fell together to her dorm room floor. Mila twisted. In the light, the shock and horror of recognition he saw in her eyes gave way to apparent acceptance. She knew her attacker. It would be okay. Ethan watched as life left her once vibrant brown eyes. Blood covered her neck and shoulder. The toe her gold ring was on quivered to stillness.

Ethan shuddered, unable to absorb what he was seeing.

The man, the monster, moved like a panther—smooth, precise, efficient. He slid out from under Mila's lifeless, slender form. Ethan prayed to turn away, but the horrific spectacle made it impossible, as if in penance for his inability to save her.

His eyes caught the twinkle of the toe ring—a gift. *But Mila didn't have … It was …*

"Oh, how beautiful you are," the madman said. "Such a shame you had to get in the way. Wrong place, my dear, at the wrong time."

The monster lifted her to her bed and laid her on her back, her pretty face tinged with the gray-blue of death. Blood seemed to be everywhere. Mila's lifeless dark brown eyes stared at the ceiling. The monster sat down on the bed and closed her dead eyes.

"If I can't have you, he can't either," the monster whispered.

Ethan knew what was about to take place.

The monster sat beside her corpse, observing it as an art lover might have studied the brushstrokes of a master. Two buttons had popped open on Mila's blood-soaked white blouse, baring more of her breasts than she would have liked. But that didn't stop her attacker, who proceeded to undo two more buttons and spread open her blouse. Blood ran down her shoulder. Ethan watched, unable to move, as the monster removed a rubber surgical glove. Like an obsessed lover, with the tip of his bare index finger, he touched—

Ethan screamed, frantic in the silence he could not defeat. His neck muscles strained to bursting as he tried harder and harder to be heard.

"Ethan!"

A voice sounded from a distance.

He was no longer in the room. There was no blood. Something was moving. He could feel her. She was yet wasn't. Something dark moved about—something raw and gnawing.

"Ethan!"

He heard his name again. The voice was closer and recognizable.

He was on his hands and knees, his hands in something prickly. His head hung between his arms. He opened his eyes to stare into a brown puddle of what looked like wet dog food. He was on grass. The sight caught him off guard. He pushed himself to get away and collided with something hard and rigid beside him.

"Ethan! Take it easy!"

The familiar voice was close.

He didn't like what he heard. "Take it easy" wasn't about to save her. But he could move. He could save her, only it was too late.

"Ethan!" his father said in a loud whisper. "She's gone!"

Ethan felt the roughness under his fingers wanting to tear his soft flesh. It hurt. The pain brought into focus the grass and the gray-pink headstone his hand was on.

"No," he said as the two worlds—the one he knew that wasn't and the one that was—came together. He could finally hear his voice. "I know."

"Let it go, Son," his father whispered. "Let her go."

Ethan raised his head and sat back on the grass, sitting with his arm across his knee, regaining his whereabouts. He turned and looked at the engraving on Mila's gravestone:

> Here lies an angel
> with broken wings.
> Her eyes still watch;
> her voice still sings.

His father's hand gripped his shoulder.

"Ethan," he said, his voice quiet, "can you hear me?"

Ethan nodded, trying to assure himself he was back. The stone and grass felt real enough. A large nearby maple provided them shade. *Shade for the buried and gravestone sentries for the trees, each unknowing of the other's charge,* he thought. It seemed odd that such a thing would come to his mind.

"You wrote that," his father said.

Ethan was facing Mila's headstone. He smiled. "I like it," he said, not remembering but finding the verse fitting for his love. "It's beautiful."

His father didn't reply. His hand remained on Ethan's shoulder.

"Were you really invited to the Maple Leafs' training camp?" Ethan asked, his question coming out of nowhere.

"What?"

Ethan was about to ask the question again when they were interrupted.

"Ethan?"

Ethan abruptly stood up, bumping into his father.

In front of them stood a man about his age, dressed in a navy jacket with a white-and-burgundy-striped necktie. His hair was bleached blond, cut short, and spiky on top. A small gold ring hung from his right earlobe. He did not smile.

Surprised, Ethan responded in the same way he'd been addressed. "Sean?"

"Yeah," Sean replied. "I didn't expect to find you here."

"Feeling's mutual, man," Ethan said, his eyes opening wider as if to better believe who stood before him. "Where did you come from? We didn't see anyone here."

Ethan looked at his father, whose eyes had narrowed in a "What's this about?" expression.

"I come out here once in a while," Sean replied. His jacket was open. His hands were in the pockets of his gray trousers. He nodded at Mila's gravestone. "So tragic and unnecessary."

Ethan turned and looked back at the words engraved in the granite of Mila's gravestone. He didn't like that their visit had been interrupted, but he didn't say so.

"What are you up to these days?" he asked, forcing himself to sound polite.

Sean looked down at his polished black dress shoes. His right foot moved as if he were nudging something forward with the toe of his shoe. "Working in a bar on Bank Street, not far from Lansdowne," he answered. Then, raising his head, he looked at Ethan. "Bogart's."

Ethan nodded but didn't reply. He didn't know the place. A long pause followed. His father stepped back.

"Sorry, Sean," Ethan said, motioning with his hand. "This is my father, Darren Jones. Dad, this is Sean."

The awkwardness Ethan remembered of Sean around Mila was gone. He appeared more relaxed as the two men—young and old—shook hands.

"Nice to meet you, Sean," Ethan's father said in his professional business voice.

"Good to meet you, Mr. Jones," Sean replied, his smile revealing braces-straightened white teeth. Ethan couldn't recall Sean's perfect teeth. Before, he'd only seen Mila.

"Do you like it?" Ethan asked as his eyes moved back to Mila's headstone.

"I suppose," Sean answered.

"Something else'll come up, I'm sure," Ethan said, trying to sound upbeat.

"Come again?" Sean asked, his voice changing pitch, causing Ethan to turn and look at him.

"I'm sure you'll find something else," Ethan added to clarify what he'd just said.

Sean squinted, a half smile redisplaying his white teeth. "I thought you were talking about the headstone." Sean laughed, breaking the solemn tone that had settled around the three men.

Ethan smiled, realizing that what he'd said had been disconnected. His father shook his head.

"Do you like bartending? That's what I meant," Ethan said, correcting himself.

"It's okay. Keeps my mind off things."

Sean didn't say any more, which gave Ethan time to reflect on when he'd last seen Sean. The police had been involved. Sean had been questioned about Mila's murder.

"Sean," Ethan said, breaking their silence, "I don't even know your last name."

CHAPTER 7

"Wayland," Ethan said as he pulled open the passenger door of the Honda. "It's amazing I didn't know that."

The three of them had left the gravesite together. Ethan wanted to stay longer but now feared being alone at the grave. Sean must have seen he'd thrown up on the grass, but he didn't say anything.

On the walk back to his father's car, Ethan saw a new silver Mustang a distance away. *Bartending must pay pretty well,* he thought. Sean must have come in another way.

"I don't remember meeting Sean before," his father said as he turned the car around in the long driveway. "I don't recall seeing him at the hospital."

Ethan fastened his seat belt and stared at the gravel drive ahead.

"Sean was with Mila when we first met," Ethan said, thinking about how different Sean looked from how he remembered him on that first night in Charly's: days-worn jeans, sweatshirt, and worn-out sneakers. He'd never pictured Sean dressed up. "Outside of a couple of brief encounters, I never saw him much."

The Accord moved slowly along the cemetery road, jostling them in their seats. It was a route not traveled often, and for those buried, it was their last, Ethan thought bitterly.

"Were they a couple?" his father asked as they approached the road.

Ethan heard his father's question, but he was remembering Mila. He thought of her long brown hair pulled back into a quick ponytail. She would work her hair into a colored band and then position the ponytail at different angles about her head. Any angle seemed to suit her. He only had to look into her brown eyes, and any thought in his head would disappear like water down a drain. Mila had held a power over him like no other—and she still did. He could do nothing but acquiesce to her wishes, yet she loved to please him. He never tired of her company. Tight jeans showed off her lean legs, which never lacked for energy or his attention. Even now, it was as if he could reach out and touch her. Her energy was almost tangible. It seemed impossible that he would never feel her again.

He saw Sean standing at her side, holding a half-full glass of beer.

His father's question—"Were they a couple?"—beckoned.

"I don't think so," Ethan said after his long pause. "Mila said they were just friends, but I did wonder whether Sean saw it the same way. Seeing him here today, I think he probably didn't. It made no difference to me." Ethan looked over at his father. "You know us guys—we never admit more than the girl. If she says we're friends, we're friends. It's all part of the game, no matter how much it hurts."

His father nodded.

They were now on the road, facing the four-hour drive back to Toronto. It would be a long ride.

The car was confining and uncomfortable despite the leather seats and air-conditioning. Sitting in one place without the ability to move around was nearly impossible. He'd been freer in the hospital. After the first hour, he wanted to stop—he needed to. They pulled into the dirt parking lot of a small roadside restaurant. Ethan opened his door before the car had stopped.

"You okay?" his father asked.

"Not really," Ethan replied, standing on the red-and-white patio stones that lined the front of the restaurant. "That was a long time to sit."

His father nodded as Ethan stood at the front of the car.

"It'll take time, Ethan," his father said, nodding. "We went too long. Old habits, you know. Sorry."

"Don't worry about it."

Ethan turned before his father could say more.

The place wasn't much to look at from the outside, but Griffin's Stop had enough food, drink, and conveniences to satisfy most travelers. They entered through an aluminum screen door. A small bell at the top of the door announced their arrival but seemed redundant to the screech the door made when Ethan pulled it open. Like the horrid sound of fingernails across a blackboard, the noise did nothing to ease Ethan's already anxious nerves. He'd managed to keep a lid on his disquiet inside the car, but the urge to lash out was edging closer.

He remembered Dr. Katharine's warning about claustrophobia.

"The feeling of anxiousness will come unexpectedly. Maybe in an elevator, maybe a car," she'd told him. "Focus on breathing. In and out. Slowly from your diaphragm." She'd demonstrated how in her office.

This was a new sensation for Ethan and not a comfortable one. Controlled breathing helped, if he could only remember.

Inside, his father headed to the restrooms. Ethan wasn't really hungry but bought two cans of Coke and two bags of Fritos corn chips from the young Asian girl behind the counter. An older gray-haired couple sat at one of the tables covered in red-and-white-checkerboard tablecloths, but otherwise, the place was empty. The glum-faced teen raised her eyes only once to Ethan, when she handed back his change. Her only words were "Thank you." Ethan walked back to the small front foyer to wait for his father. His nerves had calmed.

In the tiny alcove between the entrance and the restaurant was a magazine rack Ethan had glanced at upon entering. He'd forgotten his excitement when standing in front of a display of new magazines. The assortment was small by convenience store standards but big enough to kindle his interest and anticipation. As was commonplace, the metal rack had the adult magazines at the top. Before looking, he glanced back at the counter in time to see the girl avert her eyes. He was being watched. He was about to move on when he saw the glossy cover of *Guitar Gear*. He didn't hesitate and pulled the magazine from the rack. The guitar on the cover was a black Rickenbacker 4001 standing upright. It was that month's featured guitar. Ethan was in love. He'd forgotten how much music mattered. He returned to the cashier and bought the magazine.

"Whatchya got there?" his father asked after exiting the washroom, pointing at the brown paper bag in Ethan's hand.

"A magazine," Ethan answered, stating what he thought was obvious. "I bought Cokes and Fritos too."

"Thanks," his father said as Ethan pushed open the screeching screen door. "I'm gonna grab a newspaper. You wanna drive?"

Ethan stopped. He hadn't given driving another thought since his father had first asked. He was about to reply with the same answer, anxious to read about the new Rickenbacker, but changed his mind. Maybe he should try. It might make the car feel less confining.

"Sure, why not?" he said, thinking his father might renege on his offer.

Offering to let Ethan drive was remarkable, but allowing him to drive his new car was astounding, considering his father's usual possessiveness.

"I'll only be a minute."

As he settled behind the leather-wrapped steering wheel, Ethan went from an initial sense of apprehension to feeling renewed. It had been the previous September, coming to Ottawa, when he'd last driven a car. It seemed an eternity ago. He placed the Coke cans in the cup holders. This was the first car he'd been in that had them. They were convenient. He dropped the chips on the small shelf between the seats. He relaxed, surprised at how much he liked the luxurious comfort of the car.

While he waited for his father, he flipped through the pages of his new magazine until he found the Rickenbacker. It had been the bass of his dreams since he'd played one back when his band rented equipment at Coll's Music in high school. The red sunburst paint job of that guitar did nothing for him, but he loved the shape and sound of the guitar. He had a new obsession.

His father came back with his paper.

"She's all yours, Son," he said, seeming as eager to dive into the paper as Ethan was his magazine. Ethan set his magazine on the tray in the center of the dashboard.

He used the electric controls to adjust his seat and moved the side mirror into place with the small inside lever. As he glanced in the rearview mirror, he caught sight of the cashier leaving the restaurant, heading to a rusty Datsun behind them. Something about her intrigued him as he started the Accord. Could he have met her somewhere before? Or was he feeling something else, something more nefarious? Was he sensing something his sister, Carlyn, might have called her aura?

"Are you about ready?" his father asked, prompting Ethan out of his reverie. His father had been folding his paper and seemed to be paying little attention to his son's activities. Ethan figured he should have known better than to think his father wouldn't be watching; after all, this was his father's new car.

He did seem to be procrastinating his moment of truth, which seemed strange, as he loved to drive. At sixteen, he couldn't wait to get his license. But the excitement of driving had been replaced with a beginner's indecision.

"Yeah," he said finally.

He shifted into reverse and eased his foot off the brake. They eased backward. He stopped and shifted to drive. Now more confident, he stepped on the accelerator. The car responded instantly, lurching forward, sending them both back against their seats and sending his magazine to the floor. On reflex, his right foot overcompensated and came down hard on the brake pedal, jarring them both forward. Their seat belts locked, which saved them from smashing their heads into the steering wheel and dashboard. Flustered, Ethan reached for his magazine, threw it into the back seat, and then grabbed the steering wheel with both hands.

He could feel his father's stare. He didn't dare turn his head.

"Relax," his father said in the professional, patronizing tone Ethan knew and hated. "Just take it slow."

Ethan pursed his lips tightly. He was mad at himself and his incompetence and was sure his father thought the same. He hated making the foolish mistakes a pimply faced teenager would have made when getting behind the wheel of the family station wagon for the first time. Maybe he wasn't ready, but he wasn't about to admit it.

Easing into the highway traffic, Ethan was in awe of how different the Honda was to drive compared to his father's last car. When he so much as nudged the steering wheel, the car reacted. In his father's Chevy Caprice, the steering wheel could float an inch or more before there was any movement in the front end. The engine sounded different too. The roar of the Chevy's V8 was replaced by a sound akin to an industrial sewing machine. There was no less zip from pressing the accelerator, but the response was instantaneous. There was a feeling of intent with the new car. Ethan liked it.

As he settled in behind the wheel, a Dodge pickup came up behind them. They were no longer the last car in the train. Ethan noticed little after that. He slowed and accelerated in sync with the car ahead. The Honda drove like a dream, following the curves in the road as if on rails, begging him to go faster.

They'd been on the road for about half an hour when his right hand dropped to his thigh and his left slid to the bottom of the steering wheel. He rested his elbow on the driver's-door armrest. It was wonderful to be driving again on such a nice day. For the first time, the fears he had of leaving the hospital and reentering the real world were second to the joy of his freedom. The confines of the hospital faded as the outside world took over. A smile shaped his lips. The sunshine made everything a little better.

"Okay if I turn on the radio?" he asked, his hand already in motion. He hadn't listened to any music in a long time. It wasn't encouraged in the hospital.

"Sure," his father answered without raising his head from his newspaper.

He didn't know the song that was playing, but what followed carried a longing he'd thought forgotten. Bob Dylan was singing "Like a Rolling Stone." It was as if the song spoke only to him.

After Dylan finished, the disc jockey came on. Ethan didn't want to hear any more. Something in the song had affected him. He couldn't help but think about his band in high school. He turned off the radio. As his hand came back from the radio, he touched a piece of paper stuck between his seat and the center console.

He pulled it out. Doing his best to keep watching the road, he looked at the piece of paper. It appeared to have been torn from a coil-ringed notepad. He turned the paper over to find a neat handwritten note:

> I'm older than I look. If you have a band and need a guitar
> player, call me. Sydney.

He saw a phone number just before the shocking blast of a car horn blared by.

The Accord was riding the double yellow line down the center of the highway.

CHAPTER 8

Friday, May 25, 1984

The steering wheel turned in his hand. Though the reaction time of a twenty-year-old was quick, it wouldn't have been quick enough to save them from colliding head-on with the passing car. Unbeknownst to Ethan, his father had reached across the center console, put his hand on the wheel, and steered them back into the right lane and out of harm's way. Ethan thought he was lucky to get off with only the blast of an angry motorist's horn.

He saw the dust cloud from the other car's ride on the gravel shoulder in his side mirror. With both hands tight on the steering wheel, he slowed. The distance between him and the car traveling ahead of them lengthened. He started to shake, envisioning the accident they'd narrowly missed.

He directed the car toward the shoulder, wanting out.

"No," his father said, his tone sharp, as the passenger-side tires popped and crackled in the gravel of the shoulder. "Keep going."

"No," Ethan replied. "I need—"

"You need to drive," his father said emphatically.

Ethan clenched the steering wheel in his fists. Pink lines showed on his knuckles. He didn't want to keep going; his earlier confidence was now gone.

His dad was right, though Ethan didn't want to admit it. He couldn't quit now. He pulled back onto the highway, doing his best to push the near miss out of his mind.

They drove in silence for a while as he settled back into the rhythm of the road. His father spoke first.

"That was pretty close."

Ethan didn't think his father had looked away from the road in front of them or at his paper since the incident.

"Yeah," Ethan replied. His father's words were a reminder of what he was trying to forget. He stared at the car in front of them.

"You doing okay?"

"Yeah," Ethan repeated, not wanting to say more. He didn't turn his head, as he might have done earlier. But it wasn't the driving that made him uneasy now. He felt unsettled at the thoughts the song and note had triggered.

"You want to keep driving?"

"I think so."

The inside of the car again went quiet, except for the hum of the car's engine and the outside wind noise. The Dylan tune was stuck in his head; it seemed to be making his future a little less foggy. *But where did the note come from?*

At Raymondville, his father directed them south down Highway 37. That would take them to the 401; the 401 would take them the rest of the way. To Ethan, it was the halfway point. The second half of the trip was always the better half. He put the destination ahead of the journey, in spite of the saying.

His father broke their silence for the second time.

"So what was so important to read while driving my new car over the speed limit?"

Ethan knew better than to think the incident would go unnoticed, but he didn't like the reminder either. Why couldn't his father just leave it alone? Ethan was curious about the note but not about to share it with his father.

"I don't know," Ethan replied. He knew his answer wouldn't be enough but would give him time to think of something more. There were laws that governed the exchanges between sons and fathers. He kept looking at the road ahead.

"That's it?" his father said, his voice rising. "You nearly run us head-on into another car, and you don't know? Come on, Ethan. Don't insult my intelligence."

There was another drawn-out silence that Ethan refused to break.

"I wondered how long it would take you to make a mistake. I only hoped it wouldn't cost us our lives."

Ethan listened, his resolve not to say anything slipping with each word from his father. *God, I made a fucking mistake. It happens to humans, you know.*

He could feel his father turn to look at him. In spite of what he might have been thinking, he'd uttered his last thought out loud.

Why had he said anything? It was as if the paper was still in his hand. Then one image seemed to fade into another as if part of a movie. The two-lane highway ahead of him replaced the scrap of paper he thought he was holding. They passed a sign indicating the next service center was just ahead.

"What do you say we take a break and get something to eat?" his father asked, sounding congenial, his reproachful tone gone.

"Sure," Ethan replied, his stomach still tight after his father's earlier comment.

"Pull into the next stop."

As they approached the exit, Ethan edged the car into the ramp lane and then drove into the parking lot of the service center.

"How are you feeling?" his father asked. Before Ethan could answer, he added, "You did well, having not driven for so long."

Ethan turned off the car, surprised by what he was hearing. The feeling of waking from a dream flowed over him. He couldn't help but notice how his father's condemnation had turned to concern. He then realized he couldn't remember anything they'd passed on the 401 or even getting to the 401 from Highway 37.

"Are you coming?" his father asked as he climbed out of the car. "I need to stretch my legs. They get stiff now when I sit too long."

"Yeah, in a minute," Ethan replied, not sure he wanted to move.

He stared at the steering wheel in shock, realizing he didn't remember anything from the last hour or so.

And the note?

He didn't want to look down, because he knew with certainty that he wouldn't find it. He'd gone away again while driving. The feeling was unmistakable. Yet again, he'd come out of it. *But I was driving!* He opened the door and climbed out. With the courage it took to look for something a person didn't really want to find, he squatted down and slid in between the steering wheel and the seat. On the beige carpet between the driver's seat and the center console was a clear BIC pen and nothing else. Relief flowed over him. There was no note. There'd never been a note. Maybe the Dylan song had been what set him off.

A number of things flashed back—the guitar magazine he'd tossed into the back seat, the passing car, the Asian girl at the cash register, the jumpy start in the parking lot.

He took the pen. There was something about holding a new pen that felt good. After closing the door, he saw the magazine in the back seat. He opened the back door and grabbed it. He'd take another look at the black Rickenbacker; he wanted that guitar.

After closing the door, he locked the car, slipped the keys in the front pocket of his Levi's, and started toward the service center entrance. The chorus to "Like a Rolling Stone" was in his head.

He passed the magazine from one hand to the other. A piece of paper floated to the ground from between the pages.

He knew what was on it before he reached down to pick it up.

It wasn't possible.

PART 2

PORTAMENTO

Deep in the human unconscious is a pervasive need
for a logical universe that makes sense. But the
real universe is always one step beyond logic.
—Frank Herbert, Dune

How you gonna know for sure, everything was so well organized.
Hey, now everything is so secure,
And everybody else is satisfied.
—Billy Joel, "James"

CHAPTER 9

Thursday, July 12, 1984

God, it was a long day. The humid afternoon heat didn't help. It was past three thirty in the afternoon. Their break was over. They had eight postholes to dig before calling it quits. Ethan didn't want to drill one. The guy he was saddled with—Nigel, the boss's nephew—didn't want to work, let alone drill postholes, so he didn't. When his uncle wasn't around, he sat with his long hair hanging over his eyes, indulging in what appeared to be an unending supply of weed. That left Ethan to drill most of the holes—each four feet deep—by himself with a two-man gas-powered auger in the hot sun. It was all he could do to hold the heavy machine steady as it cranked a spiraling metal auger into the hard ground. Ethan's arms were repeatedly yanked as the engine's torque spun him around whenever the auger caught the edge of a buried rock or tree root. The holes were intended to hold four-by-four posts that would support a fence around the periphery of a soon-to-be in-ground swimming pool. The pool installation would start next week. Nephew Nigel sat in the shade of a big oak tree at the back of the large property. He inhaled as Ethan gulped the last of the water from his yellow Coleman thermos, which he'd already refilled once that day. Sweat ran down Ethan's forehead and off the tip of his nose.

Ethan resented the kid. He was getting paid minimum wage—same as the kid—and doing all the work. His boss had made it clear he could put up or get out; jobs were not plentiful. He was lucky to have this one, he supposed.

Nigel wasn't mean or malicious and was always offering Ethan a hit. Ethan usually declined, not because he didn't want it—it might cool his frustration—but because he feared anything that might trigger him away from the present. Nigel was a stoner. His parents had had enough of their degenerate son and sent him to work with his uncle Al, as if it were some kind of Outward Bound program: "Send us a boy; we'll send you back a man." Just thinking about it made Ethan smile as he pulled the cord to start the auger again. Uncle Al was straightening Nigel out all right. He was stoned all day and God only knew what at night. Ethan could see Nigel was pretty messed up. Was there any help for kids who couldn't find their way?

"Nigel!" Ethan shouted across the lawn, adjusting the choke on the small engine. "Give me a hand here."

Nigel trudged across the yard in his undone Kodiaks, kicking clumps of clay that were in his way on the lawn. Nigel didn't say a word and never argued. He was just slow and disinterested. Unless asked, he didn't do anything. Nigel grabbed the auger's handle opposite Ethan. Ethan squeezed the throttle. The engine responded loudly. He engaged the auger and started twisting dirt out of the ground.

With Nigel's help, he finished the remaining holes in less than an hour. At five, Uncle Al's rusty Ford Bronco showed up. He backed up the paved driveway and stopped beside the garage of the two-story house, just in front of the backyard. The truck was filled with lumber—and more work.

Al opened his door and put an undone new work boot on the truck's running board.

"What's up, boys?" he shouted, stepping onto the driveway. The boys had been waiting for fifteen minutes. Ethan was anxious to get going.

Al was thin, with big hands and feet. His face looked weathered. A cigarette constantly dangled from between his lips. A straggly gray beard exacerbated his worn-out thinness.

Nigel was somehow always the first to speak.

"Finished all the holes," he said in the most enthusiastic voice Ethan had heard all day. Ethan was exhausted and didn't care. His thoughts were on the gig that night. He was making his way to the passenger side of the Bronco to drop his thermos onto the seat through the open window. The words to the song his band would open with that night were on his lips.

"Good to hear," Al answered, heading to the backyard. Nigel followed like a dog out for a walk with its owner. Ethan stood still, hoping they might skip inspection that night but knowing it wasn't likely.

Al walked the periphery of what they had completed that day. He kicked some of the largest clumps of clay, as Nigel had earlier. He bent down, picked up a hunk of sod, and shook his head as he tossed it aside. The backyard looked as if a bomb had been detonated.

"You boys should clean up a little better," he said, turning to look at Ethan, who was now standing at the back of the house. Ethan didn't say anything and only nodded. He was unsure what might come out of his mouth if he opened it. He didn't need to be spoken to like a child about something as stupid as dirt. Tomorrow they'd be cementing in the posts. The place would look even worse.

"The holes look good and deep," Al said as he approached the last one they'd drilled, near where Ethan was standing.

"Thanks," Nigel said.

Al's remark surprised Ethan. It was odd for him to say anything nice about their work.

None of it changed the fact that Ethan needed to go. He looked at the dirt under his fingernails. He still had to get cleaned up.

They all walked back to the truck.

"Can you guys unload the wood," Al said, "while I see if anybody's home?"

Nobody was home. Ethan knew it and was pretty sure Al did too. They hadn't seen anyone all day. But Ethan knew they wouldn't be going anywhere until the lumber was unloaded.

Al's hard-soled boot heels clapped on the asphalt as he headed across the driveway to the front of the house.

"Come on, Nigel," Ethan said, his hands already on one of the four-by-four posts sticking out the back of the Bronco. "Let's move this shit before he thinks of something else to do."

Ethan figured he'd be doing most of the lifting, but Nigel surprised him. They had most of the lumber out and stacked before Ethan heard Al's boots on the driveway. There were two posts left in the truck.

It had taken them less than five minutes to unload the wood. *Asshole*, Ethan thought as he grabbed the last two posts and piled them on top of the others on the ground.

"Nobody's home," Al announced, rejoining them, brushing his hands together as if he'd just finished a big job.

No shit, Einstein, Ethan thought.

"You boys done?"

Ethan was sick of hearing the man's voice.

"Looks like it," Nigel said, answering his uncle's obvious question.

"Atta boy," said Uncle Al like a Little League coach cheering on a scrawny kid who'd just hit a pitch for the first time.

Al slammed the Bronco's tailgate closed. They were done. Ethan was more than anxious.

Al was the first one in; Ethan and Nigel climbed in the passenger side. Ethan sat between Al and his nephew. It was an odd arrangement, but sitting by the door was one thing Nigel did care about. He sat taller and even looked confident. Ethan guessed it might have been the only time he felt important. But to Ethan, it wasn't Nigel's position in the truck that gave Nigel his importance.

Al drove forward into the vacant street.

They were half an hour from Ethan's parents' home.

CHAPTER 10

Thursday, July 12, 1984

Ethan closed his eyes and went through the set list for the evening while Al drove him to his parents' house. The band now had three original songs to add to the cover tunes they'd been rehearsing for weeks. They had sixteen altogether. Half of those had become a little stale to Ethan. He wanted to write more.

He also wanted to perform the songs, not just sing them. It would make their show more unique and not just four musicians playing onstage. The band was strong musically, but he didn't think more music was the answer. They needed to perform in a new way.

It was hard to believe the supposed teenager he'd bought *Guitar Gear* from was any more than an immature kid working the counter at her mom and dad's restaurant. Sydney had come to Toronto and blown him away with her chops. Though her slender five-foot frame would make her look childlike onstage, Ethan wasn't about to pass up the chance to work with a dream musician.

Meeting Sydney coincided with his return to a certain level of normalcy. It helped push him back into the world before he got used to hiding from it. The drive home from Ottawa had convinced him to form a new band. Witnessing Sydney play a guitar had locked it in. It hadn't been that long since he'd forfeited the plan to make music his life's pursuit. He'd give it another go.

Not unlike the serendipity of meeting Sydney was discovering that Greg, his high school buddy, was back in town. MIT was not the Shangri-la Greg had envisioned. His first semester had turned into his last. Unbeknownst to his parents, he'd stayed in Boston not for school but to experience the subculture music scene. He was back in Toronto a month before Ethan arrived. After meeting for lunch, Greg was game to meet the female guitarist from Ottawa and talk about forming a new band. Ethan was a little surprised at Greg's eagerness to start, as he'd been the instigator in breaking up their first band.

In love with the black Rickenbacker from the magazine, Ethan saw himself as the bass player. With Sydney coming out of nowhere and Greg's reappearance, he saw everything coming together; he'd have the power trio he'd always imagined.

A few days after meeting with Greg, Ethan was mowing his parents' front lawn when he ran out of gas. While refilling the tank, he heard the pound of music coming from the house across the street. Unable to ignore it, he went over to investigate. His ear picked up a busy bass line. At the front door, there was no mistaking the live bass playing alongside the Bee Gees' "Nights on Broadway." He was a little surprised, as it was not his usual fare in music, but the originality of the bass fills captivated him. They made the song better—not a dance tune but real rock. Whoever was playing knew the fret board of a bass guitar.

Curious to see the player, he waited for the song to end and pressed the doorbell. Almost at once, he heard the electrical clunk of a guitar unplugging from an amp. Someone was coming. The front door opened to reveal a longhaired, black-bearded man a couple of years his senior. The man was new to the neighborhood since Ethan had left for university. Ethan introduced himself to Gus Petrovsky. As he shook Gus's hand, two things became apparent: his plans of bass playing in his new band were over, and the band would not be a trio.

Ethan opened his eyes. He liked remembering how the Release had come together.

Al slowed the Bronco and pulled into his parents' subdivision. The last stanza of their newest song, the verse from Mila's headstone, was in his head:

Here lies an angel
with broken wings.
Her eyes still watch;
her voice still sings.

He loved the words. The melody he'd written with Sydney made them more beautiful. It was the perfect song for Mila's memory and made him proud. Mila had put the right words in his head. He felt her smile each time he sang the words in rehearsal. They would debut the song that night in their second set. He couldn't wait.

The truck pulled into his parents' empty driveway. His father was out of town, and his mother was likely on her way home from the school.

Nigel opened the door and climbed out. Ethan slid across the bench seat, dragging his thermos behind him. He heard Al open the driver's-side door. Nigel climbed back into the truck.

"See you tomorrow," Ethan said.

"You're on," Nigel called back, closing the door.

Al met Ethan at the front of the Bronco.

"Say, Ethan," he said, putting his hand on the front fender. He picked at some rust on the edge of the hood and then raised his head. "I'm not gonna need you for the next little while."

His words caught Ethan off guard. Al's worn face seemed to tighten. His eyes seemed to get smaller.

"Business isn't booming," Al added. He held out a white envelope and nodded for Ethan to take it.

Ethan didn't move.

"Here's last week's pay," Al said, continuing to hold the envelope in front of Ethan.

The moment grew. Ethan didn't respond; he only stared at the man.

Al kept talking. "I'll send this week's in the mail."

"No, you won't," Ethan said, rage lighting up behind his eyes.

"What?" Al replied, his face darkening.

"No, you won't send it to me in the mail." Ethan's bottom lip quivered as he did his best to contain his sudden anger. "I need this job, Al," he said, his evening forgotten for the moment. This was his second job that month. It was as if his return had coincided with a collapse in the job market. He needed money. It had taken weeks to get this job. His parents' handouts were a kind gesture, but he was beginning to feel awkward taking their money. "You haven't said anything about not needing me."

"Things change. Customers cancel. People change their minds. All kinds of shit. This is the only job we have this month."

Ethan shifted his weight from his left foot to his right. "What about Nigel?"

Al turned and looked toward his nephew in the truck. He put his hand in the front pocket of his dirty jeans. "There's still stuff to do," he said. He placed the envelope on the hood of the Bronco. He put his other hand in his pocket. "Nigel will work with me."

"Fuck!" Ethan said, anger getting the better part of his tongue. "You know I'm three times the worker he is. What gives?"

Ethan knew the answer, whether Al was willing to admit it or not. Nigel was his wife's sister's son. Family was family, no matter how Ethan might argue his side. There might have been all kinds of issues behind Nigel's behavior, but none of it helped Ethan's case. Whether he liked it or not, his game was over, no matter how unfair he thought it was.

"I want what's mine before you leave."

"I haven't got it," Al replied.

"Then we have nothing left to talk about."

He grabbed the envelope off the Bronco's hood and stepped in front of the truck. He pulled out the pen he now kept handy in his pocket and wrote Al's license plate number on the back.

"What the fuck are you doing?" Al asked, his voice rising.

"Calling the cops," Ethan replied matter-of-factly. "You may not care about paying me, but I'm sure they'll be interested in your suspended license."

Al's cheek twitched. He looked as if he'd just been caught touching himself.

"How the fuck?" Al growled. A meanness surfaced Ethan had only seen once before, when Nigel had dumped a wheelbarrow of fresh cement onto a patch Al had just finished smoothing. Ethan didn't care; his own anger was rising. Somebody was going to pay. Ethan turned and looked at Nigel sitting in the truck as content as a stoned angel.

"Guess," Ethan said, looking back at Al.

Al's jaw stiffened under his two-day stubble. Ethan folded the envelope and stuffed it in his pocket. Not done, he turned and walked to the right door of his parents' two-car garage. He yanked it open. Behind the center pillar separating the two doors were his father's golf clubs. He set his thermos down on the cement floor and pulled out an iron.

He walked back, past Al, to the rear of the Bronco with the club in his hand.

"And to make your truck easy to fucking identify ..."

"You little shit!" Al shouted.

Ethan paused, gripping the club with both hands, ready to take a full swing at the red lens.

"Hold up a fucking second!"

The meanness Ethan had seen in Al's face faded as the consequence of what was happening became apparent. Ethan doubted Al would fight him.

Ethan lowered the club as Al hustled back to the driver's side of the truck. It took him seconds to grab something inside and come round to where Ethan was standing beside the back of the truck.

"Okay," Al said, handing over a number of twenties, "here's what I owe you."

Ethan took the money and set the club against his hip.

"Happy now?" Al added snidely.

"Almost," Ethan said. He pulled the envelope out of his pocket and counted the money. "Last week had five days in it. You're short."

Ethan held out the open envelope and put his hand back on the grip of the golf club. Al pulled a thick black wallet out of his back pocket.

"You'll never fuckin' work for me again, ya little shit," he said, sliding two twenties out of his stuffed billfold.

"I wouldn't get my hopes up," Ethan replied, having no desire to say anything else to the jerk standing in front of him, let alone work for him again.

Al didn't say a word. He turned and got back in his truck. Ethan, with the club in hand, was tempted to take a swing at the rear taillight anyway but held himself in check. He had what he wanted. He'd save his energy for the show. He stepped onto the lawn as the Bronco's engine revved. The truck shot backward into the street, skidded to a stop, and then roared forward. Not looking at him, the coward then gave him the finger.

Ethan didn't respond. He walked back to the garage, satisfied he'd stood up to the bluffing coward and had money in his hand to boot. It was a small victory but a victory nonetheless.

CHAPTER 11

Thursday, July 12, 1984

Preshow excitement had Ethan on edge, and he hadn't left the house yet.

His altercation with Al had used up much of the little time he'd had to get ready. Once in the house, he'd grabbed a Budweiser from the fridge and gulped down half the bottle on the way to his bedroom. The alcohol hardly touched the anxiety stirring his stomach. He was angry at what he'd had to do to get what was his and angry that a lazy, dope-smoking nephew had beat him out of a job. But he had $140 more in his pocket for his efforts; it wasn't all bad. Proud of standing up for himself, he was now unnerved by how far he might have gone had Al called him on his threat. The upheaval was now jostling for space in his head with the songs that would make up their first set of the night.

After a quick shower, he grabbed clean jeans and a denim shirt from his closet. He hustled down the hallway to the front of the house, swallowing what was left of his beer. As he passed the kitchen, the phone rang. He wasn't going to stop, as he thought Sydney might be in the driveway, but he realized it might be Gus or Greg calling to find out where they were.

"Is that Ethan the Actor?" replied a familiar voice after he said hello.

Ethan hadn't heard himself referred to as the Actor since leaving Ottawa. He could hear the smile in Randolph's voice.

"The one and only," Ethan answered, "who is running late."

"I won't hold you up," Randolph said. "Just wanted to see what you're up to."

"Time flies, doesn't it?" Ethan said, holding the receiver between his ear and shoulder while buttoning the shirt his mother had cleaned and pressed. "Seems like only yesterday that I left."

"Get used to it," Randolph said, "'cause it's not about to slow down."

Sydney pushed open the front door. He waved and pointed to the phone.

"Yeah, there's a lot going on, but I really do have to go," Ethan said as Sydney passed him and walked into the family room. "I will call you back."

"Yeah," Randolph said, "check's in the mail too."

Ethan could hear Randolph laughing at his own joke. He made a mental note to call Randolph back.

"Talk to you soon," Ethan said.

After hanging up, he heard Sydney start in on his Yamaha acoustic.

"We should get going," he said, entering the room. "Gus'll be freaking."

Sydney was sitting cross-legged on his parents' brown-suede ottoman. He loved listening to her make his old acoustic come alive.

"What's that?" he asked.

"What's what?"

"The thing you just played," Ethan said, excited. "That run. Da, di, da, di, do. Sounds like being scolded with love."

Sydney shook her head while her fingers moved along the neck of the guitar. "You confound me with your descriptions. Scolded with love? What is that?"

Ethan didn't reply, intent on listening as Sydney went back over what she'd played. The scenario had become habit between them. She was always playing. He was always listening, picking up bits here and there like scraps of fabric to stitch into a quilt.

"Wait!" he said, all but shouting. "That's it! Right there. Play that again."

Anyone watching might have looked for a cord connecting them; his motions were in sync with the notes that flowed from her fingertips.

"La-la-lu-lala-li-la," he scatted. "Shamala de da-da."

Sydney stopped playing; her dark eyes widened. It was an expression Ethan had come to understand as her way of asking "What the fuck was that?"

"No! No!" Ethan pleaded. "Don't stop. Please!"

He was on his knees in front of her. His hands were in motion as if trying to draw the music from her fingers through some kind of wizardry.

He often used the word *magic* to describe how a song came together. How else could he describe creating something from nothing? Thinking too much almost seemed to deny it. He was learning to listen to his imagination, that and his intuition. It would always take him somewhere unexpected if he let it, unless he tried to control it or figure it out. There was no model or process to follow. It came and went like the wind, and if he were lucky, he'd catch a spark to hold on to. Ethan was beginning to see the world as made up of two mind-sets: those who believed there was a universal model that would eventually be figured out and those who believed there wasn't—at least not one mere mortals understood.

Sydney's playing was just such a moment.

"Play it again," he repeated, feeling more was outside them than between them. It wasn't about him or her. It was beyond them—a glimmer of something, a gift that, if willing, he could have and grow into something. It was raw, primitive, and his for the taking—truth, pure and innocent, melding the heart, mind, and soul in an unadulterated place where rules and procedures didn't exist. Creativity was like that. It revealed the soul in glimpses on occasion. Having everything in order didn't matter. It was a choice to take the gift, but it wouldn't show itself again.

Sydney played the bit again but added something else.

Ethan shook his head. "No, no, no. Take it higher, like ta-ti-ti-ta."

Sydney's fingers seemed to float over the strings, one note flowing into the next, as Ethan's hands followed along in unison like a hawk taking unseen air currents to a new height. Unlike the hawk, Ethan closed his eyes.

"It's there. I can touch it," Ethan sang, the words flowing with the notes under Sydney's fingers. "But it won't let me in."

He stopped and jumped to his feet maniacally in search of a pen and paper.

"The fear stops me moving," he sang as the words came to him, blind as to what would come next, terrified they would stop. It was like trying to catch something he couldn't quite see.

He grabbed an envelope and pencil from a drawer in the kitchen.

"No. The last is the second," he said to himself. His fingers worked the pencil across the blank white envelope, writing, "But she's not mine." He scratched it out and wrote what he'd sung:

> It's there. I can touch it.
> But it won't let me in.
> The fear stops me moving.

He finished by saying, "I don't know where to begin." He scribbled down the words to complete the four-line stanza.

"Play it again," he said, scared he would miss what was screaming by.

These special moments—or clouds, as Ethan thought of them—came and went like dreams. If he didn't write them down, they were gone.

Sydney played the notes exactly as she had before.

"Play it again," Ethan repeated, counterpointing the notes she played by humming a forming melody. When she finished, he wanted her to play it again. This time, he sang the words he'd jotted down.

"Yes!" he shouted, driving his fist into the air. "That's it!"

Fist pumping, he danced beside her. "I love it!" he cried, unable to contain himself. "Play it again!"

Sydney added a little front end and played it again. Ethan sang along.

"Wow!" he yelled.

"Wow is right," Sydney said, setting down his guitar. "We gotta go."

CHAPTER 12

Thursday, July 12, 1984

They quickly got into Sydney's yellow Corolla and headed to the gig.

Things had changed considerably since their accidental meeting en route from Ottawa. The gifted twenty-two-year-old graduate of Ottawa's School of Art seemed able to play almost any tune Ethan could think of with little effort. From an early age, she'd trained to play the cello, but while touring as a fourteen-year-old cellist prodigy with the Ottawa Symphony Orchestra, she'd discovered the guitar and rock. Her obsession with both shook the foundation of several generations of music tradition in her family. Her defiance—which Ethan soon learned was unwieldy and fierce—led to an exile from music and serving behind the counter of the family restaurant as penance for her insolence. The distress that followed took her away from music despite her graduating with top honors from the college. If she couldn't have it her way, she wouldn't have it at all. Modern music and the electric guitar were in her blood. Smitten, there was no going back. It all was working out as far as Ethan could see.

"Gus will be having a shit fit," she said as they passed slower traffic.

Ethan was paying little attention. The tune they'd started was wreaking havoc in his head.

"Why aren't you?" Sydney asked, her words bringing him back to the night's show.

"I am," he replied, smiling. He loved the magic of writing a new song. He didn't want to stop.

"Sure as hell doesn't look like it," Sydney said. Ethan knew her preshow jitters made her talk more than usual. "Your head is someplace else."

"Just goin' through the show," he lied. In truth, he was trying hard to lock in the tune they'd come up with. Writing down the words helped, but that didn't always capture the music or the feel. He feared losing the groove of the song. It was like chasing a shadow. He could see it and reach out for it but not quite touch it. Playing it over and over usually locked it in, but still, it could vanish, returning only when and if it wanted to.

"Yeah, sure you are," Sydney replied, "and I'm fucking Diana Ross. You're like glass you're so transparent. Don't be playin' fucking poker."

He laughed uneasily, as he could almost feel the tune fading. They really had to play it. He wished they hadn't left so quickly, show or no show.

"You're still working the damn song, aren't you?"

"I hope you fuckin' remember it, 'cause listening to all your talk is pushing it out of my head."

"You worry too much," Sydney replied, turning the car onto the exit ramp. They were close. "It's locked up tight right here." Her right hand came off the wheel as she pointed to her temple.

"Tight or not, if you don't keep your hands on the wheel, it won't fucking matter."

"You're an asshole," she said, and the car surged forward. "I can't believe I joined a band of dicks."

"Feeling's mutual, my dear."

"Always have to have the last word. You're fucking pathetic."

A minute later, Sydney turned into the gravel parking lot of Benny's Bar and Grill. Greg's gray Nova was parked beside the roadhouse.

"How does Gus find these places?" Sydney asked, frowning. "We're gonna need fucking helmets if they don't like us."

"We'll soon find out. I hope everything's set up."

"It will be," Sydney said, sounding a little more upbeat. "What's up your sleeve tonight?"

"Have to wait and see," Ethan answered, thinking of his earlier episode with Uncle Al. "I've got a little anger to blow off tonight."

He smiled, not quite sure himself what he might do.

Sydney parked at the side of the building, beside the Nova. Ethan grabbed his Shure mike case off the Corolla's floor and got out. He'd taken to the habit of carrying his mike so he knew where it was. Sydney pulled the case holding her prized white Gibson ES-355 off the back seat. When he'd first seen her play, the polished white guitar had looked as big as she was, but it didn't take long to see who was in charge. Onstage, five-inch heels helped offset her physical size against that of her guitar, but when she started to play, there was nothing small about her. Ethan pulled his duffel bag out from behind his seat. He followed her to the rear entrance at the side of the building.

Greg opened the steel door in answer to Sydney's knock.

"Where the fuck have you been?" he cried. "We were supposed to be on ten minutes ago."

"Fucking traffic," Sydney answered, looking at Ethan, "but from the looks of the parking lot, nobody fucking cares anyway."

"Fuck you," Greg said, and he turned away.

In the entranceway behind Greg, Ethan could see Gus shaking his head. Whether at their lateness, the exchange between Sydney and Greg, or both, Ethan couldn't tell. Gus was standing beside the door to what would serve as their dressing room for the night. Greg held the door as Sydney and Ethan stepped into the small alcove. Left of the door was the kitchen, which led into the back of the barroom.

It was early by Thursday night standards and still light outside. Inside, they entered the bar's dim smokiness, which was intended to keep the patrons in perpetual night, away from the world of bills and responsibility. The few cars in the parking lot matched the number of customers inside; the place felt like an empty cavern. Opposite the long bar was the twelve-by-twelve platform that would serve as their home for the night. Gus and Greg, with the help of Gus's friend Scott, who did their sound and lights, had the stage all set. Greg's drums, the two amps, and a small keyboard filled the space. Gus and Sydney would be in tight against the equipment. Ethan would spend little time on the stage. The setup was pretty much the norm on the local bar circuit. Often, there was no platform at all. Only the high schools had stages that afforded a band room enough to move around.

Sydney walked across the room and set her guitar case on the stage.

"Let's suit up," she said when she came back.

"I'll tell Scott we'll be ready in five," Gus said.

"Okeydokey," Ethan responded as he headed toward the makeshift dressing room. The room, the men's washroom, had a single toilet and urinal. There, Ethan's transformation to rock star would take place, an inauspicious start to the evening.

He put on the white T-shirt and black leather cowboy vest he'd tucked into the duffel bag at the house. He decided to leave his jeans on instead of wearing the multicolored tights he'd brought along. He figured flamboyance might be a little over the top for the night, considering Sydney's helmet comment. Besides, he'd had enough confrontation for one day.

As he pulled a red headband out of the bag, the back of his hand caught the sharp edge of the toilet paper dispenser. The pain was sharp and quick, but he couldn't get the cut to stop bleeding. He was wiping the back of his hand with the small square sheets of toilet paper when he struck on an idea. After wiping away the blood with his index finger, he dabbed a horizontal line below each eye. As the cut continued to bleed, he marked short vertical lines beside each eye that connected with the horizontal lines. He looked in the mirror above the sink. The markings gave his face an angled Adam Ant–like look. He liked it. He stretched on his headband. His hand continued to bleed, but he stopped thinking about it, absorbed in his new look. He wrapped a red tie—one of several in his bag—around his neck. He was ready.

Sydney came out of the adjacent washroom the same time he exited. White platform shoes made her six inches taller and changed her walk to a strut. How she cavorted onstage in such footwear, he'd never know. Her straight black hair extended at varying angles from her head. White mascara and black eyeliner accentuated her dark eyes, and deep red lipstick made her look even taller. A white scarf completed her ensemble.

"You shine up pretty good," Ethan said, staring at her transformation and not for the first time. "I only hope people can hear what we're playing over what they see."

"Or be fucking scared," Sydney retorted, staring at his face. "Who the fuck are you?"

"I'm your fucking worst nightmare," he answered, grinning.

Her sparkly black spandex pants showed off her slender figure. Her look appealed to most males in the audience, but if any gave her a hard time, they did so at their own peril. She wasn't one to mess with. Ethan had seen her in action at one of their first gigs. A guy had decided to get a little too friendly. Close to the stage, he'd slid his hand down her back while she faced Gus. She'd turned, held up her hand, and shaken her head, her expression for "Not interested." Not getting the message, the guy had smiled and touched her arm. A second later, before either Ethan or Gus could react, Sydney had been on top of the guy with her knee on his chest.

Ethan was anxious to perform. They hadn't played since Monday. At that show, Sydney had played through her new Marshall cabinet, which sounded pristine and loud. Greg and Gus had been tight. Recalling the night charged him up.

Standing in the little alcove outside the washrooms, Sydney stepped past him and peeked into the barroom.

"This may be a rehearsal night," she said, stepping back. "Lots of empty fucking tables."

"We'll do what we came to do," Ethan said as Greg joined them, crowding in the tiny space.

"Let's get this party started!" Greg shouted over the din of the last bars of Van Halen's "Panama" playing through the PA.

Greg headed to the drum kit. Gus, already at the stage, grabbed his black Fender Jazz off its stand. Ethan watched in envy as he strapped on the bass. Sydney seemed to float to the stage in a stream of white and black. Ethan smiled as he watched the eyes of the few people in the bar follow her. In seconds, she had her white Gibson on and ready to play. She handled the instrument like an experienced cowboy wrangling a calf to the ground with both grace and confidence.

As "Panama" came to an end, the house deejay's English accent took over.

"We're going to change things up a bit," he said over the murmurings of the few people drinking. "For two nights only, please welcome the Release!"

Sydney counted them in and then struck down the opening chords to Boston's "Don't Look Back," which were studio perfect to Ethan's ears and as good as what Tom Scholz had played on the record. Sydney repeated the opening phrase a couple of times, until Greg came in on his hi-hat. Gus pumped out a bass line more intricate than the original, which Sydney couldn't help but attack. Ethan moved to the side of the stage, doing his best to stay hidden behind Gus's bass amp. His voice came on strong, but he remained unseen until the second verse, when he burst out beside the small stage.

Ethan was so into his part and hitting his cues in the songs that it wasn't until the first song was over and they were into the second—Aerosmith's "Walk This Way"—that he noticed maybe a dozen people in the bar. All eyes were still watching Sydney.

Midway through "Don't Tell Me"—a song the band had written to Ethan's lyrics—Ethan looked down to find the red tie he'd brought onstage tied to his mike. He pulled the mike from the stand. Without thinking, he tossed the mike sideways and began to swing it in a circle beside him. He caught it just in time to sing the chorus. Sydney was watching and winked her approval. The Eagles' "Life in the Fast Lane" followed. Gus's rhythmic bass riffs matched Sydney's guitar dexterity. Ethan thought their arrangement was kicking. The Eagles would have been jealous. They rounded out the first set with their version of Tom Petty and the Heartbreakers' "Refugee" and Greg's favorite, Alice Cooper's "School's Out."

In the closing notes of the song, Ethan knew what he would do to end the set. Using the edge of the stage as leverage to get higher, he leaped into a flying scissor kick, imitating what he'd seen Van Halen's David Lee Roth do on *Don Kirshner's Rock Concert*.

As he jumped, he saw his right leg go up high, but that was all.

CHAPTER 13

Thursday, July 12, 1984

"Don't move," said a woman's voice softly. The voice was direct and almost familiar. It made him feel safe—a nurse's voice maybe. A hand touched his arm. "How do you feel?"

"Okay," he said, questioning whether he did or not. His head was sore. His arm hurt. Where was he? The hospital? It didn't feel like his room. It was dim and smelled of smoked cigarettes and spilled beer. There was nothing white or hospital-like he could see. It was too dark. No, thank God, it wasn't the hospital.

Soft fingertips brushed the side of his head.

"Really?" the kind voice asked.

"I think so."

He tried to lift himself up.

The soft fingers turned firm and held him back.

"Don't try to get up," the comforting voice said.

He stopped. Faces surrounded them. Some he recognized.

"You have blood on your face," the woman said, her face close to his, examining, "but I don't see any ..." Her voice trailed off.

Fragments of what had taken place were coming back. He could see Sydney behind the nurse woman. He saw Greg. Then, as if he were waking from a deep sleep, everything came back—the stage, Benny's Bar and Grill. They were ending their first set. He was jumping.

"You have a small laceration on the side of your head," the woman said, her warm hand brushing his cheek.

"A what?" Ethan replied. It sounded serious. The woman's fingertips pressed against his head. Ethan raised his hand to find a painful lump.

"Sorry," she said, her gentle voice in control. The tone was familiar, but he didn't know why. "You've cut your head."

Ethan turned. Their eyes met. There was an instant of recognition, followed by a sudden need to turn away, as if he were seeing something he wasn't supposed to, but it was too late to avoid it. He didn't know why he had the feelings he did. Something was familiar, but he couldn't place from where.

"Do I know you?" he asked, knowing the answer before the woman replied.

"No, sorry," she said quickly. "I'm a nurse. I saw you fall."

Ethan got the sense there was more, but he only looked at her. Her hair was tied back. Her pretty face was unsmiling, a face of concern. There was something familiar in the way her fingers touched his bruised head, as if she'd been there before comforting him.

"Do you feel dizzy or light-headed?" she asked, her eyes looking everywhere but into his. Her closeness charged the air, as if electricity passed between them.

"No, but my head's a little sore. I think I'm okay."

More people seemed to be standing around them. Maybe the bar was filling up. He wanted to get up.

"Give this man a drink!" someone shouted through the chatter that hovered in the air above him.

"But the blood on your face," the woman said, rubbing her thumb and fingertips together.

"It's okay. It'll take too long to explain." Ethan smiled.

He sat up. The wood floor in front of the stage was dirty, not that he cared. Gus and Sydney squatted alongside the woman. Greg was standing at his feet. Ethan looked up at the overhead stage lights, but nothing looked out of place.

"You're a fuckin' hardheaded bastard," Greg said, shaking his head.

Ethan then looked at the unknown woman. What he said next, he'd never said to a woman before.

"Can I buy you a drink?"

CHAPTER 14

Thursday, July 12, 1984

"No," the woman replied, recoiling as if he'd offended her.

"I'm sorry," he said, trying to recover as best as he could from what he couldn't believe he'd said. "Ethan Jones."

He stuck out his hand. The woman did not reciprocate. He felt awkward; he couldn't say what he wanted to, and what he did say seemed wrong. She didn't look at him. Those around them began to disperse.

Ethan spoke again, unable to remain quiet, self-conscious of his bruised body and now bruised ego.

"What's wrong?" he asked, not knowing quite what to say but feeling the need to say something. "I didn't mean ... Please don't ... You're so ..."

He stopped. He was mumbling.

"I can't," the woman said as her brown eyes swept past him like a giant hand he was powerless to escape from. The moment both shook and exhilarated him. It was like looking over the railing of an open balcony twenty stories up. *It only takes a second to jump.*

"You feel okay?" she asked again.

"Yes," he replied, wishing that more of the right words would come.

The woman stood up and left.

Ethan, dumbfounded, got to his feet. His head was sore. Sydney was behind him.

"Strange," she said, flipping back her hair as she looked at him. "Kind of an odd response, don't you think? How's the head?"

Ethan couldn't shake what had happened and hardly noticed his hurt head. The caring concern of a nurse followed by such sudden derision—he seemed to have confused schoolboy infatuation with professional care.

"What?" he said, looking from the entrance back to Sydney, trying to act as though nothing had happened.

"I think you're more hurt by the woman than your fucking flip," she said, and she looked away. "But beauty like that is hard to get over."

Ethan didn't say anything.

"Come on. Let's get some ice on that head of yours. You're one lucky son of a bitch. I didn't think you were getting up."

They moved to the bar. Gus and Greg were already there after retrieving his mike and making sure their equipment was in order for the next set.

"You okay?" Greg asked.

"Yeah, just fucking stupid is all," Ethan said, annoyed about not being more aware of how low the ceiling was and even more about the woman leaving.

Sydney slid two draft beers and a small bag of ice in front of him.

"This place is so small," he said.

He grabbed one of the glasses. Beer helped a lot go away. He held the bag of ice against the lump on his head.

"Here's to taking one for the band," Gus said, raising his glass.

"Ooh-rah!" shouted Greg, using an expression he'd picked up in the States. Raising his almost empty glass, he clinked it against Ethan's. "Right on, bro!"

"It was a pretty awesome jump," Sydney said, "before the light got in the way."

"It was fucking fantastic!" Greg said. "Without that, it was just another set."

Ethan didn't want to talk about it. In his mind, they'd performed their best set yet. He didn't want his overexuberant move to take away from the show.

"It was a killer set," he said, punching Gus's shoulder. He looked at Sydney. "I don't know how you do it. You're like two players in one. 'Don't Look Back' was fucking crazy. Gus, you're funked up."

"Funked?" Gus replied, putting his beer on the table. "You sure your head's okay?"

Sydney smiled then walked back to the stage.

"You may think you can fly," Greg said, laughing, "but can you remember the words for the second set?"

"Fuck off!" Ethan quipped. He and Greg had been through a lot over the years. Greg was playing well that night and knew it.

"What did you say to the lady?" Greg asked, picking up the other glass of beer. "She left pretty fucking fast after rushing to your side. Thought you had a new friend."

"Dunno," Ethan replied. "She wanted nothing to do with me after knowing I was okay."

The bartender wiped the bar in front of them.

"Thanks for the ice," Ethan said, and then he thought of his throat. "Do you have any tea and honey?"

"You're welcome, and yes," the bartender answered, dropping the cloth in her hand behind the bar. "Need a minute for the tea, though. You sure you're okay? Looked like you hit that light pretty hard." She smiled—another kind face.

Ethan nodded. "It wasn't planned."

He kept the plastic bag of ice on the side of his head. The crushed coolness was soothing. He'd have a good lump in the morning. He turned and looked back at the stage. He was lucky to be sitting there. *What was I thinking?* His tea came. The warm sweetness relaxed his throat. Even from his short time singing, he'd learned that when his throat felt dry, it was too late. He'd wake up hoarse or worse. An irritated throat had a way of turning into a cold. Lately, he'd practiced shifting the sound of his voice to a rougher, grittier sound in the likeness of AC/DC's front man, Brian Johnson. It added an edge they all liked to the songs, but it had a tendency to irritate his throat, sometimes painfully. Honey in the tea seemed to ease the tension and act as a kind of lubricant for his vocal cords.

As he sipped his tea, he watched as more people entered the bar. It was almost ten o'clock. Coincidence or not, the bar was filling up after his stunt.

The in-house deejay came by and introduced himself. He'd give them ten more minutes. If their second set was anything like the first, more people would be coming. Word got around quickly when something special was happening, he told them. The Release was special. Many of their regular customers lived close.

"Where'd you get the name?" he asked.

"He stole it from a book," Greg said, pointing at Ethan.

The deejay looked at Ethan. "What book?"

Ethan shook his head. Greg still couldn't believe they were named after a fictional band from a novel. He'd warmed up to it, though, after hearing others remark on it.

"There's not much to explain," Ethan said. "Ever heard of *Browning Station?*"

"Nope," the deejay responded. "Not much of a reader, I'm afraid."

"Well, that's where it's from."

"Fuckin' cool," said the deejay, and he picked up the glass of soda the bartender had set on the bar. "Ten minutes to rock."

Ethan took another sip of tea. His thoughts drifted to *Browning Station*. He wondered where his copy of the book had gone. He'd been unable to find it since getting back and had pretty much given up looking for it. Randolph's girlfriend had had a copy. He was sure he'd seen his in the car but now figured they'd left it behind. Funny, he didn't know where it had come from in the first place. The hospital didn't have a library. He hadn't bought it. It seemed to have appeared from nowhere and now had disappeared to the same spot. He wondered whether the band's name really had come from the book. He'd never finished reading it that he could remember.

Sydney rejoined the three of them at the bar. She held a yellow piece of paper listing the songs for the second set.

"I've got an idea," she said, holding out the paper. "Want to hear it?"

"Does it involve me?" Greg said quickly.

"You're in the band," she replied, "so yes."

"Then no," Greg said, as any of them would have predicted. Unless it was his idea, he was usually unreceptive. Any suggestion from Sydney was always a no.

Sydney ignored him, as was her usual response. "You doing okay?" she asked Ethan. The bag of ice was on the bar.

Ethan nodded. "Can't get rid of me that fucking easily," he said, touching the lump on the side of his head. "Does that change your plan?"

"Nope." Sydney leaned over the bar to sit down. "But it does make it possible. Let's start with 'American Woman,'" she said excitedly, appearing to vibrate as she spoke.

"Ah, come on," Greg groaned. "That's our grand finale."

"Just wait," Sydney said, raising her hand. "Gus goes on with a simple growing bass line. You come in after six or eight bars on the hi-hat and snare. Chic-ka-chic-ka tu, chic-ka-chic-ka tu."

As she spoke, her hands moved in rhythm to her words, as if playing his drums.

Greg didn't say anything, nor did anyone else.

"I'll come in with the guitar," she said with the coy smile Ethan knew they all recognized meant she had some magic up her sleeve she wasn't about to reveal until they played it. The look also reassured him that whatever it was would likely blow them away. "Ethan, you come in screamin' the chorus with your ties flying."

She paused and looked at each of them. "The crowd's small. If it doesn't work, no one will fucking know anyway."

Sydney was convincing when she had a hot idea going off in her head.

"But if it does ..." She didn't need to finish.

No one said a word. They'd all witnessed a few of Sydney's moments of genius already. Ethan's senses tingled. He knew each of them understood what was about to happen in making another of her ideas real.

"And, Ethan," Sydney said, tilting her head forward as if looking over the top of a pair of reading glasses, "no jumping."

"I'm in!" He grinned. "Fucking bring it on."

CHAPTER 15

"Please welcome back," announced the deejay fifteen minutes later, "to Benny's stage for the second time tonight, the Release!"

There was a brief cheer that was all but extinguished by Gus's pulsing bass line. Greg followed with his hi-hat-to-snare rhythm, just as Sydney had described. As if they'd rehearsed it for weeks, Sydney's searing guitar split the air like a jet on a flyby with the famous "American Woman" riff. She'd discovered a mix of sound from her plethora of guitar effects that combined fuzz and flanger pedals to stretch the notes she played like an elastic band. After she repeated the iconic riff for the third time, Ethan emerged from the darkness, screaming the song title popularized by the Guess Who. The crowd, which had now grown from the few they had started the first set in front of to a couple dozen, erupted as if some kind of disaster had taken place inside the bar. The Release played on, hitting each part of the song as they'd rehearsed over the past weeks. Ethan's vocals captured the urgent feelings of hurt, anger, and escape in the lyrics. By the end, the cheer that had greeted them at the beginning of the song had grown to a roar. As Sydney hit the final chord, she looked over at Ethan. Her eyes said it all: "We done good!"

They paused between songs only long enough for Ethan to take a quick sip of water, and then they broke into their arrangements of the Police's "Don't Stand So Close to Me" and Steve Winwood's "Higher Love." Both highlighted Greg's growing prowess on the drum kit. Ethan gulped down more water as they went into another band original, entitled "Confusion," which he sang his heart out on. At one point during the song, he opened his eyes to see the woman who had helped him standing alone at the back of the room. She was beautiful; her eyes surely could melt whatever might have been protecting his heart. He hoped she'd stay until the end of the set.

When the song ended, he glanced at Sydney, who was already counting them in for their version of T. Rex's "Bang a Gong." He knew Sydney loved the opening, with her flair for dizzying finger work. The crowd loved it too. Ethan tried to find the woman again, but she was gone, and with her this time went something in his heart. He pulled out everything he had to finish the song and the two that followed. They closed with Foreigner's "Feels Like the First Time." They owned the night. The crowd's ovation brought them back for not one but two encores. The last song in their repertoire was Aerosmith's "Sweet Emotion." It was their least-rehearsed number, but it seemed to coalesce them as a band; their groove was unbreakable, led by Gus's bass line. Benny's was full. The hardwood portion of the barroom floor in front of the small stage was packed.

With the motto "Leave the audience wanting more" whispering in his head, Ethan smiled, realizing they had little choice. They didn't have any more songs.

"That was fucking crazy!" Sydney shouted, following Ethan into the men's washroom after they'd finished. Ethan was at the sink, throwing cool water onto his face. A pretty good-sized lump had formed on his head.

"Sydney!" he shouted with playful disdain in his voice. Her top was off when he turned to look at her. He looked away.

"Like it matters," she said, laughing. "We're in a fucking band for God's sake—like an old married couple, except our best years are ahead of us."

He laughed too. *Leave it to Sydney to bring new meaning to an age-old expression.* Ethan looked in the mirror. The blood he'd smeared on his face was almost gone. He ripped off a section of brown paper towel from the dispenser and wiped off the rest.

"We fucking killed it tonight, Ethan," Sydney said, more serious.

He could see her reflection standing behind him in the mirror. Leaning forward, she shook her head, taking some of the hairspray stiffness out of her hair. He thought it amazing how such perfection could reside in such a tiny package. For an instant, he imagined her petite body standing in front of his, her tiny breasts pressed against his chest in a warm embrace. But it couldn't happen. Intuitively, he knew it wouldn't work. Bandmates falling in love were doom to a band. At times, he wondered whether she might like girls. She'd taken down the guy who had bothered her in quick order. He'd watched her eye other women dancing to their music. Even that night, she'd remarked on the beauty of the nurse. The Release couldn't have gotten a better gift. If it were true, it would explain her inhibition in front of him. But it didn't stop his attraction to her. He looked away.

In a matter of minutes, Sydney transformed back to her teenage look of jeans, a jean jacket, and sneakers, looking barely old enough to be the neighborhood babysitter, let alone of age to be playing bars. Without fail, a request for ID would follow a drink order at the bar. She became unrecognizable as the genius who created their unique arrangements of established hit songs. She was much shorter without her heels and stage getup, and he doubted many in the bar would have any idea she was the guitar aficionado, except she was the only Asian chick in the vicinity. The irony never changed, no matter how often it was demonstrated. The terrorist and serial killer were never the monsters who stood out from the crowd. They were common folk, the man or woman next door. It was easy to be fooled, he thought. People were unpredictable, despite the propensity to think otherwise. It seemed a paradox that in spite of everyone's uniqueness; the similarities were forever searched out. But Sydney was an outlier.

"Almost ready, singer man?"

Ethan shook his head as Sydney pulled on her jean jacket. It was her look even if the outside temperature was too hot for a coat.

"Yeah, almost." His throat was tender, irritated enough to make his voice sound raspy. "Wanna grab a beer with the guys?"

"Sure, I'll be at the bar then."

Ethan grabbed his gym bag and pulled on what he'd packed: a pair of faded jeans and a T-shirt with Rush's star man on the front. The show had pumped all of them up. Ethan didn't want to abandon the feeling and just head back to his parents' house. There was nothing that could touch a great performance—not alcohol, drugs, or even sex. It was pure adrenaline that danced on the line between life and death. Music connected them with an audience and could turn into moments of incredible exhilaration.

He ran his fingers through his messed-up hair, touching the lump that quickly reminded him of his jump. He leaned toward the mirror and looked more closely at the small cut and swelling. Some dried blood was caked in his hair. He moved back and shook his head. It was a small mishap for a kicking show. He wanted to celebrate.

Gus and Greg were deep in conversation at the bar. Sydney seemed distracted, her slender fingers drumming out some melody that only she could hear on top of the polished bar.

"Ethan, my man," Gus said, turning away from his conversation. "What a fucking night!"

"That's one way to put it," Ethan said, pulling out a barstool beside Sydney.

Ethan was scanning the bar, hoping. It had been a long time since he'd felt anything akin to how he felt looking into the eyes of the woman who had helped him. Maybe his heart could love again, he thought hopefully. The pervading guilt that accompanied even thinking about someone after Mila was finally dissipating. He was ready, only to be disappointed. The dispersing crowd left no sign of the woman.

"What can I get you?" asked the bartender he'd spoken to earlier. "On the house."

"I'm on my second," Greg said, holding up a half-full glass of beer.

"Gin and soda," Ethan answered, his eyes moving from the bartender across the barroom again, still hoping.

"You were something else tonight," Gus said, shaking his head. His eyes were wide and lit up, something Ethan hadn't seen since their early rehearsals. "Like a magician making the imaginary come to life."

Gus moved closer to Ethan. "During 'Don't Stand So Close to Me,'" he said, putting his hand on Ethan's shoulder, "it was like Sydney was the student, and you were the helpless teacher. How you showed your feelings about this vulnerable young schoolgirl. How you couldn't help yourself. Nabokov was here with Lolita. You were mesmerizing. The whole place was deliciously uncomfortable." Gus slapped him on the back. "It's a gift, dude. Better than Sting—and Sting's the best."

"Thanks, man," Ethan replied. He was smiling. It was humbling to be praised by someone he respected as much as Gus, even though he hated that Gus was the bass player he would never be. He turned to Sydney. "We reinvented 'American Woman' tonight. I don't know where the fuck you pulled that from, but keep pulling."

"Just stay away from the fucking stage lights," Sydney said, grinning.

The bartender laughed and placed Ethan's drink on the bar in front of him. "We haven't had a crowd like this in months," she said. "You'll be back."

Ethan raised his glass. "I'll drink to that!" He took a sip of the cool liquid. He'd hardly noticed the heat of the night. "We're here again tomorrow night," he said.

They chatted about the night for the better part of an hour. Several customers came over and shook their hands, praising their show and saying they'd be back.

"Last call," the bartender announced. Ethan had finished his drink, and he ordered another. He didn't have to get up for work. Greg ordered another beer. Sydney and Gus abstained.

It wasn't long before Benny's crowd was back to the size it had been when they'd started the evening. Gus and Sydney were talking. Greg was looking in the direction of two women near the front entrance. Ethan looked again for his mystery woman and then turned, picked up his drink from the bar, and stood behind his three bandmates.

"I've got something on my mind," he announced.

Gus and Sydney turned on their stools.

Greg, already sitting sideways to the bar, turned to look at Ethan but didn't move. "Shit," he said, expressing what his eyes were already saying. "You're not going to fuck up this night, are you?" Greg slid off his stool and stood eye to eye with Ethan.

"What?" Ethan said, staring at Greg. "How the fuck could you even think that?"

"'Cause your tone is fucking serious, dude," Greg said.

Ethan shook his head, remembering his earlier confrontation in the driveway at home. "I'm not about to fuck the night up. But thanks for the vote of confidence."

"Okay, I'm tired of this mystery shit." Sydney sighed. "What's up?"

Ethan took a sip of his drink. "We need to move in to together," he said, looking at Sydney in answer to her question.

"You and me?" she asked, her eyes widening in apparent shock. "Are you—"

"No, no, no," Ethan said, shaking his head with his hands open in front of him. "Us—us as a band."

There was a long pause before anyone spoke.

"Really?" Greg said, his voice rising.

"Yes," Ethan said, looking from Greg to Sydney and then to Gus. "If we're serious about this thing, we need to be together—live together."

The extended version of "Do You Feel like We Do" from *Frampton Comes Alive* was playing in the background. Gus lit a cigarette.

"Give me one of those," Ethan said. Gus popped out the butt of a Camel cigarette from the soft brown package he was holding and extended it to Ethan.

"Man, this is serious," Greg said as Gus flicked his BIC lighter in front of Ethan's cigarette.

Ethan watched the tip of the cigarette light up as he sucked on the other end. He didn't smoke much but enjoyed the pleasant buzz it gave him.

"Wow," Sydney said, staring at Ethan with the cigarette in his hand. "I didn't see that coming."

"It's all part of the night," Ethan replied in defense of his smoking. "You haven't seen me get close and personal with a stage light before either."

Sydney glanced sideways at Gus. "Give me one of those fuckers, pusher man."

Gus patted the pack again, directing a cigarette to Sydney. He pointed the pack at Greg. Greg shook his head.

"Abstaining, thanks, but I'd like Cigarette Man to elaborate on this fine idea of his," Greg said, looking at Ethan.

Ethan blew out the smoke he'd inhaled. The buzz kicked in sweetly.

"As serious as we all are," Ethan said, and he gulped down a mouthful of his gin and soda. He could see Sydney's eyes locked on some spot in the bar behind him, taking in what he said. She had a particular focused stare, Ethan had noticed, whenever listening to something she thought important.

Gus blew a plume of smoke toward the ceiling. Greg continued to stare at Ethan. He was the only one now who had a day job.

Ethan didn't think anyone knew he'd lost his. "We need to commit."

"Did you have something in mind?" Greg asked. "Like a place maybe or even a fucking plan?"

Ethan shook his head as he sucked in another breath of smoke from the Camel cigarette. They were stronger than the Player's Special Blend he usually chose.

"No," Ethan replied, exhaling smoke through his nostrils. "I just thought about it before the show. Sydney played something cool at the house. I put some words to it."

Ethan took another short draw from his cigarette. "We get fucking ideas all the time," he said, speaking through the cloud of smoke he breathed out. The words came quickly as his thoughts came together. "While we're doing something else—like digging fucking postholes—we think we'll catch it later, but we never do, 'cause later never comes, or when it does, we can't remember what it was."

Sydney was drumming her fingers on the bar again. She stopped and looked straight at Ethan.

Ethan took another drag. "If the Release is going to be real, we have to live it," he said. He set his cigarette down in the small tinfoil ashtray on the bar top. "It's gonna take everything we have and then some. I mean fucking everything. We gotta eat, drink, and sleep fucking music all the time. We're gonna fucking hate each other and write music. We're gonna be hungry, thirsty, and wasted together and write music. We're gonna fuck our brains out and write more music."

"Hey now. Whoa there, maestro," Greg said. "Just how do you see us fucking paying for all this? Only you and I have jobs."

"I don't know!" Ethan shouted. "But that's a fuckin' excuse, and you know it! Everybody uses it. Money, money, fuckin' money—the fucking dream buster!"

He picked up his cigarette and took another drag. "You know what?" Ethan said, reminded of a *Circus* magazine article he'd read. "Aerosmith lived together as a band. Steve Tyler said it was their secret recipe."

Gus turned and looked at Ethan. "You know, I remember reading something like that too. I didn't think it was Aerosmith, though."

No one said anything, but Ethan knew he had their attention. The few minutes he'd sat with Sydney at his folks' house should have been the norm, not the exception. If they wanted the music world, they had to live it. If they didn't, they were destined to end up goofing around like most who decided they wanted to start a band. In a way, the secret to success in the music business seemed too simple, and yet it really was that simple: they had to play and live music. Few seemed to have what it took to make that commitment.

Sydney stopped drumming on the countertop. "I'm in," she said. "I'm fuckin' in!"

Gus and Greg turned and looked at her. Ethan wondered if they were surprised she was first to agree. He wasn't. If anybody was ready, it was Sydney. She'd left home for the band and was living with her aunt in Toronto. To Ethan's mind, she was already committed.

"I'm in too," Gus added, clenching his fist and pounding the bar top like a judge pounding a gavel. Gus looked at Greg as if to say, "Well?"

"Oh, and so you know, Greg"—Ethan gave him a small lips-together smile—"you're the only one with a day job. I got fired today."

CHAPTER 16

Friday, July 13, 1984

Sydney and Gus stared at Greg. Ethan didn't need to say any more.

"So," Greg said, his hand on his beer glass, "you're proposing we live together as a band. Any thoughts on how we might do that? Like where we're gonna fucking live? Or how we pay rent when only one of us has a fucking job?"

Ethan felt for Greg. He'd had a peek into Greg's life over the years, and that was enough. From the outside looking in, he knew Greg's family was the envy of most. They lived in Queenston Heights, a gated community on the outskirts of Toronto; had a cottage in the Muskokas; had Cadillacs and Mercedes in the driveway; and took cruises to exotic places around the globe. They were rich by most standards, and the stress that the lack of money brought most didn't really exist for Greg. That was the belief. But what Ethan had seen in being around Greg in high school was the exact opposite. The expectation that accompanied what money represented was crushing. Making money and keeping the family's fortune intact never seemed to leave Greg's conscious mind. Ethan figured that pressure likely filled his dreams and nightmares too. Greg's apparent arrogance was really inverted fear. The guy was scared—freaked out was closer to the truth—most of the time. There was an incredible assumed pressure to be successful. Subsequently, he never made decisions that were really his, and Ethan knew now that the band—Greg's place of refuge—was forcing his hand. For possibly the first time in his life, he was being asked to decide what he wanted to do and who he wanted to be. Ethan began to suspect why Greg had really quit MIT shortly after meeting him for lunch. People went to MIT with commitment. Greg was smart, top of their graduating class, but he wasn't committed, no matter what his parents thought. Now Ethan's proposal was asking for that commitment. For Greg, that commitment had to pay off far beyond the expectations any of the other band members had placed on them—imagined or otherwise. Compared to MIT, the Release was a pipedream that Ethan was asking him to believe in. He didn't envy Greg.

"Why the fuck are you so worried about that?" Sydney asked, bringing Ethan out of his thoughts.

"Somebody has to," Greg said like a fighter backed into a corner.

"I don't," Sydney retorted, "and I get along just fine."

"Let's sleep on it," Ethan said, wondering if he really did understand Greg's concerns. "It's a big deal, and we've just had the night of our lives."

He looked at Greg, who stared back at him. The Cars' "Let's Go" was playing in the background.

"I don't need to sleep on it," Greg said, looking from Ethan to Sydney and then to Gus. "It's a moment of truth for the Release, isn't it? I get it. I'm in."

Sydney was first to respond, jabbing her tiny fists back and forth like a boxer in front of her. "I knew it! I fuckin' knew you'd see the light!" she cried.

"That's awesome, man," Gus said, reaching over and shaking Greg's hand.

"It scares the shit outta me," Greg replied, "'cause I have no fucking idea how it's all gonna work."

"None of us do," Ethan said.

"But I'm fucking supposed to," Greg said as Sydney stood up and gave him a hug. "That's the Schmidt way."

Ethan had his hand on Gus's shoulder, smiling. "Maybe the Schmidt way isn't the Greg way," Ethan said.

"It's how I was brought up," Greg answered, "but if Boston taught me anything, it's that things don't always work out as planned."

"They fucking never do," Ethan said, and he raised his hand to the bartender. "Four shots of tequila, please."

"We're supposed to be closed," the woman answered, turning to the liquor bottles lining the wall behind her. "But I'll make an exception tonight if I get to join in." She grinned and pulled down the shot glasses.

When she'd finished pouring, Ethan took a filled glass, raised it, and moved between Greg and Sydney.

"To the Release!" he said over Pink Floyd's "Another Brick in the Wall." They simultaneously brought the shot glasses to their lips and gulped down the contents.

"We're in this together, like it or not," Ethan said, and he set the small, heavy-bottomed glass down hard on the bar.

He looked at Sydney. She was smiling.

"It's time to crash this Popsicle stand," Ethan said, surprised at his use of an old high school expression. Tequila had that effect on him.

"Okay," Gus said, giving him the eye. "Whatever."

Ethan watched as Sydney picked up his bag and tossed it at him. She picked up her own and headed toward the door they'd come in.

"Bus is leaving," she said.

"You guys good to go?" Ethan asked, looking at Greg, as he was the one with the car.

"We got it, man," Gus said, motioning his head in the direction Sydney was headed. "Don't keep her waiting. It's a long walk."

Ethan shook their hands with the thumb-lock grip of brotherhood and started toward the door.

"Excuse me," the bartender called to Ethan. She was holding something in her hand. It looked like their bill.

"The man with the beard," Ethan said, trying to be helpful. "He's got the money."

"No," the woman said, shaking her head. Ethan quickly clued in and readied himself for an awkward moment. He'd returned the woman's smile each time she looked at him. Had he given her the wrong impression?

"Sorry. I meant to give you this earlier," she said, handing him a note. "I put it down and forgot about it. Lucky I saw it now."

Ethan took the note and shrugged as though to question its origin.

"A woman passed it to me earlier," she said in answer to Ethan's unasked question. "Asked me to give it to the singer."

Ethan nodded. "Thanks," he said. With note in hand, he headed again to the door, thinking of Sydney's note in the guitar magazine.

Sydney was already out the door.

CHAPTER 17

Ethan couldn't wait to get to Sydney's car before looking at the note. In the dim cone of light cast by the single lightbulb above Benny's Bar and Grill's back exit, he read the neat, tight script:

> To Ethan:
> I'm not supposed to talk to you. But I can't help myself.
> I don't come to these places often, but we all have our
> moments. I recognized you in the photo posted in the lobby.
> Call if you want.

There was a phone number written below the note.

"Are you coming?" Sydney called through the open driver-side window of her idling Corolla. "I can hardly keep my eyes open."

"Yeah," Ethan said, and he walked around the rear of the car to the passenger-side door and climbed in.

Sydney backed away from the wall and drove to the parking lot exit. She turned onto the roadway, which was lit only by the car's headlights.

"So," Ethan said before they'd gone far. He held the note out in the sparse light from the dashboard. "What do you make of this?"

"Make of what?" Sydney asked, returning his question with her own. "I'm driving."

"I can drive," he said, knowing the answer before he said it.

"Yeah, sure you can, but not my aunt's car."

Ethan didn't reply, looking at the note. He didn't want to drive anyway. He wondered who had written the note, guessing it could be but one person.

Her abrupt departure still puzzled him. Something in her eyes was familiar. He couldn't explain it, and it was gone the instant he thought about it, blocked by what felt like a heavy, immovable door inside his head. She was a nurse and had a duty to care for people, but there was something more; of that he was certain.

"Whatever you've got there has you fucking stumped, doesn't it?" Sydney asked, the red light of the speedometer reflecting in her dark eyes.

They drove on in silence before Sydney laughed.

"What's so funny?" he asked.

"You. You and that note."

"You know?"

"I saw her talking to the bartender afterward."

"You didn't say anything."

"What was I gonna say?" Sydney asked, taking a curve marked by a series of reflective yellow arrows, which pushed him against his door. "Just call her."

"You think so?"

"Worked out pretty good last time," Sydney said. He could hear the smile behind her words. "She probably just wants a few tips on jumping."

"Fuck off," he said, nodding invisibly in the darkness. "But you're right. I'll call her."

They were ten minutes from his parents' home. He could barely keep his eyes open.

"You really think we can live together?" Sydney asked, breaking their silence. The excitement of the show had dissipated like the calm that followed a tempest.

Her question brought him back to life.

"I do," he said. He turned in his seat. "There's a lot of talent in this band. You. Gus. Even Greg's beginning to surprise me. He's practicing hard. But talent's not the answer. It's never enough, no matter what we think. And it's not enough just to be different. Everybody's different. Different, in a way, makes us all the same. No, part of it is being different, but the difference has to be original and for the music. I'll quit when it isn't."

He stopped. Sydney didn't say anything. She stared at the road in front of them.

"Look at Kiss, Tom Petty and the Heartbreakers, or Alice Cooper. Even Rush. Every one of them is original, and their music matters. It's always about the music; when it goes, it takes everything with it. Maybe bands get lost or distracted, like the Eagles. I don't know. But we're climbing the mountain.

The music has to come first. Kiss might seem more about the show than the music, but Alice Cooper sure isn't, and Rush and Tom Petty—they're all music." He paused to take a breath and then added, "And guess what—they all live together. Mostly on the road, as they're always touring, but still—livin' and workin' together all the time."

For the second time in less than twelve hours, the vehicle Ethan was riding in turned into his parents' subdivision.

"We have to do this, Sydney," Ethan said, staring at her profile through the darkness. "We can be a bar band like everyone else and just dream about it, or we can do something extraordinary."

Sydney pulled up in front of the garage doors. She shut off the engine and headlights. Her hands returned to the steering wheel.

"I'll be honest, Ethan," she said, looking through the windshield as if she were still driving. "I think the idea is fucking nuts. I can't imagine living with the three of you."

Her words hung in the air like invisible bombs ready to explode. Ethan didn't know what to say.

"But I want this so fucking bad," she said. Tears glistened in her eyes, reflecting the house lights. "I've given up everything to be here." Her hands left the steering wheel and wiped the tears from her cheeks. "Do you understand? Fucking everything!" she cried. "My family doesn't understand. My aunt can barely stand me. I have no fucking job. You guys and the music are all that's holding me together."

Ethan didn't say anything. His hand rose to touch her shoulder. Onstage, she transformed into a music mecca behind her white Gibson, but out of the lights, without her guitar, she seemed to shrink into the tiny person he'd first met behind the counter of her parents' restaurant. Sydney was the most talented one in the band, and although he wouldn't admit it, treating her like one of the guys made that fact easier to accept. Females weren't supposed to be better at this male game of rock. He didn't make the rules, and Sydney made them even harder to accept.

He was speaking before he'd figured out what to say.

"Sydney," he said, turning sideways to face her, "we're a band. You're a quarter of it. But it's not just the four of us playing. Anyone can do that. We've got something. You can feel it. I can feel it. We all feel it. If we didn't, we wouldn't be talking. You know that better than any of us. Music is in your blood. If it weren't, you wouldn't be here. It has to come from inside us, and that's not just about playing and practicing. It comes from living and breathing it. It comes from how we live, where we eat, where we sleep, and what we think about when we're not playing. You don't get to the core by polishing the outside. You gotta go deeper. We have to live inside. Live the good and the bad. It's all gotta come out. However the fuck it wants to."

Ethan stopped. Sydney was staring at him. There was something in her eyes, a twinkle maybe. Some might have called it love and mistaken it for something it wasn't. It could destroy the possibilities of what the union of two minds could create. Ethan had begun to understand how love changed the game. But love between man and woman—between people—could be misleading. Love created. The love between two created the miracle of life. But the love *in* people created all the rest. Confusing the two devastated lives—maybe that was the court evil liked to play on.

In the darkness, Ethan felt his face tighten. "Sydney?" he said, trying to figure out whether she understood what he was saying.

"Yes?" Her lips curved into a smile. The tears were gone.

"Does it make sense?" He shifted in the seat.

"Already said I was in, didn't I?"

Her mouth hardly opened. Her left hand went back to the steering wheel. Ethan turned and looked through the windshield, wondering whether he'd missed something.

"I guess I said all that for nothing."

"It wasn't for nothing. I think it's clearer to you now." She grabbed the steering wheel with her other hand. "I'm fuckin' tired and still have to drive to my aunt's."

"You can stay here if you want," Ethan said. Not wanting to insinuate the wrong idea, he quickly added, "Mom always has the guest room ready."

"My aunt needs the car in the morning, but thanks."

Ethan opened the passenger door and climbed out. "Great night, Sydney. 'American Woman' was fucking amazing."

Sydney restarted the car. "Thanks." She waved her hand.

Ethan heard the transmission clunk into reverse as he closed the door. The car started to move backward and stopped. Ethan remembered his microphone case and hustled back.

"You know what fucking scares me the most?" she said as he opened the door.

Ethan shook his head. He felt his own tiredness coming on but sat back down in the passenger seat.

"It's you," she said, her dark eyes on him like those of a mother warning a child.

Ethan straightened his shoulders and leaned his head back. "Me?"

"Yes, you." She took her right hand off the steering wheel and pointed her index finger at him. "You do something I've never seen before. It's something in the way you perform. Everyone watching feels it. I know. I've asked. You're able to touch something inside people."

Sydney opened her hand as if to offer him something he couldn't see. "I've seen a lot of performers, some with even more talent." She stopped, raising her eyebrows as if what she said might be true. "But they couldn't touch that inside part. I don't know what it is. It's hard to describe. You just know when you feel it. You have a way of reaching people they can't turn away from. Look at tonight. Sure, 'American Woman' and 'Don't Look Back' were spectacular." She smiled. "But it was how you sang and performed the songs that had everyone responding. You're like a spectacle we can't turn away from."

"But—"

Sydney raised her hand. "Let me finish. I have to get this out. It scares the fuck out of me, Ethan. You can say what you want about our music and playing, but it's you who connects everything—the audience, the music, us. It's you people will come to see, 'cause it's you who makes them feel. You make us fucking feel when we're playing. You have that thing. I don't know what to call it. Charisma? It's that thing beyond us. It makes Robert Plant Led Zeppelin and Mick Jagger the Rolling Stones. Yeah, we love the music and the bands, but it's the stars performing their art that makes it fucking magical."

She stopped for a moment, as if to emphasize her point. "That, Ethan, is what fucking scares me."

She turned and appeared to stare at the backs of her hands, which were clutching the steering wheel. "Someone else will see you. I saw it at art school—and in high school. Someone with money and fuck knows what else. They will steal you away from us. And without you, we're just another band—great musicians, mind you—filling the air with song."

She smiled at her last comment but didn't look at him. "Don't say anything, Ethan. It's like attending your own funeral. You can't see you. It's a gift—a special gift from God. You can only see your reflection. You can't feel how you make others feel. It's such a fucking paradox."

Ethan didn't say a word. Sydney had framed her words so that a reply would only have demonstrated her point further.

He couldn't refute what she was saying. Ethan knew there was something special about the way he performed, but instead of trying to figure it out, he just went with it. The words he sang took him away to another place. It was like being back onstage, rehearsing *Another Color Blue* with Mila, going somewhere else—creating another world—unable to realize what it did to others. Despite feeling alone, he wasn't alone at all.

"But," Sydney added, looking right at him, "I'm in regardless. I'll start hunting for a place tomorrow—and it's tomorrow already."

"Good," Ethan said, climbing out of the car for the second time. He was too tired to think of anything else to say. He closed the door and watched Sydney back out of his parents' driveway.

He wondered what Sydney knew that he didn't. He unlocked the front door of his parents' house and pushed it open.

CHAPTER 18

He saw her.

It wasn't possible, yet there she was. Her silky brown hair was shorter. He was in IGA, grocery shopping. She stood at the checkout counter. It was like seeing a ghost. His thoughts seemed to prompt her. She turned to face him. Her brown eyes were magnificent in their power over him. Her smile pulled at something attached to his heart. Something was written on her T-shirt. He recognized the script:

> Here lies an angel
> with broken wings.
> Her eyes still watch;
> her voice still sings.

Her lips moved, but he couldn't hear her. A mist-like smoke came between them. When it cleared, her lips were still moving.

"Beware, my dear," she said. It was her voice—Mila's, a voice he would never forget. It was perfect in its melody, yet he sensed warning in its tone. He was certain of what he heard: "Deception is near."

Then, as if discovering that familiar face was instead a stranger's, she picked up her purchases and walked away. She did not look back.

Alarmed by her aloofness, he wanted to catch up with her, only to find he could hardly move, as if his legs were immersed in deep water. He tried to call out, to make her wait, but like his leaden legs, his mouth refused to move. Everything around him appeared normal as he watched her disappear; one moment she was there, and the next she had vanished. It was as if he alone were stuck in a viscous medium.

His whereabouts grew about him, and he felt the hard surface of the counter against his thighs. His hand was on the rubber conveyor that moved the groceries to the cashier. He recognized the cashier who stood behind it. It was someone he hadn't seen in a long time. She smiled. Her olive skin would have been velvety smooth to touch. Her chocolate-brown eyes pulled him in, melting something inside. Gold hoop earrings—elegant, not gaudy—hung from her ears, shining their sparkling reflection of sunshine he didn't see.

This is a dream?

He didn't think so but couldn't tell. He didn't want it to end. He was frustrated and saddened that he couldn't remember her name. There was something else about this statuesque woman standing in front of him. She looked up at him. Her eyes, rimmed in dark mascara, opened wider and seemed to light up.

"Ethan," she said, her crimson lips inviting his.

"Christa?" he whispered, reading the black-and-gold name tag pinned to her cotton blouse. He knew her better than the name tag suggested.

"Ethan, it's me," she said, leaning forward to bring her face closer to his, implying a familiarity he did not share.

He stepped back, caught off guard.

The woman frowned but quickly regained her composure, as if understanding something he didn't. "Christa."

"Christa?" he heard himself say, though it sounded as if it came from somewhere else—someone else. Something shifted—like missing frames in a movie reel causing a scene to shift unnaturally on the screen. For an instant, he thought he would throw up, feeling nausea at the back of his throat. But the feeling passed. Sweat broke out across his forehead and ran down the sides of his face. As he wiped the wetness away, light-headedness came over him, forcing him against the counter and then down. He slid sideways against the counter, unable to get a grip on anything to stay upright. Gravity sucked him to the floor.

Unaware of how long he'd been down, he opened his eyes to the same brown eyes that had pulled at his heart before. Concern contorted the woman's pretty face. Her thin eyebrows were close above her caring eyes.

"Are you okay?" she asked, gently touching the side of his head. "You took quite a tumble."

She moved back to give him space, pulling her hair back as she did. Her long hair touched his face. He did know her, but how? His head was like a programmed calculator with the wrong program loaded in his memory.

86

She's dead, Ethan.

"I was never dead," the woman from behind the counter, now kneeling beside him, replied, as if he'd spoken his thoughts out loud.

Never dead?

He wasn't talking.

"Did you see a coffin?" she replied, a smile on her red lips. She leaned in closer. "Did you see me in it?"

Ethan tried to remember a funeral. He recalled wisps of a family, a big man, and a sad absence. He couldn't recall a coffin or her.

It's not possible.

"It's possible because it's in your head. But I'm not."

"Ethan!" He heard someone call his name from a distance.

"And *Browning Station?*" the woman with the Christa name tag asked. He was on a floor hard like cement, but it wasn't cold. The book was beside him.

What about Browning Station?

"It's important to you," she replied, again answering a question he'd only thought about.

Two things were in his hands now: a script in his left and a book in his right. Both had the title *Browning Station*. He was on the spotted tiles of the small bathroom floor in his hospital room. He felt saddened; he didn't want to be there, but he'd found his copy of *Browning Station*.

"Exactly," she said as she pulled her brown hair back into a ponytail. She wrapped something elastic around it. "Your dad put it in the car when you left."

"How do you know?" he asked, hearing the words come out of his mouth.

"Because you know," the woman said. She leaned in closer to him. "How do you feel?"

He wanted to feel her silky hair against his face again, maybe for the last time. It wasn't a dream, and it was perfect.

"Better," he said.

He moved to get up. His head seemed clear, but the woman was gone. He was alone on the hard floor of the gray bathroom.

"Ethan?"

He stirred. Maybe he wasn't where he'd thought he was. He was on his stomach; his head was on a soft pillow. He was in bed—his bed.

He opened his eyes. The room was dim.

It was hard to take in where he was and what had happened. Even with his eyes open, he was disoriented, but thankfully, he wasn't in the hospital.

The door to his room opened.

"Ethan, for the last time," his mother said, "you're going to be late for work."

As he fought to bring his head together, his brain was like a vacuum sucking through his thoughts to find the right ones. He looked up.

"No work today, Ma," he answered, thinking of a golf club, a pretty woman helping him off the floor, and the large stage lamp. He turned his head back into his pillow and smiled.

He wasn't in the hospital.

CHAPTER 19

Friday, July 13, 1984

Ethan woke up a few hours later. It was almost noon. He vaguely remembered the dream. He had a fuzzy memory of a woman, but even that was fading. He recalled no who or what, only a feeling—a good feeling. It was hopeful, but he didn't have enough memory of it to re-create an image or even where he'd been. What had happened was like a mirage and now gone. He wished he could remember more.

He pushed down his covers and the waistband of his pajamas, exposing himself to the open air. He was hot, almost sweaty. His sleep had left him erect. The cooler air felt good. He touched himself, but the dream was gone. He was left with only the sweet feeling of want that had begun to fade as the emptiness of Mila's absence returned. Once again, failure and inadequacy flooded his heart. He often woke that way.

He forced himself out of bed, as if the physical act would push away the thoughts hijacking any remaining sweetness from his dream and pulling him into the dark abyss of self-loathing.

The events of the night before crowded in—Uncle Al, the show, the nurse. All that had led up to sitting with Sydney in her aunt's car in his parents' driveway. They'd talked a lot.

A place the band could call home would be cool. But could they really do it? Everyone had bought in last night, but things had a way of changing, especially after a night of adrenaline and drinks. Thinking of the band living together made him remember the song he'd started with Sydney and the words he'd written down. Where had he put the envelope? In seconds, he was digging through the pockets of his jeans. Relieved, he pulled the white envelope out of a back pocket and headed to his bedroom door. As he passed the mirror above his bureau, he saw the blood on the side of his face. He stopped and looked closer, remembering the cut on his hand and what he'd done. He touched the still-tender lump on his head. The stage lamp had done a job. The swelling had gone down, but his head was still pretty sore. He licked his fingers and wiped the bit of blood from his face.

Still staring in the mirror, he remembered his promise to Randolph. He'd better call before he forgot.

As he'd hoped, he was alone. There was a note on the refrigerator, wishing him a good day and ending with "We have to talk." He poured himself a glass of orange juice and dialed Randolph's number.

"Randy Baseman," Randolph said after the first ring.

The name caught Ethan off guard. Despite knowing who was on the other end, he replied, "Randolph?"

"Of course," Randolph said, seeming to know Ethan's voice right away, "and to what do I owe the privilege of speaking with the Actor today?"

As usual, Randolph was ahead of him.

"Randy Baseman?" Ethan asked, his voice becoming distant as he spoke. He felt as if he were trying to hold on to a handful of sand that was slipping through his fingers in slow motion. But it wasn't his fingers it was slipping through; it was his mind. "You use Randy often?"

Ethan did his best to focus and push away the strangeness that seemed intent on taking him somewhere else.

"All the time," Randolph said. Something in the timbre of his voice smiled.

Ethan liked that. It helped stop the pulling-away feeling that was preying on him.

"That's what you called me in the hospital. Rachel says it's cute. Kinda catchy for this new world I find myself in."

"Really," Ethan said, still feeling himself pushing back at whatever seemed intent on pulling him out and trying to overrule what he was thinking, leaving him with the feeling of forgetting something.

"Yeah, really, dude," Randolph replied, laughing. "So what's happening with you?"

"Lots," Ethan said, excited by Randolph's question. Thinking of the band helped push away whatever else was there. "I've put a band together. We played last night."

Ethan talked of his chance meeting with Sydney on the way back to

Toronto, his discovery of Gus while cutting the lawn, and his high school friend Greg's return from Boston.

"And you?" he finally said, realizing Randolph hadn't said anything.

"Thought you'd never ask, but I want to know more about this band thing. How does the Actor-turned-Musician thing work?"

"Pretty simple. I was in a band before coming to Ottawa. Thought I'd try again."

"Really?" Randolph sounded surprised. "I didn't know."

"Yeah, kind of crazy, isn't it? We're called the Release."

"The Release? From *Browning Station*?"

"Yeah. You've read it?"

"Pretty much," Randolph said, saying his words unusually slowly, as if he were savoring their taste. "You got anything to listen to yet?"

"We've got one song on tape and are working on some more."

As he spoke, Ethan wished the band had more happening besides the few lines he'd written on the back of the envelope in his hand.

"Can you send me a copy?"

"Sure," he said, unsure of whether Gus or Greg had the tape and feeling the strange pull coming back. "So what's up with Randolph—Randy Baseman?" he said.

As the words left his mouth, a rush of images blew through his head: a yellow taxi, a manila envelope, and the image of a woman he recognized but didn't know. Immense monolithic buildings were close around him. Bright colors of fire engine red and canary yellow flashed by. There was no apparent order to any of it; he simply saw a dizzying array of marvel that raced through his mind like the chaotic LSD scenes of *Easy Rider*.

"It's fucking amazing, Ethan," Randolph was saying. "I'm almost finished. It's a big comic book—the clash of good and evil in everyday life. I'd have never considered it if I hadn't seen it on your father's dashboard. Then Rachel had it in her hands. For God's sake, it was on your nightstand for weeks. It was all there right in front of me. The story is disturbing in its ordinariness."

"You're talking about *Browning Station*," Ethan said, interrupting, engaging back in the conversation.

"You bet your ass I am. It's fucking extraordinary!" Randolph roared, his voice exploding over the phone. "I don't know how it'll work out exactly. A couple of guys, Corben and Metzger, started calling them graphic novels in the seventies. It's like a novel-sized comic book."

"Cool," Ethan said, trying to put together *Browning Station*, Randolph, and the many sordid images flying through his head.

"There was a paperback called *Blackmark* two guys put together—Gil Kane and Archie Goodwin."

Randolph kept talking. He was excited. Ethan tried to listen but had a hard time. *Browning Station* had been in the car, but where had it gone? He hadn't seen it since the hospital.

"*Blackmark* is recognized as the first graphic novel but wasn't called that at the time."

Randolph's words trickled past him as he tried to remember unpacking the car back in May but instead remembered the book's character William Avery. *That bookstore downtown with the giant letters in the windows … Books at …*

"I don't know what's gonna happen."

Ethan wasn't quite sure what Randolph had said, but he noticed Randolph had stopped talking.

Ethan didn't say anything.

Randolph's voice returned. "So what do you think?"

Ethan could feel himself being pulled by some kind of current intent on sweeping him away. It seemed as if things that were otherwise unrelated were drawing him somewhere else. It dawned on him that he hadn't taken his medication, as he'd slept late. He figured that might be the culprit leading to the bombs dropping on vulnerable places in his head, each targeted to knock him off center. He'd dodged them all so far. He'd take an Orap as soon as he hung up.

"Ethan?"

He didn't reply; it seemed he couldn't.

"Ethan?"

Conflicted, his thoughts jumped between how to answer and where his copy of *Browning Station* lay. He remained silent, as words eluded him.

"Ethan?" Randolph asked a third time, his voice lower and less enthusiastic.

"So you like *Browning Station*?" Ethan said, his mouth finding the words that his brain couldn't.

"Yeah," Randolph said, his tone flat and colorless, "there's so much that's visually appealing. I could draw from it all day."

"Cool," Ethan said, trying to push away *Browning Station* and whatever else was pulling him.

"Fuckin' right it's cool," Randolph said, almost shouting. "It's manna from heaven."

He paused, as if intentionally waiting for Ethan to say something. Ethan didn't.

"Your call couldn't have been better timed," Randolph said, his voice rising. "I'm in Toronto next week. You around? Maybe we could grab dinner or something."

"I am," Ethan replied, seeing his way out. It wasn't that he didn't want to talk to Randolph; he just needed a break to get his head straight, take his medication, and stop whatever was trying to take him out. "What day are you thinking?"

"Midweek. Wednesday or Thursday."

"You're on," Ethan said, putting his hand in the front pocket of his jeans. He found another piece of paper—the note from the bartender.

"I'll call you Tuesday," Randolph said, his voice sounding more businesslike.

"That works for me. It'll be good to see you."

His reply sounded rehearsed, but it was the best he could do.

"Right back at you, guy," Randolph replied, his voice again sounding excited. "See you next week."

"Ciao," Ethan said, and he hung up.

He couldn't remember ever being so relieved to end a phone conversation yet didn't know why. Randolph had triggered something in his head he didn't like. He needed his pills.

But there was something else. He could feel it again. The big, heavy padlocked door keeping him away from something. There was no sign on the door. There was no need. The size of the door and lock were clear enough: Keep Out. It was a door only for him, likely intended as a reminder, Dr. Katharine had tried to explain. She'd encouraged him to open the door— to find a way in—but instead had helped close it more tightly and made the padlock feel even bigger. Nothing was getting in, but seemingly more important, nothing was getting out. The medication was there to serve and protect him against that happening.

Don't disturb what you don't understand.

He looked at the note he'd pulled from his pocket, bringing him back from where his thoughts wanted to stray. He read it again. The questions started before he'd finished the first sentence: "I'm not supposed to talk to you."

Why? He couldn't imagine anyone stalking him, but seeing him must have been important enough to risk losing a job over. He didn't know anyone who wasn't supposed to talk to him. The notion sounded crazy but not that crazy. He knew what real crazy was. That crazy didn't write notes. If it was from the woman who had helped him, why the note? Why hadn't she just talked to him? But maybe it wasn't from her.

Maybe it was Mila.

The big door and lock loomed in front of him again.

Why did he always come back to Mila? Grief? Did it ever give up?

It's not Mila! He all but shouted to himself. He looked back at the note.

It wasn't the note's message that filled his head. It was the padlock. The padlock had a keyhole, and that keyhole seemed to stare at him like a single eye that could see right inside him. Where there was a keyhole, there was a matching key, and he was certain he could find it if he really wanted to. What would he find?

The note came back into focus, as if to warn him of his thoughts. It ended with "Call if you want," as if the decision were really his.

He picked up the phone and dialed the number.

CHAPTER 20

"Hello?" said the sweet voice Ethan recognized from the night before.

"Hi," he replied.

"Ethan?" The voice resonated with familiarity he couldn't miss.

"Yes," he answered, "this is he."

"You called," said the woman, her voice rising in pitch, sounding surprised. Before he could reply, she added, "I'm glad you did."

"Your note gave me the option," Ethan said, excited upon hearing the woman's voice.

"Yes, I did," she said.

Ethan waited for more and was about to speak when the woman went on. "This is not easy for me. It's not what you think."

"And what do I think?" Ethan asked, his words sounding terser than he intended.

"This goes against all I believe in as a—" She stopped, causing Ethan to wonder what she hadn't said and whether he should have even called.

"Who is this?" he asked.

He was all but certain what he was about to hear. *It's Mila*, he imagined the voice saying. *I'm surprised you had to ask.* He could feel the invisible strength of an undertow pulling his feet out from under him, threatening to sweep him into the open ocean inside his head. He could feel the heavy wood door and the padlock. The giant black eye of its keyhole stared him down, daring him, beckoning him to step forward. *Oh, come on, Ethan. You know it's me.*

He pushed back hard, as if his back were against the door, his legs locked, holding the door from opening.

The note was still in his hand. He raised it. "I'm not supposed to talk to you," it said.

Then why are we talking? he thought.

"What was that?" the woman asked, her voice jarring him from the heavy padlocked door at his back to the phone in his hand.

"Who is this?" he asked again, his patience thinning.

"You don't know?" asked the woman, avoiding his question with her own. Her voice was quieter.

"No," he said, picturing the woman at Benny's looking down at him. There was something between them outside of his attraction to a pretty woman, but what it was, he couldn't figure out.

"I knew the note was a mistake," said the woman.

There was an audible click in the line. She'd hung up.

He still didn't know who she was.

CHAPTER 21

Friday, July 13, 1984

Ethan was flustered by the short-lived phone call. There was probably more there than he wanted or needed to deal with right now. There were some big messes lurking behind some pretty faces. *Beware of the beauty*, he thought, wondering where he'd heard that before. Curiosity had driven him beyond his better judgment in making the call in the first place. He likely was lucky she'd just hung up.

It was almost four o'clock by the time he was back standing in the kitchen again. He'd showered and found his right elbow bruised and a little swollen. The right side of his ribcage hurt when he took a deep breath, as did his back when he bent forward. His tailbone was tender, but sitting down didn't seem to bother him. The bump on his head was still sensitive but almost gone. It was amazing he'd escaped without more serious injuries. He looked at the phone on the counter and, to his disbelief, considered calling her again.

Before he could decide, his mother walked in the front door, carrying a brown paper bag of groceries.

"Fancy meeting you here," she said cheerily upon entering the kitchen.

She looked tired. Worry had aged her prematurely during his months in the hospital. Though she never acknowledged it, he sensed she'd prepared for the worst—that her son might never recover. Every day, it seemed, she treated him like a gift that God had returned to her, making allowances for his varied comings and goings she never would have before. He found when she was around now, all the problems of his world seemed fixable; that had not always been the case.

"Yeah," he replied, sticking both hands in the front pockets of his jeans, "I suppose I owe you an explanation."

"Not if you don't want to," his mother answered matter-of-factly, setting her brown leather handbag, along with the bag of groceries, on the extended counter that often served as the breakfast and lunch table. There was a small black-and-white television on the corner nearest the wall—a new addition prior to his return. A silver antenna stretched toward the ceiling. The new TV had been a surprise, as before, TV had always been forbidden at mealtime. It was another of his mother's adjusted rules.

Ethan leaned against the speckled gray countertop and took a glass from the cupboard beside the sink.

"The fence guy—Al—ran out of work," Ethan said, "and chose to tell me just as he dropped me off."

"That's disappointing," said his mother. "What kind of notice is that?"

"It's none, and that was my point," Ethan said, pushing the lever on the water faucet. He rinsed his glass and then filled it and turned to face his mother. "He tried to stiff me for a week's pay. Said he'd send it to me. I didn't buy it."

"Good. You stood up for yourself," she said, moving in beside him to wash her hands in the sink. "Any preferences for dinner? Your father won't be here. Your sister'll be late."

Ethan shook his head, but he was hungry.

"So what are you going to do?" his mother asked, opening the refrigerator and pulling out a head of lettuce and some celery. Whether he liked it or not, salad was on the menu.

"We're going to move in together," he said, surprised at how quickly the news came out of his mouth. Each time he said it out loud, it seemed more real.

His mother set the vegetables on the countertop and turned to look at him. "Who is moving in together?" she asked, her face tightening and her lips shrinking to a thin line.

Ethan knew at once what his announcement must have sounded like to his mother. He remembered Sydney's response.

"The band," he replied, smiling. "We agreed last night."

"Oh really, and how are you proposing to do that? You don't have a job."

"We haven't got that all figured out yet," he said, a little surprised by her frank reproach to his idea. She'd always been suspect of new things she didn't know about or understand. "But we will. A band that lives together becomes more than the sum of its parts."

She returned to the head of lettuce on the counter and pulled off the plastic shrink-wrap. "And Aristotle is the new name of your band," she said, placing the lettuce under the faucet with one hand and turning on the water with the other.

"Not quite," he said, unable to keep the smile off his face, as he wasn't about to get anything by a schoolteacher who taught English. "Too much to live up to."

His mother reflected his smile with a fake one. "You're gonna find rent is like that too." She snickered.

Ethan was surprised by her wit; she looked tired, but she was on it. He knew his plan sounded crazy. His mother obviously thought the same, but that was okay. This crazy wasn't the institutionalized crazy she'd lived through. This was the crazy behind every dream that sat outside the boundary of normal expectation. But the more he thought about it, the more it didn't seem that crazy. It wasn't much different from a group of college kids renting a house off campus, and most societal standards deemed that quite acceptable. There would be challenges, but anyone living together had those.

"You can laugh, but I think you're missing my point," he said, not as comfortable as he'd have liked to be with the reality of his mother's point. "The Release has talent, but that's not enough. We have to become more than just four people playing a bunch of songs. You should have seen us last night. We rocked the place."

"Can you get three salad bowls down?"

Ethan pulled three glass bowls from the shelf above his head and set them on the countertop beside his mother.

"Greg's the only one with a job, so we really—"

"Whose idea is this?" his mother asked, interrupting.

"What do you mean?"

"Who thought you should move in together?"

"Me. I did," Ethan said, preparing to defend his idea. "Why?"

"Because it doesn't sound like you. Sounds like Greg."

Of the band members, his mother really only knew Greg. It was no secret she didn't like his influence on her son. On several occasions, she'd commented that Greg had never once contacted Ethan in the hospital. "What kind of a friend is that?" she'd asked. It wasn't the only thing that bothered her about him.

"Just so you know, Greg was the one least excited about the whole thing," Ethan said.

His mother didn't reply for a moment and pulled open the refrigerator door. "What's the timing on all this?" she asked with a tomato in each hand.

"As soon as we can find a place. Sydney started looking today."

His mother rinsed the tomatoes and pulled a knife out of the cutlery drawer. "You haven't looked at any places yet, have you?"

"No, we only agreed to the idea last night," Ethan said, feeling defensive. He'd thought his mother would be glad he was trying to get on with his life and out of the house. Figuring his mother out was nearly impossible.

She put the rinsed tomatoes on the cutting board and set the knife on the counter beside them. She slid open the door on the breadbox. "Burgers okay?" she asked, taking out a package of buns.

Ethan nodded. "We're gonna look closer to the city," he said.

"The city," he thought, sounded more mature and businesslike, a demonstration of his seriousness to make a go of the band. He wanted to imply they had more worked out than they actually did.

"Not around here?"

"We need to be closer to the action." He was building a case for what he thought they needed to do. "Part of the downtown music scene."

He had a picture in his head of what the place might look like, remembering the apartment from the *Three's Company* sitcom—a sofa in the center of the living room, surrounded by their equipment. He smiled, thinking of a recent episode with Jack tripping over the couch.

"What are you thinking?" his mother asked, sounding a little more interested in the idea. "An apartment?"

"Yeah, something like that. We really haven't talked about it."

His mother opened the refrigerator again and pulled a box of frozen hamburger patties out of the freezer. "How many?" she asked, one part of the conversation weaving into another.

"Two," Ethan said before thinking about how hungry he was. "No, make that three. I'm starved."

"You haven't eaten, have you?"

"I thought about it and had some orange juice," he answered, watching her reaction. "I made a couple of phone calls. I don't know where the time went."

"Getting out of bed after one o'clock didn't help," his mother said. She wasn't angry.

"That's true." He didn't have the nerve to say it had been closer to two. "I talked to Randolph today. Remember? From the hospital?"

His mother stopped trying to separate the frozen hamburger patties when he said Randolph's name. She handed him the frozen stack. "If you want three, you can pull them apart."

"I was wondering when you'd ask." He laughed. He pulled a table knife from the cutlery drawer and pried apart the frozen disks. His mother took a Teflon fry pan out of the drawer below the oven and placed it on the stovetop.

"Such a thoughtful son," she said. "You could have offered, you know."

She switched on the burner and, out of habit, sprayed the pan with Pam. She then turned and looked at him. "You know, the four of you might want to consider a house."

"How so?"

"You could likely rent a small house for the same amount as a four-bedroom apartment—if you can even find an apartment that big."

Ethan listened. He hadn't thought much about living arrangements, but a house made sense. They would need space to rehearse.

"We'll be talking tonight," he said, pulling apart the last two frozen patties, which he handed to his mother. "It's a good idea."

The four frozen disks started to sizzle in the pan. His mother tossed the salad. "What kind of dressing do you want?"

"Thousand Island," he replied, and he decided to tell her about the previous night's show. "You know, Sydney and Gus are unbelievable musicians. Sydney came up with this new beginning to 'American Woman.' We'd never rehearsed it, but it was incredible. She knows how stuff sounds before we play it. She brought new life to a killer song."

"You expect me to know what you're talking about," his mother said, shaking her head.

Ethan kept talking. "I hate to say it, but Gus is a much better bass player than I could ever be. I don't know how he plays so many notes. His fingers hardly look like they're moving."

His mother pulled a spatula out of the drawer and flipped the burgers in the pan.

"What's cool is Gus has made Greg pick up his game." Ethan watched as his mother raised her eyebrows and frowned. She wasn't about to change her opinion of Greg.

"Get what you want for your burgers," she said, pulling the hamburger buns out of the package.

It was his turn to open the refrigerator, but he kept on about their night at Benny's.

"The crowd liked us too," he said, searching for the ketchup, mustard, and relish. He put the condiments on the counter beside the plates. "The place was full when we ended."

His mother nodded as she served him his salad. Ethan thought to mention his jump and the woman, but then his mother spoke. "Well, you've answered my note from this morning."

He smiled and didn't say any more. He didn't need to; the rest was in the past now. He was setting a course for the future and didn't expect her to understand; he wasn't sure he did. He couldn't know how hard it would be.

PART 3

AFFANNATO

And I'm here to remind you
Of the mess you left when you went away
It's not fair to deny me
Of the cross I bear that you gave to me
You, you, you oughta know.
——*Alanis Morrisette, "You Oughta Know"*

I stole this from a hockey card,
I keep tucked up under
My fifty mission cap, I worked it in
To look like that.
——*The Tragically Hip, "Fifty Mission Cap"*

CHAPTER 22

"Where's the fucking milk?" Greg shouted from the kitchen. He was mad.

No one answered, at least not that Ethan heard.

"I bought a fuckin' carton!" Greg said.

Ethan couldn't believe it. He hadn't been in bed three hours. He could barely move. Greg no doubt was still coming down from whatever he'd imbibed that night. Hard drugs and alcohol were an extracurricular he'd picked up in Boston that had come to light now that they were all living together. He was doing tequila shots with a girl who had been dancing in front of the stage when Ethan left the bar.

Try as he might, Ethan couldn't keep drugs from the band or out of Greg's hands. They were bad news—end of story. But Greg used Ethan's prescribed medication against him whenever the subject came up.

"Doesn't count?" Greg had retorted when Ethan had confronted him and defended his own drug use by saying that doctor-prescribed medication didn't count. "You might get yours prescribed, but I gotta get mine off the fuckin' street. Give it a fuckin' rest."

Greg had then shaken some white powder from a Ziploc bag onto the glass inlay of the coffee table in their living room. With the edge of his American Express card, he had portioned a small amount of powder from the pile into a line, and then he'd lowered his head to the tabletop and snorted it up his nose.

Ethan hadn't liked Greg's response. Orap wasn't a choice if he didn't want to live in the hospital. He was likely stuck with it or something similar for the rest of his life. Orap was the brand name drug for pimozide, intended for patients with delusional disorders. Dr. Katharine and her colleagues

105

prescribed it as the best solution to allow him a return to normal life. Part of his stay in the hospital had been to figure out a dosage that would minimize the depressive effects of the antipsychotic drug while stabilizing his ability to cope with the world. Ethan never mentioned his spells to anyone after leaving the hospital. His medication was a requirement to live in the outside world; he wondered whether Greg's self-medicating was too.

Ethan wasn't about to let drugs or anything else break up the band. Sydney smoked and made no bones about her dislike for Greg's habits. Gus didn't seem to get perturbed about anything and often smoked a joint after an intense rehearsal. "Whatever gets you through the day" had become Ethan's motto. He did his best to ignore the drug habits.

"Fucking shut up!" Sydney shouted from her room across from his. Ethan wasn't the only one awake.

"Use some goddamn water!" Gus shouted from somewhere else. "And shut the fuck up!"

They were all awake, but with Gus's last words, calm returned. Greg went silent. Gus was a couple of years older than the rest of them. With his jet-black hair and beard, he seemed almost godly in his steadying influence on the rest of them. "Shut the fuck up" or "Exactly what's your fucking problem?" had a way of settling things down.

Things had turned out different from how Ethan had imagined they would. Each show, they played more together—more connected, tighter, better—but each day in the house seemed to tear them further apart. It was as if bad stuff in the day made for good stuff in the night, as if they needed conflict to grow. Their repertoire had grown to almost a dozen original songs, all of which had come into being with at least one of them threatening to quit. The latest bout had started with Sydney the day before last. She refused to play the notes of a riff he liked the way he wanted her to. Each time he got ready to sing the words to what she was playing, she played the run just a little differently, as if intentionally trying to mess him up. Searching to find whatever she was looking for, she ignored him. Each time they played it, he grew more agitated.

"Come on, Sydney—just once!" he yelled over the hum of the amps.

She played the part leading up to the bridge just the way Ethan wanted, only that time, she stepped on her flanger effects pedal, stringing the notes together as if they were elastic.

"Fuck, Sydney!" Ethan screamed. "Just play it once!"

She was shaking her head. "It's not right. It doesn't fucking fit."

"You haven't fucking played it yet!"

"I don't have to play the goddamn thing to know what it sounds like!" she shouted back, looking up from her fingers on the fret board. "You're such an idiot."

"Look who's talking!"

"Asshole," Sydney huffed. He could see she was mad, but so was he.

Ethan didn't care. He was ready to call it quits. Gus was unplugging. Greg was twirling a drumstick between his fingers, seeming to pay little attention to the lot of them. As mad as Sydney was, the neck of her guitar remained in her hand like a friend she was afraid to let go of. As if cued by some secret signal, she turned away from Ethan. Her right booted foot came forward and, with masterful precision, depressed one of the effects switches on the floor in front of her. Then, with the virtuosity of someone who'd played the riff a million times before, she ripped off the notes in a fashion different from anything she'd been playing. It was as if a giant wave hit Ethan, knocking him from hell into sweet paradise.

"You fucking babe!" he screamed, the surge of joy making it nearly impossible to hold on to his mike. "Play that fucking magic again."

If there was one thing Sydney could do better than anyone Ethan had ever seen, it was repeating something exactly as she'd played it the first time—if she wanted to. Like a photographic memory, she had a replay memory.

"That's it!" he said, jumping up and down like a baseball player watching his home run ball soar over the fence in left field to win the championship. "That's fucking it!"

"So much for your shitty little riff," she said, hinting at a smile.

Sydney was right more than she was wrong, but it didn't stop the screaming matches. The good stuff didn't come about without their first puking up their bad emotions. Ethan became convinced it was a law of the universe, but that didn't make it any easier to accept. He doubted most could have put up with it. But good songs came out of it.

They played the song through. Hearing the song come along, Gus plugged back into his amp. Greg found a beat.

"That's how it's done," Ethan said when they'd finished. He turned and looked at Greg.

"So," Greg said, as if Ethan were talking to him alone, "when are we going to fucking record an album?"

The question had come up several times as their catalog of original songs grew. Ethan knew they all thought about it. Sydney was usually the one to comment after a missed note or screwup, "We're not ready yet." They all knew what she meant. But mistakes were becoming less frequent. They had just played something new for the first time and gotten it.

"I think you're scared," Greg said, pressing his chin with the heel of his hand to an audible crack of his neck. "Our songs are fucking good—we sound great. What are we waitin' for now?"

"For you to keep the fucking beat steady," Sydney snapped before anyone else had a chance to react.

"Blow me!" Greg said. "You're fucking scared, and you know it."

"I'm not fucking scared," Sydney said in defense, but Ethan could hear fear in her voice. Her drive for perfection made being wrong next to death. "You're still not coming in right on 'Lonesome Body.' We're not charged up enough with 'Held in Chains.' The words aren't right in 'Taken.' Shall I go on?"

"I don't know," Ethan said. "Is that really the point? Greg's right. We're close."

"Who died and made you fucking king?" Sydney said, looking at Ethan. The whiteness of the skin around her fingernails showed how tight a grip she held on the neck of her guitar.

"It's not about me," Ethan said, feeling Sydney's wrath. She was an important part of the Release, as were the others, but she wasn't always right. The Release was a band. They had to figure things out as a band. One person couldn't make all the decisions, even if differing opinions mired them in indecision and frustration. Recording was only one of those decisions. "It's about us. Everyone has a stake in this."

"And just what fucking tree is the money falling from to get in a studio?" Sydney asked.

The question caught Ethan off guard—it was the first time Sydney had used money, not their playing, as a reason. She'd argued the opposite with Greg regarding getting a place and moving in together. Money was always an excuse for something else, Ethan thought.

"We have money in the bank," said Gus, who'd taken on the band's finances. Everyone was responsible for an equal share of the rent and food, such as the milk Greg was now complaining about. Each month, they split what their gigs paid, with an equal portion going in the bank. But Ethan knew there couldn't be much.

"What are we looking at?" Ethan asked, figuring quickly in his head what two months of being in the house might have amounted to. "Five hundred bucks?"

"Almost eight—seven hundred eighty-seven dollars," Gus said, unstrapping his bass.

"We need three times that to record," Sydney replied, letting go of the neck of her guitar and stretching out her arm in front of her. "Where the fuck are we going to come up with two grand?"

Ethan still couldn't figure out where the money thing was coming from. Sydney's line of thinking had never been about money.

"I may be able to offer some assistance," Greg said, spinning a drumstick through his fingers confidently. His lips curved into a closed-mouthed smile. Ethan couldn't help but think of Lewis Carroll's Cheshire Cat in *Alice's Adventures in Wonderland*.

"How so?" Gus asked.

"Here we go," Sydney said. "I don't wanna fuckin' know."

"Let's just say I have a few ideas."

Ethan wasn't excited about the source of Greg's ideas, but he was excited about making a record. Recording was a dream for all of them. He could feel it getting closer. As with the house, there was always a way. Money wasn't about to stop them.

Sydney's next words made it real.

"Great, but can we talk about this tomorrow?" she said, adjusting the strap on her Gibson. "We've a fucking show tonight, and 'Taken' is not ready for public consumption."

Without hesitation, as she often did when wanting to get things going, she started without a count. The sound of her guitar shot off like a rocket blast, starting the song with its spinning riff. The sound she created charged up the others. Gus quickly returned his guitar strap to his shoulder and played a skip bass pattern that Greg followed with syncopated drumbeats. A month before, the rhythm would have been beyond what Greg could play. Sydney had shown him a trick to balance the separate patterns. The offset had taken a while to learn, but he'd pegged it. Ethan watched as Sydney did a little foot dance in front of her pedals, beaming as if she'd just given birth to a new life. He then reasoned that in fact, she had.

That night, they owned not only the stage but also the world.

That had been the night before last.

Ethan didn't hear Greg complaining anymore. Water must have worked, or Greg had simply run out of steam.

Ethan had too, and sleep took him away.

CHAPTER 23

"Ethan?"

"Randolph," Ethan mumbled through the spoonful of Cap'n Crunch in his mouth. It was just past two o'clock in the afternoon. He dug something crusty out of the corner of his eye with the tip of his index finger. He swallowed and more clearly repeated, "Randolph."

"You're never going to stop calling me that, are you?"

"You know how it goes—hard to turn what at first we learn," Ethan replied, liking what he'd said. He scanned the kitchen for a pencil and paper. They'd bought a bunch of pads and pencils to put around the house for when ideas struck, but one or the other still seemed to be absent when he needed them.

"I didn't know that was a saying," Randolph said, his voice growing quieter, as if he'd moved away from the mouthpiece.

"Nor did I." Ethan laughed, trying to write and talk at the same time. He paused briefly to write down the line. "I just made it up. What's up? It's been a while."

"Yeah, tell me about it. When did we have dinner—three months ago?"

Ethan had to think. It had been at least that long. When he'd last seen Randolph, the Release hadn't yet found a house.

"At least that," Ethan replied, looking at the words he'd written down.

"I just finished," Randolph said.

Ethan had to think for a moment what Randolph was talking about. The pause was enough for Randolph to prompt him.

"*Browning Station*, man. Don't tell me you've forgotten. It's your book."

Randolph's words coincided with his thoughts. Having been so wrapped up with the Release, he'd lapsed on the book Randolph had become so attached to. It brought back the question of his lost copy of *Browning Station*.

"No, just a lot going on," Ethan said, trying to sound as if he hadn't forgotten, though he had.

"What else is new?" Randolph said, the speed of his words quickening. "Listen to this. Venture's so happy with the comic that they've optioned a movie."

"You're kidding," Ethan said, losing a bit of his enthusiasm. He was surprised by what Randolph had going on. Good fortune had turned its favor in Randolph's direction since the hospital, but Ethan could think only about how the Release still didn't have their record together. Between living, sleeping, and gigging, there wasn't much left. He was happy for Randolph but envious of what Randolph had happening. "When are you heading to Hollywood?"

After he said the word, the heavy door he hadn't sensed in a while seemed to rise beside him.

"Not Hollywood. Most of the work will be done in Toronto, seeing where the dollar's at. But that's not why I'm calling."

Ethan didn't say anything. The door was fading. He underlined the word *learn*.

"Well."

"Well what?" Ethan asked, wondering what Randolph was about to tell him.

"Aren't you going to ask me why I'm calling?"

Ethan was finding it hard to stay excited. Maybe he had too much on his mind. He stared at the words he'd written down, thinking they might fit into "Taken," a song that was taking way too long to come together. Not wanting to disappoint his friend, he followed Randolph's lead.

"Okay, why are you calling?" Ethan asked, hearing his own flippancy.

"You're such an asshole," Randolph responded.

Ethan smiled and wrote down "We can never go back." He liked it. "Are you going to tell me or not?" he said. He wanted to move on. The words were coming, and he didn't want to miss them.

"I want the Release to do a couple of songs for the soundtrack," Randolph blurted out.

Ethan imagined a cork popping from a bottle of champagne.

"One of the producers asked if I had any recommendations. The budget's tight, but there is some money. I keep talking about you guys. You blew my mind in Toronto."

Randolph had Ethan's full attention.

"That's fuckin' cool!" Ethan cried, as if the air around him suddenly had gotten thinner. A million things ran through his head, none of which he could articulate. This was their way into the studio! He regretted his earlier jealousy. Only Randolph would have gone out on a limb for a friend on a project that was so important. The Release was good, but still.

Randolph was talking again. Ethan didn't catch the first part, but the second caused things to slow down.

"There is one catch," Randolph said.

"Catch?" Ethan asked, the word coming to his lips before he had time to check it. *Catch? Okay, here it comes,* he thought, ready to renege on his thoughts on Randolph.

"It's not really a catch—it's more timing," Randolph said. He continued before Ethan could say anything. "They want to hear two songs in two weeks."

"Really?" Ethan said in disbelief. "We've been trying to record for a while. You've got horseshoes up your ass and a crystal ball."

There was silence for a moment on the other end before Randolph came back on.

"I think the fuckin' horseshoes might be yours."

CHAPTER 24

Monday, November 26, 1984

Ethan had dreamed of recording in a studio since before their band in high school. Now he was going to live it. But dreams had a way of changing in their realization.

He had pictured something closer to the stills he remembered of the Beatles at their Abbey Road and Apple Studios sessions. The Release were in much more cramped quarters at Focus Sound. The four of them could barely squeeze into the recording room, never mind being comfortable. Greg's Slingerland drum kit was set up farthest from the door to the studio. Sydney's six-string acoustic was in its stand beside one of her black Marshall cabinets on one side of Greg's drums. Her amp sat on top. There was no room for her other cabinet, which remained in the van out back. Her ever-present jean jacket was slung over the end of her amp. Her dim yellow Stratocaster, which she rarely played, was leaning against the cabinet behind the acoustic. Gus was set up on the other side of Greg. His Ampeg head and cabinet behind him were a little taller than Sydney's two boxes. Ethan stood between Sydney and Gus, opposite Greg.

Cables like a tangled nest of black snakes ran everywhere across the floor, between mikes, guitars, effects pedals, electronic boxes, and amps to the omnipotent mixing console, separated from the musicians by a big picture window. In the middle, on top of the mess of black spaghetti between all of them, sat the binder of their handwritten lyrics and chord charts. Several sheets from the binder were spread across the floor. A blue bowl filled with cigarette butts sat on top of the binder. Squeezed in behind Gus and Greg was the rented Yamaha keyboard. There appeared to be no plan to the arrangement of equipment. They would play, listen, talk, move something,

113

and then play again. Out of this chaos would come the music, the songs, and then the record. The dream was never messy, but creativity sure was. Ethan wasn't dreaming anymore.

They had arrived at Focus Sound following their late Sunday night show at Tormo, a small bar in Markham, north of Toronto. Three of the four songs they were to record came off like clockwork. The fourth, "You Don't Know What You're Saying," didn't fare as well. Gus wanted to make changes before they recorded it. They played until midnight and ended the night with Sydney's blistering arrangement of "American Woman." Then they packed up with hopes of starting to record around three o'clock in the morning. Adrenaline got them through most of the teardown. They were on fire. They were dragging their butts by the time they left Tormo.

Gus drove the van while Greg passed around a bottle of caffeine pills. They were booked until noon. For the next five days, their routine became: Tormo, Focus Sound, house, and Tormo. Sleep would be second priority to getting the four songs recorded.

They arrived at the back door of Focus Sound just after three, but setup took another hour. At four thirty, Gus and Sydney were plugged in and working through "You Don't Know What You're Saying." Greg's snare had loosened up during transport. Ethan could see him getting frustrated at not finding the pop he wanted. Sometimes it took a few minutes, but other times, no matter what he did, he couldn't get the right sound.

"Let's lay down a song," Raj, their sound engineer, said.

Raj Mahar was hired to engineer and produce their songs. Someone Randolph knew in Ottawa had recommended him. Raj was from Nashville, but the first thing out of Greg's mouth was "I'm not drumming to any sitar shit!" But after listening to a couple of tracks Raj had done with other bands, Greg backed off. Raj would be the most expensive part of recording, but they needed help. Raj was their man.

"Sydney, is it, and Gus?" Raj asked, his tone sharp through the intercom speaker. They nodded. "What do we start with?"

Sydney and Gus were in the recording room behind the large pane of glass that Ethan and Raj looked at them through. They might have been all of six feet away, but the intercom connecting the rooms made the distance seem like an illusion.

"'Never Say Never,'" Ethan said without looking at either of them. "We killed that tonight. Start with what we know."

Sydney answered by winding through the opening riff, which hadn't changed from the first time Ethan had heard it in his parents' living room, the same night Ethan had proposed they all move in together. That now seemed like an eternity ago. Gus followed Sydney's lead. They were into it. Raj nodded to the beat, moving slides on the long multitrack console in front of him. Ethan half expected Raj to stop them to get a count in when Raj was ready, but he didn't. Ethan soon saw that Raj loved the spontaneity of live performance as much as he did and wanted to capture it. Some of their best stuff was off the cuff, when things weren't all set up. They could always go back and adjust things later, but it was nearly impossible to duplicate a moment of magic. That was what recording was about to Raj.

Ethan could see Sydney's tiredness. Her face was flush with color high in her cheeks, but her fingers didn't seem to notice. She was a spectacle to watch. The two had played almost the whole song when Gus threw in a new bass riff that lit up Sydney's bloodshot eyes.

"Awesome, guys!" Raj shouted over the intercom after they'd finished, giving them a thumbs up. "Sorry, miss, but I don't know what else to say."

"Works for me!" Sydney shouted back, looking at Ethan.

"She's one of the guys," Ethan said.

Ethan smiled at Raj's politeness and was sure they'd see another side of Mr. Mahar in time. He figured Raj's high recommendation had come with a few frayed nerves and hurt feelings.

For the next hour, Gus and Sydney played on. Gus broke his D-string near the end of "Don't Tell Me." Raj raised his hands, signaling them to keep playing. "That was cool," he said. "We'll use it."

"The Angel" caused them the most grief. Raj told Ethan to squeeze in with Sydney and Gus and sing.

"It doesn't work," Raj said when they'd finished.

Ethan returned to the sound booth. He could see Raj's fists clenched on the board.

"Something's not right. It's beautiful but not like this." Raj shook his head. His long, straight black hair shimmered in the overhead fluorescents.

Ethan looked at his watch. It was almost eight o'clock.

"It needs piano," Raj said suddenly. "Maybe some strings."

Ethan saw Raj had one focus: to make a great song. Good wasn't enough.

Greg squeezed into the booth with them, a can of Mountain Dew in his hand.

"How's it goin'?" Greg asked.

"Damn fine," Raj replied. "Ready to play some drums?"

115

"Yep," Greg said, and sipped his soda. "Replaced the skin. Spent an hour tuning the fucker, but we're good now."

Greg had taken the snare somewhere else to fix it.

"Let's do it," Raj said. "Drums were a pain on my last project. I must think good thoughts."

Greg looked at Ethan. Ethan smiled and shrugged.

"Big kit. Squeeze in, and we'll see. Sound'll bounce less. Gotta hear it. Cross that bridge," Raj said, speaking fast, and then he stood up. "Show me what you've got."

Greg went into the room, where Gus was unstrapping his bass. Sydney joined Ethan beside Raj. Ethan was always amazed at how tiny she was offstage. A couple of barrettes held her hair in place at different angles, giving her an edgy Laurie Anderson look. The fingers of her left hand were moving as if she were running through another riff in her head. If he asked, Ethan knew she'd shake her head and say something like "What goes in must come out."

"Let's get something to eat," Sydney said, interrupting Ethan's thoughts about her. Her love for music did not include the drums, and Greg was not on her favorite-people list, which didn't help.

"I wanna hear Greg for a minute," Ethan replied.

"Suit yourself. I'm going for a smoke."

Greg slid in behind his constantly expanding drum kit. Ethan had difficulty seeing it as just drums and had begun to refer to it as the Kit. Greg had to crawl under two cymbals to get to his stool.

Raj moved a couple of slides and stuck a piece of masking tape at the bottom of each slide. He wrote a number on the tape to indicate which mike the slide controlled.

Greg struck the snare with his drumstick. "That's fucking unreal!" he yelled.

Ethan smiled; when the snare was good, Greg was good.

Raj nodded, acknowledging the comment, but his thoughts seemed elsewhere. He appeared to stare out a side window that wasn't there. Ethan hadn't stayed to hear Greg drum. He was concerned about Greg clashing with Raj. It was like watching clouds darken before a storm. Greg disliked change more than most. Ethan wanted their first recording session to go well. The Release was unknown, unsigned, and unrecorded, and no matter what Randolph had said to those backing him, there would be little tolerance for personality conflicts and delays. They couldn't screw up this opportunity.

Raj watched through the glass as Greg made his never-ending adjustments.

"All right!" Raj yelled over Greg's pops on the snare. "I'll run 'Never Say Never' to your ears."

"What?" Greg called back.

Raj didn't repeat himself. He shook his head.

Ethan could feel the tension growing.

"Yer da boss," Greg replied in some kind of mixed accent, seemingly to intentionally antagonize the man at the controls.

An instant later, Sydney's blistering riff filled the room. Gus's pounding bass line followed. Greg started and then stopped.

"Stop. Stop. Fucking stop!" he shouted, but the music kept playing. "Start it again!" he yelled, raising his sticks in the air.

"Just play!" Raj shouted back, but Greg didn't start and shook his sticks at Raj behind the glass. Raj punched the board. The music stopped.

Greg was more structured and process oriented than all of them put together. Sydney liked to say he was a robot. He could follow instructions like nobody's business but was devoid of passion. Playing drums was a process for Greg. He saw himself as an elaborate metronome. Playing was more science than art. He had a point, as his job was to keep the band in sync. It drove Sydney nuts. "Drummers are a different breed," she'd say, "and Greg's fucking special to the breed." But love them or hate them, bands didn't exist without drummers.

"I need a count in, dude!" Greg said loudly, defiant in his caffeine-and-whatever-else-induced exhaustion.

Ethan believed that Greg, out of spite, would have stopped again if Raj hadn't given him one.

Ethan again saw that Raj was all music; nothing else mattered. He had no patience for bullshit and whining. As if by magic, Greg drummed "Never Say Never" like Ethan had never heard before. He watched, waiting for the mishit, but it never came. He didn't notice Sydney and Gus squeeze in behind him.

When Greg finished, he stopped, clenched his sticks together in one hand, and bent down to adjust something. The action seemed like his subconscious acknowledgment of playing well. When he returned to his upright position on his stool, he flipped his hair to the side. Raj was standing with his thumbs-up approval.

"Wow!" Raj cried. "Right on."

Greg, smiling, placed his sticks on his snare. He roughed up his hair with both hands as if he were washing it and then raked it back between his fingers, one hand following the other. It was another ritual Ethan had witnessed time and again over the years. He knew when Greg was pleased with himself.

"We've a couple hours left," Raj said, and he sat back down. "Here's what we'll do."

He explained his plan for the next three hours. He wanted to use the electric piano and find Sydney a twelve-string Fender. The Music Place down the street would be open and likely have one.

When Raj finished, Sydney left to chase down the guitar. Gus went for a round of coffees.

Raj wanted Ethan to sing "The Angel" to the piano, but Greg was to drum out "You Don't Know What You're Saying" first, and he did so flawlessly. Greg smiled when Raj stood up and pressed his thumb to the glass separating them.

It was Ethan's turn.

CHAPTER 25

Ethan was anxious.

While Sydney was gone, finding the twelve-string guitar, Ethan fingered out a new version of "The Angel" on the upright piano in the lounge area. It took him half an hour to get the mix of chords and arpeggios he could sing to. Raj was right. It did sound better on the piano. In a matter of hours, Raj had become like a fifth member of the band. Big-boned and chubby, he was unlike many of the skin-and-bone music types Ethan had come across in his short time immersed in the Toronto music scene. Like the rest of them, he said what was on his mind. His direct outbursts kept them on their toes. The recording session was already like an extension of life at the house, edgy and uncertain but productive.

Greg crawled out of his kit and said he needed a cigarette. Ethan sat down at the Yamaha electric and played. Sydney walked in just as he finished, carrying a guitar case that looked big enough for her to climb into to go to sleep.

"I fell in love with a Martin," Sydney said, setting the case down on the floor. She undid the latches quickly.

"Martin! I said Fender!" Raj said, his sharp tone piercing the quiet studio like shots from a pistol. Ethan's hunch regarding Raj's other side was evident in his reaction to Sydney not following his request.

"I know, but the Martin felt better," Sydney replied, Raj's terseness having no effect on her.

"Get the Fender!" Raj said, speaking even louder.

"Fuck you!" Sydney said, on the attack and not about to retreat.

"I want the Fender."

"You want the Fender? Get the fucker yourself."

Exhausted, Sydney was mad, and Ethan knew it. She had the guitar strapped on and was already strumming through the chords of "The Angel" as if no one else were there. Her eyes were closed.

Raj threw up his arms. "Let's go," he said, shaking his head, appearing to realize he should choose his battles.

Ethan sat down at the keyboard and played a few chords. Sydney stopped and looked at him.

"I changed it a bit," he said.

He liked the opening and repeated it twice before starting to sing:

Here lies an angel
with broken wings.
Her eyes still watch;
her voice still sings.

The words fit better with the notes he played, as they often did when he wasn't trying to fit them to some kind of structure. A smile stretched the width of his face as he looked at Sydney. She started to strum to the melody he was playing. Incredibly, the two instruments were in tune and sounded beautiful together.

"Okay, okay," Raj said, "we gotta get this on tape. That's close! My bad."

He ducked out of the room and back into the booth to hunch over the mixing console.

Raj's thumb went up behind the glass. Ethan started, already more comfortable with the song. He repeated the opening two bars as he had before, readying to sing, feeling the words. But something changed. The heavy padlocked door was back. It scared him, yet he refused to stop playing. His eyes closed as they did when he was trying to focus on something he couldn't quite hold on to. The words left him. What came out was different from what he'd written in his parents' living room:

It's there; I can touch it,
But it's not mine to have.

He didn't get to the next line. It didn't sound right. He stopped.

Raj was quick on the intercom. "It's okay. Start over."

Sydney was sitting on the stool beside him, her slim black-denim-clad left leg stretched out in front of her. The Martin rested on her right thigh; her foot was elevated on the stool's footrest. Her hands were on top of the twelve-string body; her chin rested on her hands. She was frowning. Her eyes were closed. Ethan knew her look: pathos.

But in looking at Sydney, he saw Mila. Mila was not there, though his heart said differently, breaking all over again. He felt love he'd thought was dormant—love that would never touch the one for whom it was intended. The performer and creator were unable to enjoy the beauty of their work as others would. His fingers would never touch her softness again; his ears would never hear her sweet voice.

Ethan, start again, she said in his mind.

He watched her speak. They would have been only words to anyone else, yet he craved to hear but a whisper.

"Ethan," Sydney said, her eyes wide like those of a person questioning whether another was listening.

Ethan blinked.

"Start again. We don't have all day," she said.

"From the top, man," Raj said over the intercom.

Ethan looked at the piano keys as if they'd suddenly appeared before him. His fingers played the first chord. The sound seemed to touch him as she might have. He hoped it might touch Mila.

He raised his head and looked at the ceiling. His fingers moved across the keys in familiar territory again. They seemed to know where to go on their own. The melody came and then the words:

Here lies an angel
with broken wings.
Her eyes are watching as he sings.
It will never really end.

"Fuck!" Sydney said.

Ethan kept playing, trying to match his voice to the piano, rushing the words to bring the song around.

"Okay, okay!" Raj came on the intercom. "This needs work. Ethan, let the vocals go. We don't need them right now. Just play. Time's almost up."

Ethan stood up and then sat down again. He was in a moment and knew it. He wanted to capture the vocal but followed Raj's direction. He hadn't intended to play the piano in that song and wasn't ready, but now that was all he was going to end up doing. For some reason, he suddenly remembered his meds, which he hadn't taken for two days, going on three. His mother would have had a conniption if she'd known.

"Ready?" Raj asked, his electrified voice coming through the intercom. Ethan nodded. "Let's do it."

Sydney faked a smile. Ethan could tell she was already somewhere else. It was clear she didn't like what was happening. Her lips were pressed into a line.

They'd been up for almost twenty-four hours.

CHAPTER 26

Ethan hoped day two would be better. It wasn't.

They all went to bed after returning from the studio. They slept until six and somehow played their hearts out that night at Tormo. They were already dragging by the time they reached Focus Sound. Their equipment not only seemed heavier, but they seemed to have to move it farther.

Ethan sang "Never Say Never" to what the rest of the band had recorded the day before. Standing still and singing into a bulbous black foam ball that encased the microphone took some getting used to. He was always moving on stage, holding the mike. In the studio, he felt constrained and, consequently, sounded that way. He couldn't find his groove. "Never Say Never" came out flat and dreary, missing the emotion of his stage performance. It was as if he were singing someone else's song instead of his own.

Midway through the second take, Raj signaled him to stop. Angered, Ethan jumped up and screamed the line he was singing.

"Whoa," Raj said through the intercom. "What the fuck was that?"

Ethan turned.

Raj beamed. "That's it!"

Ethan shook his fist. He knew it too. It felt wonderful.

It was three thirty in the morning.

By ten o'clock, nothing else had gone right. It was as if that first take had taken all they had. Raj proposed they give it a rest. They packed up and left.

They headed to McDonald's, where Ethan and Sydney rarely ate, but they were so out of sorts they didn't care. They were hungry, tired, and down. The Golden Arches satisfied at least one of the three feelings.

Back at the house, Gus helped Ethan move the electric piano inside.

Ethan had decided he would practice "The Angel" until it was right. There was something missing when he sang while playing the piano. Maybe it was confidence. All morning, he'd felt off key. By three o'clock, he still wasn't happy but couldn't keep his eyes open. He fell into bed. The others had already crashed.

His sleep was restless and short. By five thirty, he couldn't stay in bed any longer; he was unable to stop picturing the melody he played with his right hand out of sync with the rhythm he played with his left. Still in his plaid boxers, he went to the Yamaha, plugged in the headphones, and played. Gradually, the song began to feel like his. His heart had to be in sync with the notes he played. The music seemed to come through him—love in play.

Absorbed in working the song out, he was surprised when Sydney sat down beside him on the shaky bench. He unplugged the headphones.

"Sorry," he said. "I didn't hear—"

"Try this," she said. Her soft hand brushed against his. The notes she played fit beautifully.

His eyes filled. Joy overcame him as tears rolled down his cheeks. He shuddered.

Sydney turned and looked up at him. "What's wrong?" she asked, her voice sweet and caring.

"Nothing." He rubbed his cheeks with the back of his hand, embarrassed. He didn't know what was wrong, only that her notes completed his.

Sydney turned, touched his arm, and then moved closer and kissed his cheek.

"No, we can't," he whispered to no avail as Sydney touched his face. She kissed the tears on his cheeks and then his starving lips. His lips melted into hers. A hunger overcame him as he lost himself in her caresses. He couldn't help but respond, knowing it wasn't right. Her mouth was hungry and welcomed his. He felt reluctance, confused between love for her and love for her genius. He needed her—her energy, her body. He wanted to feel and hold her. It was as if she had become the music. Their coupling was inevitable, working as they did with the forces of love that fed creativity, one born from the other, creating not only art but also, in essence, who they were. Their attraction to each other was undeniable in spite of his reluctance.

But the love they shared was music and its creation.

His mouth opened, permitting her entry and succor, her hungry tongue matched only by his own yearning. Her musical hand moved to his boxers, touching his body's anxious, willing hardness—he was beyond ready, beyond need. Sydney stood as Ethan shifted on the bench, moving closer. Her chest was against his; their lips were inseparable. Her petite size was perfect for his seated height. His fingers slipped between her thighs; her loose underwear allowed his fingers to slide between her sweet folds into the liquid smoothness inside, exciting him to near bursting, her inner secret no longer veiled to imagination and infatuation.

Ethan closed his eyes.

He was again coupled with his beloved Mila, but something was wrong—something he couldn't stop. *How could something so beautiful be wrong?* His Mila, her forever-deep brown eyes that took him to a place he never wanted to leave. Her gentle, loving fingers that discovered an exquisiteness he never knew existed. Her mesmerizing body that when entwined with his was the embodiment of heaven itself.

His eyes opened—another vanishing act.

Sydney pulled down his boxers as he lifted himself off the bench. Her underwear slid to the floor. She raised her leg over his and straddled him, her lightness unimaginable as she sat on top of him. He entered her effortlessly; the feeling was nearly enough to make him ejaculate upon penetrating her. Their mouths remained locked, their tongues, like their hands, searching for more. As his fingers moved, they discovered a lovely newness in her breasts, her chest rising to his touch. She sucked his tongue between her lips. For a moment, they were inseparable, locked together on the edge of eternity.

"Ah, fuck!" a voice said behind them.

Greg walked into the living room. He was barely awake but awake enough to see them together and know.

It was their common room, like the kitchen. It was their rehearsal space.

"Shit!" Sydney said, leaping off Ethan like a jack-in-the-box. She swept up her underwear and dashed to the couch. Ethan stood up pulling up his boxers.

"Shit! Shit! Shit!" she repeated, her words fast and furious.

"Fuck you guys," Greg said. "You could at least go to a bedroom."

"Shut up!" Sydney shouted, pulling on her underwear and grabbing the gray blanket off the arm of the couch. "Fucking shut up. Don't say another word!" She wrapped the blanket around herself.

But it wasn't Greg's fault. It was Ethan's, and he knew it. He'd put the band together and broken the solemn promise he'd made to himself and the band—there could be a female member, but there would be no messing around. It would break the band's democracy, change the dynamics, and end in disaster, he'd said. Now he was the hypocrite.

He was disgusted with himself after feeling incredible only moments before.

Too angry to say anything, he turned and adjusted his boxers. It wasn't supposed to happen that way, and he'd allowed it to. It had taken an instant, but the Release would now be different. *What doesn't kill you ...*

"Christa," Ethan said, immediately confused as to why that name had come out of his mouth.

"What!" Sydney cried. "What did you say?"

"Syd—I said Syd," he replied, as surprised as Sydney was but for different reasons.

"No, you didn't," she said. "Who the fuck is Christa?"

Hearing the name Christa said out loud alarmed him. The living room seemed to tilt as his head spun with a rush of different images—his hospital bed, gold hoop earrings, a toe ring. He sat back down on the shaky piano bench.

"Somebody," he said, hesitating as his memory pleaded to take him deeper. The presence of the heavy wood door was beside him. He couldn't recall how the name meant anything.

"What?" Sydney sneered.

He couldn't say any more. A door opened in the hallway. Sydney seemed to sink farther into the couch as Gus, pulling back his long hair, came into the living room.

"What's up?" he asked.

"Just some fuckin' sex," Greg said. He grinned, looking at Gus and then at Ethan. "That I interrupted."

"Fuck off, Greg," Ethan said, his anger helping him to think quickly and push away the looming door. He had to confront what had just happened and get it out in the open before it festered and grew into the end.

In a split second, he decided, intuition telling him to go on.

"Okay," he said, "group meeting. Now! Sydney, that means you too."

He hated himself as soon as he said it.

CHAPTER 27

"I've broken my rule, our rule," he said, his heart shrinking as he looked at Sydney curled up on the couch. There was nothing in her eyes. "Syd and I had a moment a few minutes ago."

He couldn't remember calling her Syd before.

"I don't know what's going to happen," he said, looking from Sydney to Greg and then to Gus, "but it was my mistake."

He was sure Sydney cringed as he spoke.

"We're a band—the Release. We're a fucking good—no, a fucking great band. And now we're going to find out how great. What just happened between Sydney and me wasn't right. I'm sorry, Sydney. This band is why we're here—the only reason why we're here."

Surprising Ethan, Sydney spoke next. She spoke as if she'd prepared for it.

"I'm sorry, Ethan," she said, staring first at him and then at the floor. Her voice cracked. There were no tears; Sydney wasn't one to cry. "I love this band. It's why I'm here. We—I—had a fucking weak moment. That's all. I am fucking human. It won't happen again."

Greg was silent and nodded.

Gus, his black hair now tied back, barely had his eyes open. "Interesting way to wake up."

His comment broke the moment. They all laughed. It was a serious laugh.

"We've a lot of work to do," Ethan said, "and a long night ahead of us."

He waited to see if anyone would say anything, but no one did. They all looked at him. He needed to say something.

"Okay, group hug."

They all came together, with Sydney on his right, Greg on his left, and Gus in between.

"What doesn't kill us," he said, trying to think of what to say next. He felt Sydney's hand on his back. He closed his eyes. "Allows us to live another day."

Gus was first to break from the hug. "I gotta take a piss."

Greg and Sydney headed to their rooms. They still needed sleep, even a little.

Ethan knew sleep was over for his day. He headed back to the piano. He had to figure out "The Angel" before they went back to Focus Sound.

He sat down, but all he could think of was the name Christa. It wouldn't go away. The name meant something—he was sure of it—but why? He would have understood if he'd blurted out the name Mila, not that her name would have been any less hurtful, but Sydney at least knew that name. But Christa? He couldn't connect the name to anyone, but he didn't like how it made him feel either.

He sat down and looked at the keys on the piano. It was a place he'd gone to for years. In high school, he'd sat at his parents' old Heintzman upright and played when he needed to clear his head. It seemed to bring order to whatever disorder was disrupting his life. He'd play notes that became melodies, which pleased him and made what didn't please him go away.

He put on the headphones and started to play "The Angel," but the name Christa wouldn't go away. He tried the notes Sydney had played, hoping they were still there, but only the name kept coming back. After half an hour, he was closer but still not there. He couldn't get it. He dropped the headphones, stood up, stretched his arms out, and cracked his knuckles. He couldn't wait any longer. The name and the melody—one was there, and one wasn't.

He took a step from the piano, and it suddenly came to him: Christa was the nurse, his nurse. Randolph had mentioned her in Ottawa. Ethan had never met her after returning, but that was her name. He didn't like how it made him feel. The heavy door was in his midst, but there was something else, something warm, inviting, and gentle, as if he were being wooed. He shook his head. He didn't know why he would have said that name, but now he had the answer. He still needed the notes.

He headed to Sydney's room. Whether asking Sydney was a mistake or not, he had to get the song figured out—chase it out of hiding. Sydney could do that.

Approaching Sydney's door, he could hear her playing "Never Say Never" on her acoustic. He wasn't the only one who couldn't sleep. He knocked.

Nothing varied in her guitar playing. He knocked again, a little harder. The music stopped. He heard nothing for a few seconds. Then the guitar started again. He knocked again.

"Go away!" she said over the music she was playing.

"No," Ethan replied. "I'm sorry, but 'The Angel' needs your notes."

He leaned his head against the door and stared at the white paint on the doorframe. Its many coats had rounded the sharp edges of the frame. The doorknob needed painting. None of the bedroom doors had locks. They had respected each other's privacy.

"I don't have them. They fucked off."

"I need your fingers," he said, but as soon as he said it, he wanted to take it back. In trying to be cool, he was anything but.

"Really? It didn't seem that way half an hour ago."

"You know what I mean," he said. "I need the parts you added."

Sydney didn't say anything. He heard a couple of final strums of the guitar. "Give me a sec," she said finally.

"I'll be at the piano," he said. He walked back to the living room. Their music stuff was strewn everywhere, yet there was comfort in the mess.

He was playing "The Angel" when Sydney joined him. Gray sweatpants and a black-and-white Lycra top had replaced the nightclothes she'd been wearing before.

"I liked you calling me Syd," she said quietly.

He stopped playing. "Okay."

"My mother calls me that most of the time." She was behind him to his right. She rarely mentioned her family. "So what are you missing?"

"Your notes," he said, and he played the two bars leading up to the part he was searching for. "Right here."

He stopped and moved his hands back from the keyboard.

Sydney leaned over and, without hesitating, played the notes she had played before—without touching his hand.

"So why can't I get that?" he said, his hands returning to the keys. His right hand brushed against hers. Her warm skin was tempting, like Eve's forbidden fruit, sweet but prohibited. She moved her hand away.

"You'll have to figure that out," she replied, lingering for a moment longer at his side. Uncomfortable yet wanting, Ethan straightened up from his slouched position over the keyboard. He arched his back, his hands on the keys.

"I'll get the Martin," she said, and she left while Ethan played the exact short phrase she had just shown him. Finally, he had it.

He played it twice more before starting over.

Sydney returned with the rented twelve-string.

"Thanks, Syd," he said, and for the first time, he saw her as Syd.

"We have to get this right before we leave," she said, moving the card-table chair closer to the piano.

"Tell me about it," Ethan replied, realizing he was playing without the headphones. He stopped.

"Keep playing," Syd said, sitting down.

"We'll wake Gus and Greg."

"It's fucking time they got up."

Ethan started playing, working his way up to the new part. He came into the first notes only to miss the beat.

"Shit!" he said, splaying his fingers across the keys. "I thought I had it."

"Play it again, Eth," she said. She chuckled at her joke as Ethan rolled his eyes. "I'll help you through it. I won't play."

He started again. Syd's right hand moved to the music as if she were holding a magic wand. She, if anyone, knew the notes weren't what he was having difficulty with. The song changed time signature, though the change was subtle and easy to miss. Learning it wrong had made it doubly hard to correct. He watched Syd's hand and used its rhythm to cue him. That time, the awkward part vanished.

"I got it!" he cried. "I fucking got it! Stay there. Do that thing again with your hand."

He played it half a dozen times more. Each time was better. Syd joined him on guitar for the last two.

"Okay," Syd said, adjusting the guitar on her lap, "let's do it from the start and sing this time."

Ethan started, each part like an artist adding new color to a painting. He loved the song. The new arrangement and words were much better. Syd came in on cue. Out of the corner of his eye, he saw Gus come into the room. He kept playing. Syd played the final riff, synchronizing perfectly with the notes he played on the piano.

"That was great," Gus said. "It's a beautiful song."

"It is," Greg added, surprising Ethan from behind. "Let's hope you can get it fucking right tonight."

His words sounded less than genuine.

CHAPTER 28

Wednesday, November 28, 1984

They all arrived at Focus Sound just past two o'clock in the morning.

The first thing Raj had Ethan do was sing "Never Say Never." It was a repeat of the night's performance. Ethan sang easily, adjusting his tone and volume like an actor modulating his lines onstage. Raj was smiling. Ethan didn't think he could sing it any better. The others clapped when he finished. It was a good place to start the session. He hoped it wouldn't be a repeat of the previous day's futile efforts. It was also a good sign that they had moved on from the incident at the house, at least for the time being.

They spent the next four hours putting together "Don't Tell Me." Ethan didn't think it was their best song, but Raj really liked it. It pushed their musicianship to the limit.

By seven o'clock, Ethan was repeating his previous pattern again with "The Angel" for the fourth time. Again, he couldn't bring the piano and vocal together the way he had at the house. Frustration was taking him on a downward spiral he couldn't seem to stop. Nothing sounded right.

"Leave it!" Raj shouted over the intercom. "Fucking leave it. Now!"

"I can't leave it!" Ethan shouted back.

"You leave it if I tell you to!" Raj exploded over the speaker. "We'll come back later. Next song."

"I need a fucking break," Syd said, and she disappeared out the door.

After waiting a bit, Ethan stood up, an unexpected rage upon him as if he'd taken a punch to the nose.

"Fuck!" he screamed, clenching his fists in front of his face. Blood rushed to his head, as if his body were trying to squeeze out his anger. He went to the door. How many times was he going to get it wrong? They didn't have time for that. They had a deadline. He was supposed to be leading the way, not slowing them down. He yanked open the door.

"I don't give a fuck!" Syd shouted. Greg was standing in front of her with the hint of a smirk on his face. "You're such an asshole!"

Gus was sitting on the worn leather couch in the lobby. His head was back against the wall. He was staring at the ceiling.

Raj came in from the control booth at the same time as Ethan.

"Okay!" Raj shouted, splitting the tension in the room wide open. "Enough, enough. Enough! If you want me here, you fix this. I'm taking ten!"

He turned and left out the street entrance.

Ethan looked at Greg. Greg's eyes were red; his pupils were pinpricks. He turned as Syd picked up the black case that held her white ES and her small Pignose amp beside the couch Gus was on. She didn't say a word, but Ethan knew where she was going. Syd played her frustrations out.

"Take a tape recorder," he said. Even in his angered state, he knew she was about to play stuff they would never get to hear.

"Fuck off!" she snarled, and she backed out the door.

Ethan headed to the back door. He could only think to walk. He had to get away. A coffee would help too. He was ready to blow up. Outside, he was surprised how warm and sunny it was for late November. Snow easily could have been on the ground at that time of year.

The walk did him good, as did the coffee. He picked up coffees for everyone from a little place around the corner.

On his way back, he found Gus in the front seat of the van with his eyes closed. Ethan didn't disturb him. When he opened the back door to the studio, he found Greg flopped on the couch. He was out. He wondered if Greg had slept at all before their show. Syd wasn't there. He hadn't expected her to be.

"Where's Sydney?" Raj asked, coming out of the recording booth. He stared at Ethan as a parent might stare down a kid who'd missed curfew.

"Dunno," Greg grumbled more to himself than in answer to Raj's question. He turned into the couch.

"Give me a few minutes," Ethan said, putting down the cardboard tray of coffees in his hand. He had a feeling he knew where he'd find Syd and was surprised Raj hadn't run into her. He went out the front door, which faced St. Clair Avenue. It was almost eight o'clock.

Across the street, a few doors down, a small crowd was gathered near a place called Nancy's Restaurant. As he crossed, he could hear the sound of Syd's playing. She was winding through "You Don't Know What You're Saying." The group seemed captivated by the magic taking place in front of them. Nobody was moving past.

Ethan squeezed between some teenagers who looked mesmerized by the playing of this girl who didn't look any older than they were. Syd's fingers were weaving up and down the neck of her Gibson. Blinding flashes of the morning sun reflected off the ivory body as she moved. Her guitar looked mammoth resting against her thigh in front of her. Music flowed from her fingers as if the guitar were part of her body. The crowd, mostly older teens and twentysomethings, seemed awed by the guitar aficionado in their midst, as if they were seeing a Joni Mitchell or a Neil Young en route to celebrity. Ethan was inspired while watching her play. She was in her element. Then, as if interrupted by his presence, she looked up and saw him. Her reaction was immediate; she drew in the melody and brought the song to what seemed its natural conclusion. The amp echoed her final notes.

The small crowd clapped, whistled, and shouted their pleasure, tossing coins into her open guitar case.

"I'm afraid my time's up," she announced to groans of disappointment. "But," she added, nodding at Ethan, "I'll leave you with this."

People turned as Ethan shook his head, his nerves once again on edge, but he couldn't say no. He had to perform.

"We're part of the Release," Syd said, adjusting the position of her guitar. "We're recording our first songs across the street. Come out and see us sometime, and buy our album when it comes out."

Ethan made his way forward as Syd spoke. As he turned to face the crowd gathered around them, Syd started to play "The Angel." He was about to wave her off to play something else but stopped. He wasn't ready, but the moment was here and now. *The show must go on, Ethan.* The words came to him as if Mila were standing at his side, whispering in his ear. But as he started to sing, he saw her—not Mila but the woman from their night at Benny's. He felt something more than just familiarity. It was an old feeling, a feeling of comfort, like seeing a close friend after a long absence.

It was the feeling of love.

CHAPTER 29

If there was an autopilot to performing, Ethan engaged it. Though the piano was missing, Syd played their new arrangement. Ethan watched the woman move along the back of the crowd. On starting the second verse, he caught her eye. There was that instant of recognition that one desires more than the other but both know it. Syd played on, working the song like a master beyond her years. Ethan sang as if his miscues in the studio had never happened. He looked from the woman to Syd, who was gleaming with the joy of performing well. Her eyes signaled him to turn back to the crowd. There seemed to be even more people; people stopped on their way to work, school, or breakfast, captivated by the unexpected spectacle. But Ethan searched only for the eyes he had fallen for.

Unbelievably, they were gone. Two unknown faces filled the spot where he'd seen her. Panicked, he scanned the many faces that surrounded them, but the face—the eyes, the smile—had vanished. Had he imagined her? It seemed too much of a coincidence for her to be there without having any way of knowing he would be, yet he felt certain his eyes had not deceived him. She was real. He had seen her. She had seen him, only to vanish like a wisp of smoke moments later.

As he sang the last words, Syd wound through the last guitar riff. His eyes darted from one person to the next, trying to find the lost brown eyes and the person they belonged to. The crowd clapped and hooted as Syd played the last chord.

"Thank you!" Ethan shouted, hearing Syd reiterate the same words. Coins plunked into her guitar case like large pellets of hail.

As the crowd dissipated, Ethan's eyes met Syd's.

"You should have done this before we started recording," Ethan said, nodding at the money in her guitar case. "Look at that."

Syd looked back at him, her eyebrows raised. "What do you mean?" she said. "There were only a few coins in there ten minutes ago. This is for you."

Ethan shook his head. "Yeah, right."

She unplugged her guitar as Ethan bent down to collect the money, thanking those who passed by dropping more coins.

"Did you see her?" Syd asked, squatting beside him.

"See who?"

"Ah, come on. You didn't see her?"

"See who?" Ethan repeated, pretending not to know whom Syd was talking about, afraid the answer would trick him again.

"The nurse woman from Benny's," Syd said.

Ethan smiled, still hesitant to admit whom he thought he'd seen but relieved he could trust she was real.

"You saw her too?" he asked, turning around and looking again, hopeful she might reappear. The sidewalk where they'd performed was nearly clear. Two teenage girls were walking into Nancy's Restaurant. They were wearing shorts and T-shirts in the unseasonably warm weather.

"Only for a moment," Syd replied. "I knew I'd seen her before but couldn't remember where. When I remembered, she was gone."

"Strange. Why would she be here?"

"Stalker," Syd joked.

Ethan looked up to see Gus waving at them urgently from across the street.

"Fuck. What now?" he said.

Syd didn't reply. She picked up the few coins he'd missed and set her white ES inside the case, cradling it like a piece of fine china.

"You think you can sing 'The Angel' now?" Syd asked as they crossed the street. "That was quite a performance. Talk about recording. That was the one."

Performing live was different from the confines of the studio. It was like the difference between talking to someone he liked and talking to someone he didn't.

"It's different out here," he said. "It's like I'm someone else."

"Then fucking close your eyes and imagine." Syd laughed as they stepped onto the opposite curb in front of the studio.

"It's like I feed off who they want me to be," Ethan replied, surprising himself with his response.

"Then pretend you're who they want," she said. "Like an actor."

Ethan stopped. Her words hit him with an unexpected suddenness. *Like an actor.* He was back at the hospital. He saw the tunneled corridor and the gray tile floor he'd shuffled down too many times. "How's the Actor today?" someone asked.

"You know what?" he answered, somehow jerking himself back from where his mind seemed intent on taking him. "You're fucking right."

Syd smiled and pushed on the front door of Focus Sound.

Raj was leaning against the doorframe of the console booth when they came in. His right hand was on his hip in a fed-up stance.

"We're gonna do 'The Angel' again," Ethan said before Raj had a chance to speak, "and if it's anything like we just played, you're gonna be happy."

Raj stood upright and shrugged as if to say, "I doubt it." Losing Raj would put an end to their biggest break to date and, worse, Randolph's confidence.

Gus pointed at Greg, who was still crashed on the couch.

Ethan shook his head. They'd deal with Greg later.

"Let's get the show on the road then," Raj said, pushing open the door to master control of their future. "We've only a couple of hours left."

Ethan followed Syd into the recording room. Her Gibson would replace the twelve-string Martin. Ethan walked to the microphone, not the piano.

Ethan watched Raj behind the glass glance at the piano and back at him. Ethan didn't respond and stared at the six-inch black-fabric disk in front of the mike, which had replaced the big black foam ball.

Ethan turned to Syd. "Whenever you're ready."

He closed his eyes. Syd started to play. The music sounded just as it had on the street. Ethan started to sing.

"Here lies an angel ..."

CHAPTER 30

A Place without Time

Her hair fell through his fingers like the white sand on the beach they'd walked along. Like the beach, it seemed natural that they were there together. She was magnificence in his arms.

"Where have you been?" she asked.

"Been?" Ethan replied. "What do you mean?"

Something wasn't right; something was missing, like a family photo with all the eyes removed.

"You've been gone a long time."

"I have?" he said, suddenly realizing that the person he thought was with him couldn't be.

"Ethan, I've been searching for you," she said, her brown eyes melting him from the inside out.

Ethan paused and looked around. He was in a room he recognized—the cinder block walls, the chains hanging from the walls, the chair—but he couldn't remember the name of the person in the chair.

"I know you recognize me," she whispered, "but you don't remember me, do you?"

"What do you mean?" Ethan said. "I'll never forget you."

"But you have, sweetie," she said. Her soft hands were on his cheeks. "There's something missing, isn't there?"

Ethan turned his head and again looked around the room he was standing in. Behind him was a bed with a small table beside it. There was a commode. *A name much more appealing than a toilet.* They weren't his words, but he knew them as if they were. The man sitting in the chair wore only a white T-shirt smeared with brown stains and blood. A towel lay across the top of his legs.

"You're singing now," she said.

"I'm in a band."

"You're a beautiful singer," she said, smiling, "and you sing pretty good too."

She was no longer in his arms but standing beside him.

"But it's not your singing, Ethan," she said. "It's how you bring songs to life. You are the Actor, Ethan."

At first, he found the scene strange, but as he looked more closely, he could see everything was intentional. People he didn't know stood around, watching them. There were wires, lights, and equipment—equipment the likes of which he'd never seen before. He saw movie cameras. People were moving about, busy in what he could only describe as chaos. Many eyes were watching him, almost touching him, but he liked it; he loved it. He was there for their entertainment—to make them happy.

There were people around a man sitting in the chair in front of him. The chains from the wall were fastened to the man's arms. The towel across the man's thighs was gone.

"Keep searching, Ethan," she said.

He could no longer see her. He turned, but she was gone, along with any chance of her name.

"Keep digging," she whispered, as if her lips were beside his ear, and he felt her breath on his skin. "Dig deeper, Ethan. Find me."

The room faded into something else.

He was singing words to a melody and then nearly screaming, *You've made me do this to you! It's all self-inflicted!* But the words were in his head.

Then he heard his voice singing, "With eyes still watching, her voice still sings." He sang as if the words were the last he would ever utter.

CHAPTER 31

Wednesday, November 28, 1984

"Ethan! Ethan!" Raj shouted through intercom. "Un-fucking-believable! Where did that come from? Ladies and gentlemen, we have ourselves a star!"

Raj was jumping up and down in the control room, doing a shake-and-shimmy routine behind the console. It was strange for Ethan to open his eyes to such exuberance. Everything looked a little fuzzy, as it did when waking from a deep sleep. He looked over at Syd. Her smile said it all.

"I'm with Raj," she said, her voice quiet with respect. "Where the fuck did that come from?"

Ethan shook his head. He didn't know. He couldn't remember even singing. Only the last words remained on his lips: "her voice still sings."

He felt awkward stepping back from the black fabric disk he'd sung into. He turned and walked to the door, feeling like a stranger in the room.

Gus was standing outside the door when he came out.

"Couldn't take my eyes off you," Gus said. "Like something from the fucking cosmos."

Greg was rising from the couch, looking no less haggard, as Ethan tried to come to terms with what had just happened.

Randolph coming in the front door cleared his head.

"Ethan, what's up?" Randolph said, closing the door. His hand was extended. Ethan shook it. Dressed in a tailored navy suit with a burgundy tie loose around the unbuttoned collar of a white cotton dress shirt, he was leaning forward, a posture Ethan had come to recognize as intent. Randolph had things on his mind. It was the first time Ethan noticed Randolph had put on some weight.

Before Ethan could answer, Raj opened the sound booth door.

"What timing," he gushed, his cheeks rounded into a smile. "Ethan just blew us away." Ethan's hand was still in Randolph's. "It's a bit ballady, but what a song."

"Ballady?" Randolph repeated, his eyebrows rising. "Is that a real word or industry lingo?"

"It's my word. It's a Rajism."

Everyone laughed. When things worked, everything worked.

As his head cleared, Ethan introduced the others to his friend. They all shook Randolph's hand. Greg was last, straightening the waist of his jeans as he stood up from the couch. He looked as if he needed to sleep for a week. Ethan couldn't help but wonder how Greg was going to drum to anything.

"How are the songs coming?" Randolph asked. He still looked and sounded anxious, as if something else were on his mind. "Is the ballady one of them?"

Ethan was about to answer, but Raj jumped in.

"The ballady will make the cut. It's pure fucking magic."

Raj talked fast. He seemed anxious to Ethan, probably not wanting to interrupt the roll they found themselves on.

Ethan stared at Raj as he spoke, reminded of the hospital, where Randolph would tell him things he had done in his other world. There was only a feeling, no memory of having been there. He wondered whether an actor felt that way when hearing someone describe a movie he or she had been in—the watched as opposed to the watcher.

"You broke into falsetto while Sydney matched you note for note, up, up," Raj said, his fingers mimicking his voice, rising higher and higher in the air in front of him. Syd nodded. Raj shook his head. "Those moments never come twice."

"I want to hear the song," Randolph said. "Sounds perfect for when Avery knows something's up—a perfect contradiction."

William Avery, Ethan thought, from *Browning Station*. Sadly, he still didn't have a copy, and the book was why they were there.

"So what else have you got?" Randolph asked, looking from Ethan to Raj and back to Ethan again.

"We've recorded parts of four songs," Ethan said.

"Yeah, but there's still tons to do," Raj added.

"Right on schedule," Randolph said. "Good."

"Yeah, the best is ahead of us," Raj said.

Ethan smiled. Raj had come around.

"We need two," Randolph said. "The rest is gravy."

Ethan was doing his best to stay with the conversation, but the gap left in his memory during "The Angel" still disturbed him.

"All four will be good, though," Ethan said, interrupting his own thoughts.

"That's okay," Randolph said, patting Ethan on the shoulder. "We need two, and if Raj is happy, I'm happy."

Raj turned and clapped his hands. "Okay, okay," he snapped. "Enough chitchat. We've got work to do."

"Yeah, I gotta go," Randolph said, looking at Ethan. "I've been here too long already. I was in the neighborhood and couldn't help myself."

In the neighborhood? That's odd, Ethan thought. *Why would that be?* Randolph lived in Ottawa. There was no "in the neighborhood" about it. No doubt Randolph had wanted to know how his baby was coming along. Futures were on the line. He knew it. Ethan knew it. But why not call? Ethan didn't like being checked up on, as if they couldn't be trusted. It was like being watched—like the woman from Benny's on the sidewalk. No, that thinking didn't seem right. Ethan figured it best to leave the matter alone. He looked at Greg. There was enough to worry about as it was.

"We've two hours before we get kicked out," Raj said. He'd moved back to the open door of the sound booth. "Time is money, and ours is a-wasting."

Randolph stepped forward and shook Raj's hand again. Ethan thought he saw a look pass between the men. It was hard to read but likely something between "We'll get it done" and "This is pretty fucked up," he thought. He was also sure he knew what end of the scale Raj was at, despite "The Angel." But from what Randolph had told him, Raj always delivered. Ethan figured Raj had dealt with bands much more screwed up than the Release. He would overlook all the antics, but they had to play. How they got there didn't matter as long as they did. Ethan realized that was all Randolph cared about too.

"Let's play 'You Don't Know What You're Saying,'" Greg suggested, causing everyone to turn and look at him. He was standing beside the couch behind Gus. "Syd and Gus can start. See if we can get something down that the star can fucking sing to."

"Right on," Raj said. "See you later, Randy."

Randy? There that name was again. The feeling was immediate: the heavy locked door seemed to rise beside him. Ethan did his best to push it away, stepping forward with his hand extended to shake Randolph's.

"Can't wait to hear what you've got."

"You won't be disappointed," Ethan said as confidently as he could, his real feelings contrary to his words.

"I know. That's why you're here." Randolph smiled and left.

The door hadn't quite closed behind him before Syd was at the door to the recording room. Gus was right behind her, his black bass in hand. Ethan headed to the control booth behind Raj. Greg turned into the one-toilet washroom.

Syd and Gus checked their tuning. Raj gave them his thumbs up. Gus counted them in and was off with a new bass line he'd worked out. Ethan hadn't quite figured out how Gus coordinated his finger movements on the neck to create a skip-flip rhythm that sounded so cool. After four bars, Gus had found a groove. Syd followed with a winding guitar intro that heightened Gus's bass line—once again, musical evidence that the whole was much more than the sum of each instrument.

Ethan closed his eyes. The lyrics came to his lips as if they'd always been there. He was in the nightclub. His hands were on the mirror-polished surface of the bar's countertop. The woman tending the bar had her back to him. Her shoulder-length hair shimmered, reflecting the flash of light behind them.

"Ethan," Raj said, "ya gotta stop."

Ethan opened his eyes, surprised to be standing in the recording booth.

"I can't record you in here, and you're too good to miss. Just wait."

Ethan sat and listened, startled at how quickly his head had taken him away.

He watched Syd and Gus perform through the glass. He was getting so used to what they could do that he expected something new every time. He remained envious of Gus. It was hard to call himself a bassist with Gus in the band, but that didn't stop his love for the sound of the instrument. The low, understated power still sent tremors through his chest. There was never enough bass, and Gus had a way of making the music all fit together and feel right. Ethan had taught himself the mechanics of playing and could perform some pretty good riffs, but he never seemed able to put it all together without getting messed up. He'd listened endlessly to the records of Geddy Lee, Chris Squire, and Jaco Pastorius in high school, attempting to copy their chops to the sold-out stadiums of his imagination, but Gus could play anything and add his own nuances to make the riffs and the songs sound even better. It was captivating to watch how Syd could feed off Gus and make everything sound fuller.

Ethan turned to Raj, who was all but vibrating at the board. His body moved to the beat of unheard drums. His hands glided across the console of dials like a third musician playing what he wanted to hear and how he wanted to hear it. There was little doubt in Ethan's mind that Raj knew what he was doing and would find the best way to orchestrate their work. He was wired to do what he was doing.

They would do as many takes as Raj requested. Ethan was still mouthing the words to the song Syd and Gus were playing but doubted he'd sing again that day. He didn't want to sit around and watch and decided a walk would do him good.

As soon as he stepped out the front door of the studio, he spotted her. Half a block down the street, he saw her walk into an art gallery.

He didn't hesitate and hustled up the sidewalk to the gallery. Inside, he found her in seconds, already at the back, talking to a woman he guessed was the owner. With straight black hair and bangs cut straight across her forehead, she resembled art that might have been on display. He was about to speak when the sound of the woman's voice stopped him, its familiarity nearly stopping his heart. *How do I know this woman?*

Perplexed and suddenly unnerved, he backed away. He could feel the presence of the big padlocked door. He recalled seeing her brown eyes in the crowd on the sidewalk and, at Benny's, hearing her speak. He remembered the voice on the phone and again felt the uneasy feeling of sinking in deep, sucking mud. It scared him. He took another step backward and turned.

"Excuse me," said the other woman. "Can I help you?"

Ethan kept moving. The pictures on the surrounding walls seemed to spin.

"No, just looking," he said, not turning but feigning an interest in a painting he'd yet to look at. "Thank you."

Confront her, he told himself as he grabbed the handle of the front door. But it didn't feel right. The padlocked door seemed right in front of him. It was too much.

Outside, he headed up the sidewalk in the direction opposite Focus Sound. He didn't get to the end of the block before he changed his mind. He'd head back to the studio. Maybe they'd be ready for him.

The words to the second verse of "You Don't Know What You're Saying" were on his lips:

You tell me what you think is true,
but the words you speak are not from you.

143

He wanted to shout them out, to scream them.

He was mouthing the second line of the song as he passed the door of the art gallery. The door opened.

It was too late to bolt past or retreat and run for cover.

CHAPTER 32

Wednesday, November 28, 1984

Coming face-to-face with her brown eyes scrambled his thoughts and melted his heart. Their recognition of each other was instant. Locked in each other's gaze, they embraced without touching one another.

"Hi," the woman said, breaking their silence. "I figured we'd run into each other eventually."

She spoke so matter-of-factly that Ethan was caught off guard.

"You did?" he said.

"Of course."

Her voice was like the sweetest music he had ever heard. He didn't want to admit how good it made him feel.

"Why do you think I know you?" Ethan asked, speaking what was on his mind, too mesmerized to do otherwise.

"Because you do," she replied, smiling. "We met at the bar the night you tried to knock the light off the ceiling with your head."

Her smile sent a warm comfort through his body. Her eyes said she'd known him much longer than that.

"I think we should go for a coffee," she said.

Ethan nodded but didn't say anything. He couldn't.

"This isn't a two-minute 'How ya doin'?' conversation," she added, and she turned to look across the street. "By the looks of it, we'll need to be sitting down. Come on."

She directed him across the street. Ethan practically stumbled over the curb, feeling bewildered yet excited. His mind was spinning as if in search of crevices that might reveal some hint of where they'd met before Benny's. The padlocked door was close. Her brown eyes held something he couldn't quite put together. He'd looked up into them at Benny's but known even then he wasn't looking into them for the first time. He stepped on the curb on the opposite side of the street, not far from Nancy's Restaurant. They walked quickly toward the restaurant. It was evident that was where she intended to go. Seeing her pretty profile as she opened the door brought back the night at Benny's.

"What would you like?" she asked as they approached the counter, where a blonde teenage girl stood ready to take their order. "I'm buying—no questions."

Ethan didn't dare attempt to disagree. He could have listened to her voice all day; it was not only soothingly familiar but also one he could fall in love with.

"Coffee. Black."

"Anything to eat?" she asked.

Ethan shook his head. "No, thanks."

"You might need something. This could take a while."

Ethan hesitated. He could always eat. He hadn't had anything since leaving Tormo.

"A chocolate doughnut then," he said, smiling at the girl behind the counter. His hands found the front pockets of his jeans. "I don't want to upset things."

The woman said, "It won't be you upsetting things."

The blonde poured their hot drinks and used plastic tongs to pull his doughnut and a blueberry muffin from behind the glass display. Ethan followed the woman to a small table at the front window.

"I'm sorry, but I am in the middle of a recording session," Ethan said as they sat down. "I can't be long."

"Yeah, that's why you're out visiting an art gallery with your hands in your pockets. Your time's real tight."

He smiled, not knowing what else to say.

"Ethan," she said.

It surprised him to hear her say his name when he didn't know hers. The misgivings he'd had on the phone and in the gallery faded. Now that they were across from each other, he couldn't stop looking into her dark brown eyes, which looked as if they were trying to tell him something.

"I may as well start at the end. I'm Christa White."

CHAPTER 33

Wednesday, November 28, 1984

Ethan heard her say her name.

For an instant, there was silence. Then he remembered. It had been only hours since he'd said her name out loud—the nurse from the hospital who'd left before he came back. Then he felt the door again, as if it were right there beside him, waiting. Only this time, he felt something was behind it, both sad and bad. Still looking in her eyes, he felt a strange sense of comfort as her name repeated in his head.

"Christa!" he said, all but shouting. "You're Christa?"

He could feel those around them turning their heads at his unexpected loudness.

"Yes, I am," she said in a loud whisper, seemingly pleased with his acknowledgment of who she was.

"I shouted out your name yesterday," he said, lowering his voice before a confusion of emotions took over. Joy flipped to upset as one emotion fed the other, from the incident with Syd at the house that he remembered, to what might have happened in the hospital that he had no recollection of.

Tears filled his eyes and rolled down his cheeks. Something hard and constricting grew in his throat. Embarrassed in front of this stranger, he turned away to hide from what he couldn't understand or explain, only to realize he loved—and had loved—the woman sitting in front of him, whom he didn't know or even remember.

"Why didn't I know your name?" he asked with a million other things scattering all at once inside his head. "How can I not know you and feel that I do?"

Talking to her was like becoming part of a fairy tale. It wasn't real—it couldn't be—yet he'd taken his meds. His eyes shifted to Christa's lips, which were dark with crimson lipstick. How could he have known what it was like to kiss them? But he did.

"I'll answer your first question," Christa said with a forced smile. For an instant, it seemed Mila had risen from the grave like Jesus before Mary Magdalene. "Then I'll explain some of the story—my story."

Ethan continued to stare at her, switching between the lips he wanted to kiss and the brown eyes he didn't want to turn away from. Sitting still was agonizing.

"Ethan," she said. She stopped. Her eyes had become wet glass. A tear rolled down her cheek. "I'm sorry. I hadn't expected to feel this way. This is not easy for me."

If it was hard for her, Ethan thought, it was nearly unbearable for him.

"I was your nurse, Ethan," she said, brushing away a tear on her cheek. "At the Royal. I had to leave."

Ethan nodded. He loved listening to her voice.

"I was giving you the best care a nurse could give," she said. "We had such wonderful times. You were the perfect patient. But I—"

She didn't finish as tears ran down both her cheeks. Her hands clenched into fists on each side of her cup of tea.

"I didn't mean to," she said. Her hands shook.

Ethan reached forward and put his hands on hers. He knew her skin, the warmth her fingers could give.

"I know your story, Ethan. The murder. Your roommate. I'm so sorry. Oh, this—"

She stopped again. Ethan was swimming in feelings. It was all he could do to keep his head above the surface of whatever seemed intent on pulling him under.

"Are you all right?" Christa asked, her hands turning to take his. The touch of her fingers was electric, giving him strength to fight whatever was pulling him away. Her brown eyes stared intensely into his.

"Yes, but something's stirring," he said.

"We should do this another time," Christa said with a weak smile. "Give us some time to—"

"Are you nuts?" he replied, squeezing her hand. "I'd rather die than stop now. This is a chance to figure myself out."

Christa's hands squeezed back. She was real.

"We talked a lot," she said, her eyes wide, seemingly intent on controlling her emotions. "I knew you were somewhere else and not where I was, but you were fun to talk to. The doctors encouraged us to talk to you, especially Dr. Katharine. You didn't talk to everyone."

Christa let go of his hands—disappointing him—and, with both hands, raised the white cup of hot tea to her lips. He wished his lips were the cup.

"Eventually, every time I was in the room," she said after placing the cup back on the table, "you'd start talking."

Ethan didn't say anything.

"I don't know when exactly," she said, putting her forearm on the table. "In February or early March maybe, you started to say personal things."

Her brown eyes looked down at the tabletop as if suddenly seeing something of interest.

"Ethan, I couldn't take it," she said, unable to control the tears that again trickled down her cheeks. "You'd already stolen my heart, and I knew I couldn't have you. You were locked in a box and out of my reach."

Christa took a breath and then looked up at Ethan. "I was off for almost a month before I finally took leave and eventually quit. There were all sorts of rumors. The hospital did nothing to deny them. I'd kissed your forehead to say goodbye once as another nurse walked in. She asked what I was doing. I knew it was over. I'd—"

She couldn't finish.

Ethan pulled a couple of serviettes from the chrome dispenser on their small table. He handed them to her.

"I'm sorry," she said, patting her cheeks with the white napkin, sniffling. "I thought I could do this, but—"

Then, as abruptly as their accidental meeting across the street had occurred, she stood up and left. Ethan was shocked. She was out the door before he even reacted. He sat in a stupor, as if he'd been slapped across the face.

The beige leather strap of her purse brought him to his senses. It was slung over the back of her chair. He got up quickly, knocking into the table and spilling both their drinks.

"Sorry," he said, as if she were still there, and he hustled to the entrance, carrying her purse. Christa was already past where they'd crossed the street as he stepped out of the restaurant.

"Christa!" he shouted, breaking into a run. "Wait! You forgot your purse!"

It didn't take him long to make up the distance between them.

"Ethan, don't!" she cried when he caught up with her. "I just can't."

"Can't what?" he asked, handing her the purse.

"Thank you."

"You're welcome, but what can't you do?"

"I can't bear to go through this again," she said, her arms rigid at her sides.

Before Ethan knew what he was doing, his hand moved to brush her hair back from the side her face. He saw the small gold hoop dangling from her earlobe.

"Dorian's Coffee Emporium," he said.

CHAPTER 34

Wednesday, November 28, 1984

"What?" Christa asked.

He didn't answer but leaned forward and kissed her. It was a light kiss, over in seconds, but found a depth that had been missing from his life since he'd come back. If love at first sight was a cliché, so be it. It felt wonderful, though this wasn't really love at first sight, from what he'd just learned, though this would be the first time he would remember. It was a moment of truth between them as pure as the birth of a child—innocent from the ways of the world, genuine in its virtue, and right and glorious.

"Ethan?" Christa asked, breaking the sweet moment between them.

"Yes," he answered, joy bursting inside him.

"Why did you say that?"

"Say what?"

"Why did you say, 'Dorian's Coffee Emporium'?" Christa asked, a hint of accusation in her voice. It felt like the moment after he'd said her name in front of Syd.

"I don't know," he said, looking at her earrings. They brought back a feeling he could almost see. The sense of the padlocked door was there but different. He was inside. He saw the plate-glass window; Christa was behind the window, looking away from him. Gold hoops hung from her ears. The neon sign in the window was bright: Dorian's Coffee Emporium. He didn't know how he knew what it said, but he did.

When had he been there?

"You're here, Christa," he said, looking into the face he loved.

"I am," she said, shaking her head, "but are you?"

"Did we have coffee there maybe?"

Even as he asked the question, he knew it wasn't right. He didn't know any place by that name. A person passed beside them on the sidewalk.

"No," Christa replied.

Ethan looked back into her eyes. "Your earrings," he said, moving back to point to them. "I've seen them before."

"You have. I wore them at the hospital."

Ethan smiled, thinking, when he heard "I don't give a shit!" from across the street. He knew the voice before he looked to see Syd smashing the rented acoustic guitar against the front entrance of Focus Sound.

"Holy shit!" he said. He'd all but forgotten about their recording session. Syd was out-of-control upset. "Fucking Greg."

"What?" Christa asked, sounding alarmed.

"Christa," Ethan said, "I'm sorry. I have to go."

"What?" she said again.

"Can I meet you later? At one? For another coffee?" he shouted, already moving across the street, pointing to the restaurant they had just left.

"Okay," Christa said. She waved her hand. "Goodbye."

CHAPTER 35

Syd was around the corner by the time he caught up with her.

"What's going on?" he asked, running up behind her, out of breath.

"Like you give a shit!" she shouted without slowing down.

"Where are you going?"

"Away—away from this fucking bullshit!" she yelled, turning to look at Ethan but still not slowing down.

"Can you wait a second?" he said. "What the hell happened? I step out for a few minutes—"

"A few minutes! You've been gone for a fucking hour! Greg's all cranked up, sayin' we sound like shit! Raj is fucking furious."

"Fuck. You know what?" He stopped. Syd kept walking. Ethan looked at his watch in disbelief. Their session was over—and maybe more. He'd let her go. Nothing was getting fixed. They were supposed to be recording a couple of songs but instead seemed intent on destroying themselves.

His head was swimming, his emotions reeling, and it was all his fault. Less than an hour ago, his world had seemed to be coming around. Now it had flipped upside down. Syd was enraged. Christa was confused. Raj had likely quit. God only knew about Greg and Gus. Chaos had suddenly taken over his world.

As he turned the corner to the street side of the studio, he saw Gus crouched down on the sidewalk, picking up pieces of the smashed Martin.

"I don't know, Ethan," Gus said, shaking his head. "Syd loves guitars, but she's out of control."

Ethan didn't say anything as he picked up a few pieces of splintered wood. Even to his eyes, the demolished guitar was a sorry sight.

"Greg treats everyone like shit, but Syd gets the worst of it, especially when you're not around. He's got a real hate on for her, like he's jealous or something."

"Jealous?" Ethan said. "Of what?"

"You and Syd."

"I thought we put that behind us," Ethan said, knowing that what Greg had walked in on wasn't something easily put behind them.

"Yeah, right, you fucking fixed everything with your magic wand. Are you shittin' me?"

Ethan could feel a sudden rage coming on. He wound up and threw the pieces of wood in his hands onto the sidewalk.

"Fuck. I don't need this shit either," he said, seething. He glared at Gus, indignant that things had gotten out of hand so quickly.

Gus shrugged and looked at the pieces of guitar Ethan had thrown down.

"We've got two fucking days to get our shit together, or we're fucking through," Ethan said.

"No kidding," Gus said, brushing hair from his eyes.

"Listen," Ethan said, picking up the wood pieces he'd thrown onto the sidewalk. He stood up and pushed open the front door of the studio. "I'll talk to Greg. If he's got to go, so be it, but it's too late to find another drummer. We gotta fucking get through the next two days."

Ethan held the door for Gus, whose hands were full of the broken guitar pieces. Ethan shook his head. Money was tight. Replacing a $500 guitar wouldn't help.

"Where's Raj?" he asked, closing the door behind them.

"He left when Greg laid into Syd."

Gus took the remnants of the guitar out the back door of the studio. A jazz ensemble was squeezing into the recording room, lost in tuning their instruments. Ethan didn't recognize anyone from the day before. He waved at the recording engineer and followed Gus out back.

"Where did Greg go?"

"Who knows? I don't really care," Gus said, opening the van.

They loaded Greg's remaining drums and Syd's amp and left for the house. They were halfway there when Ethan realized what he'd done.

"Holy shit!" he shouted. "Turn around. I'm a fucking asshole!"

If he could have, he would have cried.

CHAPTER 36

It took twenty minutes to get back to Focus Sound. Ethan ran across the street to Nancy's Restaurant but knew before he got there he wouldn't find her.

"Fuck, I'm a jerk!" he said, climbing back into the van.

"Hard to disagree," Gus replied, half a smile on his face.

"I'm serious, man," Ethan replied, more gut-wrenchingly disappointed than angry. He didn't know how he would find her; he was sure he'd thrown her number away. "There's this girl—"

"Yeah, I know," Gus said. "There's a lot of them but one you gotta deal with now."

Ethan turned and looked at Gus. Gus didn't say any more. He didn't need to.

Ethan rethought what he was about to say. "Yeah, I know."

"She's hurtin' bad, dude. You messed her up. Ya gotta fix it."

Ethan didn't know what he was going to do or what to think. He had to fix things with Syd, but Christa was the one on his mind. He'd let her down too. The last thing in the world he wanted to do was jeopardize what they had started—or restarted—yet he'd already done so.

Gus drove them back to the house. Neither said much on the way. Ethan was exhausted and figured Gus was too. There was no sign of Syd or Greg when they reached the house. Ethan couldn't think much beyond Christa. The Release had another show to do at Tormo that night.

Gus was first to break the silence while they unloaded.

"Why don't we go through 'You Don't Know What You're Saying' and 'Don't Tell Me'?"

Ethan smiled. He knew Gus wanted the Release to happen as much as any of them. It was all he had too. Being older, he'd brought perspective to what they were doing and how impossible it was. But that didn't seem to deter him. His alternative was working in a factory alongside his father. He'd told Ethan when they first met, "Anybody can do the possible, but the impossible is extraordinary." Ethan wondered if he still felt that way.

"I can show you what Syd and I worked on. I think I can manage most of her parts."

Ethan wondered what look he had on his face, as Gus stopped and quickly rephrased what he'd said.

"I can't play it like she can," he said, "but it'll be good enough to sing to. Raj seemed to like it, even though it took a while."

Gus picked up Syd's acoustic in the living room. Ethan had seen him play a few times. He was good and knew what he was doing, but he wasn't Syd.

Ethan started to sing and was soon lost in "You Don't Know What You're Saying." It seemed but a moment before he opened his eyes. Gus was staring at him.

"I'll be pissed if you don't sing like that tomorrow," he said as Ethan blinked. "That was unbelievable. Raj'll hate missing that one."

"Yeah, if he's even there."

"He'll be there," Gus said, nodding. "I don't know where you go when you close your eyes, but the way you can portray a song can change the world. You, my friend, have a gift."

Gus then set the guitar in its stand and opened the case to his bass. The black Fender Jazz was his baby, as the white Gibson was Syd's.

"Seeing as that went well, let's try something a little different."

"A little different?" Ethan said, smiling as he stood in front of his mike. "You directing is a lot different."

Gus laughed. "We've got two fucking days. We gotta do something different."

Gus wanted Ethan to sing to his bass line for "Don't Tell Me." Ethan took a bit to find the melody, but once he had it, he was off. At first, it was as if they were trying to play two different songs at the same time, but gradually, his singing seemed to couple with Gus's bass notes. Midway through the song, he closed his eyes. He could feel Christa's hand in his and see her cheeks wet with tears. His words were kind and gentle:

> You can't know what I'm feeling.
> You can't know who I am.

You can think that you know me,
but don't tell me again.

When they'd finished, Gus screamed, "Ethan! That was crazy!"

Ethan's eyes flashed open when he heard his name. He knew crazy. His hand was on the side of his leg—empty.

"Raj would be dying right now," Gus said, adjusting the volume knob on his bass.

As if Gus's voice were the prompt, their front door suddenly banged open. The sound startled Ethan as he tried to figure out where he was coming back from. He looked at his watch. It was almost six. The afternoon had disappeared.

Greg walked into the living room with a girl Ethan had never seen before.

"Where the fuck is Syd?" Greg asked without saying hello to either of them. He looked like the walking dead.

"Who wants to know?" Gus answered.

"What the fuck does that mean?" Greg said, moving past the girl, who looked as strung out as he did. "I don't need your fucking attitude."

"Feeling's mutual, stud man," Gus retorted, undoing his guitar strap. "A little early to come down, don't you think?"

"What the fuck?" Greg snarled, holding his hands out in front of him as if to show he had nothing to hide. "Is it gang-up-on-Greg time?"

"I need to take a shit," Gus said, placing his bass in its case and then brushing past Greg and the girl.

"What've you been doing?" Ethan asked as Greg came into their rehearsal living room space.

Greg ignored his question. The unknown girl stood behind him.

"Where's Syd?" Greg said.

"Dunno. We've been practicing," Ethan said, his eyes moving from Greg to the girl and back again. "And this is?"

"A friend," Greg answered.

"Hi, friend," Ethan said.

The girl nodded, her big, frizzy brown hair floating forward and back like a duster. She didn't say anything.

"My room's the first door back on the left," Greg said to the girl, speaking just above a whisper.

"What's goin' on?" Ethan asked as the girl left.

"Nothing," Greg said, rubbing his forehead with his fingers. "Needed a break s'all."

"I heard something like that. What gives? Why are you hating on Syd?"

"Ah, come on, Eth. You were fucking right here!" Greg exclaimed, extending his hands to imitate Ethan holding Syd in front of him. His hips gyrated forward, simulating the act. "What's goin' on? Fuck, I should be askin' you."

Ethan rubbed his hands together as if he were trying to wring his disgust away. Greg was really high. Ethan wondered if he even knew what he was saying. He didn't know which bothered him more—Greg or his own actions.

"I said I was sorry."

"Yeah, fuck, that makes it all right, Eth," Greg said, flipping his left arm in the air as if he were shooing a fly. "You and your fucking high-and-mighty shit."

Greg's words sent a bolt of fury straight to Ethan's head. He didn't think. His left foot came forward as he swung his right arm, and his fist caught Greg unaware and hard across the left side of his face. Greg dropped as if the floor had disappeared beneath him. He looked up, stunned.

"Don't you ever fucking say that again!" Ethan hissed, his lips tight against his teeth. Rage engulfed him. He knew how people could kill; he'd never used his fists to solve anything.

As if on cue, the front door opened again, and in walked Syd. She looked horrified. It was all Ethan needed to see. His rage began to dissipate. Greg was on the floor, still in apparent awe of how he'd come to be there.

"What the fuck?" She gasped.

Ethan didn't say anything, looking from Syd back to Greg.

"So it's fucking come to this?" Greg said, rubbing the side of his face.

"Of course it's come to this," Ethan said with fight still in him but his anger fading. "We're either all together or all apart—there is no middle."

Gus came back into the living room.

"Interesting timing," Ethan said, looking at Syd and putting his hand out to Greg to help him up.

"Fuck, that hurt," Greg whined, rubbing his jaw.

"Better get some ice on that," Syd said, surprising Ethan and staring at Greg with what looked like genuine compassion.

Ethan figured it was more guilt than care, as she likely felt partly responsible for what she could only surmise had taken place. Either way, Ethan was glad to see her reaction.

"You're gonna look like fucking Frankenstein tomorrow," she added, taking the pizza box she'd come in with to the kitchen. "I thought we could use a bite before we got started."

She returned with a bag of ice. Nothing more was said. They each grabbed a slice of the pepperoni pizza. After one slice, Gus slung the strap of his bass over his shoulder.

"I want to start with 'Don't Tell Me,'" he said, flicking his amp's power switch. "Ethan did his thing—it's hard to call it just singing—while I played. It was stunning."

He plucked his strings a couple of times as his amp came on. "I'd like to work out something different with the guitar," he said, looking at Syd. "I'm telling you—it was fuckin' cool."

He played the opening riff with a flourish at the end. Ethan started.

"You can't know what I'm feeling," he sang.

"Hey, can I not finish my pizza?" Greg complained. He was nursing his injured face with the ice in one hand. A slice of pizza was in his other.

Ethan stopped. He looked at Greg's swollen face. He'd wronged his friend.

"Sorry about the punch."

"Fucking deserved it," Greg replied. Ethan saw Syd raise her eyebrows.

"Prob'ly," Syd said, standing up. It was obvious she was itching to get at Gus's proposal.

As Greg stood up, Gus started to play, pressing the thick strings precisely against the fret board of his bass. Ethan looked on with envy. It was like watching how a sculptor molded clay into an imagined shape—inspiring to watch.

As he played, Syd stepped in, shaping sounds that accented Gus's bass line. Ethan realized that was what completed Syd as a musician—she had the uncanny ability not only to step up and lead with aplomb and style but also to make other players sound even better.

Ethan knelt down on their worn gray carpet to listen.

They were coming together after another eruption to create something new, as if they were discovering a place they'd never been before. Creating wasn't a process. It was about being together, coming in sync and doing, and then changing and doing again. Emotions of anger, joy, rage, and love mixed in a batter of frustration, beauty, and wonder, determined to find something and maybe nothing—but maybe truth. Creativity involved feeling it and doing it over and over again, intuitively knowing something was there yet not knowing what it was or wasn't until it was. It was having the courage to keep going, close to the edge, an instant or eons away from paradise or doom. It was surviving to discover new and better places. If it didn't die, it lived. There was a power in seeing belief come to fruition, creating a thing from nothing. Living together, sticking to what they believed in their hearts, made it possible. If they could only get through the other stuff, the stuff that separated the great from the mediocre, they could do things that were unachievable any other way.

To Ethan's amazement, Greg picked up his drumsticks and started what sounded like a click-track on the rim of his snare. He wasn't just a metronome. It was part of the music. Syd was smiling as her fingers eased across the neck of her Gibson. Gus was leading the song with his bass line. Syd played slowly and then, for an instant, ferociously fast, her musical instinct breathtaking. It was just enough to bring brilliance to Gus's playing. All the while, Greg kept tapping—once on, a triple, once off, once on—in rhythmic unison.

Enthralled in the privilege and magnitude of the moment, listening to three totally synced musicians, Ethan suddenly realized the need to record what he was witnessing. Raj would have been coming apart. Gus had a small cassette recorder in his room.

Moments later, Ethan had a new cassette recording the music blossoming around them.

Gus winked at Ethan, cuing him to sing.

Ethan grabbed his microphone and closed his eyes.

> You can't know what I'm feeling.
> You can't know who I am.

Christa was in the window. Light from the streetlamp reflected off her gold hoop earrings.

CHAPTER 37

"I haven't a clue where to find her," Ethan said.

They'd finished recording their last song at Focus Sound. Ethan was sitting with Syd at Nancy's Restaurant, in the same seats where he'd talked to Christa. He was questioning whether their meeting had even taken place. Had it all been an episode? In truth, he knew it hadn't been, because he couldn't remember what happened when he went away, except for the space left in his memory. He remembered everything with Christa. His discovery of who she was, the tears, and his aching heart were evidence enough. She dominated both his conscious and unconscious thoughts. Their meeting had been as real as the conversation he was having with Syd.

Christa was real.

"Did you try the hospital?"

"Syd," Ethan said, sighing in exasperation, "that's where I started. They don't give that kind of information away, especially to past patients."

"You know the saying 'If she's to be with you, she'll come back'?" Syd said after a sip of coffee.

"No, I don't know that saying," he said, his lips curved tightly with smugness.

Syd rolled her eyes. "I'm trying."

Ethan suddenly remembered that his six-month appointment with Dr. Katharine was coming up. He was taking the Orap pills she'd prescribed but had reduced the dosage—under his own guidance. It was something he'd become comfortable adjusting. Orap made him feel drowsy, withdrawn, and distant. It still scared him to think of disappearing into one of his episodes and never coming back, like an ocean wave sweeping him out to sea forever. Maybe Dr. Katharine could help him locate Christa.

"You know, it's like writing a song," Ethan said after taking a sip of his tea, an unusual drink selection, as he usually preferred coffee. He had ordered something different because he wasn't with Christa. "You get a tune in your head that won't go away. You grasp for notes that just aren't there." He held his mug of tea with both hands.

"Let's write a song," Syd suggested, smiling. "Find the notes that are hiding. Maybe she'll come back too."

Ethan looked back at Syd. He knew this situation was not easy for her, despite how she talked. He should have been more aware of her feelings, especially after what she'd done to get there. Before he could think of what to say, like planned choreography, Randolph walked into the restaurant, wearing his usual smile.

"Raj said I might find you here," he said, pulling up a chair from the empty table next to them. "You sure have Raj fired up; that's not easy to do. Believe me, I know. Things seem different from two days ago. You know, he was ready to drop you guys. He was fucking fed up."

Randolph looked at Ethan, then at Syd, and then back at Ethan. Neither said a thing. Even without talking, they knew. What happened in the Release stayed there. Differences of opinion were never easy to deal with among those who really cared about the never-ending pursuit of a vision. If the dream of their vision was strong enough and they could find whatever special glue kept them together, they could achieve anything. The converse could also happen; they could explode and come apart. Odds favored the latter; history demonstrated it. Syd and Ethan weren't about to expose any of it to anyone.

"Did you like what you heard?" Ethan asked, knowing the answer from what his own ears had told him. It mattered what Randolph thought, but his opinion wouldn't change what they'd created. It was their best, and they loved it.

"Like?" Randolph replied, his eyes widening. "It's perfect. I haven't heard everything, but the song 'Don't Tell Me' is something else."

Ethan watched as Randolph signaled the waitress behind the counter for a tea, pointing to Ethan's cup.

"It's perfect for the end of the movie," Randolph said.

Ethan nodded, not sure what to say. He didn't remember how the book ended.

"But that's not why I'm here."

Ethan turned and noticed how sunny it was outside.

"You guys need a manager," Randolph said, "and visibility. Your songs need to be heard and promoted. You need exposure. So here's my pitch."

As if imitating Ethan, Randolph turned and looked out the window. He turned back as the waitress brought his tea. "We'll use at least two of your songs," he said, looking at Syd. "You'll get lots of PR as part of the movie's promotion. You can even use it to help launch the Release. But you need your own."

Randolph paused and leaned forward, his forearms supporting his growing bulk on the table. He took a sip of his tea. "I'm no expert," he said, looking again at Syd and then back at Ethan. "Raj has a recommendation you should consider. You're ready."

Ethan looked at Syd. The band had talked many times about hiring a manager but had never come to a decision. Early on, one of Gus's friends had helped out, but that had ended after they didn't get paid for a high school dance. The guy had seemed to make up problems that didn't exist and then explain how he'd solved them. They had seen him as the problem and decided to handle things themselves—Gus primarily—until they really needed outside management. Ethan was hearing that that time had come.

"How come Raj never said anything?" Ethan asked.

"Don't know," Randolph replied. "He seemed a little unsure of what to make of you guys as a band until yesterday."

Randolph's right eyebrow rose. He was seemingly curious as to what had gone on. Ethan was sure Randolph knew a lot more than he let on.

"We grew up a lot," Ethan said, trying his best to sound confident that everything was now good, knowing it really wasn't.

Syd didn't say a word. Ethan knew her response. She'd been against dropping Gus's guy, simply because they'd had no one else. Gus wasn't a manager—an amazing bass player, yes, but not a businessman. They needed someone to manage them. Syd brushed away something on her forehead Ethan didn't see.

"Is Raj still around?" Ethan asked.

"Yeah, he'll be around for a while. He claims the real work is just starting." Randolph pulled a card out of his shirt pocket. "The guy's name is Jonah Vetch," he said, passing the card to Ethan. "He'll hear your songs tonight. He'll want to see you play. Got anything in the works?"

Ethan nodded and thought for a moment. They were back at Tormo again on Tuesday for a couple of nights and then downtown at the Gasworks on Friday and Saturday. Nothing more was confirmed, though he'd made countless unreturned phone calls.

"Call him," Randolph said, pointing at the card Ethan held in his hand. "Who knows? Maybe you'll like him. I'm headed back to Ottawa tonight. I can't thank you enough for doing this. I picked the right band."

"Fucking right you did," Ethan said, smiling and looking at Syd, "but we need to thank you. We've finally recorded some material."

"Yeah, thanks, Randolph," Syd said as Randolph stood up.

"You really have to stop this Randolph stuff," he replied, smiling at her. "Ethan's started something that seems contagious, but I prefer Randy. Randolph sounds like a stuffed shirt."

Syd smiled.

"You're one amazing guitar player, Sydney," he said. "Your guitar work makes 'Don't Tell Me' something extraordinary."

"Thank you," Syd said, shaking his hand. Ethan was sure he saw the look of a young girl's crush in her reaction to Randolph's compliment.

"See you, man," he said to Ethan, shaking his hand.

Ethan nodded as Randolph turned and left as quickly as he'd arrived.

"I don't think I'm going to stop calling him Randolph," Ethan said. "It seems to be working just fine."

CHAPTER 38

"Okay" was all Jonah Vetch said before he hung up. They'd talked for less than five minutes.

Jonah was professionally polite after his assistant finally connected Ethan, who had pleaded with her regarding how important it was that he talk to Mr. Vetch. Ethan's confusion started shortly thereafter. Jonah said he'd not spoken to Raj, which caused Ethan to wonder what he'd missed in talking to Randolph. He almost thought he needed to explain who Raj was. Jonah was forthright in indicating he didn't think he had time to handle another client but said he'd try to stop by the Markham gig. He knew the place. Ethan couldn't help but sense the man's disinterest, which was different from what he'd anticipated after Randolph's recommendation. But he trusted Randolph. He hadn't steered him wrong yet.

After wrapping up with Raj at Focus Sound, the band agreed to take the night off and take a break from one another. Syd drove Ethan back to the house and went to visit her aunt. Gus headed to his parents' for dinner. Greg was out with a girl he'd met at Tormo. Ethan stayed at the house, wanting to make the call to Jonah alone, but he wished he'd taken Syd up on her offer of dropping him at his parents' place instead.

Amid the excitement of recording, Ethan was ready to sign with Jonah Vetch, but the call deflated that enthusiasm. After the call, he didn't want to spend the night alone. He wanted to talk to Christa but had failed to find her after several attempts with the operator. He decided to call his folks.

His father surprised him, agreeing to meet halfway. Ethan took the bus to Finch Station.

He'd been there all of five minutes before his father drove up in his Accord.

"Hey, young fella!" his father shouted out the open passenger window. "Lookin' for a ride?"

"Yeah, mister." Ethan laughed and tried to hold his own with his father's humor. "So I can steal your car and wreak havoc on your house and family."

The joke was weak; comedians they weren't. He pulled the handle on the passenger door.

"Maybe, on second thought," his father said as Ethan climbed into the car. His father's hand was already out. "Long time no see."

"It has been a while," Ethan replied, shaking his father's hand.

"You know your mother and sister are fussing together a special dinner for you," he said. "Your sister's pretty excited to hear what you've been up to. She might be your biggest fan, next to me and your mom."

Ethan smiled. It sounded odd hearing excitement in his father's voice about what he had chosen to do. The music world was not one his father had encouraged but likely was an easy alternative to losing his son to an institution.

"We're playing Tormo next week. You should come by one night."

"Maybe we will," his father answered, surprising Ethan. Ethan caught his father's side glance; his father was smiling. Maybe he liked his son's earnestness in pursing at least something, Ethan thought.

"We're hoping to show a potential manager our stuff," Ethan said, encouraged by his father's interest. "We'll be playing the songs we recorded this week."

"Recorded?"

"Yeah."

"You've recorded songs?" his father said, sounding astounded.

"Yeah, that's where I was this week. We just finished." Ethan found himself excited and decided to go on. "A couple of the songs will be part of a project Randolph's working on. Remember Randolph? He came by as we were leaving the hospital."

"I remember Randolph," his father said. "Had a girl with him that day."

"Yeah, Rachel," Ethan replied, thinking Randolph hadn't mentioned her on his visits.

"Randolph—as you call him—spoke to us a lot while you were in the hospital," his father said. "I could never quite understand why he was there. He seemed more sad than ill, but I guess that's sometimes the same thing."

Ethan shrugged. "I don't know, but he's got things going on now."

"Like?"

"The songs we recorded are for his movie."

"His movie?" his father said, his voice rising, sounding incredulous.

"Yeah, his movie, an animated film based on *Browning Station*."

"Why do I know that name?"

"'Cause it was in my room at the hospital," Ethan said, looking over at his father. "You know, the book I couldn't find when we got back. I was sure we packed it. But I've never seen it. I've been meaning to pick up a copy."

"You know, I do remember it," his father said, rubbing the side of his jaw.

"That's what his movie's based on," Ethan said. "I guess I performed a lot of it on our floor, not that I remember."

They were close to the house now. Ethan looked out the window. Someone was walking a black dog on the sidewalk. Ethan looked back at his father. "I gotta get a copy."

"I've never seen it here," his father said, turning into the driveway.

It had been a while since Ethan had been to his parents' house, despite his living less than an hour away. Proximity had no bearing on frequency, his grandma—God rest her soul—had once told him. She'd lived three hours from them, in the country near Long Point Bay. When he was a kid, she had told him she saw his family more often than his aunt's family, who lived three concessions away. Geographical proximity might have carried the sense of always being together, but reality often showed that closeness not to be true.

"You got a new front door," Ethan remarked, looking up at the house.

"Yeah," his father replied, "a month ago. Your mother's idea."

"Nice," Ethan replied, wondering what had been wrong with the old one but knowing better than to ask. The door probably had cost more than the rent the Release had paid in November.

In less than a minute, he stepped into the aroma of his mother's pepperoni and anchovy pizza, which carried with it reminiscences of good memories and happiness. Carlyn was standing in the living room. He couldn't remember the last time he'd seen his little sister. She'd not been there on his previous visits. Her social calendar was full, leaving her little time for school or home, as their mother was quick to mention during his occasional call home.

He gave his sister a hug. "How's Sis?" he asked.

Her blonde hair was pulled up and tied on top of her head, resembling a fountain. Everything about Carlyn pointed to her being a sports jock; spandex pants, a sweat top, and running shoes adorned her athletic physique.

She had more energy than two people combined, and the times he'd seen her, she'd never stopped moving. He sometimes wondered how his ordeal had impacted her. He figured parents in constant worry over her brother's uncertain prognosis would have taken a toll, not to mention wondering herself whether her brother would ever return to his former self—not that they were close. It seemed to have shrunk the five-year difference in their ages; she seemed older.

"Sis is good," Carlyn said with spunk in her tone. "How's Bro?"

"I guess I deserve that," he said, walking over to give his mother a kiss on the cheek. "It smells delicious in here. What's the occasion?"

"Oh, come now," their mother said. "When's the last time we were all together?"

Ethan's eyebrows rose as he looked at her. Strangely, he hadn't thought of it that way, but he wasn't surprised that she did. It had been a long time.

"Glad to see you're as excited about it as we are," Carlyn said, putting a hand on her hip, unimpressed.

"You know, all you have to say is 'Mom is cooking pizza,'" Ethan replied, "and I'll be here."

"Yeah, right. Well, I made your favorite dessert."

"Apple crisp," Ethan said, his hazel eyes lighting up. "Now, you wanna talk about the last time for something? I don't even remember what it tastes like."

"Oh, come on, you two," their mother said. "You'd think you didn't know each other."

Ethan hadn't realized how hungry he was until he sat down in front of two steaming slices of his mother's pizza. In years past, he'd joked that his mother's Italian heritage ran deeper than she let on.

"You look like you've lost weight," his mother said as they started to eat. His diet at the house was that of a student and consisted mostly of popcorn, hot dogs, and macaroni and cheese—staples of a low-income lifestyle.

"A little maybe," he replied after swallowing a mouthful of pizza. "It kind of goes with the territory."

"How so?" she asked, staring at him, a furrow of concern in her brow. He hated to think of what she'd gone through and was still going through because of him.

"The artist's life. Doing what you love but really can't afford," Ethan replied, smiling, liking what he'd said and wanting to write it down.

"What was it like recording?" Carlyn asked, her green eyes as vibrant as ever. Ethan wondered if he might draw energy just by looking into them.

"How did you know?" asked their father.

"Mom told me."

Their father looked at their mother, who shrugged and raised an eyebrow. Ethan went on before they could say any more.

"Most of the time, it was kinda like a storm," he said, thinking of Syd destroying the Martin outside of Focus Sound and then Christa. It was the last time he'd seen her. It jarred him to think he still couldn't contact her. "But then it clears, and you find a treasure."

"Oh, come on," Carlyn replied, an earnestness coming through her tightened facial expression as she leaned over the table across from him. "What's that supposed to mean?"

"It's what seems to happen," he said, shrugging, remembering his moment with Syd and his fight with Greg. "We all play our parts of the songs. The engineer records them; Raj was our engineer. Then he goes away and puts it all together."

"When can I hear it?"

"How about Tuesday night?" Ethan said, looking at his mother as if for approval. He didn't know why; it was as if he had a need to get her buy-in. "I was telling Dad. We're at Tormo for a couple of nights next week."

"No way!" Carlyn shouted, having left the table to take her plate to the kitchen. "I was just there!"

"You were?" their mother asked, the pitch of her voice rising.

"Yeah," Carlyn said from the kitchen, her voice losing its excitement.

Ethan figured she'd let slip more than she'd intended. He knew the feeling.

She stepped back into the dining room. "Jocelyn's brother's friend was in the band who was playing."

Ethan watched as his sister looked to their mother for acceptance of her story. He was aware of where things could go if she didn't accept it. To Ethan, Carlyn was growing up faster than their mother was willing to accept. He watched as his sister played to their mother's reaction.

"We were there to help carry equipment," she added, wiping her hands on a dish towel. "We can't get in a bar."

Carlyn looked at Ethan. There was no indication in her face that she had been trying to hide something.

"Blaze was their name, but they were shit," she said, her language getting away from her. Ethan couldn't tell whether the cursing had been intentional or not, but she quickly corrected herself. "I mean terrible."

"We won't be terrible," Ethan said, "but we will be loud."

Before their mother could say anything, he went on to explain what he'd told his father in the car about a potential manager coming to see them.

Ethan could see Carlyn had already decided she was going, underage or not. Their mother then said she'd like to go too. It was hard to tell whether Carlyn liked the idea or not. Ethan was certain he saw a subtle frown cross his sister's face.

He'd not intended to stay overnight, but his father was driving in to his office in the morning—he often worked on Saturdays—and offered to drop him at a bus stop closer to home. It beat going back to an empty house that night.

Ethan hadn't slept in his old room in months. It brought back memories of a time when his world was smaller and less complicated—a time when all he had to worry about was what book to read next or what album to listen to. But he couldn't go back; time was like that and only permitted memories backward. His mother kept his room much tidier than he remembered it. He looked at the few books she'd set neatly together on the bookshelf his father had mounted on the wall beside his bed. *Serpico,* one of the first books he'd ever read, sat beside *Atlas Shrugged,* one of his favorite books. His small collection of Hardy Boys and half a dozen Zane Grey paperbacks sat beside them. He'd read all of them growing up.

He sat down on the corner of the new green duvet that covered his old bed. The bed was in the same place it had always been: along the wall opposite the door. The brown wallpaper, an imitation wood-paneling pattern, still covered the walls. He looked at the spot on the wall beside his bed he used to pick at when he couldn't sleep at night. It had been glued flat but was still visible. He stared at the wallpaper, but his memory seemed to be after something else.

He turned to the wood desk where he'd done much of his homework in high school. Many a late night, he'd sat there poring over calculus and physics, readying for a world that now seemed nothing more than a magician's illusion.

The desk was old. His mother had rolled her eyes when his father had brought the piece of junk, as she called it, home from an auction sale. But his father had refurbished it to uncover a beautiful cherry desk with a classic lift-top center section and drawers on both sides. It had found a home in Ethan's room. He'd used it for more than homework; its hidden compartments had been ideal to stash cigarettes, adult magazines, and the occasional mickey bottle, now all but memories.

Several of his record albums were neatly piled on the desktop. David Bowie's *Young Americans*, one of his first albums, sat on top. Glenn Campbell's *A Satisfied Mind*, a birthday gift, was underneath it, followed by Alice Cooper's *School's Out*, Kiss's *Destroyer*, and Stevie Wonder's *Talking Book*. He had listened to each one endlessly. They had made him feel invincible, as if anything were possible.

He picked up and stared at the back cover of *Young Americans*, remembering the song "Fame." It was a good song. He smiled, imagining the treatment Syd might give it. He put the album back on the pile and searched for a pen and paper. He'd forget to bring the idea to the band if he didn't write it down. He pulled open the right-side desk drawer and found a pencil among a bunch of other things—a sparkly lime-green Hot Wheels car, several different-colored blocks of Lego, a miniature deck of cards—but no paper. He turned and looked back at the books on the shelf, reminded of *Browning Station*, half expecting to see the title on one of the spines. He had probably looked a hundred times for the book in the desk but couldn't help looking once again. He pulled open the drawer on the left side and found the paper he was looking for. He pulled out a sheet of the lined binder paper and jotted down, "David Bowie—Fame." He was about to shut the drawer when he saw the crumpled paper.

He knew what it was before he grabbed it. *Christa's note!* Elation lit up his heart.

To Ethan:
I'm not supposed to talk to you.

He didn't need to read it. He headed to his parents' phone.

Everyone else was in bed, which made him hesitate. It was past midnight, maybe too late, but he couldn't wait.

He dialed the number and wondered if she'd answer.

After five rings, already disappointed, he hoped for an answering machine.

"Hello?" answered a croaky voice he knew right away.

His heart swelled with its sweetness.

"H-hello?" he stammered, irritated by the sound of his voice cracking. He coughed, but it didn't help. "Hello."

"Hi," Christa replied in little more than a whisper.

"Hi," Ethan repeated, instantly at a loss for what to say. "Sorry to call so late. It's Ethan."

"I know," she said, her tone flat. "You found my number?"

"You won't believe what happened," Ethan said, holding the crinkled paper in front of him. "I just got lucky."

"I can't do this, Ethan."

He felt his heart pound upon hearing her words. What he couldn't believe in the first place was quickly turning into what wasn't going to happen anyway.

"Please don't hang up," he pleaded.

Silence was all he heard.

"Christa?" he asked, praying she'd hold on and answer. He could feel the heavy door. "Please say something."

"Why?"

In a fraction of a second, his mind scanned a thousand answers, none of which seemed right. "Because …"

There was a lot that could follow the word, yet nothing did. A dead inertness enveloped him.

"After all I'd said, Ethan," she whispered, speaking a little louder. Emotion rattled her voice. Still, he loved the sound. "And you couldn't even show up."

"But I did!" Ethan cried into the receiver, tightening his hold on the mouthpiece as if it had the power to bring her closer. "You were gone."

A longer pause followed. He tried to hear her breathing but couldn't. The heavy door was in his midst.

"I stayed for half an hour," Christa said, the pain in her voice almost more than he could bear. It seemed to reach inside his chest and squeeze his heart, threatening to stop its beating.

"Oh, Christa," he said, "I was there. I promise you. Things got really messed up."

He stopped. This conversation wasn't about what had happened. It was about what he wanted to happen.

"Can I see you again?" he asked. He heard something rustle in the background. Christa was saying something, but he couldn't make out what it was.

"Ethan, I can't do this," she repeated.

"Wait. Just—" He couldn't think of what to say and then blurted out, "Come see us Tuesday at Tormo."

He waited to hear the click. It didn't come. There was a chance she'd agree. A slim chance, but he was hopeful.

"Ethan, I have to go."

She hung up. Ethan held the phone to his ear as if the sheer willpower of doing so would bring her back.

Something felt different. The feeling of the heavy door was gone.

She hadn't said goodbye.

CHAPTER 39

Tuesday, December 4, 1984

They were upstairs at Tormo. Their last rehearsals had left them feeling relaxed, and as a result, they were tighter than ever. They'd all returned to the house on Saturday afternoon. They'd rehearsed that night, hitting their cues and playing together as if everything were new again. The songs, perfected from the studio, seemed more alive each time they played them. Ethan didn't get hung up on "The Angel." Things felt good. They were a family again. If only the music didn't have to stop. That night at Tormo would be a good night.

"What time will he be here?" Greg asked, again adjusting the tension rods on his snare.

"Didn't say," Ethan replied, "but likely early, before the club gets too full."

"Yeah, right. Ya think he'll even fuckin' show?"

Ethan let Greg's comment slide. Maybe he could keep peace a little longer. Their heads had to be in the game when Jonah arrived. They needed everything to come together, with both luck and hope working in their favor. They all had to be fully present, playing their best both singly and as a band. Performing in front of Jonah Vetch was a chance they'd only get one shot at.

Ethan was anxious and knew it. Jonah Vetch was the person they thought could and would change their lives and possibly the break they needed to bigger and better things. Yet his call with Jonah had left him uneasy. Was Jonah really who they thought he was? But Jonah and performing well weren't the only things on his mind.

Over the last day, he'd been having trouble focusing. It wasn't that he wasn't excited for the Release; he was. But thoughts of Christa wouldn't go away. She was there when he closed his eyes to sing. Now, minutes before he was to put on the performance of his life, he was all wrapped up in the hope that she would, by some miracle, show up. There was much between them he didn't know. It was strange to feel deep love for someone without the memory to understand why he felt that way.

Hearing Greg's snare drum's succinct pop from the strike of his drumstick brought him back. Not unlike Gus or Syd tuning their guitars, Greg had a tone and resonance he strived to achieve. As with tuning a stringed instrument, during which one string vibrated its sound while the next was stretched or loosened until it matched, a process repeated until all strings were in tune and ready for magic, Greg would adjust the tension on his snare until the pop was just right. Math and physics explained the science of how it worked, but hearing and feeling the vibrations brought the musical experience. The experience defied explanation; it spoke to the soul. Greg was ready.

Ethan looked at Syd. He thought of Carlyn and his parents. Carlyn was coming for sure, but would his parents come? Maybe his mother would come with Carlyn; neither had seen him perform in years. He doubted his father would show. Would Christa show? Would they distract him? Syd would keep him in line.

They started the set at eight o'clock. As with previous shows, only a few were in the audience; none were their guests. Ethan kept reminding himself it was Tuesday, not a big night. They finished their first song, a cover of the Beatles' "I Feel Fine," to a less-than-raucous response. They broke into their own "Don't Tell Me," which was now one of their favorites to perform.

Ethan noticed a middle-aged man in a wrinkled white dress shirt alone at the bar and wondered if it might be Jonah. He closed his eyes. The music carried him off.

Torches appeared to light his way in a forest cloaked in a heavy fog. He could only see a few feet ahead, but as he left one, another torch appeared to direct him. He kept walking. Time did not matter, nor did progress. Concerned he might be lost, he quickened his pace, though he did not know the way. The faster he walked, the less sure he was. He thought to turn back yet felt compelled to go on, closing on wherever he was destined to arrive. Whispers to turn back grew in his head, as did his anxiety, further speeding his step. He came to two torches showing separate paths. Not knowing which way to turn, he went right.

"This is not the way."

He turned, shocked that someone could be talking just behind him yet be unseen.

"Come this way," said the sweet voice that comforted him. "This is the way; this is your hope and your truth."

Then he saw her standing there, just visible on the edge of the mist in front of him. Mila was directing him.

A rod appeared in his hand. He was trying to speak. No, he was speaking—and then singing.

"Don't tell me."

He opened his eyes. People were standing and clapping, staring at him. A couple dozen people were standing up in front of him.

There was no mistaking her. Standing near the end of the bar, where he'd seen the man in the wrinkled shirt, was Christa; she was clapping.

Excitement was on him in a sudden burst of joy. He could barely breathe.

He turned his head and nodded to Syd. She shrugged. They'd only started, but he wasn't about to let Christa get away again. He turned back to his mike and said, "We'll be back in a minute."

His eyes locked on her as she moved away from the bar. She knew he'd seen her. He didn't wait. From the small stage, he crossed the floor. Most had returned to their seats. People were watching him. If Tormo had been more crowded, he wouldn't have gotten there soon enough. Christa had left the room and was headed downstairs to the front entrance. Why was she leaving? By the time he reached the front and the top of the all-but-barren stairwell, the entrance door below was closing. He jumped down the steps two at a time, faster than his hands could grab the steel handrail. At the bottom, he jumped onto the black floor mat in front of the opaque glass entrance. Momentum took him to the door, which swung open, and he nearly collided with the couple coming in.

"Sorry," he said, his eyes searching for Christa.

"Slow down there, buddy," he heard the guy say behind him. Ethan ignored him. Christa was halfway down the sidewalk that fronted the plaza.

He ran. There was no way he was letting her get away.

It broke his heart to watch her run, her chestnut-brown hair streaming behind her. In the club, she'd stood out like a starlet in the dim desolation of the barroom. Now, seeing her in tight designer jeans and a waist-cut brown-leather jacket, he just wanted to stop and watch her slender form run. He was certain she knew he would chase her.

"Christa!" he shouted forty feet behind her.

She didn't turn or do anything to indicate she'd heard him. It was impossible she hadn't heard him.

He caught up with her near the end of the strip plaza.

"Christa, please," he said, out of breath from his sprint.

He ran in front of her and stopped. She didn't try to maneuver around him. "Christa," he said.

Unable to say anything else, he leaned forward, put his hands on his knees, and, for a second, caught his breath. He then stood up and, without saying a word, brought his hands up to the sides of her face and kissed her. If a man could melt into the lips of the woman he loved, Ethan did. It was as if he'd kissed her a thousand times before, his lips finding their natural place against hers. Though new and electric, the kiss was like discovering something that had always been and was supposed to be. He didn't want to let her go.

When their lips parted, the first few moments seemed an eternity where time was not measured by human clocks. It was as if he'd left the world, had returned, and was unsure where he was. His eyes locked on hers.

"Ethan?" Christa asked, seeming to look as hard into his eyes as he was into hers.

"Yes," he replied, forcing himself to concentrate on what she said.

"Are you—" She stopped, as if rethinking what she wanted to say. "Do you know where we are?"

Ethan heard her but didn't want to break the moment by speaking; he wished for eternity.

"Yes," he answered, knowing he had to reassure her. "I'm with the most beautiful woman in the world."

He didn't think it was the answer she wanted, but he wasn't about to jeopardize the good fortune of being with her. He held her hand. She was a stranger yet seemingly much more than a friend.

"Ethan," she said, her body already less resistant.

He could see she was trying to make a point. "Yes," he said, feigning impatience for this woman he barely knew.

"Where are we?" she asked with increasing earnestness in her voice. Her face was beautiful to look at—soft and understanding, like how he'd imagined an angel's. She didn't pull away, but she didn't soften either. It was as if he were holding on to his own life.

"Why are you asking me that?" he asked, turning serious.

"Because I have to know," she said.

He squeezed her hand as if to confirm he wasn't dreaming. "We're in Markham," he answered, hoping to understand why she was asking. "The

Release just played a couple of songs at Tormo. I'm standing with you on the sidewalk out front."

Christa kept staring into his eyes.

"Christa," he said, trying his best to find the right words, "why are you looking at me like you're trying to find something?"

Christa blinked and stepped back.

He wanted to kiss her again.

"Because I have to know," she said, her eyes not wavering from his.

"Have to know what?"

"That you're really here," she replied, frowning, her eyes fixed on his.

Ethan looked away. "Where else would I be?" he asked.

"Los Angeles maybe?" she said matter-of-factly as he looked back at her. "Hollywood?"

"Hollywood?" Ethan asked. "What do you …"

His voice faded. Something felt different. He didn't know why, but something was there. He could feel the heavy door and padlock looming again.

"I can't answer that right now," she said.

Ethan had moved back unknowingly. His eyes never left hers.

"But I will," she said.

"Will?" Ethan asked. Now he was asking the questions.

"Yes," Christa replied, her hands stretched open in front of her. "I don't know how to explain it yet. I didn't think this would ever happen. I'm still not sure it is happening. You have to believe me."

Their kiss was fading like a sunset. Ethan couldn't bear it. He didn't think. He stepped forward and kissed her again. She kissed him back.

"I love you, Ethan," she said, pulling away, her eyes pouring into his. "Please trust me on that. I know things. But slow down. This is so hard."

Ethan's head was spinning. He didn't know what to think, but he couldn't take his eyes off the woman standing in front of him. He loved her but didn't know why. The feeling was like connecting with his soul.

"There you are!" cried Syd, breaking their moment. Ethan turned and looked back toward the entrance to Tormo as she added, "He's fucking here!"

Ethan was about to ask who was there when he remembered Jonah and what that night was all about.

"Fuck!" he said, speaking just above a whisper.

"Let's go!" Syd shouted. "He doesn't look—"

The rest was lost on Ethan. His eyes were on Christa.

"Big night," he said, not wanting to go but knowing he had to—for everyone's sake. "Come back with me, please?"

"I can't," Christa replied. "I've stayed too long already."

"But—" Ethan stopped himself and kissed her again. He didn't want to let go of her hand or let her out of his sight. "I'll call you."

"I'd like that."

CHAPTER 40

Tuesday, December 4, 1984

Ethan was so excited he flew up the cement stairs three at a time back into the club. Inside, Syd was standing in the shadows beside the stage, holding the neck of her white Gibson while talking to Gus. Beside her, the guitar looked the size of a cello. On seeing Ethan, she raised her guitar and wrapped her arms around the body as if she were hugging a date. She smiled and flashed her eyelids. He knew what she was insinuating. Greg was behind his drum kit, sticks in hand.

"Where's Jonah?" Ethan asked as he came up beside her.

Syd nodded toward the bar. Ethan turned and saw the same guy he'd almost hit with the door downstairs balancing two drinks in one hand and looking at a pager in the other.

"Where's your friend?" Syd asked. Gus was adjusting his guitar strap. More people had come in since Ethan had left, but Tormo was still far from full, which surprised him. He'd hoped for more. He didn't see Carlyn or their mother.

"Had to go," Ethan replied, and he grabbed his mike. "Let's go."

They started the second set with Syd's arrangement of "American Woman." Syd's first chords filled the bar. As the stage lights came up, he saw his mother and Carlyn come in. They added to the joy of seeing Christa, which helped bring on a surge of energy that he wasn't about to try to contain. Kissing Christa had brought magic to the evening; anything was possible.

Syd ripped apart Boston's "Don't Look Back" and the Bee Gees' "Nights on Broadway," but when Ethan opened his eyes, he couldn't see Jonah. Alarmed, he scanned the room. He stepped off the small stage, still singing, but saw no sign of the man they were playing for. Though disheartened, he didn't slow down. The tables were filling up as more people came in. He saw Carlyn—no longer beside their mother—talking to a couple of girls at the bar. It was soon evident that invites had gone out to a lot of her friends. Gus and Syd came together at the end of their Bruce Springsteen cover of "Born to Run," bowing forward in time with Ethan's leap into the air.

The cheering crowd got louder but was no match for Syd's guitar and Marshall amp in the Release's version of Led Zeppelin's "Kashmir." Ethan loved the song Gus had brought to the band, and he emulated Robert Plant's epic vocal and stage moves. He pulled his shirttail out and went somewhere else when Gus started on the keyboard against Syd's Jimmy Page chords. At times, when they played, the ghosts of rock seemed to find their way onto the Release's stage.

At the end of "Kashmir," Ethan noticed even more people in the audience. The tables were full; Ethan saw more people than the Release had ever played to at Tormo. The crowd added fuel to Ethan and the band's already high-energy night. Greg was playing better than ever, flipping his sticks in the air—at least as high as the ceiling would allow—and twirling them through his fingers like batons, a trick he'd refined during lulls at the studio. He hit his toms hard, pounding out Prince's "Little Red Corvette." The high-pitched crunch of Syd's guitar's distortion set Ethan off every time, putting rockets in his legs and a raspy edge to his voice. Nothing could touch him when he performed at that level. That night, the zone was all theirs.

"You Don't Know What You're Saying" was up next, and though the crowd was hearing it for the first time, it was hard to tell. Girls were dancing in the small space in front of the stage. Ethan didn't care if they were Carlyn's friends or not; they were enjoying the Release's music. Their original plan had been to finish the second set with "The Angel," but Ethan wasn't feeling it. Instead, they played Aerosmith's "Sweet Emotion." It slowed things down, but Gus's bass groove kept those on their feet dancing. When the song ended, Ethan nodded to Syd and mouthed, "Angel."

Holding the mike with both hands, he spoke into its wire mesh. "We're gonna slow things down a bit more for a very special song we recorded last week. It's called 'The Angel.'"

He didn't close his eyes until they'd reached the part that had given him so much trouble. He saw Christa sitting at the table beside the front window of Dorian's Coffee Emporium, sipping tea. He watched her until he found the mike back in his hands, having just sung the last verse. Syd was beside him, playing, her fingers busy winding the song in for him to sing the final words.

"We'll be back in a few minutes," Ethan announced to groans from the crowd after they'd finished. "But don't go away. We've got a little surprise when we come back."

Ethan hustled around the stage. Greg was standing behind his floor tom in his sleeveless T-shirt, showing off his biceps. A short, empty hallway led to the rear of the club. Scuffed light blue walls and worn gray floor tiles led to a stairwell and the back entrance they'd hauled their equipment through earlier that day.

He stopped near the top of the stairs, thinking about how to end the show; his adrenaline was screaming, mixing thoughts of Christa, Jonah, and their performance.

"Syd?" he said. She was right behind him. "Let's not stop."

Greg and Gus were there too. They all reflected his excitement.

"Let's go back on," he said. "We'll start with what we left out of the first set: 'Don't Stand So Close to Me' and 'Higher Love.' We'll wrap up with 'Feels Like the First Time' if they let us."

Syd was nodding. "Works for me."

"Right fucking on!" Greg shouted.

Gus was beside him, jumping up and down. "Let's go."

Ethan was already moving toward the stage with the rest of the Release right behind him.

CHAPTER 41

Tuesday, December 4, 1984

It was hard to believe such a turnabout could take place. The week before, he'd watched Syd smash an expensive twelve-string Martin to smithereens and seen a band on the brink of collapsing. But as Ethan was beginning to learn, emotions were revealed in different ways and seemed to come out more prominently when people really cared about what they were doing. The line between love and hate was almost indistinguishable when things really mattered. Despite their faults, when they were onstage or rehearsing, they all cared. They seemed to love not only what they were doing but also the people they were doing it with. It was their creation.

Their last set was to be short, even though they came back to unexpected cheering. They tried to ascribe to the adage "Always leave them wanting more" but decided to follow "Feels Like the First Time" with their original "Never Say Never" to end the show. Ethan knew it was a risk, but greatness didn't come from playing it safe. Besides, it was better for people to leave with the Release's music in their heads.

Like something from a Hollywood script, Jonah Vetch returned midway through the Foreigner song. Finishing with "Never Say Never" was ideal. The enthusiastic crowd made it even better.

But Jonah was gone again before they finished "Never Say Never" to a standing ovation. This second disappearance was unexpected but quickly forgotten when Ethan stepped down from the stage and heard Carlyn say to one of her friends, "That's my bro all right."

The sound of pride in her voice caught him by surprise. He turned and hugged her without saying anything. She was his little sister, yet he hardly knew her.

Their mother still was sitting at the table she'd been at since arriving. She wore a frilly pastel blouse he'd not seen before. A half-full glass of what looked like water was on the table in front of her. Her coat hung on the back of her chair. She smiled as he caught her eye. He wondered if she was smiling for him or smiling at seeing her children together—maybe both.

Carlyn's friends stood around them, squeezing out any room for silence with their constant talking, most of which was about what they'd seen and heard.

"I'm so proud of you," Carlyn whispered in his ear before she stepped back among her friends. Ethan moved to sit down in the empty seat beside his mother. Strangers patted him on the back or extended their hands to shake his, as if they were friends from his past. As he sat down, his discomfort grew. He felt like a narcissist who needed to feed on attention.

"It was very loud," his mother said.

"I warned you."

His mother wiped her mouth with the white paper napkin on the table. "I wish I could understand what you were singing," she said, "and Greg hits the drums like he's trying to kill something." She wrapped the napkin around her glass and took a sip.

"Greg plays hard," he said. "Everyone does. Want to meet the others?"

"Not tonight. I'm pretty tired. Tomorrow's a school day for me."

"Thanks for coming, Ma," he said. He didn't want to push it. "Hope you can hear tomorrow."

He stood up, leaned over, and kissed her on the cheek.

"Sorry your father wasn't here," she whispered, rubbing his arm.

Ethan didn't say anything. He didn't know why she'd said that. Whatever her intentions, he wasn't about to let her comment mar his evening; he wasn't having any of it.

He turned and waved to Carlyn, who was beside the stage with a group of her friends, talking to Greg and Gus. Ethan wondered how her friends had gotten in. The thought was gone as quickly as it had come. He wasn't about to interrupt.

He followed Syd back to the office they were using as a dressing room at the top of the back stairs. They were there only a few minutes before the door opened.

"Holy fuck!" screamed Greg as Gus followed him in. "What a night!"

They slapped each other high fives that ended in a group hug. That was as far as they got together. There was a knock at the door. Ethan shook his head to leave it, but Syd was already turning the doorknob.

Jonah Vetch stepped in.

"That was something to behold," he said, nodding as if trying to keep some kind of internal rhythm going while he shook each of their hands. Then, in a rough Ricky Ricardo imitation, he added, "Raj has some splainin' to do."

He laughed. They all smiled at the stranger who had just entered their midst. Small talk came easily with this stranger, who seemed different from the man Ethan had talked to on the phone. Syd had met him quickly before their second set.

Jonah then told them how he knew Raj. He didn't mention Randolph. He loved their songs. He couldn't stop talking about their arrangements of "American Woman" and "Kashmir." He'd only heard a little of "Never Say Never" but liked it. The cassette Raj had given him would be the next one in his tape deck.

"You guys are tight," Jonah said, speaking fast, as if something were burning up inside him. Genuine excitement seemed to shape his voice.

Standing in the small office beside him, Ethan was surprised at the man's height. He wasn't much taller than Syd. Gus had him by a couple of inches, and Gus wasn't tall.

"You actually know how to play," Jonah said.

"Thanks," Greg said and smiled.

"So," Jonah said, rubbing his palms together as if he were about to perform some kind of magic. The collar of his white shirt was buttoned to the top. He didn't wear a tie. "Can you guys be in Chicago next Tuesday night?"

The question came as a surprise to Ethan and likewise to the others, judging by the glances that went around the room. They'd all expected him to say something more along the lines of "So you're looking for a manager?" But Ethan liked his response. Without explaining or filling their heads with a bunch of wishful ideas, Jonah seemed to want to do. It had been a great night—why stop?

"Chicago?" Ethan replied, trying to think how they could manage the Gasworks Saturday and Sunday and make it to Chicago Tuesday. He didn't want to give anything away, but inside, he was screaming. Jonah wasn't yet their manager and had a gig for them. Ethan could only suppress his emotions for so long. "Are you kidding?"

"I've a spot on the bill," Jonah said. "My opening act just canceled. You need five songs. I know about four."

"'Confusion,'" Ethan said as the others turned and looked at him. They'd played it once.

"We're going to fucking Chicago!" Greg shouted, thrusting his fist into the air.

"Just a minute," Ethan said, suddenly uncomfortable with how fast it was all happening. "You're not our manager yet."

"No, I'm not," Jonah replied quickly, looking at Ethan, "but it's how I roll. I've seen what I need to see. I'm ready if you are."

Jonah's reply could have come off as arrogant, but it didn't sound that way. He likely knew more about the Release than he was letting on, Ethan thought. They had planned to spend much of the next week booking shows. Those gigs might land in their laps with Jonah Vetch. It didn't seem possible. Jonah had a way of speaking that made Ethan want to listen; he represented hope. The Release would make music; Jonah would manage them. As hard as it was to believe, everything seemed to be coming together.

"This is fucking it!" Greg shouted, looking to the ceiling. "Where do I sign?"

Ethan's head was buzzing. Less than a week ago, they'd almost packed it in. Now a potential manager was in their midst with work. They had recorded four good songs—two for a soundtrack. They'd played one of their best shows. He'd seen Christa. As his mother said, nothing ever went as planned.

"Are we just looking at Chicago Tuesday night?" Ethan asked, needing to ask something before his insides exploded. Was there a catch to Jonah's offer?

"Tonight, yes," Jonah replied. His voice trailed off.

Ethan's lips tightened. He thought he might be onto something. The Release was filling a need for Jonah Vetch—likely getting him out of a jam. The Release would turn their world upside down to get to Chicago. Would that be the end of it?

Jonah's right hand went in the front pocket of his designer jeans and then came out as if he'd pulled something out of it.

"There'll be more," Jonah said, looking up at Ethan. "Much more if things work out as I think they will."

Ethan's mind was racing. They'd never been stateside as a band. How was that going to work?

"You've all got passports?" Jonah asked, as if reading Ethan's mind.

Ethan didn't and shook his head.

"Birth certificate?"

"Yeah."

"That works," Jonah said. He looked at Syd. "You?"

Syd twisted her face in a "Really?" frown.

"I'm as fucking Canadian as anyone in this room," she sneered.

"Sorry," Jonah replied, and he tried to recover. "Bad on me. Won't happen again."

"Sure," Syd said, and she faked a smile. "Better not."

Ethan looked at Gus. "The van'll get us there?"

"Sure," Gus answered. He hadn't said anything yet, and Ethan wondered whether he was buying into Jonah becoming their manager. The Chicago thing did seem a little far-fetched, given their current circumstances.

"How do we know you're not full of shit?" Gus said.

"You don't," Jonah answered, stepping back and putting his hand on the doorknob. "I can walk right out this door, and you'll never see me again."

"Whoa!" shouted Greg before anyone else had a chance to speak. "That's not gonna happen. We're going to fucking Chicago if I have to drag everyone's ass down there myself."

"You're not dragging my ass anywhere, drummer boy," Syd said.

"Okay, just a minute," Ethan said. "Nobody's dragging anybody's ass."

"I'm fucking going," Syd said.

Jonah handed each of them his business card.

"What's next?" Gus asked.

"We'll get to Chicago first," Jonah said, and he looked at Ethan. "I'll be in touch tomorrow."

Jonah pulled open the door and left as swiftly as he'd arrived.

Ethan figured Jonah had known before he walked in that the Release was going to Chicago.

CHAPTER 42

Thursday, December 13, 1984

Jonah, to his word, had called Ethan the next day. He said the Release had to be in Chicago by noon on the Tuesday. Ethan also learned the destination wasn't exactly Chicago but Peoria. Ethan didn't mind. None of them did; it was a gig stateside. If they drove straight, it would take them nine hours.

The Release finished the week at Tormo and, as planned, played the Gasworks in downtown Toronto Saturday and Sunday night. They stayed at the house for most of Monday, rehearsing the four songs they knew and an arrangement of Ethan's "Confusion." They left just before midnight. The van was packed with gear. Gus and Greg did most of the driving. A friend of Greg's Ethan hadn't met before came along to help them load and unload. They were on their way to Peoria, USA.

Even if they'd been told, they wouldn't have believed what was ahead of them. They went from playing small clubs to the Peoria Civic Center, which held twelve thousand people. They didn't know until they saw the marquee in the arena's parking lot Tuesday morning that they were opening a show that one of the top bands in the nation—REO Speedwagon—was headlining. Like a dream, the show passed in a flash. Outside of watching backstage and receiving a few pats on the back when they came off the stage, they didn't see the members of the headliner at all, and just as Jonah had said, they played their five songs and left. For the Release, the arena crowd was monstrous. They'd never heard such a loud response to a performance. But it was a murmur compared to thunderous ovation REO Speedwagon received when they finally took the stage an hour late. Neither Ethan nor the rest of band paid much notice to the difference. They were pinching themselves just to be performing in front of a stadium crowd and not booed off the stage. It was the first time they'd played all their own material.

Most of the show was a blur to Ethan despite his attempt to savor each moment. He remembered little after grabbing the mike to sing "Never Say Never" in front of an audience of thousands. He had become increasingly self-conscious of his singing but unaware of what he'd sung or where he'd gone afterward. He said as much to Jonah after the show. Jonah responded, "You've quite a presence on stage, young man."

On their return home, though exhausted, they talked about writing more material. The song ideas started to come, but it wasn't long before they discovered that ideas were not the problem; the problem was deciding which ones to pursue. They all jotted stuff down, but it was Syd who began consuming what they wrote, connecting notes and melodies to the words dropped in her lap.

The band had arrived back in Toronto midday yesterday, which was Wednesday. After a surprise call from a club owner in Oshawa they'd played again last night. They were to head to London, Ontario, tomorrow to play a new bar on Friday and Saturday. Jonah told them he would keep them booked. They hadn't signed anything, but they had their manager.

It was now ten o'clock in the morning. Ethan didn't want to be up after getting in late from the gig in Oshawa, but Jonah wanted to meet with him—alone—before the Release headed to London. Ethan took the bus to a coffee shop on Eglinton. Jonah was there when he arrived. With all that was going on, Ethan hardly paid attention to the decorated Christmas tree in the corner of the small shop. "Merry Christmas" was stenciled on the windows with spray-on snow. Tinsel and garlands surrounded them. Ethan moved his mug of black coffee back and forth across the tabletop, anxiously listening to what Jonah had to say.

Jonah's inscrutable facial expression was difficult to read. Ethan had anticipated Jonah wanting to set the terms of an agreement with the Release. What came instead proved to Ethan just how wrong he could be about Jonah.

"Ethan," Jonah said, leaning forward and hooking his index finger into the handle of his coffee mug. He leaned back and took a sip of coffee. When he set the coffee mug down, he seemed different to Ethan. "Ever done any acting?"

CHAPTER 43

Thursday, December 13, 1984

The question was so out of sync with anything Ethan had anticipated that his first response was an incredulous "Pardon me?"

Jonah's eyes widened. "Acting—like in the movies."

"Why are you asking me that?" he answered, still thinking about a contract and a tour for the Release.

"Because I have to."

Jonah shifted his chair forward, causing the wood legs to scrape on the coffee shop's beige ceramic floor tiles. He suddenly looked much more interested than he had in anything else they'd talked about.

"Why? What's that got to do with the Release?" Ethan asked.

"Nothing," Jonah said. His open right hand slid palm down across the tabletop as if he were smoothing its hard surface. "Nothing at all." He picked up his coffee, this time without using the handle. He didn't drink.

"I don't follow you," Ethan said when it became apparent Jonah wasn't about to say more.

"Randy's told me some of your story." Jonah stopped. His eyes didn't leave Ethan's.

Something trembled in Ethan's head when he heard the name. It was the first time Jonah had mentioned Randolph.

"It's kind of amazing, don't you think?" Jonah set his mug back on the table.

Ethan was disappointed not to be talking about the band. Acting didn't play a part in his life anymore. He didn't feel good even thinking about it, as Mila's memory was always close by when he did. "The Angel" expressed how he felt.

"That time has passed. I really don't think about it anymore," Ethan said, his tone implying a finality.

Jonah nodded. "I get it. I won't belabor the point. But here's my question. Would you consider doing some?"

Ethan didn't want to answer the question. He knew where things were heading. He avoided anything to do with acting. He didn't go to the movies, rent VCR tapes, or watch TV; they didn't have a VCR or a TV at the house. He'd blocked it all out. Deep down, he wondered whether a movie might trigger him to go back. He was terrified of going away for good. He didn't want to talk about acting—or even think about it. But there it was, back again.

"Why are you interested?" Ethan asked after his moment of retrospect.

"Because Randy lit up when he talked about you. He told me you were remarkable."

Ethan held Jonah's stare. It was the only way he could remain steady; the heavy padlocked door was already edging up beside him.

"How would that work exactly?" Ethan asked, frowning, doing his best to avoid where Jonah seemed to want to take him. "I thought we were here to talk about the Release."

"We are, and we'll get there. What are you afraid of?"

Ethan squinted, affecting confusion, but he was anything but confused. He wasn't about to take the bait. "What? Are you a doctor too?"

The padlocked door seemed to be right beside the table. Ethan's stomach tightened; his teeth ground together.

"No," Jonah replied, "but I know when I see something special. It's what I do—and I'm fucking good at it. You transform onstage. Few do it naturally; even fewer know it."

Ethan didn't say anything.

"I want to get you in front of a camera."

"What does that have to do with music?" Ethan asked. "Or the Release?"

The big door was at his side as Syd's prophetic words came to mind: "Someone else will see you, with power and money, and steal you away."

"It doesn't have anything to do with the band or your bandmates," Jonah said, "or even music, for that matter. This is about you and a gift."

"No, this is supposed to be about the Release and our future," Ethan said, leaning over the table on his forearms. His fists were clenched. "That's the deal. You're our guide through the fucking music business. End of story."

Rage suddenly inflamed Ethan. The heavy door was close. *Open me!* it seemed to yell.

Jonah pushed his mug across the table away from him. "I know what my job is," he said, appearing unperturbed by Ethan's sudden outburst, "but I'm not your manager yet." Jonah paused; his hand didn't leave his mug. "You have something that's rare. I've seen it. Randy confirmed it. There's no question of your talent in the band. But there are hundreds of talented musicians around. You can see them any night of the week. You have a couple of good songs. But what makes the Release special is you—your transformation onstage. It's not just about music, Ethan. It's about what you create, what so many strive for yet rarely achieve. When an audience witnesses these moments, it's magical, and they know it."

Jonah stopped and rolled his mug back and forth between his hands. He looked as if he were warming them up, but Ethan knew what he was really doing: Jonah was trying to pry open what was locked down tight.

Jonah was right; Ethan was scared. Even a peek into what might be behind the padlocked door might take him away forever. That was the risk, and he thought it was a good fucking reason to be scared. He'd gone away and had somehow come back. As Dr. Katharine had repeated, they didn't know why. The human brain was like that. He was doing his best to pretend he wasn't having the episodes, but he was, and they were real. Only Christa knew. He was having this conversation because of them. Somehow, he was controlling them. He didn't know why he could leave now and come back, but he could. The fade-outs in the studio, onstage, and even at Mila's grave—each time, he had come back. He gave one remarkable performance after another, unable to recall where he went or what happened, knowing only that he went somewhere else and that most liked what he did while he was there.

"But I'm here to talk about the Release," Ethan said, interrupting his own thoughts, "not about me and acting."

Jonah's eyebrows rose as his head shifted to the right as if to say, "Really?"

"Acting was another time—another place," Ethan said, noticeably uncomfortable. "I barely remember it. I've moved on, and you need to too—as does Randolph, apparently."

Jonah didn't move; he only looked at Ethan. His right hand covered his left on the table.

"So here's the deal," Jonah said, still not moving. "I will manage the Release under one condition, which is not negotiable. You have to audition for the work I get you as an actor."

Ethan made to stand up. Jonah raised his hand.

"Let me finish," Jonah said, his hand returning to the table to cover the other. "I will not overload you. I will pick carefully, but refusing an audition will be a breach of contract—our handshake—and result in my termination as the band's manager. Or you can decide right now that I'm not right for the Release, and I will get up and walk away."

Ethan started shaking his head before Jonah finished. "This is bullshit," he said. "Fucking blackmail."

"It's neither, but you can call it what you want. Opportunity is knocking, Ethan. It's the deal I'm prepared to make. It's up to you."

Ethan continued to shake his head. He didn't like being coerced into making a decision.

"So pack your bags," Jonah added before Ethan said anything. "The Release is going to be busy."

Ethan turned his head and stared out the front window of the coffee shop. A couple of kids were standing on the sidewalk. One looked to have a can of Coke in his hand. He was wearing a pair of red canvas high-cuts. The other kid was talking. The kid opened the can and took a drink. He then handed the can to the other kid in exchange for what looked like a couple of coins. Both kids smiled. Ethan turned back and looked at Jonah. The padlock was hanging from the door latch. The lock was open. The heavy door was slightly ajar. Someone was inside. Horrified, he recognized the face. It was Robbie, his roommate from university. The heavy door then slammed closed with shocking suddenness. Ethan blinked.

His own voice brought him back to the table.

"You know I can't say no," he said. "It means too much to the others."

"It means a lot to you," Jonah said. "Look, Ethan, I'm not here to fuck you around. There are too many who thrive on that in this business. People who do what they love to do are very vulnerable to it. They can't help themselves. The business is full of people chasing dreams. Fight your fear; you won't regret it."

Ethan was struggling. It'd been all of six months since he'd come home. Music had consumed most of that time. He loved it but fought it too, especially when he watched Syd or Gus. They were hardwired to music; to them, nothing else mattered. There was a sense of reverence in watching them. But it wasn't Ethan's musical ability that made him part of it; it was how he made the songs come to life to touch people. It wasn't something he could explain or even know that he was doing. People saw it, felt it, and lived it.

He became what they wanted to be; he gave them a chance to be someone or something else for a while.

What kind of musician disappeared from the music he was playing to become a character—to become something the audience could relate to and feel they were? Yes, it was artificial—or was it? The music was the message, the truth, but for Ethan, it was the trigger—the means—that bore something else. The war was within him; he could fight it, but he could never win because the music wasn't really him. He was just another singer, but what he could become made his singing special. He knew what he was. He'd known since meeting Mila.

"You can run away, Ethan," Jonah was saying as Ethan returned to the conversation. "You've already got a good start. But you know. Only you can know."

"How the fuck do you know that?" Ethan said. He was suddenly aware that his hands had slipped to the edge of the table. The skin around his fingernails was white with the grip he held on the table.

"It's not what I know, Ethan," Jonah replied. "It's what I see. It's what Randy's seen for a long time. He talks like you're Al Pacino. It's only a matter of time before you figure it out. You can't keep running." Jonah paused for a second. "I think you have figured it out, and it scares the shit out of you."

Jonah took a drink of his now cooled coffee. Ethan stared at him, holding back where the name seemed bent on taking him. He didn't want to even think. His plan for a life in music was crumbling, almost as if he'd known it would, and he felt helpless to do a thing about it.

"Raj said you were performing—but not music; you were somewhere else."

"Raj said that?" Ethan asked, surprised. "He never said anything to me."

"Raj makes great songs," Jonah said. "He counsels only to make a better song. He'd have fucked things up if he'd have said anything."

Ethan rubbed his chin, sensitive to the sandpaper feel of his unshaven skin. "So what now?" he asked, feeling he'd been pushed down a hill and had to find another way up.

"Do we have a deal?" Jonah asked.

Ethan knew his decision. "You already have it all lined up, don't you?" he said. It wasn't a question.

"You're on to me, Ethan." Jonah laughed. "And yes."

CHAPTER 44

Monday, December 24, 1984

To say the last few weeks had been busy was an understatement.

The day after Ethan met with Jonah, Jonah was true to his word again and had him set up with his first audition. The audition was in a warehouse east of the city, down on the lakeshore, next door to a sound stage where the film's production company would shoot the picture. Ethan hadn't known the place even existed. No one in the band knew about the audition.

That was yesterday, Sunday, the day after their second gig in Sarnia that Jonah had also booked after their meeting.

The Release had played five shows in the last week, four of which were a lead-in to a tour that would start their New Year off through southwestern Ontario. They'd also returned to Oshawa on the Wednesday to do another show at the club owner's request. The two Sarnia gigs had the Release billed with a more established band from Toronto who had become popular playing the Ontario club circuit. Smash Dickson had become a fan favorite on late-night FM radio. The Release had partied with the band after each show. To Ethan, it seemed the party had become as important as the show to the veteran band. He wondered how increasingly difficult it was to stay motivated to the music after years of trying to make it. Those who weren't in love with their art and what they created inevitably moved on or became lost in the distractions of drugs and alcohol, which were almost necessary to the lifestyle. Friday and Saturday seemed to magnify his meeting with Jonah.

On arriving back at the house late yesterday morning, Ethan was anxious—about the audition later that afternoon and about keeping it from the others—but he didn't let on. With Sarnia being their last gig until New Year's, they all were headed back to their families for Christmas. Syd left for Ottawa shortly after they returned. Gus and Greg headed out soon after they'd unloaded the van. Ethan said he was leaving for his parents' at four o'clock but had actually headed to the audition.

Now he was on his way back to where he'd auditioned to pick up a revised copy of the script he'd read from for the actual audition. They wanted to see more. After getting the script, he would head to his parents' place.

Ethan was just about to leave to catch a bus downtown when the phone rang.

"So," Jonah said before Ethan even said hello, "how did it go?"

Ethan was excited but didn't want Jonah to know that. He'd been low-key after the audition and sat around the house most of the night reading one of the copies of *Browning Station* he'd bought as a Christmas present, reliving the audition over and over again. With Jonah, he wanted to make the audition sound like no big deal and pretend everything wasn't in Jonah's hands. Ethan didn't want to admit the latter to himself, but the deal was done, and he knew it. He was certain Jonah did too. In his heart, acting was the centerpiece, no matter how much he wanted music to be. He wanted to act—needed to act, had to act—all reservations aside. It was in his blood. He had tried to ignore it, but he knew it wasn't working. He'd refused to admit it until Jonah. Like a virus, the acting bug had infected him and came out in their shows. High school drama class had introduced him to acting, but he hadn't had the wherewithal to understand or acknowledge it. But being onstage with Mila had made it so. He'd landed two loves at the same time. But his love of acting had become fear after Mila's murder: love for what it was and fear of what it might become. Yet it seemed to have been lying there all along, waiting for that moment to rise up and take over his life. Talking with Jonah had relit the embers he'd thought dead, and they'd exploded in flame at the audition. He was good, and he knew it. It didn't take long for those watching to know it too. He hit the mark and then some, but he didn't want Jonah to get wise to how right he was in reading him.

"It went well," Ethan replied, keeping his voice even and low. "I liked it."

"What kind of role is it?"

"I started reading the part for a maître d'," Ethan said, smiling into the phone's handset. "It wasn't much, but when I finished, they handed me something else. I've been sworn to secrecy."

As he spoke, whispers of something else fluttered in his head, as if he'd been there before.

"Really?"

"Yeah, really," Ethan said. "Did they call you?"

"No, why?"

"They asked me who my agent was."

"Did they now?"

"I gave them your name."

There was a pause. Ethan pictured Jonah rubbing his hands together.

"You must be fucking ecstatic," Jonah finally said.

"You could say that," Ethan replied, thinking of the character he was to play, who was shy and withdrawn and had an affinity for computers. "They asked me to come back on Wednesday. I'm headed out to get a revised script now."

"Cool!"

"Yeah, it's cool all right," Ethan said, "but I don't expect it'll go down as cool with the others."

"We'll work it out."

"By explaining what exactly?" Ethan asked, raising his left hand in the air as if Jonah were in front of him.

"Whatever you want to."

"Really," Ethan said. He didn't want to think about it.

"Ethan, it'll work out," Jonah said.

Ethan pictured Jonah looking off into the distance from wherever he was, his mind already on another trajectory. It annoyed Ethan. He was going through life decisions, and Jonah acted as if it were just another day at the office. Maybe it was. Ethan was about to say more when Jonah returned, a heightened intensity to his voice.

"Ethan, what I'm about to tell you is very important to what will happen over the next few months. No, it's more than that. It's fucking important to the rest of your life."

What Jonah explained next changed Ethan's thinking.

Several months earlier, even before Randolph had asked the Release to record songs for his movie, Jonah had, by chance, met a film executive he knew of by name only: Rom Kami. Rom produced films. He'd recently had a hand in Clint Eastwood's *Pale Rider*. Two other projects were on his plate. The first was *After Hours*, which a young director named Martin Scorsese was directing, coming off the critical success of *Raging Bull*. Rom had met Scorsese only once. The other, *Death Wish 3*, involved director Michael Winner and another star: Charles Bronson.

Rom had been in Medora, North Dakota, as part of a fund-raiser for Theodore Roosevelt National Park and had stayed in Dickinson, North Dakota. Jonah had taken a couple of days' break from his usual hectic schedule to go on an excursion into the national park, knowing little about the Badlands or Roosevelt's legacy. They'd met in the lobby of the Best Western and, both being alone, had agreed to meet for dinner. Rom had described his search for a new, unknown actor for a movie project he was producing. He'd told Jonah the search in California and up the West Coast had yielded nothing. They needed another approach. Rom didn't want a Hollywood type and was convinced they weren't looking in the right place. The actor had to come from somewhere else. He wanted someone with a set of values contrary to the Hollywood mind-set. Hollywood had become so comfortable in their packaged world that it was impossible to see things in a new way. Over dinner, Rom had become convinced Jonah was the guy who could find him the right actor. "We're all actors," Rom had told Jonah. "We just end up in different parts of society. You can find this guy."

At the time, Jonah explained to Ethan, he hadn't had a clue what to think. But Jonah, as Ethan was beginning to understand, wasn't about saying no. Jonah told Ethan watching him perform was spellbinding. He made songs Jonah knew and had heard hundreds of times before feel new. He believed the camera would see it that way too.

"You hold a magic, Ethan," Jonah said, his voice not losing any of its intensity. "Einstein said something that I quoted to Rom that evening: 'Things aren't solved the same way they're created.'"

Jonah went on to say that after meeting with Rom, his schedule had become a disaster. He'd spent no time on Rom's request and owed him an answer. He told Ethan that Hollywood and Los Angeles were remarkable, if for no other reason, because nothings turned into somethings, and the somethings were often nothing at all.

"You're like that," Jonah said as Ethan tightened his grip on the phone. "You've come out of nowhere. An offhand conversation with an acquaintance at a party I wasn't even supposed to be at."

Raj had introduced Jonah to Randolph, a new movie guy he was working with. Randolph had mentioned an interesting performer, singer, and musician. The details had been sketchy. Raj had had to push Jonah to go see Ethan and the Release. Jonah had seen only Ethan—and his answer for Rom. It had seemed unbelievable yet believable. After all, now it was happening.

"So now you know," Jonah said.

There was nothing left to say. Ethan was beyond excited.

"This year, 1985, is going to be a busy year, my man," Jonah added. "Merry Christmas."

CHAPTER 45

Monday, December 24, 1984

After speaking with Jonah, Ethan couldn't sit still. What he'd heard was hard to imagine, even if his feelings were mixed. It was like dating a nice girl only to have the right one come along. Hurt was on the horizon. But now was the season to be merry, and merry he would be—maybe the Release and acting could coexist. But finding out whether they could would have to wait. It was Christmas Eve.

No sooner had he put down the phone with Jonah than his father called, offering to pick him up. Ethan liked that. He'd bought Christmas presents for everyone, and with his clothes and everything he had to bring, he hadn't wanted to ride the bus while lugging along a full hockey bag. He didn't say anything about his chat with Jonah or the audition. He'd pick up the script and meet his father back at the house.

On their way back from Sarnia, the band had stopped at a service center in the early-morning hours to exchange Christmas gifts with each other and share a little Christmas cheer from a bottle of Crown Royal. Nobody had any money, but somehow they'd managed a little something for each other. Gus had given everyone a cassette stuffed in a white envelope. Ethan had received Led Zeppelin's debut album. A note had accompanied the cassette, thanking him for crossing the street while he was mowing the lawn. A twinge of guilt had pressed Ethan's stomach as he thought of his audition later that day. Syd had given him the latest issue of *Guitar Gear* with a note that said, "The magazine that started it all," adding further to his guilty feeling. Greg's gift had been a black-and-white photo of their band from high school. They'd come a long way since those days. Ethan had given everyone a copy of *Browning Station*, meant as a keepsake from their recording experience.

He'd also bought copies for himself, Carlyn, and Christa. He doubted he'd see Christa before Christmas, but he would at least have something if he did. The celebration was short but a nice way to wrap up the band's year.

His father's Accord pulled into their short driveway half an hour after Ethan returned with the new script. He was ready to go.

"What's new?" his father asked as Ethan climbed in.

"Not much," he said. He knew there was a lot but was unsure how much he wanted to tell and how many times he would have to tell it. Pulling the passenger door closed, he thought of their trip back from Ottawa. It didn't seem that long ago, but much had happened. Strange that he would think of Robbie. One thought seemed to nudge another, ending in silence.

"Come on," his father said, backing out. "I haven't seen you in weeks. You've been all over with this band thing. There must be something."

"You know," he said, trying to distance his memory of Robbie from everything else. Like debris from a sunken ship, things seemed to surface at the least expected times.

Two lines popped into his head: *I don't know where I'm going, only know where I've been. It's not supposed to matter, but I know that I've sinned.*

His hand shot to the pocket of his ski jacket. Pens and paper were in every corner of the house, but again, he found himself without them. Like a watch, they needed to be attached to his body.

"Do you have a pen?" His words came out sounding quick and panicky.

"In the glove box," his father said. "What's up?"

"Words," he answered, pushing the button on the glove-box latch. He rifled through the contents but couldn't find what he was looking for.

"Hey," his father said in a deprecating tone that made Ethan feel like a ten-year-old, "slow down; you're making a mess."

He finally found a pen at the back of the small compartment but still had no paper. He pulled out the car's manual and flipped it open, looking for a blank page.

"What are you doing?" his father said.

Ethan could feel his father's stare and didn't answer. He wrote down the two lines in his head. He knew if he didn't, he'd forget them as quickly as they had come. They turned onto Lawrence Avenue.

"I gotta write things down when they come to me," he said, feeling a calm come over him at having the words written down. "If I don't, they're gone."

His father didn't say anything.

Ethan tore out the page he'd written on.

"Hope I don't need that page," his father said, his tone unchanged.

Ethan knew his father didn't like his stuff being touched, never mind torn up. "It was blank."

They drove in silence for a few minutes. With pen in hand, Ethan waited for the next words to come. It was his father's words that came instead.

"Okay, let's start over. Merry Christmas, Ethan."

CHAPTER 46

Monday, December 24, 1984

"You did get something for your mother?"

"Dad," Ethan said, stretching out the word in reply to the onerous question. "What kind of son do you take me for?"

"Don't ask questions you don't want the answer to," his father said, smiling, "but it wouldn't be the first time you didn't get her one."

"It's not much," he said, ignoring his father's comment, "but I think she'll like it."

After finding Christa in the small gallery down the street from Focus Sound, he had gone back later. His mother loved the Group of Seven. A small-framed print of Lawren Harris's *Summer Houses* had caught his eye. He really couldn't spare the thirty bucks it cost but had bought it anyway. Christmas hadn't been far away. Now he was glad he had.

"You know, your mom's real excited about Christmas this year." His father had the habit of explaining how his mother felt to express how he did.

"I don't doubt it," Ethan replied.

"You know, she never thought you'd come back."

Ethan caught his father's sideways glance. "I know," he said, reminded of how he went away during songs. He still hadn't told anyone about his episodes. But it was Christmas now, and he didn't want to go there. "Tonight and tomorrow will be fun."

Bing Crosby singing "Silver Bells" came on the car's radio.

"Christmas is Bing Crosby," his father said as the warm air from the dashboard vents blew across Ethan's face. The temperature had dropped overnight. Late November and early December had been unseasonably warm, but the last week was making up for it. It wouldn't be a white Christmas, but it might be close.

"This song especially," Ethan said. The song was the epitome of Christmas, bringing back Christmases of years past. He recalled the decorated tree with gifts piled under it in his parents' living room. Christmas was a fun time. Maybe they would relive some of those memories tonight and tomorrow.

Twenty minutes from the house, they came up to a liquor store. The parking lot was jammed.

"I don't think I want to go in there, but your mother," his father said, not finishing his thought. He turned in. Ethan could see the lineups through the front windows.

"I'm okay with Coke and coffee," Ethan said, remembering the bottle of Crown Royal in his bag—his father's Christmas gift.

"Really?" his father said. "That surprises me, living with a bunch of musicians."

"What's that supposed to mean?"

"I didn't mean—" His father slammed on the brakes to avoid the car backing out in front of them. In another two feet, they would have been outside trading insurance policies.

"Dammit," his father said, hitting the horn after stopping.

It made no difference; the other driver was seemingly oblivious to what he or she had done.

"Can you believe this shit?" his father shouted.

Ethan didn't respond. He knew his father was anxious.

"You know, maybe I need some too," his father said. He pulled into the now vacated parking spot in front of the store. "Where one door closes, another opens. Gotta love it." He stopped and turned off the Honda. "You coming?"

"Nah, it's okay," Ethan said, and he pulled out the piece of paper he'd written on. Maybe another line would serve itself up.

"Suit yourself."

His father left, shutting the door a little harder than he might have if he'd been more relaxed. He was like that. One minute, he'd be talking happy thoughts, and the next minute, something unexpected would happen and freak him out, and he'd be pissed off and cursing at whatever had disrupted his expected course of events. It didn't seem to matter who was around him or whether he knew them or not. Ethan wondered what he was like to work for—maybe more like Uncle Al than Ethan wanted to think about.

Ethan looked inside the liquor store. Even the drunks would be deterred by the lineups, he thought. Only the desperate would bother, and there were more than a few.

He looked down at the words he'd written. Nothing more was there. He wrote anyway: "I'm going to be coming."

Nothing followed. He put a line through the words and put the paper back in his pocket.

It seemed more people were going in than coming out of the store. His father would be a while if he managed to stay.

There was only a day, Christmas Day, before his follow-up audition. He hadn't said anything and was glad he hadn't. It would be big news and add to the excitement of Christmas Eve. That night would be a special one, especially after last year's. He wondered what his family had done. It seemed odd he didn't know.

There was no sign of his father in the liquor store. Ethan still doubted he'd make it out with a purchase and smiled. He pulled out the paper again but didn't write anything. He thought of Christa. He'd tried her number a couple of times without success. She must have had someplace to go for the holidays, but he didn't know. He wanted to see her but knew she was struggling to see him. One didn't pick whom he or she fell in love with; love didn't work that way. He hoped she was happy.

He thought of his copy of *Browning Station* in the back. Maybe he'd read a few more pages. He'd have time.

He reached over and pulled the lever to release the trunk lid.

He'd wrapped and stacked the books together to pack in his old hockey bag to keep from damaging them. In addition to *Browning Station*, he'd bought Margaret Atwood's *A Handmaid's Tale* and Stephen King's *The Stand* for Carlyn. He'd never finished *The Stand* but wanted to. His sister might. He should have bought a couple more books for Christa too. Maybe he'd give her *A Handmaid's Tale*. He pulled out his copy of *Browning Station* and hopped back into the passenger seat.

He loved the feel of a new book—the crisp pages and sharp edges bound in a tight, neat package of another's mind. He didn't recognize the author's name—Louis Noir—written in small letters below the title. During all the time the band had spent on the songs for the soundtrack in the studio and all the discussions he'd had with Randolph on the book, the author's name had not come up. It was like that for songwriters too. Unless the performer wrote the song, people rarely knew who'd written it. People mostly cared about how the song made them feel. Remembering the title was hard enough most times. With books, unless the reader cared who'd written it, he or she cared only about the story. Outside of a select few, authors were a group of quiet unknowns. *Browning Station* was no different—at least for now.

Ethan had read the first chapter the night before. He was just getting into the second when his father opened the door, startling him.

"Damn people," his father said, sliding into the seat.

Ethan had known how his father's trip inside was going to turn out. *If you touch a hot iron, you get burned.*

"No one knows anything. We live in a world of idiots." He started the car.

Unlike his father's previous Chrysler, the Honda always started, but his father didn't seem to notice the difference; he took it for granted. Ethan didn't want to think about the explosion that would have taken place if the car hadn't started.

"You won't believe what they're doing in there," his father said. He eased the Honda backward out of the parking space. A car horn sounded behind them. The Honda jerked to a stop. His father craned his neck. Ethan pretended not to notice, but he couldn't read with his father's angst. The car then eased backward.

"They don't even have all the cashiers on!" his father said, all but shouting. "It's mind-boggling how no one gives a shit!" Then, as if suddenly aware he was not alone, he said, "Sorry, but I just can't believe it!"

No kidding, Ethan thought, having started reading the same sentence three times. *Maybe you should relax, like you always tell me to.*

"The Christmas rush is so unnecessary," his father added, and Ethan raised his head as a couple dashed across in front of them. "You'd think people might think further ahead."

Ethan smiled at the irony. Without turning his head, he could see his father continuing to shake his. They bumped over some broken asphalt upon exiting the parking lot and then were homeward bound.

"What're ya reading?" he father asked, calm returning to his voice. They were ten minutes from the house.

"*Browning Station,*" Ethan answered.

His father didn't reply. It was as if he'd asked the question as part of making professional conversation, not really interested in the answer.

"Isn't that the book you had in the hospital?" His father was listening.

"Yes, it is."

"You found it?"

"Not exactly," Ethan said, knowing his father was trying. "I found it in a bookstore."

"That book has a mind of its own."

"You could say that," Ethan replied, closing the book. He wasn't going to get any more read now. "The hospital copy doesn't want to be found, so I bought my own."

They stopped for a red light.

"I figured I should read it now that we've recorded songs for the soundtrack."

"The soundtrack?" his father asked, the pitch of his voice rising. "What's that about?"

"It's what we recorded."

"You recorded songs for a soundtrack?" His father's right hand came off the steering wheel. He opened it as if he were letting a bird fly away. "Why don't I know this?" The calm was fading from his father's voice.

"I told you about it on my last visit. Mom knows."

His father's hand returned to the wheel in an apparent exchange with his head, which was again shaking. "Fill me in. I don't remember, and it appears your mother doesn't think it important enough to tell me."

Ethan didn't like his father's disrespecting his mother. She had likely tried, as he had, and been crowded out by something else on his father's mind.

"Sure," he said. He could try to steer the conversation away from his mother—that would be easier than what saying nothing would result in. He explained again what he thought he'd said before: Randolph was working on an animated feature of *Browning Station* and had given the Release a shot at recording a few songs for it.

"Ah, now I do remember something about you recording," his father said.

They turned left off Highway 7 and onto McCowan Road. The field where Ethan used to ride his bike was full of bulldozers and dump trucks.

"Isn't recording a rite of passage for a musician?" his father said. "Like 'publish or perish' for an author. A soundtrack sounds pretty major."

Ethan couldn't help feeling that his father still viewed him as the kid who'd ridden his bike in the then-empty field they were passing.

"It's pretty big," Ethan said, "and why I figure I should read the book."

Then, as was his annoying habit, his father abruptly changed the subject, as if he were watching television and had decided to change the channel.

"Still taking your medication?"

CHAPTER 47

Monday, December 24, 1984

They were on the doorstep; Ethan had the handle straps of his hockey bag slung over his shoulder. Five minutes had elapsed since his father had asked the question. They were still talking about it.

"Why would you think I'd stop taking my meds?" Ethan asked, feeling his father was questioning his personal integrity. He was living on his own, asking them for almost nothing, yet it was as if his father still wanted to know whether he made his bed every day.

"Because you think you don't need them anymore."

"Maybe I don't!"

"Okay, okay," his father said, turning about-face. He was about to push the door open.

Ethan was standing beside the painted wood cutout of Santa Claus that had been beside the front door every Christmas for as long as Ethan could remember.

"Sorry," his father said. "I didn't mean to pry. Don't forget: this is your mother's night."

When Ethan visited his parents' house now, it was like returning to his childhood and who he'd been when he lived there. Everything, including the neighborhood, seemed smaller, something he'd noticed the first time he'd come back from Ottawa. But things had changed. For example, the black wrought-iron railing he'd painted one summer—his first paid work—was gone, replaced by landscaping and brickwork his parents had done while he was away at university. It was as if his departure had prompted the change. The new door, with etched-glass panels, held a large Christmas wreath, and an evergreen garland decorated the doorframe. As he reached for the door latch, the door opened. His mother was there, her bright, smiling eyes looking over the top of reading glasses perched on the tip of her nose.

"Ethan," she said, her arms opening wide to give him a welcome hug.

He set down his bag and hugged her. He gave her a kiss on the cheek as he felt her arms wrap around him.

"I'm so glad you're here," she said.

"Me too," he said. He liked her hugs.

"Okay, okay," his father said behind him. "I'm here too and would like to get in."

His mother stepped back. She was wearing her traditional red-and-green Christmas Eve cardigan she'd worn for years. Her graying hair was all fixed up, no doubt from her trip to the hair salon earlier that day. She was still smiling.

The house smelled incredible. The aroma of her homemade buns, which could have been a meal by themselves, filled the air. No one would leave the table hungry that night.

Ethan pulled his hockey bag inside and set it down beside a new antique desk that sat where the old shoe rack had always been in the small foyer. Above the desk was a new mirror framed in wood that matched the desk. Before he got his coat off, Carlyn came in, wearing what looked like new jeans and a red blouse. Her hair was wrapped in a matching band.

"Hello, Brother," she said, beaming.

"Hello, Sis," he answered. He was feeling a little underdressed in his day-old jeans and gray university sweatshirt. It hadn't occurred to him that his mother and sister would dress up for the occasion. Realizing his faux pas, he was about to make a comment when Carlyn stepped forward; she was a little taller than their mother.

"Do I get a hug?"

Something seemed a little awkward in hugging Carlyn. They'd hugged at Tormo too, but he couldn't remember ever hugging her before that. She was his kid sister and had been just entering high school when he'd left for university almost a year and a half ago. They had never had much of a relationship after he'd started high school, outside of her being the annoying little sister who messed with his things. She'd accompanied their father only once to Ottawa that Ethan knew of. He'd already come out of wherever his mind had taken him. Their mother hadn't thought it wise for her to visit when he wasn't the Ethan she knew. The gig at Tormo had been the last time he'd seen her; that had been three weeks ago.

Brenda Lee's famous "Rockin' Around the Christmas Tree" was coming from the living room.

"What's been going on?" Carlyn asked, barely able to contain her excitement, as if she were ready to jump in the air at any second. She made everyone else look slow and old, including Ethan.

"A few things," Ethan said. He'd planned not to say anything until dinner. *Keep a level head*, he'd told himself. *No big excitement. Full Clint Eastwood.* But of course, that didn't happen. He was talking before he had his jacket off.

"Why didn't I hear any of this?" his father said as Ethan talked, although he didn't seem too perturbed.

"I was saving the news," Ethan said, knowing it was partly the truth. His father would likely have competed unknowingly with his own news and heard little, just like when he'd told him about recording for the soundtrack.

"Tell us more," Carlyn said, "so I can tell my friends. They love the Release."

They were in the living room. Ethan looked at the Christmas tree, which was in front of the large bay window instead of in its traditional place in the corner, where his mother sat alone in their new love seat; her smile had faded a little. His father was sitting in his leather lounge chair. Ethan and Carlyn had moved to the new couch; Carlyn was still grinning like a puppy anxious for attention. Ethan had looked forward to reminiscing about the many Christmases at home. He knew those days were gone and not repeatable, but it was still nice to think about those nights before Christmas and the excitement of wondering whether Santa would bring him the new Johnny West Ranch or the Tyco slot-car racing set. Would Kenner's Easy-Bake Oven—the item pictured in the ad Carlyn had cut from the Eatons' Christmas catalog, much to their mother's chagrin, and sent to Santa—magically appear under the tree in front of the other presents? They were memories from another time, not about to be found under the artificial tree in its new location.

Ethan looked at his father in his chair. He appeared unchanged from past Christmases. But in his mother, he saw something else—a now weak smile and an unfamiliar quietness.

"This guy Jonah, who's our new manager, has a lot of contacts," Ethan said, looking at Carlyn. He paused and looked again at the unreal Christmas tree. His mother had adorned it with gold and silver decorations to coordinate with the gold window drapes that blocked their inside world from the outside. "He seems to think I can act."

He glanced again at his mother. Her expression remained unchanged. Ethan wasn't about to tell them the deal he'd agreed to with Jonah but went on with his story.

"I auditioned downtown yesterday afternoon," he said, and Carlyn sucked in her breath but didn't say anything. "They want me to come back on Wednesday."

Carlyn touched his forearm. Her excitement was contagious.

"You're going to audition on Boxing Day?" their father asked before Carlyn could speak, his voice low and stern, as if Ethan had crossed a line he wasn't supposed to.

Ethan looked at his father. "Yeah," he replied, his tone indicating there was no question that he was going.

"But it's a holiday."

"For some."

"Ethan, I can't believe it!" Carlyn interrupted, unable to contain herself. "You're going to be a movie star too?"

Bothered by his father's reaction but unwilling to fall into its play, he turned to Carlyn, who was now sitting on the edge of the sofa's cushion.

"I don't know about that," he said, smiling, pleased that at least someone was excited about what he was doing, "but I am auditioning."

"What's it for?" she asked.

"Don't know that either," Ethan said, "but I expect to soon."

"My brother's going to be in the movies," Carlyn said, standing up.

Ethan looked at his father, who was rubbing his face as if he were afraid it might not be there in a while. He was looking not at Ethan but at his socked feet on the ottoman.

Their mother spoke next. "Let's eat."

CHAPTER 48

If there was one thing that was the same as Ethan remembered, it was the place setting for dinner. There was nothing new about the dining room. His mother's idea to replace the table with a baby grand piano had not materialized. While their father's adage "You can't eat on a piano" might have been true, Ethan thought time favored his mother. But he did wonder whether the idea was more wishful thinking than something she really wanted. That obviously hadn't been the case with the living room furniture. He couldn't remember the last time he'd eaten at the dining room table.

Johnny Mathias singing "Winter Wonderland" on the stereo reinforced the Christmas ambience.

Just as he had pictured, two fondue pots were in the middle of the table, one with hot oil and the other with molten cheese. The long barbed prongs with multicolored handles they'd used for years sat at each place setting, ready to skewer the chunks of meat and crusty bread. He was sure chocolate cheesecake was hidden in the fridge.

The mixed smells of gruyère cheese and their mother's homemade buns brought back the Christmas Eves of yesteryear.

"Remember the Christmas when you looked under our bed?" his mother said in concert with his reminiscences. "You knew you were getting Hot Wheels but couldn't say anything. You were so disappointed. You loved surprises."

"You knew?" Ethan said half in jest, remembering their parents' bedroom was out of bounds during the weeks approaching Christmas Day.

"Of course. We're parents. How do you think we got here?"

Their mother was smiling again, inserting a pronged piece of chicken into the hot oil of the fondue pot. Her baby finger was raised in a daintiness she rarely displayed as she positioned her long fork among the others. Ethan knew this wasn't her preferred way to cook, but it was tradition.

The dipping, frying, and eating went on, as did reminiscing to Christmas tunes, from Perry Como's "It's Beginning to Look a Lot Like Christmas" to Andy Williams's "It's the Most Wonderful Time of the Year." It was as if the combination of music, food, and family were a secret time machine to past Christmases. Ethan remembered the Kodak Pocket Instamatic camera he'd dropped in the toilet and their mother's sugarless date squares. One night, the Christmas tree had fallen over while their father read *The Night Before Christmas*, bringing certainty that a ghost was in the room. Carlyn admitted how overwrought she'd been in asking Santa for Lego, knowing it was supposed to be a toy for boys. Even Spirograph and Pop-o-Matic Trouble came up in the conversation. Toys had a way of defining a generation. This year, it was an obnoxious cube of small, rotatable colored cubes—the Rubik's Cube.

"Have you got one, Ethan?" Carlyn asked.

"That's a revealing question on Christmas Eve," their father said.

"No," he replied, ignoring their father and thinking of Greg's frustration with the "fucking cube." "Greg has one, along with some special words for it."

"One of the girls at school can solve it in less than two minutes," Carlyn said. "I hope I get one."

Ethan skewered another chunk of beef, amazed at how quickly the little pieces had filled him up. The meal always left him stuffed, and dessert was still to come.

"We're slowing down," their mother said. Both her forks lay across her plate.

The only smart one, Ethan thought. She knew when to stop.

"One more's enough for me," their father said, leaning back in his chair with both hands on the edge of the faded red, white, and green tablecloth. "Gotta leave room for dessert."

Ethan pulled his cooked chunk of beef out of the pot and set it on his plate. Carlyn pulled out her fork with a piece of cooked chicken on the end. Their mother turned off the burner. Unable to resist, Ethan dipped another piece of the crusty french stick into what little cheese remained in the bottom of the other pot.

"Darren, can you turn off the other burner?" their mother asked their father. "Or does anyone want more?"

"Nah," Ethan mumbled, stuffing the bread smothered in the still-molten cheese into his mouth. Their mother left with the plates the meat had been served on.

Why did he continue to eat when he was already stuffed?

He wondered where Christa might be and what she was doing.

"Aren't you excited about your audition?" Carlyn said, interrupting his thought, putting the last piece of chicken into her mouth.

"A little," Ethan replied, not ready to leave his thoughts of Christa. He wondered if she might have gone to Ottawa. He knew so little about her.

"A little?" Carlyn said, sounding surprised, her voice rising in concert with her eyebrows. "I don't believe you. You were doing that in Ottawa."

Her voice trailed off, but her comment was enough to shift his thoughts from Christa to Mila, as if one could play tag with the other.

"I'm so sorry, Ethan," Carlyn said, realizing too late what she'd said. "I didn't mean to."

Carlyn had never met Mila. He wondered if she'd even seen pictures of her. The padlocked-door feeling was again in his midst.

In a way, it was as if they'd all been tiptoeing around the obvious. He was about to leave her comment alone and reply to her first question when what he'd thought about earlier came to his lips.

"What'd ya do last Christmas?" he asked, turning around what Carlyn had stumbled onto to find out what he'd thought about earlier. "Did you have fondue?"

Their mother reentered the dining room and stood behind Carlyn's chair. "I'd rather not talk about it, Ethan," she said.

Ethan looked at her. Not only had her smile disappeared, but she also looked withdrawn. The shadows around her eyes had darkened. The skin on her forehead flattened as the corners of her eyes drooped in a frown.

"I know, Ma, but we're all here now. We're all together." His hands came together, fingers spread. "We should be happy and celebrating, not hiding and pretending it never happened."

He watched as their mother's hand tightened on the back of Carlyn's chair.

"Every time I think about it, I'm afraid—so I don't," she said, grimacing and looking away.

"But I'm here now," he said. He didn't know why, but he didn't want to let go. They were too close to something. "I can't imagine what you've gone through, but you made it."

Ethan looked to their father. Their father's eyes said it all—"Remember what I told you"—but he didn't utter a word. Ethan looked back at their mother.

"It happened, Mom. Not thinking about it won't make it go away." Ethan paused, but his words wouldn't stop. "It won't stop it from happening again either." He leaned forward, his stomach against the edge of the table. "I'm scared all the time." He looked at Carlyn. Her eyes were downcast, looking at the tabletop. No doubt she'd been coached not to bring up the subject, and now she'd instigated it. By will or by accident—it didn't matter. When one was told not to do something, it often was difficult to think of anything else.

"I don't want to disappear again either. I don't know why I did. But it could happen."

Ethan was on the fringe of revealing what happened when he sang and the episode at Mila's grave.

"I don't want to talk about it," their mother replied, still standing behind Carlyn. She was looking at their father.

"We have to, Ma," Ethan said, surprised that on such a special night, they were discussing something that had remained a no-fly zone since his return from Ottawa.

"Ethan," his father said in the tone that could take Ethan to enraged fury in an instant, "I can't allow this to go on."

"You can't allow this to go on!" Ethan cried. It took but a moment to go from Christmas Eve sentimentality to raging war with his father. "This isn't just about you! It's about me! It's about Ma!"

Carlyn's face was ashen. Her hands rose to cover it. "Please! Please! Stop!" she shouted. "I can't stand it! This bickering! Dad, please stop!"

Ethan felt the abruptness of Carlyn's plea like the oomph that accompanied a large structure letting go.

"Not a day goes by that I don't think of her," Ethan said, his anger flattening as he held his voice level, still wanting to explode. "That a little piece of my heart doesn't break away and go with her. And Robbie, who it's impossible to believe was even real. He was that—"

He stopped. Tears ran down his cheeks like dammed pressure letting go. The heavy door didn't feel as heavy.

It was the first time he'd mentioned Robbie's name in front of anyone since Dr. Katharine in her office. He couldn't remember ever saying Robbie's name to his parents.

"You would have loved Mila. She was bright and happy. She made me happy." He sobbed and leaned back in his chair, trying to get hold of his feelings. He took a breath and wiped away the tears blurring his vision. "I don't want to go away again, but worrying won't stop it from happening."

Their mother sat back in her seat.

"It was my brain's way," Ethan said, extending his hand as if he were offering something visible to his family, "of dealing with a terrible thing. It wants me here."

No one said a thing.

Their mother leaned forward and grabbed his hand. Tears were on her cheeks. She shook her head.

"I can't do that, Ethan," she said. She grabbed hold of her red cloth napkin. "I've tried. I'm trying. I see you. I'm afraid I'll hear that voice—that other voice that's yours but not yours. I just can't—"

Her voice broke off. She lifted the Christmas napkin to her face.

"I can't do it!" she cried, and she stood up from her chair. "I just can't!" She left the room. Dinner was over.

"Damn it, Ethan," their father said. "I told you when we came in. You just couldn't leave it alone." He tossed his green napkin onto the table. "I don't know why you even came home."

Their father stood up and left. Ethan heard the front door open and close. He'd left the house.

Bing Crosby was singing "I'll Be Home for Christmas" behind them.

CHAPTER 49

Monday, December 24, 1984

"It's been like this for the last few months," Carlyn said, pouring herself another glass of wine. "Ma cries. Dad leaves. It's always about you."

Ethan didn't know what to say. He couldn't remember his father speaking to him so derisively before, as if he were to blame for the mess they now found themselves in. His coming home for Christmas had suddenly turned lonely and quiet. He wished for Christa.

"When did you start drinking wine?" he asked, surprised at the words that came out of his mouth.

"I don't know," Carlyn said, running her fingertip around the rim of the glass as if she couldn't have cared less what he asked her. Her vibrant excitement was gone. She leaned her head sideways against the open palm of her right hand, propped up by her elbow on the table. Ethan would have thought she was bored if he hadn't been part of the confrontation that had just taken place. "'Bout the same time they started this fucking game."

Ethan was taken aback by what she'd said. He didn't think he'd ever heard her swear before. It wasn't becoming and was likely more for his benefit than anything else.

She cupped the bowl of her wineglass in her left hand, the stem between her fingers, and took a gulp of wine. She wasn't drinking for the pleasure of it.

"How come I don't know about this?" he asked.

Carlyn shrugged, but he knew the answer. He was never there and hadn't been for a long time.

"What do you do now?" he asked. Previously, his reaction would have been to leave. In the years prior to leaving for university, during any kind of family turmoil, he'd either gone to his room to lose himself in an album or left the house. It seemed the only way he had of coping with being told what to do when he didn't want to. His mother was the usual culprit. Tonight, his naive expectation had been to have a merry and happy evening; it was Christmas Eve. He'd imagined things had changed after his short stay while convalescing with his parents before moving in with the Release. Some things maybe never would.

"Ma'll come out in a while," Carlyn said, turning the stem of her wineglass between her thumb and forefinger. "She doesn't really say anything. Dad's longer. I'll usually hear the front door sometime after midnight. I don't know where he goes. Don't really care, to be honest. When Ma leaves the table, he usually says some shitty thing about my clothes or me, like he said to you, and then gets up. I don't think he wants anyone around when he gets back."

Carlyn stopped and took another even larger gulp of her wine. She squinted as she swallowed. It looked as if she were taking medicine that didn't taste good.

"You know what's fucking weird?" she said as she set the glass down on the table.

Again with the swearing—he swore all the time, but hearing Carlyn use the word *fuck* made him sad. He didn't know why and only shook his head in answer to her question.

"They let on as if nothing fucking happened," she said, sliding her wineglass to her right hand as if clearing the passage between them might help clarify what she didn't understand. "When I ask Ma, she changes the subject. We then usually play cards or Scrabble for a while."

Saying the word *Scrabble* seemed to perk her up.

"Wanna play a game?"

Ethan shook his head. Nat King Cole was singing in the background. Ethan couldn't remember the name of the song, but it brought back the childhood feeling of Christmas he wanted to be real.

"Come on," she said, pressing him. "It'll be fun."

He really didn't want to but acquiesced for Carlyn's sake. He couldn't imagine what she'd been through because of him. Intentional or not, it was how life happened.

"Okay, but first I want a piece of that cheesecake."

"Ah, you saw it," she said.

"No, I just guessed."

Carlyn left the room.

This was not the Christmas Eve he'd anticipated. He knew that what had been could never be again, but he never seemed able to stop deceiving himself that it wouldn't be. Even while performing at their recent shows in Oshawa and Toronto, he'd kept imagining Christmas Eve at home.

He'd never imagined watching his sister get drunk while he ate cheesecake at the almost sacred dining room table.

Carlyn had just spread out the game board when their mother reappeared. Ethan didn't know what to say. He didn't have to say anything.

"I see you found the dessert," their mother said, returning to the seat she'd vacated.

"Wasn't I supposed to?" he mumbled over the forkful he'd put in his mouth.

"I gave him a piece, Ma," Carlyn said, placing her refilled glass of wine beside the board adjacent to her. She wasn't slurring her speech, but her words were elongating.

"What a good sister you have," their mother said. "She's a wonderful little girl."

Ethan all but winced at hearing the words *little girl*. He prayed the comment wouldn't set Carlyn off, even with her third glass of wine.

"Yes, I'm your sweet little girl," Carlyn said, and then she took an audible slurp, mimicking a child drinking juice. Her eyes didn't leave the Scrabble board. "We were just going to start a game. Wanna play?"

Carlyn's timing was perfect. No doubt she'd used the "Wanna play a game?" card before to keep the peace. Ethan figured he and his sister shared the same disdain for confrontation, having grown up in the same household. Some, like Greg, seemed to live for the fight, thriving on what tension and adversity they could create. Ethan mostly preferred to get along, unless what he wanted was in jeopardy.

"I think I will," their mother said, getting up from the table, "but I want a piece of that chocolate cheesecake first. Anybody want coffee?"

Ethan nodded. "I'll have one—and another slice of that cheesecake, please."

They were picking their letters to start the game when the front door opened. Carlyn looked at Ethan, her eyes widening as if to say, "Now, this is something new."

"We're not gonna have snow for Christmas," their father said, closing the front door with a whoosh, "but we won't be wearing shorts either. Sure is nippy out there."

Carlyn counted out her seven letters and handed the bag to Ethan. Ethan could hear his father at the front hall closet, hanging his coat up. He came into the dining room, as their mother had, as if his sudden departure hadn't happened.

"Dessert's been served, I see," he said, retaking the chair he'd occupied earlier. "Do I smell coffee?"

"Are you saying you'd like some or just commenting?" their mother asked.

"I'd like some, please," he said. His face was flushed from the outside cold. Ethan could feel the cold air still on him. "I see the Scrabble board has made an appearance."

Ethan still had the sweetness of the cheesecake in his mouth as he took a sip of his coffee. He couldn't get over what had taken place—not a word, not a gesture, not a "Sorry; please forgive me" or any acknowledgment that wrongs had been committed. It was just as Carlyn had described it. It almost would have been funny if it weren't so real.

The act went on—or maybe it wasn't an act at all. To Ethan's amazement, their father joined the game. He rarely played any game, cards being the only exception. He liked poker. Christmas Eve had returned with the gift of bewildering behavior.

They were about halfway through the game, and it was Ethan's turn. Carlyn had played the letters *T-H* in front of the *E* in *ending*. Ethan figured the wine was affecting her play, noting the three-letter word. Finding himself stuck, he decided to play off the *T* with a five-letter word and placed four tiles on the board, two in front and two behind the *T*.

"Actor," he said after setting the tiles in place. "Triple word score. Twenty-one plus six."

"Interesting," said Carlyn.

"The Actor," his father said, acknowledging not only the new word but also the two letters Carlyn had put down. "Hmm, that's a pretty good score for someone who doesn't go to university."

Ethan watched the letters on the board undulate like air rippling above a road in the distance on a hot summer day. His eyes widened as he stared at them.

Their father's attempt at humor didn't bring anything of the sort to Ethan. He watched Carlyn cross out his last score and add up his new total on the score pad.

"Well, that someone who doesn't go to university," Carlyn said in a sardonic tone, emphasizing her words, "is winning."

Ethan smiled. Carlyn was staring right at him. He let his father's comment slide.

"We're going to have to change that," their father responded. "Aren't we?"

It was their mother's turn.

"Are you really going to audition on Boxing Day?" she asked. She was looking at her letters on her tile rack but hadn't moved any.

It seemed like a strange question to Ethan. Why would he have mentioned it if he weren't planning to go?

"They called you the Actor in the hospital," his father said.

"Darren," their mother said, an edge to her voice, "if we heard that once, we heard it a hundred times. Why are you saying that?"

"I dunno," their father replied, pulling his tile rack away from his side of the board. "It just occurred to me."

"Occurred to you?" Her voice rose. "It didn't just occur to you. You know exactly what you're saying. You know it bothers me." She turned to Ethan. "Do you really have to go on Boxing Day?"

It wasn't a question. She was telling him she disapproved. This was his mother's other side, the one that had confronted him as a teenager every morning before school, questioning what he was up to.

"Why is it such a big deal?" he asked.

"Because Boxing Day is a family day," she said in no uncertain terms.

Ethan wished he'd kept to his original plan and not said anything about the audition. He'd thought if anyone would have been happy, it would have been his mother.

"We just got you home from all that," she said, moving her hand and spilling her tiles on the table. "Damn it." She started to pick up her letters. "You just get home and have to go—have to go acting no less. To what took you away to God knows where."

She pinched a tile between her thumb and forefinger and held the rest in her hand. "Because of her—because of that actress." She clenched her hand into a fist with the tiles still in it. "Mila, Mila," she repeated, her fist tight and shaking, as if she couldn't contain what was coming out of her mouth. "Mixed up in whatever crap that—"

She stopped and stared at the game board. She dropped her tiles onto the table in front of her. Her hands rose to cover her face.

"Even the game won't leave us alone," she said.

She stood up and again left the room. There was a moment of quiet.

"Maybe I'd better go," Ethan said.

He picked up the black bag that contained the wood tiles.

"You can't go, Ethan," said their father as Ethan slid the tiles off his tile rack and into the bag. "Your mother'll come around."

CHAPTER 50

Tuesday, December 25, 1984, Christmas Day

Ethan decided to stay after thinking about it a bit. Leaving would end his Christmas with no chance at redemption. He figured being at his parents' place was still better than being alone. Things usually looked different in the morning. After all, if Christmas wasn't hope, what was?

They said little after their mother's tirade. Their father headed to the den, where he likely fell asleep watching some old-time movie. Ethan heard him later rummaging in the kitchen before shuffling down the hall to the master bedroom.

After Carlyn went to bed, Ethan dozed for a while in the living room, but he was pretty awake once he climbed into his old bed downstairs. His thoughts took him from his parents to Christa to his audition on Wednesday. He went to sleep wondering what his acting would mean for the Release.

When he woke, it was light outside; Christmas morning had arrived. Christa was his first thought. He wished she were there. He got up to go to the washroom, only to recall his mother's hurtful comments about Mila and how impossible it seemed that Mila could have been mixed up in anything sinister, as his mother had alluded to. He wished he could be more excited about Christmas morning, but Mila was gone, and Christa wasn't there.

Before going to bed, he'd placed his presents to everyone under the tree. It was one of the first times he could remember being more excited about the gifts he was giving than what he might receive. He had no idea what might be under the tree for him.

He went upstairs to see who was up, his body and brain already begging for coffee. Nearing the kitchen, he not only smelled the coffee but could feel it. Someone was up.

Whoever else was awake wasn't there. The only sign of someone's presence was the lit red light on the coffee maker. He pulled down a bright red coffee mug from the cupboard. As he poured, he heard the suck of the front door opening. He was in no hurry to see who it was but figured it was his father. He was taking his first sip when his father stepped into the kitchen.

He was beaming. "Merry Christmas, Son," he whispered.

"Merry Christmas, Dad," Ethan said, surprised by his father's apparent joy. "You're lookin' happy."

"It's Christmas, Ethan; we're supposed to be."

Ethan nodded, remembering the less-than-congruent events of Christmas Eve.

"Thanks for making coffee," his father said, moving in to pour a cup for himself.

"I didn't make it. I thought you did."

"Wasn't me."

"It was me," said Carlyn, entering the room behind Ethan, "and you're welcome."

"Has your mother made an appearance?"

"Not yet, but I heard noises," said Carlyn. Carlyn's room was down the hall from their parents'. Ethan had moved downstairs when his parents had the basement finished during his first year of high school. They'd converted his room upstairs into a small den beside the master bedroom. Their mother had talked of knocking down the wall between the rooms, but like the baby grand, it hadn't happened.

Carlyn pulled a green mug out of the cupboard.

"Everything's ready," she said. "I just plugged in the Christmas tree."

"I saw that," their father answered, pulling off his coat. He hung it on the back of one of the wooden kitchen chairs. He didn't seem to be the same person who'd left the table the night before. He was excited and smiling, moving like a kid anxious to see what Santa had brought. Ethan wondered why he'd been outside.

"When your mother comes out," he said, rubbing his hands together, "don't let her in the living room until I give the all clear. Okay?"

Carlyn held her mug of coffee with both hands. With puffy, tired eyes she looked at their father. "Okay, Dad, whatever."

"Make sure is all. It's important."

Their father disappeared into the living room.

Ethan looked at his sister, raising his eyebrows as if to say, "What's that all about?"

Carlyn shook her head and shrugged.

Not a minute later, they heard the door to the master bedroom open.

Carlyn peeked into the living room after their father.

"He's got something going on around the Christmas tree," she said.

A moment later, their mother walked into the kitchen.

"I thought I heard someone up," she said, seeing Ethan first. "Merry Christmas, dear." She walked over, raised her arms, and hugged him.

"Happy Christmas, Ma," he said, leaning forward to give her a kiss on the cheek and a hug. It was the smart-aleck Christmas greeting he'd started in high school. She'd given him the gears about it then but now seemed to get a kick out of it. She smiled into his face.

"Carlyn," their mother said as Carlyn came back into the kitchen from checking on their father in the living room, "you're up too!"

"Yep," Carlyn said, setting her mug on the kitchen table and coming to greet her mother. "Merry Christmas, Ma."

"Merry Christmas, honey."

The two embraced.

"Well, look at this," their mother said, stepping back and spreading her arms as if she were addressing a group and not just their father's coat on the chair. "Aren't I the sleepyhead? Everyone's up."

"Ready for a coffee?" Ethan asked, knowing the answer and pulling another red mug out of the cupboard.

"Need you ask?" she answered.

"No, but it's Christmas. Still black?"

"Yes, please."

He handed her the filled mug. "You can thank Carlyn. She was up first."

She turned to Carlyn, nodded in acceptance, and blew her a kiss.

"Not ready yet!" called their father from the living room.

Their mother looked at them as if to say, "What's up?"

"Dad's preparing something," Carlyn said.

"Just like old times," Ethan added. "Gotta get that first picture."

"Well, enough with that," their mother said. "I want to sit in front of the Christmas tree." She turned and announced, "We're coming in."

CHAPTER 51

Tuesday, December 25, 1984, Christmas Day

Their father appeared to be ready as their mother marched into the living room, ignoring his instructions. Ethan and Carlyn followed hesitantly.

They found their spots, their father in his chair from the night before and their mother in the new armchair beside the love seat Carlyn sat on. Ethan chose the ottoman that Syd had sat on when they'd started to write "The Angel." As with previous Christmases, Ethan took the lead, handing out gifts to everyone. Each took a turn opening. Carlyn opened his gift to her first and loved the books. When he told her the story behind *Browning Station* and said the songs they'd recorded were for an animated movie adaptation, she immediately started reading. His mother loved the Lawren Harris print. Carlyn opened a new stereo, screaming as she ripped the paper off the box. Their mother questioned Santa's sanity. Their father nodded his approval upon tearing the wrapping paper from the purple box of Crown Royal. Ethan couldn't help but think they could have avoided the upheaval of Christmas Eve if he'd opened it then. They were near the end when Ethan caught his mother nodding to his father, who leaned back and pulled a shoebox-sized package out from behind his chair. He handed it to Ethan.

"From all of us. Merry Christmas," he said.

Ethan sat down on the ottoman. He pulled off the sparkly red paper to reveal a Shure microphone box. Inside was what he'd hoped to get in the New Year: a Shure SM58 microphone. He couldn't believe it.

"How did you know?" he said, standing up to hug his father and then kiss his mother.

"What about me?" Carlyn cried, holding up her hand as he turned toward her. "I'll take a hug."

He hugged her.

"Unbelievable!" he said, pulling the microphone, which was wrapped in protective plastic, out of the gray foam packaging. "Who told you—Syd?" He gripped the mike in his fist. "I know who it was," he said almost to himself. "Greg. He knew. While we recorded, he looked out of it, but he was taking it all in."

When he looked at his mother, she was rolling her eyes.

"He had us swear not to say anything," Carlyn said, seemingly as excited as Ethan was about the gift. "Dad?" Carlyn said, looking at their father and nodding.

Ethan looked at his father.

Their father looked at Carlyn. His hands were open as he squinted and shrugged as if to say, "What?" Carlyn pointed at Ethan. Ethan had no idea what she was up to, but then their father smiled, stood up, and reached behind his chair again. This time, he held up a larger unwrapped box. Ethan smiled upon seeing the photograph on the side. It was a black hard-shell case for the microphone.

"Man," Ethan said, standing up from the ottoman to take the larger box from his father, "you guys really want me to sound good." He opened the box and slid out the hard-shell case, which was also wrapped in plastic.

"That audition tomorrow," his mother said, "is looking a little different now, isn't it?"

The question caught him off guard. He didn't see the connection between the gift and his audition.

"Hadn't really thought about it that way," he said, not knowing what else to say.

"You must be thinking about it now, though," his mother replied, sitting up straight with both elbows on the arms of the chair. She was holding her coffee mug in both hands in her lap.

He noticed her stoic, maternal posture for the first time. It was as if she were sitting there satisfied her agenda was coming together. He didn't like how it made him feel. Memories of mornings before school surfaced, when she had demanded to know what he was up to, even when he wasn't up to anything, preoccupied with her ideas of teens and drugs and alcohol.

"Not really," he said, but of course he was thinking of it now. She'd brought it to his full attention. "One has nothing to do with the other."

He didn't want to get into it. Though his mother already seemed onto his concern about the audition and the impact it would have on the band, her concern was different from his. But it was Christmas morning. He wanted to enjoy these happy moments.

"Ethan," she said, the edge in her voice grating him like the rough edge of a fingernail caught on the loose thread of a blanket, "you can't possibly think you can do both."

His mother set her coffee mug down on the end table beside her chair.

"I haven't thought that far out," he lied, knowing he had. The situation was too complicated and none of her business. His eyes stayed on the front of his new hard-shell mike case.

"Well, maybe you should."

Ethan could feel the muteness of his teenage years returning. He now saw the gift for what it was—manipulation. It wasn't about singing. It was about acting.

"Okay, okay," his father said. "Let's not belabor the point. We're not done yet."

Ethan looked over at Carlyn. She gave him a confused frown and then looked over at their father.

"There's something else on the tree, Ethan," his father said, looking at his son with wide eyes, nodding at the tree.

Ethan set his case down beside the ottoman, stood up, and stepped over to the tree. Their father was pointing at a string dangling from the tree. Ethan had noticed it earlier but thought it was there to keep the tree upright. He reached for the string.

"Be careful," his father warned.

He lifted the string with his open hand. There was a small tag attached, which he read aloud: "To Olivia. Pull here. Love, Santa." He motioned to pull the string.

"No, no!" his father cried, flipping his hand for Ethan to stop. "Let your mother do it."

"Okay, Santa," Ethan replied, a little put off that his father saw the need to tell him something that was obvious. "Ma," he said, turning around to face her, "the honor's yours."

Ethan looked at his mother and then at Carlyn. Carlyn only shook her head, continuing her confused grimace.

"It's okay; you do it," their mother replied. She was sitting quietly—the beginning of a sulk.

Ethan closed his fingers around the string.

"No," their father said sternly, and Ethan could see he was already low on patience. "The instructions are for your mother."

"Okay, okay." She sighed, leaning her thin body forward as if getting out of her chair were a major inconvenience.

She stepped in front of Ethan and pulled the white string. Three feet of string came away without resistance. She kept pulling as several more feet came away. When she pulled again, the string came away from the tree and went down to the floor, where it was taped to the baseboard molding. As she continued to pull, the string followed along the wall behind the chair their father was sitting in, past the antique table beside him, and into the corner to follow along the wall perpendicular to the hallway. Pieces of scotch tape remained on the white molding. Around the outside corner of the living room, the string then took her down the length of the hallway and past the front hall closet, where it changed into a thicker red ribbon. As their mother moved down the hallway, bent over following the ribbon, they were all on their feet behind her. Ethan took up the rear, watching his father—the most excited—inches behind his wife. Their mother stepped into their front foyer.

"What in heaven's name are you up to, Darren?" she asked, her voice mixed tones of excitement and sarcasm. It was the first time she'd spoken since starting to pull the string.

"It's not me," their father replied, and Ethan could hear the smile in his voice. "It's Santa. I have no idea what this is about."

"I'm sure," their mother said as she pulled the red ribbon out from under the floor mat at the door. The ribbon continued under the front door and outside.

"I sure hope this isn't a new car," she said, the same edge in her voice that had cut Ethan's merry Christmas mood in half.

Ethan then knew what was waiting outside in the driveway.

CHAPTERS 52

Tuesday, December 25, 1984, Christmas Day

"I don't care!" their mother shouted as they all stared at the new dark blue Honda Civic parked in the driveway. There was a chill in the air, but it was no match for the frigid tone of their mother's voice. "Take it back! I won't have it!"

Upon stepping out the front door, their mother had continued to follow the red ribbon, leading them out past the front shrubs, which had blocked the view of her Christmas present in the driveway. The thin red ribbon ran along the front walk out to where it changed into an even wider ribbon, which eventually wrapped over the hood of the new car. The answer to what their father had been up to was clear. He'd likely gone to pick the car up from the dealership when he'd left the house after the abrupt end to their dinner. Though not the excuse he'd likely planned, it had provided an exit. He'd likely taken their mother's old Civic to the dealership, returned in the new car, and parked it around the corner. He'd gotten up early to park it in the driveway and finish setting up the surprise. Ethan was as surprised as Carlyn seemed to be at seeing the new car in the driveway.

"What do you mean take it back?" their father said, sounding hurt, not angry.

He was echoing what Ethan was trying to comprehend.

"I don't want it." Their mother scowled. "My car is perfectly fine. Take it back."

She turned and marched back into the house. She didn't look at either of her children.

Their father didn't say a word. To Ethan, he suddenly looked older and smaller. Bending forward, still not saying anything, he picked up the discarded ribbon and began wrapping it around his hand as if he were wrapping a wound. He walked toward the new car as he gathered the ribbon.

Ethan could do little but stare at the giant red bow that sat in the center of the blue hood, with a six-inch-wide red ribbon wrapped around the front fenders. It was the picture-perfect fairy-tale Christmas present.

"Dad," he said, his voice just above a whisper, "I'm gonna go."

"No, Ethan," his father replied, but he didn't stop wrapping up the ribbon.

"Yeah," he said, "Ma's got some stuff to work out."

"No, Ethan, you have to stay," his father said, turning, his hand now covered in the bloodred ribbon. "Your mother just needs some time."

"Yeah, I know, but I can't be here for that right now."

"Ethan, it's Christmas. We'll work it out."

Ethan didn't reply and walked back into the house. He'd no sooner made it to the living room than his mother came in with another mug of coffee. She went back to the chair where she'd been sitting.

"I don't know what your father was thinking," she said, leaning down to place her mug on the end table. "My car works fine. Why in God's name would I need a new one?"

She sat for a minute, seeming to expect Ethan to respond. He didn't.

"You'd think we'd come into a bunch of money or something. I don't know what gets into your father sometimes."

Ethan couldn't help himself. "Maybe it wasn't about money," he said, sitting down in the chair beside the tree, where his father had been sitting. He was looking not at his mother but at the Shure mike box sitting on top of the hard-shell case. "Maybe it was a gift he needed to give you."

"A gift with money we don't have."

"Ah, Ma," Ethan said, knowing he was going to say things that wouldn't allow him to stay much longer. "It's not just about money."

"Don't give me that," she said. "You, the man living on nothing."

Ethan kept staring at the new mike case. He didn't respond. He knew his silence enraged his mother.

"How did you manage to even buy gifts?"

He kept quiet but couldn't keep his cool. Anger was seeping around the edges like steam around the lid of a boiling pot of water.

"They were gifts, Ma," he said. "Gifts within my budget that I thought people would like."

"At least someone in the family knows what a budget is," she said, "but when you don't have the money, you don't have the money, Christmas or no Christmas."

Their father was far from perfect, but that didn't stop him from trying. A new car was an extravagant gift, but their mother was carrying on as if they were paupers—and paupers they were not. His father's business was doing well. She was a teacher. They didn't live in a mediocre house or neighborhood. No, there was something more at stake that he didn't understand, and it wasn't going away. She seemed on the downward spiral that never ended well for anyone. This wasn't new to Ethan. He'd lived through it over and over again during his teen years. Now didn't seem much different. His mother was warming for a full-out slaughter that she seemed incapable of stopping. The gift of a new car might have triggered her reaction, but it wasn't the culprit.

"Sounds a little like Scrooge, Ma," Ethan said, unable to stop himself from fueling her descent. "We're trying to make it a merry Christmas and leave the rest of our lives out of it for a bit. Especially the crappy shit."

Ethan knew as soon as he said it that it was the wrong thing to say.

"So it's come down to swearing at your mother. I thought I'd done a better job than that. You just never know how your children are going to surprise you."

It was over. He couldn't pull out and wasn't sure he even wanted to. He couldn't stay.

"And how very wise coming from the man with no money."

"Who says I have no money?" he said, fighting back. He knew he didn't, but that wasn't the point.

"Do you?"

"A little," he admitted, the question coming too fast for him to reply how he wanted.

"Actually, Ethan," his mother said, sitting up straight. She could easily have been at tea with her lady friends, though she'd never have revealed this side of herself to them. "How much do you have—a hundred dollars?"

Ethan wasn't about to answer such a specific question. The truth was, he didn't know and didn't really care. He had enough for today, tomorrow, and the foreseeable future. He would get by.

"If you're so worried about my money," he said, shaking his head, "keep the microphone. I don't need it."

He stood up. It wasn't anger he was feeling anymore. It was fury. His mother was trying to block the road he was on, but he wasn't about to be stopped. Shouting and tears were coming.

"I have a mike that works fine. At least to those listening." His feet were moving.

"Where are you going?"

"Home," he said as calmly as he could. "Merry Christmas."

He didn't wait for a response. He left the room and headed to his bedroom downstairs. He couldn't leave fast enough.

He put on the only pair of jeans he'd brought, along with his Carleton sweatshirt, and then packed the rest of his stuff in his hockey bag. He pulled the covers on his bed up to the pillow and looked around the room for anything else he'd brought. He wasn't coming back.

He heard a knock on his bedroom door. He didn't say anything.

"It's me," Carlyn said, her voice trembling.

He turned the knob and opened the door. Carlyn was leaning against the doorframe. The expression on her face broke his heart.

"Ethan, you can't leave," she said, her cheeks wet and shiny with tears. "I can't bear being alone for Christmas."

"Call up one of your friends," he said. He wasn't staying. He couldn't.

"We're supposed to be a family, Ethan," she said. More tears rolled down her already flushed cheeks.

"I know," he answered, rage and sadness mixing into an empty sense of unfeeling. He wanted to care, but caring was breaking him in two. He thought of Christa. He needed her. "But it can't happen right now. There's too much hurt going on. Love has its ugly side too."

He gave his sister a hug. "We've been given a second chance that we simply can't accept for some fucked-up reason," he said.

Carlyn didn't say anything; her earlier energy was spent. He grabbed his ski coat slung over the back of the desk chair, put it on, and picked up his hockey bag.

"Something has to change, Carlyn. Go set up your stereo, and listen to something."

He then remembered the cassette in his bag of what the Release had recorded. It was the only one he had. He unzipped the bag and rummaged around until he found it. Carlyn needed it more than he did.

"It's the only one I have, so don't lose it." He handed her the tape.

She smiled. Her cheeks glistened. "This is you, isn't it?" she asked, her eyes widening.

"You betcha," he said, rezipping his bag. "I gotta go."

Carlyn moved back to let him pass. He stopped and put his forehead against hers.

"Play it fuckin' loud," he whispered.

He headed upstairs to the front door. His mother was still in her chair. She was sitting forward as if she might get up. He hoped she wouldn't. If it hadn't been for his shoes at the front door, he would have gone out the back. As he slipped on his Converse sneakers, he glanced in the living room. His mother had leaned back, sitting like the matriarch she had become.

He pulled open the front door.

"Not even going to say goodbye?" she said. She was still trying to make her point, whatever it was. He wondered where the person who'd come to visit him in the hospital had gone.

"Goodbye," he said loudly enough for the only person in the living room to hear.

He closed the door behind him and walked down the front walkway. His father was coming out of the garage. He'd removed the red ribbon and bow from the hood of the new blue Civic.

"Ethan—"

"I can't, Dad. I'm going. Don't even try."

"I'm driving this back to the dealership," he said, as if it were just another day and the car needed an oil change. "Drop you at Finch?"

Ethan nodded and climbed in.

Christmas Day 1984 was over.

PART 4

CON SENTIMENTO

I like it when somebody gets excited
about something. It's nice.
—*J. D. Salinger, The Catcher in the Rye*

All our discontents for what we want appear to me to
spring from want of thankfulness for what we have.
—*Daniel Dafoe, Robinson Crusoe*

Where the sky begins, the horizon ends.
—*Tom Petty and the Heartbreakers,*
"All the Wrong Reasons"

CHAPTER 53

Do you know Frederick Craig?
It was July 1, 2025, when those words flashed across his Wristec, technology that five years ago had replaced his wristwatch. The note was from Francis, his young wife, in London. It was a strange transmission, as her messages usually started with *Hi* or *Hon.*
He paused for a moment and then thought-messaged back.
No, never heard of him.
He took a step forward, squeezing the grip of his black sixth-generation Glock 17. He could feel the weight of its power in his hand.
You have now.
He took another step forward.
"End it," Command One advised.
Abram was sure One knew what he was thinking before he did. Abram blinked his left eye to indicate a negative to the advice he'd been given.
What's up, hon? Abram messaged back.
He took another step forward. All signals were green in his contacts behind his standard-issue protective eyewear.
Sweetie, I'm fucking with you was the reply.
Abram couldn't remember Francis ever swearing over Messagenet. In fact, he couldn't remember the last time Francis had used a swear word at all.
Fuck! his brain screamed.
"Shut it down, Lieutenant," demanded Command One.
Abram's mind was in full gear. According to his military tests prior to enlistment, his mind worked at twice the speed of the average human's.

Abram blinked his left eye again. Negative. He took another step forward. All green.

Joke? I get it—ha-ha, he thought-messaged back.

How the hell could they have her? he thought. How many levels of protection was she under—four?

Ha-ha yourself—'cause I fucked her already.

Abram could picture Francis, the love of his life, facedown on a bed, both wrists handcuffed to the posts of a wrought-iron headboard and both ankles handcuffed the same way to the matching footboard. They'd left her bra on, but that was all.

"Don't take another step, Lieutenant," Command One said, "until your Wristec is down."

"Fuck you, One," Abram whispered under his breath.

They were in the breach. Abram was a capable tactician, but as talented as he was, he still couldn't be in two places at the same time. He'd intended to turn his Wristec off prior to the operation. It was part of how he worked— standard operating procedure. But he also believed things happened for a reason—always. This time, he'd left it on. His wife would have been dead now if he hadn't. She was still alive, because he was talking to her Wristec.

He motioned forward with his left foot as a light in his left contact went red.

"Fall back," Abram demanded. There were two other officers in the adjacent hallway. He watched them on the screens in his goggles. They stopped and then stepped back.

He'd barely spoken the command before the door they were approaching disappeared.

"Fuck!" Command One screamed into Abram's commpiece.

They knew. He didn't know how, but they knew. The compression of the blast would have blown out his eardrums if he'd not stepped back. As it was, he could feel fluid oozing from his left ear; the eardrum was no doubt perforated. The pain was staggering.

"What's your problem?" he hissed into his commpiece. "You're behind a fucking console."

His helmet cameras showed both soldiers down. He bent his head forward and saw his men. They lay on the ground, their severed legs stretched in front of them; they looked like puppet pieces in Geppetto's workshop. They were in shock but alive.

The sound that came next was beyond anything recognizable as human.

After a hissing like the sizzle of a steak on a hot grill and the bursting crack of tree trunks exploding came the insane shrieks of soldiers having their thighs pulled apart while still conscious. Abram's eyes were seized by the instant catastrophe. Boiling crimson liquid—human blood—burned into the walls. Chunks of flesh appeared to devour themselves on the floor below the waists of his bonded brothers. The training films that were to prepare them for these annihilating attacks were of little use to what took hold of his mind as he watched his fighting brothers-in-arms—the two he'd just had smokes with—dissolve in front of him.

You have no idea. The message flashed across his Wristec and subsequently through his mind. *Who you've fucked with.*

Abram glanced in the now open doorway. He'd led his men right to the enemy.

"Take the shot," demanded Command One.

You don't want to do that, Mr. Banks, said the message from his Wristec.

He thought-texted back, *No? And why not?*

"Take the shot!" shouted One. Command One could see exactly where Abrams had his Glock pointed.

Because the saw—

"Take the fuckin' shot!" One yelled into Abram's commpiece.

Is going to cut your wife in half!

Something else cut into Abram's communication.

That will be fine, young man.

"I can't fuckin' take it!" Abram said into the commpiece. "We have to get them out! I'm not fucking leaving without them." As he spoke, his finger squeezed the trigger of his Glock. The gun bucked in his hand as he gripped it tighter.

Beautiful man!

"They have Francis."

CHAPTER 54

Wednesday, December 26, 1984, 2:12 p.m.

"Ethan Jones."

"Francis?"

"That'll be fine," said a graying man in front of him.

Ethan recognized his name. Wherever he'd been was gone; he found himself standing in front of a man and woman now. He recognized them.

"We didn't expect you to have the lines memorized," said the woman in a blue turtleneck sweater, "but that's okay."

Ethan sat down on the black folding chair beside him. He felt a little light-headed. He remembered his father dropping him off at a bus stop near their house the day before. As he'd opened the door and set his foot on the asphalt, his father had spoken after driving there in silence.

"Break a leg, Son," he'd said, sticking out his hand. "It'll get better."

Ethan had replied, "I know," but his true feelings had been miles away from thinking it would.

He'd closed the car door while wondering just how awful his father really felt.

"We start shooting next week," the gray-haired man said, bringing Ethan back to the audition. "Are you available?"

Ethan nodded. "Yes, I am."

"If, of course, you're selected," the man added, as if suddenly remembering protocol after giving away what he really thought. Ethan was excited despite the heaviness of the fatigue that had settled upon him.

"We'll be in touch through your agent," said the woman, "but nice job."

Ethan didn't like how the woman stared at him, as if she were sizing up a dog to buy on display in the window of a pet store. His audition was over.

He was at the house when Jonah called. "You're going to be a busy man."

"I guess you heard," Ethan said, popping an Orap tablet into his mouth. He'd waited until after the audition to take one, as he hadn't wanted it to affect his performance. The audition had exhausted him. Alone, he'd felt a melancholy pall settle over him upon his return to the house.

"They're drawing up the contract," Jonah said as Ethan swallowed his medication with a mouthful of water.

"That's cool."

"*Cool* is a word for it," Jonah said, "but *fucking fantastic* is more like it. You're gonna be in the movies, my man!"

"Really!" Ethan said as new excitement eroded his Christmas letdown. More than ever, he wished Christa were around to share his crazy news. "It's kinda hard to believe."

"No, it's not," Jonah said. "You've got something rare, man, that only comes around once in a while—once in a long while."

Ethan didn't know how to respond. He kept trying to think that this development wouldn't mean what Syd had predicted; the Release would continue.

Jonah also troubled him. Jonah was in this for himself. Ethan knew that. The deal he'd made was evidence enough. But what bothered him most was that he was of the same ilk. He justified his actions, thinking he was more empathetic, but really, he wanted the same things. He'd agreed to go to the audition while knowing the likelihood of the outcome, but he wanted the part. Jonah knew it too, but Jonah had the edge; he could take Ethan there. Now that it seemed to be happening, what did he expect?

With his back against the yellow kitchen wall the phone was mounted to, he slid down to sit on the discolored cushion floor, his knees level with his chest. He picked at the frayed hole in the knee of his jeans.

"They start shooting next week," Jonah was saying as Ethan returned to their conversation. "I've some more dates for the Release in January, which we'll have to work around. Have you told anyone yet?"

"Just my family," Ethan replied, knowing that wasn't whom Jonah had meant. He had no plans to tell Syd, Greg, or Gus until something was really happening. "It'll come out sooner or later."

He rubbed his forehead with his fingertips, his elbow on his knee. He didn't want to think about it.

"It's your decision, mate," Jonah said, "but incredible things are about to happen."

As if in sync with Jonah finishing his sentence, the front door opened. Ethan expected to see Syd step into the kitchen, but instead, Gus ducked his head in.

"Howdy," he said. He waved and disappeared.

Ethan waved back, relieved. If it had been Syd, he'd have told her.

"Well, Dad," Ethan said into the phone, not wanting Gus to know he was talking to Jonah, "I'd better go. Gus just walked in."

"Gus is there?" Jonah asked.

Ethan nodded as if Jonah could see him.

"Put him on," Jonah said, and Ethan could hear the smile in his voice. "I'll tell him the whole story."

"Not a chance, Dad," Ethan said. He wasn't about to let Jonah say anything to Gus. *Let's not just ruin Christmas; let's destroy my life.* "Talk to you later. Merry Christmas."

"Merry Christmas, Ethan," Jonah said, and he hung up.

Ethan stood up and hung the phone on its shiny metal yoke.

"What's going on?" Ethan asked, raising his voice so Gus could hear him outside of the kitchen. "What are you doin' here?"

Gus came into their yellow kitchen. "Wasn't much doing at my parents'," he said, pulling down one of two glasses in the cupboard above the sink. He turned on the kitchen faucet. "I was missing my bass. Shoulda taken it with me. And you? You were pretty excited about Christmas." He filled his glass and took a gulp.

"Didn't quite turn out the way I'd figured," Ethan replied. "Too much bullshit going on." He curled the phone cord around his finger. "Christmas is a fucked-up time of year. Seems to bring out the best and worst in everyone."

"Tell me about it," Gus agreed, shaking his head. He took another drink. "I'm supposed to be fucking married with a couple of kids, like it's all I'm here to do. Christmas isn't much fun with three adults and a sick mother."

"I hear ya," Ethan said, thinking of his mother. "Your mom okay?"

Their parents didn't socialize, even though they lived only a few houses away from one another.

"Yeah, she'll be fine. Touch of the flu is all. But she couldn't go to her sister's. Old man didn't want to leave her alone, as its Christmas and all. Said I could go. I came here."

"Too bad for you."

"No way," Gus said, heading toward the living room. "I'd rather spend time with Fender Jazz any day."

He air-guitar-plucked his bass strings with his right hand while his left hand went into the air as if his fingers were already on the fret board.

Ethan smiled, thinking of the new mike at his parents'. It was nice but nothing like the feel of holding a guitar. He missed making music with his hands.

"Things must've been bad to come here," Gus said as they left the kitchen.

"Yeah, my mom's struggling with this—" Ethan stopped, realizing he was about to talk about the audition. He was almost ready to tell Gus but decided to leave it alone. "Me coming back. She can't stop worrying about me fucking relapsing."

Gus didn't reply and picked up his bass. He turned on his amp; the electric hum found his cabinet speakers.

"Whaddaya say we forget the shit for a bit?" Gus said, looking at Ethan. He started to play the opening to "Don't Tell Me."

Ethan started to sing. "You can't know what I'm feeling. You can't know who I am …"

CHAPTERS 55

Wednesday, January 16, 1985

One week turned into three before the movie started shooting. The Release was into a full schedule of shows. Jonah had them booked four nights of seven.

"I don't know how this is going to work," Ethan said to Jonah on the phone after Syd, Gus, and Greg had left for Windsor, Ontario, with their gear. They'd been invited to a party with the band they'd shared the stage with the previous weekend. Ethan had made up a story about having to see his parents about their will, so he couldn't go early. He would need the time to work on his lines. No one had questioned him, except to ask about his parents' well-being. He suspected Syd's intuition was up and on alert. She hadn't questioned any of his work-arounds, but he didn't expect that to last much longer.

"What do you mean? It always works out, Ethan," Jonah replied. He was talking fast, likely with half a dozen things on the go in addition to talking to his newest recruit. "It just doesn't go the way we expect it to. What did McArthur say? I think it was McArthur. All plans end when the first soldier sets foot on the battlefield. It's a good motto if you can ever get used to it."

"I don't know why I ask you," Ethan replied. He was holding the new Shure mike his folks had given him for Christmas, pressing the phone between his ear and his shoulder. He loved the clarity the new mike gave his voice. Carlyn had brought it by the house on a surprise visit a few days into the new year. She'd said it was sitting around the house, collecting dust. Their parents weren't returning it. He might as well use it.

Jonah let him go with instructions to call Jamie. Ethan put the mike back in its hard-shell case.

Jamie was Jonah's assistant and chief organizer. Ethan had Jamie's number tucked in his wallet. He didn't really know her but had a feeling he would see more of her than he did Jonah. There was nothing Jonah did that Jamie didn't know about or arrange. When Ethan called, she had his flight booked to get him to their next show on time. There would be a car waiting. His tickets would be with the driver picking him up from the shoot. She assured him everything would be fine.

Ethan only knew the working title of the movie—*Block One*—and that it would be filmed mostly in Toronto. He'd been told that Sigourney Weaver had been cast in the lead role with a new star not much older than he was, Meg Tilly. He was supposed to pick up an updated copy of the script that evening. But when he got to the rented space on Shuter Street—an hour of public transit from the house—the script hadn't arrived. They'd have the updated script delivered to him. He didn't want it delivered. He'd come back. They couldn't give him a time. He'd go with the script he had.

Low on patience, having not eaten all day, he decided to grab a couple of pizza slices and headed to Pizza Pizza on the corner of Church and Dundas. He carried the two slices and a can of Coke to an empty table. He sat down in one of the plastic swivel chairs and reread the lines from the script he'd auditioned with while he ate. It was strange not to remember what he'd done in the last audition. The words felt familiar; acting was like singing when the Release performed. After he'd gone through the lines a couple of times, he decided to head back to the house.

When he got back, he went to the living room, which looked empty with their gear gone. He started to read through the lines while sitting on the couch. About half of the scene was his. He'd gone over them again and again on the bus ride back. He pictured everything in his head in becoming someone else. He was getting nervous.

"Hi," said Syd. She was standing at the end of the hallway, looking into the living room.

Ethan all but leaped from the couch. There was no way he could hide his alarm at seeing Syd standing there.

"Hi yourself," he replied, his face already feeling hot and dark. He might have been an actor, but he doubted he could have looked guiltier of trying to hide something. He felt like a teen caught in the bathroom with his pants around his ankles.

"What are you doing?" she asked.

He thought she was trying to sound surprised. He couldn't help but think she knew his secret.

"I'm rehearsing. What are you doing?" he asked, answering her question with his own to give himself time to think of what next to say. He wasn't about to reveal what he was up to or ready for her reaction, which he was sure wouldn't be good.

"Rehearsing for what?" she asked, her voice flat and unexcited. "It doesn't sound like any of our songs."

"It's not," he said. It was a charade—his clues and her guesses. "Why are you here?"

"I didn't go," she said, her face showing no emotion. He knew she wasn't about to let him off the hook. "So what is it?"

She was trying to sound innocent and unknowing, ignoring his question. Maybe she was the real actor.

He was certain she knew. Based on what she'd told him in the car that night, she was the only one who would have suspected or put anything of the sort together. She was there to confront him with whatever it was he was up to, not that she ever would have told him that. He'd walked right into her trap, unsuspecting, like Batman into Poison Ivy's lair.

"So how are your parents?" she asked.

"They're okay," he said.

"Everything all right?" she asked, her intention beginning to seep into her questions.

"Not really, they want to move," he lied.

"I thought you stayed for their will."

That was what he'd said. She knew.

"The will led to moving," he said.

Syd forced a smile that looked more like a wince and went on, all but ignoring his answer.

"So what are you working on?" She moved closer to him.

"I'm putting some words together."

"Can I hear?" she asked, but she wasn't asking permission. She moved toward the folding bridge chair she often sat in to play.

"Sure," he replied, wishing he had more strength to say no. "Why are you here? You were on your way to Windsor."

"I was." She sat down. "But Greg was being his usual shitty self. I thought you could use some company on the long drive in your folks' car. Thought I could save you a favor with them by taking you in mine. By the way, where's their car?"

"I have to pick it up," he lied again.

He was out of rungs on his ladder and knew it. Syd's story made more sense than his. He was caught. She had stayed back to check up on him. The Release was her future. More than any of them, she had everything invested in the band. But in her words, he was the Release; he was her way out, and she was suspect of anything getting in the way of that outcome. Jonah was a big dot on her radar. She hadn't trusted him from the start.

"How's Christa?" she asked. It was another check on her list of observations.

"She's fine," he said, which was the truth, though he hadn't talked to Christa in two days. They'd only managed a couple of real dates between his schedule and hers, but she never seemed to leave his thoughts. She had been to Ottawa over the holiday but hadn't wanted to talk about it. He'd given her the copy of *Browning Station* he'd bought her for Christmas. She'd seemed amazed by the gift; a funny smile had crossed her face as she'd held the novel in her hands. After he'd told her about the audition and getting the part, she'd held up *Browning Station* and said this would be the part for him. "She might come over later." It was another lie.

"Yeah?" Syd gave a forced smile, and he knew she wasn't finished. "So can I hear what you're working on?"

Ethan was about to make up some words and create a whole story around a new song he was working out, but he didn't have it in him. He couldn't keep lying. Syd deserved better. They'd had an honest relationship up until Greg had caught them there in the living room. That had changed things. Now alone, he was in the same predicament they'd been in then. He couldn't mess with her again, not after what he'd said that night. The house was supposed to bring them to the truth, which was exactly what was happening, as emotional and hurtful as that might have been—real art, genuine and honest. Building another facade would take him even further away from that goal. He wasn't just lying to Syd, though; he was lying to himself. There was more between them than he'd understood until that night. Christa had changed things, but the situation was complicated. The truth was, his acting was the beginning of the end for the Release. Another lie would only make it worse.

"I am putting words together," he said, looking at the floor. When he looked up, Syd was staring at him. "But it's not for a new song."

Syd's eyes didn't waver.

"I've a part in a movie."

Syd didn't move or say anything. She stared through him as if he'd ceased to exist.

Ethan couldn't stand the silence. "There's something you don't know about me," he said, but before he could go on, Syd exploded.

"Fuck!" she screamed, and she stood up. "I knew it! Fuck, I knew it!"

"Syd, it's—"

"Don't say another fucking word!" she cried.

She turned and walked out of the living room. He heard her door slam. Ethan slid to the floor, his back against the couch.

He picked up the script. His heart hurt. He'd known what was going to happen. Acting would end the Release. He knew it, Jonah knew it, and Syd knew it. Acting seemed to bring an end to everything else he loved.

CHAPTER 56

Ethan knew there was a possibility he'd never see Syd again, and he certainly wouldn't that night, but in less than five minutes, he got a surprise. The words in the script were just becoming visible again to his misty eyesight when she reappeared at the entrance to the living room.

"Are you planning to quit us?" she asked.

He stood up, holding the script in his hand. "No," he said, ignoring what he'd come to realize would inevitably take place.

"Why all the secrecy then?"

"It's not a secret," he said, finding honesty a difficult place to be. "Acting's something I'm interested in. Like reading or hockey."

"Then why not just say that?"

Ethan hesitated. He knew the answer but wasn't ready to admit it. "Because I need to tell you how I came to be at your family's restaurant that day."

Syd went back to her folding bridge chair. She was wearing her faded jean jacket and tight jeans. The sleeve of her jacket was torn at the shoulder. Bright red socks had replaced her Converse running shoes. She pulled her legs up so her feet were on the seat, her arms wrapped around her shins.

Ethan sat down on the couch.

"I've hinted at it," he said, setting the script on the cushion beside him. He needed more time with his lines, but he owed Syd an explanation. "I was heading home from six months in an Ottawa hospital."

"I know that, Ethan. You've told me a few times."

"But I haven't told you why."

"Okay." Syd's eyebrows rose in concert with her shoulders. "Why? You have my fucking undivided."

Syd would tolerate him for a while, but he'd learned that any interference with what she wanted to do pissed her off and became an obstacle to get past.

"I met a girl." Ethan paused, unable to say her name.

"Christa," Syd said, filling in the blank. "I know this part too."

"No," he said. The mention of Christa's name caused him to wonder what she was doing. He couldn't let it interrupt his explanation. "Not Christa. Her name was Mila."

Syd didn't say a word. Her right leg slid off the chair.

"Mila was the love of my life," he said. He looked away, feeling his throat tighten. He couldn't break down. Tears would only misdirect what he was trying to explain. "She was murdered by my roommate."

He waited. The tears held on. Syd didn't move.

"I went away," he said, realizing after he said it that it wasn't enough to explain what he'd gone through. "I withdrew. I created a world inside my head. I can't remember any of it, only feelings."

He stopped. He was doing okay.

"When we met at the restaurant, I'd been living in my head for half a year. I'd only been back for a few weeks."

Again, he stopped and looked at her. Syd was looking at the floor, one red-socked foot sweeping back and forth.

"Okay, but why are you telling me this?"

He was going to tell her more about the hospital and his recovery but decided it was more self-serving than purposeful to what he was trying to explain about acting and what it meant to him.

"It was Mila," he said before fully thinking out what he was saying, "who brought me to acting. My ability—"

He hesitated again but went on before Syd could say anything more.

"I've been scared for a long time—scared that I will go away again and not come back next time. I don't know why I came back."

Syd didn't say anything, but her eyes didn't move from his.

"I go there now. And come back. That's what you see when I'm performing."

Ethan listened to what he was saying. In telling her, it was as if he were explaining what he was experiencing to himself.

"It bothers me how I don't remember anything after I go away. It freaked me out at first. I don't know why I come back. But I do. I get more used to it all the time. I shunned acting because of it."

He stopped, but he wasn't finished. "I don't want to stop performing with the Release, but I can't ignore acting anymore."

He held up the script. "I don't know why it's happened this way," he said, looking from the script to Syd. "Jonah threw gasoline on an ember in my gut. It didn't just light up; it exploded. I feel helpless to do anything but accept it. It's like I can't not do it. My first audition was before Christmas. We start shooting tomorrow."

A long pause followed his explanation. Syd sat quietly, seeming to take it all in.

"What about us, Ethan?" she said finally, her passion growing with each word. "What about the Release? What about what we've fucking created?"

"I'm not leaving the Release, Syd," he said, trying to convince himself as much as Syd. "I don't want to."

"But you fucking do!" she shouted. "You can't help yourself!"

She was standing and shaking her head. Her fists were clenched at her sides. Her thin arms shook, as if she wanted to strike something—anything.

"Once this acting shit gets going, it's over. Fuck the Release!"

Ethan could see the rage in her face, as he had the day she'd destroyed the guitar outside Focus Sound.

"Syd," he said, holding the script out as if he were offering it to her, "I can't change how I feel. It's nobody's fault. I'm trying to do the right thing."

Syd stood still, as if ice had suddenly filled her body.

"The right thing?" she screamed, pointing her finger at him. If a mere look could have ripped a person apart, Ethan would have been shredded. She grabbed the chair she'd been sitting in and flung it across the living room. "If I hadn't been here, nothing would have happened! I fucking caught you!"

Ethan didn't say a word. He had nothing left.

"You should have fuckin' told me—told us," she said, walking toward the hallway. "This is a shitty way to find out." She stopped and turned. "Do Greg and Gus know?"

Ethan shook his head.

Syd brushed her hair from her forehead. "I hope they hate you, you fucking coward!" she yelled, and she disappeared down the hallway.

Ethan cringed, more inside than out. Maybe he didn't know what he wanted, but he didn't want this. Acting was everything. Acting gave the Release their edge. Their original songs and new arrangements of cover tunes were good, but his acting made them come alive. Syd knew that better than anyone—even better than he did.

The door to her room slammed. This wouldn't be the end. Syd was a fighter. Minutes later, she reappeared with her jean jacket in hand and stood at the entrance to the living room. She looked at him for a second and then turned and left, slamming the front door on her way out.

Ethan didn't know what to do. He went back to the couch and picked up the script. As hard as it was, he started to read through his lines again, committing them to memory. It would take some time before his head was back to the person he was to portray. He could feel the person in the words. It wasn't long before they weren't words in a script. The feeling he got from acting again was like the balance that came back when riding a bike—a familiar comfort that was difficult to understand and even harder to explain but nevertheless real. His emotions with Syd were real but became part of his art; his hurt became his character's hurt.

He didn't want to imagine, nor could he imagine, doing anything else.

CHAPTER 57

Where his lines went, he didn't know. They were his words, but not what his character was supposed to be saying.

"Cut! Cut!" shouted Jake, directing the scene. "That was your line." He glared at Ethan. "Stick to the script, please."

"I know," Ethan replied, frustrated, shaking his head, at odds with himself for not producing his line.

"Do you need more time?" Jake asked, rubbing his bicep and then shoving the sleeve of his shirt up his forearm. His unshaven face accentuated his bloodshot eyes.

"No, I'm good," Ethan said, feeling the exact opposite.

"Okay then, let's go again," Jake said. "On script. When you're ready."

A guy in black jeans who looked about Carlyn's age raised the slate and banged the clapper.

"Action."

Ethan started. He paused before he spoke, only this time it was his character's intention to do so.

The solemnness of the church where they were shooting struck him; the hardwood pews were rigid against his thighs, and the worn wood rails were smooth in his hands. There was a musty dampness in the air.

"Cut! Great!" were the next words he heard. He saw Jake stand up from his cloth chair. "The pause works. Rewrite!"

When he came back from wherever he'd gone, Ethan couldn't remember what he'd said. He'd become the person he was portraying. It was a good feeling yet unsettling, as if his conscious mind were trying to pull together the pieces of a pleasant dream as they faded. It didn't matter. Jake seemed happy.

251

His mind might have been displaced with who he'd become temporarily during that first morning shoot, but his itinerary to get to the Release's show in Windsor now filled his thoughts.

The taxi was waiting at the gate when he came out of Lakeshore Studios. It took him almost an hour to get to Pearson from downtown. The night's set was going through his head as they drove up to the front of the terminal building. Cheap Trick's "If You Want My Love" was playing on the radio and struck him as another tune the Release could cover.

"Terminal One, Departures," the driver said, stopping at the curb.

"Thanks," Ethan said, climbing out.

"Whoa!" the cabbie shouted. "It's twenty bucks from downtown, man."

"Sorry. Thought it was paid," he said, as he'd thought Jamie had it covered. He hoped he had enough. He had only a ten and a five in his wallet. "Shit!" he said as his hand slipped into the front pocket of his jeans. A crumpled five, change from coffee that morning, brought him relief. He handed the three bills to the cab driver.

"Have a good one," called the cabbie.

After making his way through the lineup for his gate pass, he headed to the gate. He got there to find his flight was delayed twenty minutes. Jamie's well-organized schedule was getting squeezed.

Rather than sit and stew about getting to the show on time, he decided to call Christa. After finding a vacant pay phone, he dialed her number.

By the fourth ring, his mind had wandered back to his missed lines.

He'd messed up several takes. After his lapse, he could only remember Jake standing up excitedly.

"Hello?" Christa answered.

"You're home," Ethan replied, her voice causing whatever else he was thinking about to vanish.

"Just got in. Where are you?"

"At the airport."

"The airport?" she said, sounding surprised.

Ethan had expected her to be surprised. When they'd last talked, he'd just received the film schedule. Things were happening almost quicker than the plans to put them together.

"Yeah, my first scene was today."

"No way!" Christa said, all but yelling into his ear. "That's awesome! How'd it go?"

"It was cool." He was about to tell her more when she came back to her first question.

"Why are you at the airport then?"

"We've a show in Windsor tonight. With the shoot today, it's the only way I can get there in time." He paused and looked at his gate pass. "But my flight's already been delayed, so who knows?"

"It'll work out," Christa said.

"I'd expect you to say that," he said, smiling and thinking of Jonah's last words, "and I hardly know you."

"You keep saying that," she said, "as if I'm someone you met in a bar. It's not like that."

"It kinda is," Ethan said, chuckling to himself, thinking of the night at Benny's. Many things about her ran through his head. She knew much more about him than he did her; she'd mentioned things he knew nothing about. In their time together, they had only scratched the surface.

"You know what I mean. When are you back?" she asked.

"Not till the weekend," he said, knowing he was flying back in the morning for another shoot only to come back later for their second show. He thought of his lie to Syd and the guys about driving his folks' car. It hardly made sense. "We're back at Tormo next week. London after that. Then Bogart's in Ottawa. Or something like that. And filming in between."

He wanted Christa beside him and wished she could have come with him. It was strange how their relationship didn't have the anxiousness of a new one but, rather, felt like an old, established one.

"My shifts change next week," Christa said. "I'm on nights and two weeks of hell."

"I'll find you when I'm back," Ethan replied.

"Okay, I'll hold you to it."

"Do that."

That ended their call. Ethan hung up feeling good that Christa wanted to see him. Back at the gate, he discovered his flight had been delayed another fifteen minutes.

The knot in his stomach tightened.

CHAPTER 58

Thursday, January 17, 1985

His flight was an hour late landing due to snow. Five minutes after getting off the plane, he found his driver holding a sign with his name on it in the small Arrivals area of Windsor Airport. The two hustled to the driver's snow-covered car. Toronto had had no snow. There was no act too brazen for the driver to get Ethan to the arena. Red lights, the posted speed limit, and even illegal U-turns didn't slow the drive.

When they entered the arena's parking lot, groups of teenagers reluctantly moved to let them pass. Single-finger salutes and foul curses muffled by the car's closed windows followed them in. The driver stopped as close as he could to the front entrance. Clusters of kids stood outside, seemingly immune to the snow and the cold, while a line of people filed in. As they left the car, Ethan noticed the musty-sweet smell of pot in the air. The driver guided him through the crowd. Most were cooperative and let them pass unencumbered. Inside, the mixed aromas of tobacco and weed were stronger. Ethan and his driver entered the large lobby and the Plexiglas viewing area into the rink. Memories of his winters as a teen surfaced. He thought of his father sipping coffee from a Styrofoam cup at his early-morning hockey practices. It seemed ironic now that it was music, not hockey, that brought him to the rink. Moving through the crowded lobby, Ethan noticed the rink-side windows were dark, covered in black draping. There would be no watching hockey from the lobby that night, which was a little surprising, given it was the middle of January. They kept moving.

The driver, who hadn't shared his name, pushed open the swinging rubber-edged doors into the ice area. There was a growing crowd around the temporary stage that backed into the lobby's windows they'd just passed.

Rows of gray folding chairs lined the plywood-covered ice surface. A lot of work had gone into converting the rink into a concert hall. Ethan guessed the arena had a three-thousand-seat capacity and maybe another four hundred on the covered ice surface. The Living Cult had quite a following in southwestern Ontario. The crowd and the venue were evidence of that. He wondered how many in the audience had even heard of the Release, much less knew any of their songs.

Ethan felt anxious anticipation for the night's rock show. It was a little hard to believe that in a matter of minutes, he'd be performing on the matte-black stage in front of him.

"You're in dressing room two," his driver said as they descended the stairs.

"I feel like I forgot my equipment," Ethan said as they passed the red-painted handrails that separated spectators from the aisles.

"Your mike case is in the dressing room," said the driver. "I dropped it by on my way to the airport in case we were late."

Ethan smiled, as his attempt at a joke had been lost on the driver. The equipment he'd been referring to was hockey gear. He didn't bother to add that he was the only singer.

The driver knocked on the door and then pushed it open. Gus and Syd were sitting on one of the painted benches that lined each side of the dressing room.

"Sorry I'm late," Ethan said, walking into a room that immediately brought back hockey memories.

"Glad you could make it," Syd said, standing up. "We're supposed to be on in five minutes—four fucking minutes ago."

Ethan turned to thank his driver, who had already disappeared. "Where's Greg?" he asked, taking off his ski jacket.

"No fucking idea," Gus replied, shaking his head. "He partied with the Living Cult last night in London. I drove the rest of the way on my own."

"Fuck!" Ethan said. He'd thought he was the only one to worry about.

"Hans is pissed," Syd said, and she nodded in the direction of the door. "Who the fuck was that?"

"One of the arena staff I asked where to go," he lied, not wanting to get into anything before stepping onstage.

"I hope he told you," Syd said. "Like fire and brimstone."

"Hans?" Ethan asked, letting Syd's comment slide.

"A piece of work," Gus said, cracking his fingers.

"He's an asshole," Syd said. "Wasn't gonna give us a dressing room 'cause only two of us were fucking here."

"I'm sorry," Ethan said, and then he slipped up. "The plane was late."

"Plane?" Gus said. "You flew? What the fuck?"

Ethan looked at Syd. She shook her head and looked away.

The door swung open.

"Yer ready?" asked a gray-haired man with a ponytail and curly pork-chop sideburns. "Yer on in two."

"We need—"

"We're ready," Ethan said, interrupting Syd and nodding as Hans turned away. The door closed. On the opposite bench was a Detroit Red Wings cap. Ethan went and grabbed it. "We'll start with 'Don't Tell Me.' Gus, you start. Hit it hard. Repeat the first bit twice—no, three times. We'll follow and hope the fuck Greg shows up."

"That's Hans's," Syd said, pointing to the hat in his hands. "You fucking wear that, and you might just get to die onstage."

"I won't be alone," Ethan replied.

Gus didn't say a word. He didn't need to. Their set would evolve on the stage.

Ethan put the Red Wings cap on backward and then looked at Syd. "Eyeliner?"

Syd went to her bag, pulled out a small tube, tossed it at him, and then glared. A sink and mirror were behind a protruding section of cinder-block wall at the back of the dressing room. The mirror was cracked. A shower and toilet were beside it.

"What are you doing?" Syd shouted as Ethan went to the mirror.

"Preparing," Ethan replied. Despite their predicament of a missing drummer, he felt surprisingly calm. "The show must go on."

"You're fucking nuts!" Syd yelled, smiling. She knew.

Gus was strapping on his bass. Syd was holding her white ES like a teddy bear, with both arms around it. The door opened again.

"Yer on!" shouted gray-haired Hans.

Gus, with his Fender Jazz in place, looked at Ethan as if nothing out of the ordinary were happening. He nodded and left.

"This is madness!" Syd screamed as she slung her guitar strap over her head. "Absolutely fucking nuts!"

Ethan couldn't remember seeing her look more excited.

CHAPTER 59

Ethan was climbing the temporary aluminum stairs at stage right when Gus hit the first low notes of "Don't Tell Me." The house lights dimmed. The stage lit up. Gus was at center stage. Ethan could only imagine what Greg's friend Steve was going through in getting their lights and sound up from the limited access he likely had to the headliners' sound equipment. But Gus looked and sounded great. The music swelled Ethan's heart. Excitement like electricity filled the air. Gus's playing had never sounded so good. His buzz-saw bass notes had a chest-ripping resonance through the arena, like the gut-wrenching power of a race car rocketing up to speed. Adrenaline surged through Ethan. He could only imagine how Gus felt as he heard his bass rumble through the arena, shaking anything that wasn't fastened down. Ethan looked up into the darkness of the rafters and then at the crowd. Most were standing. The darkened rink and melodic thunder Gus was pounding out caused many to hustle toward the stage, silencing the din of conversations Ethan had walked into only moments before.

As he stepped on the stage, teens were moving through the open doors in the white hockey boards. Syd sauntered into the stage lights, her guitar riff ripping through the dark air of the rink. Together they sounded magnificent. Ethan climbed behind Greg's drum kit, which he figured Gus must have set up. He would pray and at least try to keep the beat. He only hoped Steve could keep up with their improvised start on the mixing console.

As Gus repeated the first part of the song for the third time, Ethan started a simple rhythm on the rim of Greg's snare. He'd keep a steady beat, sing to Syd's guitar accents, and pray Greg was just late. He kept glancing stage side. They were screwed if Greg didn't show soon, no matter what condition he was in; Greg seemed to play better high. The drugs appeared to relax him and quiet whatever was humming around inside his head.

Ethan hadn't played two bars of his click beat when Greg jumped onto the stage, opposite where the rest of the band had come on. A cheer rose from the small crowd gathered around the front of the stage, as if it were a choreographed part of their show. They could have rehearsed for weeks what happened next and never come close to what they pulled off.

Greg took over his drum stool as if Ethan wasn't there, never missing a beat in their improvised start. He looked high but lively.

"I can—"

Syd's guitar riff overpowered Greg. He frowned and shook his head.

Ethan looked up in time to see Syd glaring at Greg, playing as if her guitar were a low-slung shotgun pointed at the last person she wanted to see yet needed to see. Ethan knew she wouldn't let Greg forget she didn't appreciate his disappearing act, but their show would go on.

Gus was all over his bass. Center stage was an unusual place for him, but he seemed to relish in its glory. He was coming to the end of his groove-pounding start with Syd trailing on the guitar when Ethan raised his new microphone to his lips. He didn't move from his place beside the drum kit.

"You can't know what I'm feeling. You can't know who I am," he sang into the tight-wire mesh of his mike. No one could see the source of the voice coming through the PA except for the few standing right in front of the stage.

The crowd erupted as he broke into the second part of the first verse.

"But I'll always be here for you, no matter where you think I am."

Several people pointed at him. He took it as his cue to move out beside Gus to sing the next line. He then bent forward and closed his eyes, feeling his long hair fall around his face. He screamed the next line.

He gripped the mike tighter, its weight apparent. When he opened his eyes, Syd was beside him. He couldn't hear what she was saying but understood the words "One Thing." He turned as Gus approached her. She mouthed the same thing to him and then pounced on the final chord of "You Don't Know What You're Saying." Ethan's present had missed the set, but his somewhere else had been very present.

In seconds, Syd jumped on one of her effects pedals and was into the first chords of the Fixx's "One Thing Leads to Another" as Gus pulled the bass line apart. It would be the last song of their night.

Ethan was quickly aware of where he was. It was the first time they'd played the song live. He smiled, remembering the night of Syd's arrangement of "American Woman" at Benny's. They were pulling out everything to finish, considering their nearly disastrous start.

As they played into the final chorus, the house lights came on. Confused for a second, Ethan realized they'd worn out their welcome—but not with the crowd. Therein lay the problem: the crowd loved them too much.

They kept playing in the full brightness of the arena's house lights with no less intensity. Ethan kept singing. A moment later, the power was cut. Ethan could hear only his own voice and Greg's drums. The crowd started to boo.

At the best of times, performers were insecure out there in front of an unknown world; ego got all mixed up in the fold. The Release's playing too long and too well with the crowd cheering had surely pushed the Living Cult beyond what they could take. The Release had broken the cardinal rule: no matter what, the opening act couldn't outshine the headliner, no matter how good it felt. That night, a jealous headliner dealt with the situation the only way they knew how. Competition was the enemy.

It was the last time the Release would open for the Living Cult. It was the last time the Release would open for anyone.

CHAPTER 60

Thursday, January 17, 1985

Knowing why they'd been kicked off the stage didn't lessen Ethan's anger. But it wasn't deep and faded quickly. He was more bothered by the pettiness of the action and getting shut down while playing a good song.

"What the fuck was that?" he yelled, running down the stairs of the short corridor to their dressing room. The crowd's disdain continued; the booing grew louder. The audience was never fooled.

"What are you talkin' about?" Greg shouted right behind him. "That was amazing!"

Syd was next and then Gus. Both had their guitars, never wanting to leave them unattended at shows where someone might damage or, worse, steal them. The growing angst of the crowd made them even more cautious.

"Brilliant, Eth!" Gus cried, pulling a can of Budweiser out of the cooler that had become part of their entourage. His Fender Jazz was already in its case on the benches across from them. "What a way to start the show!"

"Saved your fucking bacon tonight, buddy," Ethan said to Greg, catching the can Gus tossed him. He pulled the aluminum tab. "Wait. Everybody get one."

Gus tossed cans to Greg and Syd. Greg's sprayed against the wall as he opened it, splashing Syd.

"You're so fucked!" she screamed, opening her can in Greg's face. She laughed as she emptied it on his head.

"You bitch!" Greg shouted, shoving past her to grab another can while wiping the beer from his face. "Without me, tonight would not have happened."

Syd turned, her eyes wide in disbelief. She stood in front of her guitar case as if she were guarding it. "Without you?" she shouted. She pointed at Gus. "Without fucking him, you mean!"

Gus smiled and raised his can. "To the Release!" he said, and he tossed another can to Syd. "And new beginnings!"

"Just like every night," Syd added, popping open her second beer.

They all raised their cans and drank.

"Let's have another!" Ethan yelled, digging in the cooler for four more after downing his first. He was experiencing a feeling like the band's name—the release of pressure built up from the show, his shoot, and his schedule. It was an addictive roller-coaster ride of never-ending ups and downs. When it seemed to be done, he knew it wasn't over, and he found himself wanting and needing to repeat it again and again. He tossed a new can to each of them.

"To what ends and then starts again," he said. He downed his second beer as if it were water. That he could only remember the beginning and the end of the show didn't bother him; it had become the norm, no longer the exception. "I don't want to open for these fuckin' guys again."

He crushed his beer can and reached for another. The first two had gone down quickly, as if he were discovering the taste of beer for the first time.

"I don't think we have to worry about that," Syd replied.

"What's up with turning on the fucking house lights while we're playing? We pumped up their crowd."

Syd raised her red, white, and blue can of Budweiser. "To the Living Shit!" she cried.

"Fucking eh, Syd!" he shouted. Ethan looked at Gus, who looked spent.

"I don't know what we'd have done if you hadn't showed." Gus sighed, flopping onto the bench against the wall. "I can't take too many shows like that." He set his beer can down on the bench beside him. The bench, like the dressing room and much of the arena, had seen its share of abuse, despite the cover of red paint. "My heart's too soft."

Ethan turned to Greg. "So," he said, feeling the effect of guzzling a few beers in quick succession, "what's your fucking story?"

"Not much," Greg replied as he pulled another beer out of the cooler. "The fucking bastards knew what they were doing. I didn't catch on till it was almost too late." He opened his can and drank. "Fuckin' wanted me to join their band, the fuckers. I took a taxi here."

Ethan looked closely at Greg, but it was Syd who spoke.

"You coulda called," she said.

"Who the fuck would I call?" Greg said, changing the tone in the dressing room.

"Our manager maybe?" Syd said, her head bobbing like a bobblehead doll, as if the answer were only too obvious.

"Never occurred to me." Greg sighed and took another gulp. "I don't have his number."

"Really?" Syd said, looking to Ethan. "Well, he is *our* fucking manager. Maybe you should."

Ethan didn't say a word; she'd said it for his sake, not Greg's.

"I still can't believe it," Gus said, looking as if he were about to become part of the bench he was lying on. "This was my best night ever."

Ethan nodded. Gus had saved them from all-but-certain disaster in front of their biggest crowd since opening for REO Speedwagon. Ethan wondered just how good Gus could be under pressure, as it seemed to up his game, even though he didn't like it.

The pounding boom of the Living Cult starting their show overpowered any more conversation.

"You know," Ethan shouted, looking to Syd and then Gus, "I've heard enough of this fucking band! Let's go for a drink. We'll come back when the show's over."

He didn't have to ask twice.

CHAPTER 61

Thursday, January 17, 1985

"Fuck off," Syd sneered above the din of the bar and ZZ Top's "Tush."

"Why the fuck do you always talk to me like that?" Greg asked, his back stiffening as she glared at him. "I've never done fuck to you."

"And you're never going to either," Syd snapped, turning to look at Ethan. "'Cause after Bogart's, I'm done. I'm staying in Ottawa."

Ethan stared back at her. She'd taken off her makeup during their brief stop at the motel and wrapped her hair in a mauve scarf. Her announcement was news to Ethan. It was no doubt in response to what she'd walked into at the house. This was her other side, her tough, get-even side. It was a side desperate to win her music and do whatever it took to win—the same side that had made her leave Ottawa to join a band in Toronto.

"You're quitting the band?" Gus said, displaying something between a question and outrage. His tone was sharp and sardonic. He set his empty glass down hard on the table and looked right at her. Disbelief seemed to sober him up. "Really? And why now?"

Ethan was silent. He wasn't surprised, but wasn't entirely sure it wasn't a bluff. Yet again, he had misjudged her. He'd explained he wasn't quitting, but that didn't seem to matter; he'd hurt her again. It was time to get his.

Gus looked at Ethan. "You fucking know about this?" he asked, but before Ethan could say anything, Gus seemed to know the answer. "You do!" he shouted. "Fuck! So much for my great night."

He stood up and walked away from them.

"So," Greg said, looking at Ethan after sitting quietly. He set his glass on the table carefully, as if it might break if he weren't really careful. "What the fuck's going on?"

It had only been a short time since Ethan had asked Greg the same question.

Ethan shrugged. "Why ask me? I didn't fucking say a thing."

"Exactly," Greg replied. "You haven't said a thing, and that's unusual. You're looking like you have nothing to do with this, and my money's on the opposite being true."

Ethan hated that Greg seemed to know him better than he knew himself. "What do you want me to say?"

"Try the fucking truth," Greg replied, and he looked at Syd.

"He's auditioning," she said.

Greg looked at Ethan. "What?"

"He's auditioning," Syd repeated, staring at Ethan, "for a movie or something."

"What the fuck?" Greg said, scrunching up his face and shaking his head as if trying to clear it.

"Tell him, Ethan," Syd said.

Ethan frowned. This was not how he'd envisioned telling the band, not that he'd imagined much. Each time he started thinking about it, he didn't like where his train of thought went, so he never got to an end. He didn't want to hurt anyone yet seemed to hurt everyone. Now the revelation was happening too fast and in turmoil. When Jonah had approached him, he'd known this scene would eventually take place. He'd tried to convince himself that what was best for him would be best for the Release, but he had known, as was now evident, success in one would lead to the demise of the other.

If he were honest—and honesty seemed all his bandmates wanted, though he was finding it difficult—he knew acting wasn't the experiment he was pretending it was. After the first audition, sitting on the bus back to the house, he'd known. He'd known when he finished the audition after Christmas. Even when Syd had found him in the living room, rehearsing his lines, less than twenty-four hours ago, he'd known. He'd known after Jonah's question "Ever done any acting?" Acting was in his heart and out of his control.

Time had mended both the sadness and the horror in his heart. Time had changed how he saw acting and remembered Mila.

"Yes." Ethan nodded. His palms flattened on the tabletop. He sat up in his chair. "Yes, I auditioned and won the part."

"What was that?" Gus said, returning to the wood armchair he'd been sitting in. He slid in closer to the table.

"Just more fucking around," Greg said, dropping to his chair's four legs after having been leaning back on two. He wore a grin Ethan recognized as the one he produced when he was trying to look relaxed but wasn't. "So what's the plan?"

"Plan?" Ethan asked, thinking he could get ahead of or at least catch up to what looked like his intention to dissolve the band. "There's no plan. A few obstacles to get around is all."

"A few obstacles?" Greg replied. His grin was gone. "Care to fuckin' elaborate on that, Eth?"

"Okay, okay!" Gus shouted. "Wait a fucking minute. I left, and Syd was quitting the band. What fucking plan are you talking about?"

Gus was angry. He usually held a pretty even temper, but Ethan could see it was fraying.

"All right, fuck," Ethan said, his voice loud above the bar's noise and Foreigner's "Hot Blooded" in the background. "Here's what happened. Last night, Syd found me at the house, rehearsing lines for the movie I auditioned for after Christmas. We shot the first fucking scene today. That's the reason I had to come down after you guys, not because I had to see my fucking parents. Syd's announcement is a surprise to me."

Syd didn't move. Her legs were crossed, and her hands were clasped together, fingers intertwined, over her knee. Her eyes hadn't left Ethan throughout his explanation. She was seething.

"You're shooting a fucking movie!" Greg yelled out. "Are you fucking nuts?"

Ethan shook his head. "No. No, I'm not."

"You shot part of a movie today?" Gus repeated.

Ethan didn't think Gus could have looked any more amazed if Mick Jones and Lou Graham of Foreigner suddenly had appeared in front of them.

"Yes, I did," Ethan replied, looking from Gus to Greg and back again. "Jonah set it up. Thought I'd—"

"Jonah? Jonah fucking Vetch?" Greg said. His voice rose in shock or anger—Ethan couldn't tell which. Maybe both.

"Yeah, Jonah Vetch, our manager."

"You're joking! You're fucking making this up," Greg said with a wide-eyed look of incredulity. "Am I missing something here, Eth?" His eyebrows rose as if trying to open his eyes wider. "Our manager is breaking us up?"

"No!" Ethan yelled, angry at what was taking place after one of the best nights the Release had ever had. "Nobody's fucking breaking us up!"

Ethan shook his head in frustration. "Syd is pissed at me. I get it. I fucking get it. Quit the band. I don't give a shit. I'm not quitting. We just had a fantastic night that we're fucking up again with our bullshit. I'm sorry I did the movie. I thought in some fucked-up way, it might make me a better performer. But this shit isn't worth thinking about for another second. I fly back for the shoot tomorrow morning. Then I'm fucking done! I'll call Jonah and tell him, all right?"

Ethan stopped. Greg and Gus didn't say a word. Syd looked at the floor.

"There it is, Syd!" Ethan growled. "Now you have it. Still want to quit? Then quit, and stop fucking us around!"

Ethan couldn't remember being so mad at the band. Every step seemed to be monumental. Instead of celebrating, they were ripping themselves to shreds again and again. No one could stand someone else's success. Success was like a sickness that grew from a never-ending series of highs and lows; quitting was incentive to keep going, and those who did achieved things beyond anything they could have imagined. Success defied logic—logic that seemed to have little to do with much outside of satisfying the rightness of one person over another. Logic killed creativity and the imagination, yet the world bought into it as if it were the only real truth. Logic was the virus that kept people from trying new things, leading them to refuse the unbelievable and believe the ability to predict an outcome was actually possible. Success was unpredictable. What looked like all the right ingredients could turn into something fruitless. Yet when nothing seemed right, defying logic, success happened. But living with success and logic was the real tragedy. The Release couldn't bear a single night of success. Ethan found himself too angry to even face his bandmates now.

"I've had enough of this fucking party," he said, pushing his chair back, scraping the legs across the worn wood floor. "I'm going to the motel. See you tomorrow."

"Ah, come on, Eth," Greg said as Ethan stood up. "We need to fucking talk this out."

"No," Ethan said, gripping the back of the chair he'd been sitting in. It was hard to hold his voice steady. "You guys need to talk it out. I'll go wherever. London, Toronto, Ottawa—doesn't matter. I'm in this band."

He didn't wait to hear more and walked away, heading to the front of the bar.

"Hey there!" a female voice shouted as he approached the front door.

He didn't know anyone in Windsor, so someone calling him seemed unlikely, yet he turned. At the end of the bar closest to the entrance, two pretty faces were smiling at him. One woman was blonde, with straight hair cut just above her shoulders; the other had wavy red hair in full Farah Fawcett–esque bloom. Both were wearing loose blouses with the top buttons undone. The redhead looked to be the one who had spoken.

Ethan hesitated. He wanted to be alone to think about what had just taken place with the band. Talking with two women together at a bar without any apparent male company was not a means to that end.

But curiosity led him toward them as the redhead waved him over. He glanced back to see if the others were watching. They were face-to-face in conversation.

"That was an awesome show," said the redhead as he approached, her voice loud above the background music of the Rolling Stones playing "Satisfaction." "You guys were amazing!"

"Thanks," he said, standing behind them.

The redhead stared and smiled.

"I'm supposed to review the Living Cult for the paper," said the blonde, turning from the bar with a brown bottle of Canadian clutched in her hand. "She said they were good."

Ethan smiled, not knowing what to make of the two. "Really?" he replied, his right eyebrow rising. It was too early for the show to be over. "That's why you're here now?"

"Yeah," the redhead said. She paused. "But your band changed all that."

The two laughed.

"Lauren," the blonde said, "you can't fake anything."

"It's not what I do," said the redhead, who then smiled at Ethan, revealing dimples he hadn't noticed before. "He's here, isn't he?"

"Not really," Ethan said, not wanting to stay, "but it was nice to meet you."

"Your show was great," Lauren replied quickly, turning to look at him. She seemed to know she was a knockout, and that made her less attractive to Ethan. "Loved your songs. Can we buy you a drink?"

"No, thanks, but the rest of the band is in the back, and they're thirsty."

He pointed in the direction he'd just come from.

"If it makes any difference," said the blonde, who now faced him, "we left because we'd already seen the best act."

She went on to say they'd loved the start of the show.

Ethan savored their compliments along with their closeness and perfume. Their presence was intoxicating, like too many beers. But it was Christa he was thinking about.

"Ladies," he said, turning to look at the door, "I can't imagine this ever happens to you, but I have go."

Neither woman replied. The woman named Lauren seemed to wince a smile. Ethan extended his hand and shook theirs.

"Again, it was nice to meet you. Come out and see us again sometime."

He then turned and left. As with his earlier thoughts on success's burden, he could at least try and steer clear of temptation.

He didn't make it to the door before the situation with his bandmates returned. Whether there was logic in success or not, he knew he couldn't keep the promise he'd made them.

CHAPTER 62

He thought of taking a cab back to the motel but realized he'd given the cabbie in Toronto most of his money. It would take him half an hour to walk. He thought the cold air would do him good. What little snow had fallen had melted.

Things were crumbling, no matter how he looked at it. For a time, he'd thought the Release had rescued him from acting, but life seemed to have other plans. In spite of his attempts to block it out, he was ill prepared to deal with the power acting held over him. It was there, recognized or not, bold, steadfast, and beckoning—not unlike his love for Christa. He was powerless to its appeal. Understanding where it came from was like trying to understand why he'd been born into the Jones family in the first place.

Even now, walking alone down the sidewalk along an unknown street in the cold, he could feel his character from the morning shoot. The desire—the overwhelming propensity—to transform into someone else was captivating. He longed to get a glimpse into someone else deeply enough to understand why that person did things—to go below the surface and do things outside of his own rules, values, and behavior. To go somewhere someone else went—somewhere he would never choose—and to do so for reasons different from his own was a chance to re-create life and, in essence, become who he might really be. It was love, a feeling of connection that even music didn't bring him. He loved making someone else's thoughts, words, and feelings into his own. He loved acting.

Both hands were tucked in the front pockets of his worn Levi's. It was cold. The frayed holes in the knees of his jeans didn't help. He'd worn the same jeans onstage, having intended to change into the newer pair he'd brought. He wished he had now.

The jeans brought him back to thinking about his day, a day that shouldn't have happened. Filming in the morning, to most, would have been more than enough. His plane's delay had seemed like a sign their show in Windsor wasn't to be. But living life wasn't about having everything in check. "The show must go on" wasn't just a cute adage. It was a way of living. There was always a way with a willing participant—adjust here, rearrange there, remove, revise, and improvise, but keep going. Maybe second chances were just part of what was supposed to happen anyway—part of a plan to reach an end that wasn't really an end at all but, rather, a point in time, unknown and uncontrolled, not human to understand but fitting with a grand master plan that wasn't his to know but instead his to discover and love. Maybe second chances were the infinite, uncountable points that together made a life, that one could only make sense of looking backward and that were little more than guesses looking forward.

He came to the end of the street. A late-model Volkswagen Beetle passed, followed by a yellow taxi. He paid little attention and turned right. The motel was another ten minutes toward the center of town.

No doubt the band was good; their original songs were really good. Syd and Gus were great musicians. But he was an actor, not a musician. Somewhere between his conscious and subconscious selves, he could transform himself. It was a gift he was only beginning to realize. Acting had his heart. He hadn't chosen it; it had chosen him. To fight its power was futile. He'd tried.

He crossed the street after another car passed. It wasn't snowing, but he thought it could. As he approached the motel, he noticed most of the parking lot was full. He saw Syd's Corolla. The place was quiet, asleep, like he wanted to be. He climbed the stairs to the second floor balcony and stopped at the number on his key. After unlocking the door, he walked into the partially lit room; they'd left a floor lamp on beside the television. As with most motel rooms he'd stayed in, the TV was the focal point and sat in the middle of the wall opposite two single beds. They'd flipped a coin to see who would sleep on the sofa against the wall at the end of the room. Greg had lost, so he would be in no hurry to get back, not that he ever was. At the beginning of road life, they'd agreed that Syd would have her own room whenever possible. Most of the time, it worked out. Occasionally, Syd wanted to mix things up and have one of the guys take the single; she'd stay with the other two. It was only fair, but one big, happy family they were not.

Ethan was glad for the warmth of the room. He didn't realize how tired he was until he pulled off his sneakers. It was painful to stay awake. He wondered what might have happened had he stayed with the blonde and redhead. Curious temptation might have kept him there given different circumstances. He dropped onto the bed.

The real reason he hadn't stayed was Christa. She was a phone call away if she wasn't working. His eyes closed as he thought of her and the meds he hadn't taken that day.

He was on the cusp of sleep when the phone beside the bed rang. The ring was like the sound of a fire alarm, startling him from the spongy motel pillow.

Instant rage made him lunge sideways, and he swiped the phone off the nightstand between the beds. *Unbelievable.* He turned over.

The room returned to silence, with an occasional car passing outside in front of the motel. He closed on sleep again.

But in the quiet, as he was on the borderline of sleep, someone was talking. The person was not close enough for him to make out the words but was loud enough to hear.

God damn it. He just wanted to sleep, but sleep wouldn't overrule his trying to hear.

It was a single voice, not quite out of earshot.

He rolled onto his back to listen.

Was he hearing things? He opened his eyes. It was still there, quiet and tinny like a transistor radio. He wasn't imagining it.

"Hello," he heard.

He rose up on his left elbow to listen closer. He hadn't turned off the light beside the television. He slid his legs off the bed and sat up.

The phone had landed on the floor between the two beds. The handset, its cord a lifeline to its base, sat just beneath the adjacent bed.

His rage at the phone ringing simmered to agitation. He leaned over, hooked his fingers into the base, and returned it to the nightstand, the handset banging against the bottom of the bed.

"Hello?"

He heard the voice again, plainly this time. He grabbed the phone. "Hello."

"It's about time."

"Christa?" Ethan shouted his surprise into the phone.

"Were you expecting someone else?" she said.

"No," he said, at once feeling guilty about his thoughts of the two women, "but I wasn't expecting to hear from you either."

"Didn't think so," she said. He could have listened to her talk all night. "Surprised, huh?"

"You could say that," he said, sleep already losing ground to the sweet sound of her voice. "What's up?"

"Nothing, really," she said, but something in her voice told him different. "Want another surprise?"

"Do I have a choice?"

"Why don't you come down to room 212?"

Ethan sat up. "No way!"

"See you shortly, my dear."

CHAPTER 63

Thursday, January 17, 1985

Ethan couldn't get to room 212 fast enough.

He slipped his sneakers back on and found a clean T-shirt, the one with the Who's black-and-white album cover of *Quadrophenia* on the front. He packed up his duffel bag and locked the door behind him. Christa's room was eight doors away. He half ran and half walked down the balcony. Small cones of light illuminated the room number beside each door. He could feel the cold, but it didn't matter. Outside of a car passing, there was no activity in front of the motel. There was no sign of his bandmates.

He reached number 212.

The door beside it was slightly open.

Ethan stopped as if he'd been lined with a two-by-four across the chest. He couldn't explain what he felt or why; he didn't understand it, but he knew he'd been there before. Bad things were behind the door.

His heavy door was back and close. He'd faced the door in front of him before. He knew there were things behind it he couldn't bear to see—agonizing things that, like a giant claw, would rip open his chest and squeeze the life out of his heart. He was too close. The padlock on the heavy door was open.

He didn't move; he couldn't. The three copper-colored numerals marking the room seemed to shimmer in the dim light. The numbers meant nothing, only that he'd been there before. His heart pounded, pulsing in his ears. He couldn't catch his breath. It was all he could do to put his hand on the door. The surface was cool and smooth. He pushed it. The door didn't seem to move, yet the strike plate in the doorjamb was visible; it had to open.

He could hear his own breathing. He attempted a deep breath to control the pounding in his chest; an aching pulse began behind his eyes. He feared what he was going to find behind the door. There would be blood and carnage, but he had to go in.

She was inside.

He pushed harder, forcing the door off the jamb. His vision blurred. He could feel the door moving. He pushed harder. The door faded. He kept moving, continuing to push.

The room was dark, yet he knew where he was. He remembered. It seemed such a long time since he'd been inside the room yet not long at all. He knew what he would find. He could feel the blood.

His fingers were sticky. There was a fragrance in the air, her fragrance—Givenchy. Then he saw the destruction. Her apartment—no, their apartment—had been destroyed. Shards of broken glass from their full-length mirror were on the parquet flooring. A lamp was upended, its lampshade crushed. The bookcase was on its side, its books a jumbled heap on the floor. The television screen was smashed. Her green antique vase was in pieces on the floor. *Her?*

"Ethan! Ethan!"

Someone was shouting. It hurt to listen. It hurt to hear.

He kept moving forward on feet that didn't seem to be his.

The upended white plastic deck chair was near the doorway. He didn't turn his head. He knew what was there. Blood was on the walls. He couldn't bear the sight again. He could hear her name repeated again and again. It was his voice but coming from someone else.

"Ethan!"

The scream was chilling and close. Had it been louder, his head might have exploded.

"Christa! Christa!" he heard. He was crying out her name.

His feet stopped moving. There was crimson on the wall, shaped into what looked like a giant red apple.

"Ethan! Stop!"

The image on the wall shattered into a thousand fluttering pieces.

He turned toward the voice, looking in the direction he had avoided only a moment before, sure of what he would see.

She was in front of him, lying in the vibrant crimson that filled her bed. Broken hands with fingers at inhuman angles were clasped behind her head. Her long, beautiful hair was tangled in a mess of blood, bone, and skin. He wanted to turn away. He had to.

"Ethan!" cried the voice, which seemed to come from inside his head. "Ethan, you're here! It's—"

He couldn't look away. Christa was in front of him. He saw the blood-smeared chalk-white bone and the skin torn from her skull. Streaks of blood were on her face.

God, please! his brain screamed.

"Ethan! Please come back."

He dropped to his knees; his whole body trembled. Her fingers were now locked in his.

"You can't take her again!" he yelled in a voice that was his and not his.

"Ethan, I'm here," Christa sobbed. He could see her brown eyes inches from his own. "It's okay."

Her voice was little more than a whisper.

The broken glass and the books were gone.

"Ethan?" Christa whispered, her tenderness melting his heart.

Could it really be? The destruction he'd seen was no longer there.

"Ethan?"

"Yes," he answered. He was on his knees. Christa was kneeling in front of him in pink pajamas.

"Are you here?"

"Yes, I am," he said, remembering the door and seeing the room number. He continued his stream of thought out loud. "I don't remember the door opening." He paused, thinking hard to remember what was already gone. "Or coming in."

"You know where you are?" she asked.

He nodded. He was in her motel room, but he had gone somewhere else. He'd been there, and now he was here; the in-between had become impenetrable space in his memory.

"Yes, but it's unbelievable."

"It is?" she asked, worry pulling the corners of her mouth down and lining her forehead. She turned her head, her uncertainty apparent. "Why is that?"

He laughed. "Are you kidding? You? Here in Windsor?" He shook his head and put his hands on her thighs. "You," he said, squeezing her legs, "right here. Unbelievable."

Christa grabbed his hands and pushed them away. She stood up and moved to the bed.

"Wait a minute," she said with a strained smile.

"What?" he replied, knowing something wasn't right but choosing to ignore it.

She sat on the beige bedspread that covered the bed. It was identical to the one on the bed he'd been lying on in the other room.

"Ethan," she said, "are you really here?"

"Yes, I'm here, Christa," he said as if needing to convince himself. "I see the TV, the bed, the night table, and a beautiful woman."

As he said the words *beautiful woman*, Christa seemed to relax and leaned back, her arms behind her on the bed. The hint of a smile curved her lips.

"I know you don't understand," she said, her words seeming to bring her comfort. "You probably think it's funny, but a minute ago, you weren't here."

It was anything but funny, but he didn't reply. Tight-lipped, he looked into her eyes, thinking they were the only link to the gap left in his memory.

"To most, you don't look any different," she said, sitting up. Her feet were on the floor. "But I know that look in your eyes. That absent look—your body's here, but your head isn't."

"How can I make you believe me?" he asked.

He got up to sit beside her. Despite his calmness, the hole in his memory was troubling. It was like waking from a deep dream and remembering nothing yet feeling different. He remembered coming to her door and touching it and then hearing his name and being on his knees in front of her.

"Kiss me," she said, staring into his eyes, not studying him like before but searching for something he knew only she could find. "You are here, aren't you?"

Ethan didn't answer. It wasn't a question but an affirmation. He nodded. They'd spent little time together—or at least little that he was aware of—but their chemistry was undeniable. He felt no anxious nervousness on what he should or shouldn't do around her. It was as if she were part of him. He'd found the missing piece of his puzzle that for so long he'd thought was gone forever. An excitement and energy came from just sitting beside her. Things were supposed to be this way. He didn't need to understand why.

Christa leaned against him. The smooth, warm skin of her forearm grazed his. It was the best feeling in the world. He turned. His lips touched the softness of hers, at once both new and age-old. They came together as naturally as two people could. The kiss was soft and momentary, over before it seemed to begin, unveiling a hunger he could not imagine ever being satiated. The intensity was instant. Their lips hardly separated before she kissed him again, harder and longer.

Ethan slid his hand along her thigh, melting between her legs. Her mouth opened with his, as hungry for him as he was for her. Her warm, impossibly soft hand touched his face like a sculptor molding him to her.

Time hardened.

His arm encircled her back. His hand touched the velvety smoothness of her arm and moved down her side and under her pink pajama top. He pulled her closer, her lips melding into his, her sensuous tongue searching for his. He was beyond needing her. They were finding each other as only two souls could.

She pulled his T-shirt over his head; he couldn't pull his arms through the short sleeves quickly enough. His fingers touched her warm, soft breasts beneath the pink fabric of her top. His palm brushed her nipple, her trembling body matching the exquisite sensations passing through his. His tongue sought more, deeper, anxious for what he had to give and she had to receive.

He guided her sideways, but she resisted, instead pushing him back. Without speaking, she stood up and slid off her pink bottoms. Ethan remained on the bed as she knelt down in front of him, her brown eyes not leaving his. She undid the top button of his jeans. In love's choreography, he lifted himself off the bed as she pulled off his ripped Levi's. With what seemed like frustration, she yanked off his sneakers and crumpled jeans together. Standing, she turned and backed into him, the backs of her long, slender legs smooth atop his bare thighs. She bent, her sculpted curves sliding along his strong legs. To touch her was magnificent; each time felt like the first, again and again. Ethan couldn't help himself; he traced her heaven-soft thighs from hip to knee and back again with his fingertips. As he caressed her, she pressed against him, harder and harder. His fingers then slipped under her thigh into the hidden softness between her legs.

Ethan was having difficulty holding back; he wanted her. Still, Christa pushed into him. He kissed her unblemished back and lean shoulders. Her perfume was intoxicating; her skin was hot to his lips as his tongue tasted her salty skin. They turned together, and with Christa lying on her back, he squeezed her thighs and kissed her velvety softness.

Her slender fingers slid up his back, tracing paths he'd never known existed. She pulled him on top of her, her fingertips and nails pressing their way down his sides as if knowing the pleasure their play gave him. Her fingers were strong. When she touched his erectness, exquisite rapture enveloped him, unbearable to endure yet impossible to refuse.

He moved to cup her breast. She pushed his hand away and slid out from under him. In front, she took him into her mouth. An unearthly gravity he was incapable of resisting forced him backward onto the bed. Her hands moved along his thighs as her lips massaged him before she plunged him back into her mouth.

Seeming to sense his imminent climax, she let go and pulled herself on top of him. He slid inside her. It was heaven. He could have died there, held tightly within her femaleness; their love was perfection. Each movement was glorious in its beauty and delight; each moment embodied the innocence of two souls together, the essence of love's purity.

Each downward thrust of her hips took him somewhere else. She fed the ravenous animal inside him. She cradled his face in her hands, carrying him away with her blissful kisses. He fed on her tongue and lips, unable to relinquish either as he pushed deeper and closer to her soul as she closed on his.

At the moment, he could climb no higher; the sense of his own mortality bore down on him. He was so close, as if birth and death were converging for a single instant during which he might glimpse the meaning of his own life. In the next instant, he climaxed as she clutched him, ejaculating again and again with all the life he had to give.

He groaned as he held her tightly chest to chest, knowing the moment was over yet not wanting to let it go. She slid her legs down along his, holding him inside her, not ready to part. He wanted to stay there forever.

He moved to roll out, only to meet her resistance again.

"Not yet," she whispered.

He opened his eyes to find her staring at him.

Her brown eyes answered his as she whispered, "It's okay. I want to be with you."

Ethan smiled and closed his eyes.

CHAPTER 64

Morning arrived to pounding on the door.

"Yeah?" shouted Ethan, groaning before he saw Christa beside him.

"That you, Eth?" shouted Greg through the door.

"Yeah," Ethan called.

"Who's that?" Christa mumbled, lying on her side beside him. A bedsheet covered them.

"We're fucking done here," Greg said.

"Yeah, yeah," Ethan said, speaking barely loud enough for Christa to hear, let alone Greg standing outside the door. Sitting up, he spoke louder. "Just a minute."

It had been a long time since he'd awakened beside the woman he loved—a very long time. But that didn't seem to make any difference to the usual plethora of thoughts that crowded his mind upon waking.

He'd promised to tell Jonah he was done with acting after the day's shoot.

Yeah, as if he could. Syd was quitting the band—was she really? Weren't they playing in London next week for two or three nights? It didn't matter; they would be back at the house that night. *Rehearse and tomorrow go back to Tormo—no, that isn't right. And Christa. How did she get here? Drive?* If he could only go back with her. Gus and Greg would take the van. Syd would drive alone, as she'd come. *Likely wants to be alone anyway. Wonder if she'll really quit.* Had they already packed up the gear? They'd be pissed that he hadn't helped. Had they tried to find him? How had they found him? Was his mike case in the van?

He looked at the time on the room's clock radio.

The taxi to take him to the airport would be there soon. He'd better get to the door. Greg would update him on last night. At least he was still talking to him. Gus would be in the van, waiting. Syd was likely on the road already. He couldn't remember his starting lines for that day's scene.

"Ethan," Christa said as he pulled on his canvas sneakers. Her warm hand flattened against his naked back. Her touch felt good. She spoke just above a whisper. "Will you drive back with me?"

Ethan's mind reversed upon hearing her invite.

"I'd love to, but I can't," he said, leaning back across the bed to kiss her. "A taxi is coming to take me to the airport. I have another scene to shoot just after lunch today."

He didn't want to leave even for a second. Her hand remained on his back. At least he didn't have to come back for another show.

"Things are going to change," he said, standing up. The light sheet covering Christa slipped from her shoulder. She did not try to cover up. Looking at her made thinking of anything else nearly impossible. He just wanted to touch and hold her, run his fingers across her smooth skin, and press his skin against hers. He closed his eyes. He didn't want to leave but had to. It was all he could do to put on his T-shirt and tie his shoes.

"Christa," he said. He didn't want to think about all the other things running around in his head.

"Ethan," Christa said. She sat on the bed, uninhibited, the sheet around her waist, looking at him. "That was the best night of my life. I didn't think it would ever happen."

She smiled with lips that seemed to cry out for his.

"I'll catch you back in Toronto in the next few days," he said, feeling awful that he was leaving after she'd traveled so far to see him.

Unable to resist, he went back to the bed and kissed her as if it were the last time he would get the chance. His hands caressed her shoulders. He wanted to stay and talk. There was much still to talk about. *What was I like in the hospital? What have I told you? What have you told me? Who are you?*

"I gotta go," he said as if he were convincing himself. He stepped away.

Christa pulled the bedsheet up around her neck. "You know my number," she answered. "I didn't expect you would stay. Was it a good surprise?"

He looked at her again, his eyes widening. "Are you kidding?" he answered, again questioning his own sanity to leave. "I still can't believe it."

"I can't believe it either," she said. She stopped yet looked as if she had more to say.

Ethan, wearing the shining grin of a man in love, didn't reply.

"I imagined it but never thought you'd come back," she said.

Ethan leaned over and kissed her again. His eyes didn't leave hers. "I did, and I will again," he said, and then he opened the door and left.

PART 5

BATTAGLIA

But Oz never did give nothing to the Tin Man
That he didn't, didn't already have.
                    —*America, "Tin Man"*

Yesterday's gone down the river and you can't get it back.
                    —*Larry McMurtry, Lonesome Dove*

CHAPTER 65

Thursday, February 7, 1985, The Last Day

The words were in his head, but they seemed mixed up. "Good Times Bad Times," their last song of the night, was what he was thinking about, but the words were from "When the Levee Breaks": "Cryin' won't help you; prayin' won't do you no good." Both were Led Zeppelin, but they hadn't played both—or had they?

He didn't know where he was. He was shaking around in some kind of truck. *Al's truck maybe*, he thought, but that wasn't right. His eyes were open, or he at least thought they were, but he couldn't see anything. Something covered his mouth and was stuffed in it. Squinting, he tried to see, and he was quickly alarmed when he couldn't. Something was stuck to his face and wrapped around his head. Greg's long baby fingernail and silver cylinder were images in his head.

"Where the fuck are we going?" a voice said. It was Syd.

"Shut the fuck up" was the angry male reply.

"No!" she screamed.

Oh fuck, Ethan thought, becoming more terrified with each passing instant. He remembered Bogart's back hallway. Strong hands had grabbed him.

"I'm not part of this, you fuck!" Syd shouted. There was an audible slap.

"He said to shut the fuck up!" growled another voice.

Ethan tried to move but couldn't. He was on his right side and being shaken about on a hard-ridged floor. He pictured the inside of a delivery van. They were moving. He couldn't feel the arm underneath him, but his other arm was bound behind his back to something. His ankles were tied together, his left above his right. With all the shaking about, he figured they must be

285

on a rough road. He could hear and even feel the rumble of the engine. His right side hurt.

"He's fucking moving!" shouted the first male voice, which seemed close.

"Shove the cloth in his face," answered the gruff voice.

"Fuck!" Syd's shriek pierced the air. "This wasn't the deal!"

"You are the deal, sister," snarled the same ugly voice, "and if you don't fucking shut up, I'll cut out your tongue and feed it to you."

Ethan jerked as something was mashed into his face. Not seeing anything and then feeling the sudden contact brought a terror that shocked him nearly unconscious. He tried to move against whatever he was tied to but couldn't. He was helpless—a feeling he'd never had in his life. *What could possibly have happened? It can't be real.* Whatever was stuffed in his face had the sweet smell of rotting garbage. It brought back the hallway, the fluorescent lights in his face, and Greg and Gus in the dressing room. Whatever they were riding in lurched sideways. His body bounced painfully across the ribbed surface he was lying on. His shoulder glanced off something sharp. Pain flared in his knee.

The sweet, acidic aroma of what smelled like tequila floated around his head.

CHAPTER 66

Eyes Open—First Time

Ethan knew the song. It was popular. Fleetwood Mac's "Don't Stop" was playing somewhere around him.

Why not think about times to come
And not about the things that you've done?

He heard every word.

He opened his eyes. He was lying on his side with his head on an ugly green carpet. The carpet fibers dug into the side of his face, prickling his skin. He could feel the hard surface the carpet covered—probably cement. He recalled the carpet that covered his parents' basement floor. Maybe there was some underpad in between, but he doubted it. He was somehow fastened to the floor. He couldn't move.

Four pieces of wood were in front of him at right angles to the carpet—legs of a chair. The toes of two polished black boots were in front of the wood pieces, a foot from his face. He couldn't see above the black laces. He had no idea where he was or who was in front of him. It didn't matter. He was in trouble—for reasons he didn't know. Fear evaporated any fog that had been in his head. He was awake. Fleetwood Mac playing in the background did nothing to comfort him. He'd never been so scared.

His mind was racing, trying to figure out why he was there. The words of the song seemed to contradict that it was because of something he'd done: "And not about the things that you've done."

But how could he think he was there for any other reason?

His mouth was covered. The covering felt like heavy duct tape. He could only breathe through his nose. His knee hurt. More memories were coming back with each second—the back hallway at Bogart's, his face close to the ceiling lights. Still on his right side, he couldn't feel his right arm. He could feel his left arm, but it was bound behind his back. They'd been in a moving vehicle. Syd had been there. He'd heard her voice; she'd sounded scared.

"Good evening, Ethan," said a voice he didn't recognize. It was deep, electronic, and horrifying, similar to Darth Vader's voice. A person—at least he thought it was a person—was speaking through some kind of device. Its creepiness was terrifying.

"Welcome to your new home."

The voice sounded real, but he tried hard not to believe it. He closed his eyes. If he could have spoken, he would have screamed.

His mouth was stuffed with something that felt like a sock against his tongue.

"You don't need to speak," said the altered voice. "I will refrain from asking you questions that might suggest you have to respond."

Ethan opened his eyes again, praying he would wake up in his room at the house, ending the nightmare. He didn't. The green rug, the chair legs, and the black boots were real. Because of the way his head was positioned on the carpet, he couldn't see through his right eye. What he saw was real—all of it—but that didn't stop him from hoping it wasn't. He might still wake up. The polished shine of the black boots looked militaristic. They didn't move.

"This will be where you will live now," the unreal voice said, "until, of course, you're dead."

There was quiet except for Fleetwood Mac in the background.

He'd never been told such a thing.

"You made me do this," the voice said. "You. You brought this on yourself. In time, you will come to understand that. You could have prevented all of it."

Something akin to a chuckle followed and turned into a sickly cackle. If it hadn't been so real, Ethan would not have believed the terror it carried.

"Are you religious, Ethan?"

Ethan could do nothing to respond. A titter followed the question.

"Oh, there I go already. The questions do slip out. I'm sorry. My bad. I did say I wouldn't ask you any questions."

The boots didn't move.

It is a nightmare. The boots never move.

"This doesn't seem real, does it?"

This time, triumphant laughter followed the question. Christine McVie was still singing in the background.

"Well, let me tell you this, my friend: it is!"

The last two words were screamed into Ethan's left ear.

"All you need to remember, Ethan," the voice said, calmer, "is—"

The voice stopped. The shiny black boots parted slightly. *The boots move. But this can't be real.* Ethan pictured the person wearing them standing up.

"I am now your hope, your fear, and your truth."

The voice spoke calmly. The sound was unreal.

Ethan tried to straighten his legs. To his amazement, he could move them.

"Please don't," said the voice, "although I'm a little surprised you haven't tried to already."

Ethan moved his legs again.

"Stop moving!" shouted the voice.

Ethan stopped.

"See this boot?" the voice asked as the toe of the right boot moved closer to Ethan's face. "Of course you do. Why am I asking you anything?"

There was another pause.

"It's important you remember this boot, Mr. Jones. Here, behind the black leather, is a piece of steel. It's meant to protect the wearer—me in this case—but in here, it's meant for you. Its purpose for you is opposite its purpose for me. It's not to protect but to inflict."

The toe tapped Ethan's forehead four times. He counted. He didn't know why. Each tap was a little harder; his fear escalated with each one.

"Remember," said the distorted voice. It paused as if knowing the horror it instilled. "I am your hope, your fear, and your truth. Don't forget it. It will help you understand—maybe."

The shiny black boot hit Ethan on the forehead again. The blow was much harder this time, connecting just above his left eye. It hurt with the maddening pain that followed a strike to the nose. His instinct to fight was immediate. He struggled to move his head. His fear, for an instant, became frustrated anger.

The black boot rose above his head. The wearer placed the clean black sole gently on the side of his head.

"Are you listening, Ethan?" the voice asked in a tone of care and kindness, softer despite its electronic synthesis. "I know you can't speak, but you're still answering. I said to stop moving. You're not listening."

The pressure of the boot on the side of his head increased. The sole pressed against the curled skin at the top of his left ear. As the force grew, his ear began to scream with agony, as if someone were pressing a burning cigarette against his skin. He watched the weight transfer from the boot on the green carpet to the one on his head. The heel of the boot still on the carpet rose as the other pressed down on his head even harder; his ear went numb. The force was like having his head clamped in a vise. Just how much could he take? The boot on the carpet was on its toe. He closed his eyes. He couldn't bear to watch the boot come off the floor, as was sure to happen. He hoped his legs wouldn't move.

"Enough?" asked the voice, which seemed to come from a distance far above his head.

Ethan prayed it would end.

"Oh, my bad again."

The pressure was released. His pain eased. He opened his eyes. The boot on the carpet had come back down. The bottom of the other boot remained on the side of his face.

"Sorry. I forgot you can't answer. But you did listen. You're a fast learner, Ethan."

The background music had changed. It was an old tune—classical, famous, almost familiar.

"Time will tell, as time always does—just ask William."

The titter-cackle that followed sounded like the Wicked Witch of the West in a pool of water.

"Get it, Ethan? William Tell."

Ethan—barely coherent in his fear—scarcely comprehended what was said. As the voice made reference to William Tell and the boot came off his face, Ethan knew the music.

"I always felt bad for poor Tonto," the electronic voice said, as if talking to a dinner guest. "He does all the work, while his masked companion gets all the glory. And we all bought into it."

Ethan remembered the show he had watched as a youngster. He hadn't known the theme song was "William Tell Overture" when he'd watched *The Lone Ranger* on his parents' black-and-white TV set.

"I think that's enough for now," said the voice. "Let's call this the end of lesson one."

The boots moved away from his face to a position beside the legs of the wood chair, or what Ethan thought was a chair.

"I probably went a little further than I would normally," the voice said, trailing off into electronic silence, as if the person behind the voice had started to think of something else. "But you're an advanced student. Aren't you, Ethan? You're what's known as a quick study."

Ethan's fear grew, as he sensed something more was about to happen—something painful. He did his best not to move.

"No, that doesn't quite fit," the voice said. "This was more of an introduction than a lesson. Lessons need to leave their mark on a student. There's no mark here—except for the red one on the side of your face. No, that wasn't a lesson."

There was another pause. Ethan already hated the so-called lessons.

"Yes, we will call this the introduction, though the two of us are in no need of an introduction. I need only introduce what this is all about."

Though Ethan was listening, he only caught "the two of us are in no need of an introduction."

They knew each other? How was that possible? Then a thought plagued him: he'd heard somewhere that most victims knew their attackers.

"Now, before I go," said the voice, controlled and direct, speaking as if reading from a script, "I must confess I'm calling these lessons because they will be lessons. Not lessons learned from others' mistakes. No!"

The voice stopped after yelling the last word. It seemed irritated and was quiet for a moment while the charge of the overture went on.

Apprehension readied Ethan for what might come next.

"No!" shouted the synthesized voice, crackling the speaker it was transmitting through. "No, no, no! It's not right. It's so, so wrong. We learn nothing from the mistakes of others."

There was another pause. Ethan waited, his terror growing with each silent second. He didn't move. He was doing everything he could to stay still despite his distress.

"Ethan," the voice said, sounding calmer, "how do we learn?"

The voice asked the question as if they were a couple of guys shooting the shit over a couple of beers.

The overture played on.

"There I go again," said the voice, "asking you a question you can't answer, but you've already learned from your failure, haven't you? That's the key! Do we learn—I mean really learn—any other way? We have to live it—experience it. It has to become part of who we are. We don't learn that from others explaining what they learned. We don't feel anything that way. Their feedback is information, to be sure—it's knowledge—but we don't learn until we do it!"

The last three words were screamed so loudly that whatever device was reproducing the voice couldn't contain it and broke into distortion, driven beyond its capacity.

"Look at this, for instance," the voice said, regaining a calmer mien. "I can read about kidnapping and confinement, about torture and killing. Picture it vividly in my mind. Plan it meticulously. Even write it down in a detailed plan. I could even role-play it. Ah, maybe that would be a little difficult, given the material. And yes, I'd be prepared and well intentioned, but that's all. I've imagined what to do and what will happen. But I won't learn a thing about kidnapping and confining a person against his or her will until I actually do it. Until I'm in the real situation, I really know almost nothing. It's all talk and no action—sound familiar? I wonder what the ratio of bullshit to action is. A hundred to one? A thousand to one? Who knows? But I'm going to find out. When this is over, I'll know what it's like to kidnap a person, confine a person against his or her will, and bring another life to its end. I'm going to fail along the way, and when I do, I'm going to learn."

The electronic voice stopped. Ethan closed his eyes, terrified. *God, if you're there, please help me.*

He waited.

"So an introduction is what we'll call it," the voice said. "An introduction to life in captivity—a confined life. I like that. An introduction may, and often does, include an example of what's being introduced or the subject matter, but it's still an introduction."

The voice paused again. Ethan blinked. The black boots were still there and seemed very real.

"I feel good about this, Ethan—really good."

Ethan was sure he heard the clicking sound made when the tongue was flicked across the roof of the mouth—real but electronic.

"What about you, Ethan? How does the actor turned musician feel?"

The voice stopped, and the last words churned inside Ethan's head with the accompaniment of the overture in the background. Focused on not moving, he tried to recall where he'd heard "the actor turned musician" before. *In the hospital maybe?* He knew only that he had. But the phrase brought something else that wouldn't leave him alone. He knew hurt was coming. How did he know—precognitive fear? Maybe. The music continued as he tried to decide whether he was obeying by not moving or disobeying by not answering—which he couldn't. Rationale was not a partner here. Would knowing who had said those words help him?

"Aha! You are listening and learning," said the voice. "You passed. You know something? I'm going to add to this story. You know, in grade school … What am I saying? Of course you know in grade school. We're the same age. The textbooks we read from, and hated, often had questions at the end of a chapter to test us little people on whether we'd paid attention, which most of us hadn't. I'm going to change my plan here. You see, Ethan, all plans change when we start to do. Until we start, we're only imagining. I imagined all this, but that was different from having you, my captee, present. You know, I've wondered about that word. Is it really a word? It's used in the book I'm reading, but I can't find it in the dictionary. But it does work! I'm your captor, and you're my captee. It's beautiful, no?"

The voice stopped again. The music changed to Steve Winwood's "Higher Love." The Release played that song. He sang it. It usually made him think of sunshine, wind, and freedom, but he felt sickened now to think those things might never be real to him again. His stomach turned. *Don't think.*

"So I'm going to add a test question at the end of each lesson."

The voice seemed excited, talking quickly at a higher pitch.

"Yep. And that question will be for you, Ethan—my captee."

There was a momentary pause.

"My captee!" the voice shouted, the electronics crackling.

Like a gunshot going off close by, it startled Ethan. His legs shifted, as did the contents of his stomach, which moved up into his throat. His cheeks bulged, pressing against whatever covered his mouth, as his vomit erupted. There was no exit but through his nose. His eyes closed with the sudden pressure as he gagged. Pain exploded in his head as the hot, acidic contents of his stomach exited through his nose. He opened his eyes to see a brown mess soiling the green carpet in front of his face; his head was still fixed to the floor.

"Oh fuck!" the voice screamed. "You moved! I thought you were learning, you retard!"

Ethan's left eye was open as the puddle of puke from his nose grew. A large knife blade flashed before his eye.

He started a silent scream.

CHAPTER 67

Left Eye Stays Open

The knife blade moved quickly, slicing an opening into whatever was covering his mouth. A prick of pain lit up his lip, but it was nothing compared to the exit of vomit through his nose.

"What is wrong with you?" demanded the voice. It wasn't a question. "You're like a pathetic little girl who ate too many SweeTarts from the candy store. You're not choking to death on my watch."

The hole cut in the material was not big. Some of the puke left in his mouth extruded through the sliced opening like diarrhea.

"One minute, I think you're learning," the voice said, "and the next, you make me lose all confidence that you have any ability to learn whatsoever. Is that why you couldn't finish your first year of engineering?"

The voice sounded angry, as if what was happening were Ethan's fault.

"You're weak, Ethan. Do you hear me? W-e-a-k. Weak."

Gary Numan's "Cars" started to play in the background. Ethan couldn't help but notice the vocals' resemblance to the voice speaking to him and recalled the lyrics "Nothing seems right in cars."

Ethan could see the shiny blade of the knife. The part of the polished steel not covered in brown puke glistened. Fear was turning him inside out, yet he could do nothing to hedge it. Expecting the knife to slice into his neck next, he prayed. The blade remained not four inches from his nose, as if the voice wanted him to inhale the smell of his own gastric juices. His sinuses burned from what had gone through and now blocked his nasal cavity. He could take the pain, but watching the razor-sharp blade in front of his face, held by some lunatic who seemed beyond anything approaching rational, would not be bearable for long.

"Something just occurred to me, Ethan," the voice said, calm and smooth again, like the voice of someone sharing an opinion on a new flavor of ice cream. "This hunter's knife is your savior. Without this knife, you might have choked. That duct tape is wrapped on pretty tight. Nothing is coming through without some help. Never mind the piece of sock that's stuffed in there."

Ethan didn't dare move. His left eye stayed fixed on the knife blade.

"I take it by your stare that you agree," the voice said. "We'll keep this baby nearby so you can pay homage to it."

The knife disappeared from Ethan's field of sight, as did the black boots. It was all he could do to suppress puking again. Fire seemed to burn behind his eyes. Not seeing the boots and knife, he focused on breathing. He tried blowing through his nose. It hurt, but he managed a small amount of air, as with a cold. Breathing in was a different matter. He breathed in through the hole cut in the tape covering his mouth. He did his best to swallow some of what had come up and stayed in his throat, careful not to trigger puking again. It burned in his throat. He tried again to suck air through his nose but stopped, starting to gag on what was in his throat. He breathed out through the hole in the tape as the polished black boots reappeared, stopping inches from his face.

"You've made quite a mess, Ethan," the voice said. It sounded closer this time, as if the owner were bending down close to his head. Was the voice scrutinizing him to see if he'd moved? "I barely have the stomach for it. Never was good at watching someone vomit. When did you last eat?"

Ethan wasn't about to move or do anything beyond staying stock-still, but his brain wouldn't stop. *When did I last eat?* It seemed eons ago. The question wasn't intended as real conversation, but Ethan struggled to remember. Like his nose, his brain was clogged, only with different thoughts. Fear swirled among them all. The band had been staying in a cheap motel somewhere in Ottawa. They had planned to go to Swiss Chalet, but Greg hadn't wanted to. But where had they gone? Why couldn't he remember?

Greg had wanted a burger. The van had stunk of weed. Ethan had been worried that Greg wouldn't be able to play at Bogart's he was so high. Greg was in descent, using all the time. They'd all been hungry. Then it came back. Not really wanting another burger, as their diets were mostly fast food, Ethan had ordered onion rings, coleslaw, and a tea to go.

"Just so you know, eating's going to be a little different," the voice said, bringing Ethan back to where he was. "I'm going to leave you now with one simple instruction. Don't move!"

The scream was horrific, but somehow he kept himself still.

"Very good, Ethan. There may be hope for you yet. I'll know if you've moved. Moving will not be tolerated!"

The voice was loud and again sounded angry. There was a longer pause this time. Then the voice seemed to settle back into its instructional tone.

"Not moving will be rewarded and will prove to me that you have learned. We will celebrate."

Another song registered with him. Joe Walsh was singing "Life's Been Good." It was as if the music were making fun of him. Maybe that was the intention.

Ethan prayed again for the voice to leave. He needed some time to put some semblance to this unimaginable situation, if that was even possible.

"Remember, Ethan," the voice added, "I am now your hope, your fear, and your truth. You've messed with things long enough!"

The voice's scream was piercing, but Ethan didn't move. It was as if he were ready for the scream. The nightmare monologue couldn't end quickly enough.

The black boots again moved out of his sight, somewhere above his head. He was certain he could hear the sound each boot made pressing into the green carpet. They stopped somewhere behind his head.

"And, Ethan," the synthesized voice said from behind him, "there are consequences when one takes something from someone else."

Ethan had only a second to think about what the voice had said before the pain struck the base of his neck. The force jarred his shoulders forward, but he was restrained by whatever held his head to the floor.

"You will only dream of freedom now," said the voice, coming closer. A cloth covered his face. The smell of sweet rot came again, followed by darkness as Ethan lost consciousness.

CHAPTER 68

Eyes Open—Second Time

"It's about time," he heard. The voice was familiar yet unwanted. His head ached. His right shoulder ached. It seemed as if a stick were in his mouth. He tried to lift his left arm but couldn't. His eyes flashed open as he remembered where he was. A dry brown puddle lay in front of his face.

The nightmare was real. He could see it.

There was no sign of the black boots, only the four wood legs.

"Have a drink, Ethan," the electronic voice said.

Ethan tried to push out whatever was in his mouth and then realized what it was. His mouth was still covered, but nothing was stuffed in it. What he'd thought was a stick was a straw. His tongue touched it. It was in a white bowl of liquid. His throat was dry and burned when he swallowed. His nose was full. His nostrils felt crusty, as if he'd had a runny nose that had dried.

At once, he was thirsty. His tongue, dry and sore, found the tip of the straw again. He could drink. He sucked on the straw. He was swallowing before he tasted the burning alcohol that came back up his throat, gagging him. The vodka followed the path of least resistance. Some exited through his mouth and the hole cut in the tape, but the rest was forced up through his nose. The agony was stupefying. A stifled groan came from somewhere inside his head. His sinuses screamed as if fire had erupted in the space behind his eyes.

In his agony, he heard the opening to Boston's "More Than a Feeling" play to the macabre scene around him. He wanted to cry.

"Can't really handle your liquor, can you?" the eerie electronic voice asked over the music. The distorted titter-chuckle returned, as irksome as an unreachable itch under a cast.

Ethan lay in wait as the rawness of the pain in his head began to subside. Though clearer, breathing in through his nose was like rubbing sandpaper against the sensitive tissue of his nasal passages. Each breath burned, the pain relenting only when he stopped. Breathing through his mouth eased the discomfort but was not without effort through the small hole in the tape.

"I thought a rock and roller like yourself could handle his booze," the horrific voice said. The person behind the voice seemed to be enjoying the discomfort he was inflicting on his victim. Ethan was doing everything he could to keep his terror in check, but he needed fluid. He didn't know how long he'd gone without drinking.

Think of something else, Ethan.

He forced himself to think about his physical position. He'd been lying on his right side the whole time—he didn't know how long. His right arm was still underneath him and numb. He wondered how long the blood circulation in his arm could be interrupted before permanent damage took place. Was that even possible? With his left arm at his side, he could feel the weight of what he thought was his right arm, figuring his wrists were tied together. Part of his right shoulder was sore, but most of it was numb to any real pain. The area between his shoulders hurt from where he'd been kicked. His legs were bent and tied together at the ankles. Something bound his calves and thighs to the carpeted floor. He didn't attempt to move them. There was something around his waist too. Because of how his head was fastened to the floor, he couldn't see any of this. His mouth was covered with duct tape, which seemed wrapped around his head. It felt like a mask stuck to his skin. Straps of some sort held his head to the floor. He couldn't move it; he didn't even try. The electric voice demanded he not move. Fear of more pain, or death, kept him rigid.

"That was pretty mean, wasn't it?" the voice said, now sounding empathetic in its electronics from somewhere behind him. "But if you were me, you would have found it hilarious too."

The Electric Light Orchestra's "Mr. Blue Sky" began tapping in the background. For an instant, he thought it might be a good song for the Release to cover, and he was then amazed he could think of such a thing—an instant of hope squeezed into a mass of fear. He came back to describing his situation in his head.

The black boots reappeared—not as close as before and sideways now. Then they turned in front of the chair legs and stopped, as if the voice were sitting down. Ethan tried to see as much as he could. Midway up the voice's shins, black denim pant legs were tucked into the tops of the laced and polished boots. *Army issue,* he thought. His vomit on the green carpet in front of his face had dried into a shape much like that of Greenland as seen on a topographical map of the world. He guessed a couple of hours had elapsed since he'd vomited. Looking beyond his mark of Greenland, the black boots, and the wood legs, he could see the lower portion of what looked like a freshly painted beige cinder-block wall.

"Well, Ethan," the voice said, again interrupting his mental descriptions, "you've made it through the first twelve hours. Congratulations."

Ethan stayed still. The metronomic clapping of "Mr. Blue Sky" in the background made him picture a deserted road lined on both sides with smiling male dancers with Dixieland hats and white canes, tapping their shoes to the beat of the music. On the road, he could see a crawling, desperate man, starved and thirsty, being ignored by the happy dancers. The foot tapping brought back the soreness at the bottom of his neck and an urgent need to pee. His want for relief soon outweighed his ability to think of anything else.

Roxy Music's Bryan Ferry singing "Love Is the Drug" was next to distract him—but only for a moment. Every bass note seemed to add pressure to his bladder.

The black boots pressed into the carpet in front of him. The voice was rising to its feet.

"Ethan, how are you feeling?" the voice said over Ferry singing, "Stitched up tight; can't break free."

The voice behind the electronic one seemed kind, as if it were speaking to a lost and frightened child in a department store.

Ethan didn't dare move or blink. *Another test.*

"How are you feeling!" the voice screamed, as if the question were a bomb the synthesized voice had decided to detonate.

The shock of loudness was so sudden it caused Ethan to wince and involuntarily close his eye.

"This just isn't going to do," the voice said in professor-like mode, as if addressing a class of students who'd all failed a recent exam.

Ethan's eye opened as soon as he realized he'd closed it. The black boots were on the move and stopped in line with Ethan's waist. Before he registered what was happening, his jeans were being undone. He tried not to move, but was uncertain what the voice was doing.

"You're not learning, Ethan!" the voice barked. The pull on the front of his pants stopped. "This is aggravating, you know. My patience has limits!"

Ethan blinked with the scream. The boots moved again.

He never saw the kick, but the pain was excruciating. Fury overtook him as he fought against his restraints to strike back. He was unaware of where the pain was; he only knew it was there. He screamed against the tape across his mouth, trying to shake free from his immovable position. Instinctively knowing he had to get control of himself, he felt his left arm tugging against his right. Given its current numbness, he could have broken his right arm and never known it. He had to stop tugging and stop moving. Then agony struck his abdomen. He tasted blood at the tiny hole in the duct tape over his mouth. He opened his eye to see blood on the carpet in front of him, not knowing where it had come from. Though his nose was clogged, he blew out anyway, sending a spume of snot and vomit to the carpet and a shock of pain to his forehead, as if the knife had been jabbed between his eyes.

"You, Ethan," the voice said sternly and slowly, "have to stop moving. You're not going to live long enough to learn anything else if you don't."

Ethan heard the voice, but that was all. He was focused on breathing. He could take air in through the hole in the tape if he breathed slowly; otherwise, his breath seemed to suck in the tape and close the hole. Slower breathing lessened the pain and seemed to calm him, opening a passage for air to pass. He had to be mindful of his breathing. It seemed to help balance the fine line his pain was on.

He struggled with what caused the pain and blood in his nose, but that discomfort masked the pain in his abdomen. But as his breathing became more controlled, his stomach started to hurt.

"If you haven't figured it out," the voice said. He couldn't see the boots but was sure he could hear them moving on the carpet behind his head. "I was trying to give you some relief so you didn't mess your pants. Too bad."

With the mention of messing his pants, his need to pee grew worse. The pressure hurt. He could remember the cramps he'd experienced as a kid when holding it in class, an unfortunate result of being too shy to ask to be excused. There was no raising his hand here.

His thought ended abruptly as a cloth with the smell of rotting garbage was stuffed in his face. The green carpet with his dried puke of Greenland and blood darkened. The wood legs and the beige cinder-block wall became one.

CHAPTER 69

Eyes Open—Third Time

Ethan awoke with something stuck in his mouth again. In an instant, he knew what it was. Without trying, he felt cool water trickle into his mouth. *Water!* His eye flashed open to find the white bowl in front of him, filled with clear liquid. *Not again.* He stopped.

Journey was singing "Don't Stop Believing" from somewhere behind him. He tuned in and out of the background music, which wasn't loud but was always present.

"It's okay, Ethan," the electronic voice said, thrusting him back into his nightmare with nauseating speed. The voice came from somewhere behind him. It sounded kind with its duping tone of empathy, as if the person behind the voice had the ability to care. "You need to drink. You've been too long without water."

Ethan, still reluctant to draw from the straw, sucked carefully, uncertain what he would taste and consume. It hurt to even think of the bitter burn of alcohol down his throat and the witch-cackle shriek that was sure to follow. The thought struck him that he might have a way out. Could he not drink and wage a hunger strike? Surely the voice wouldn't expect it. It wanted control. His refusing to drink would turn that around. Was the voice already concerned inside its feigned empathy? For Ethan, the idea brought hope, as if a ray of sunshine had found its way into the room.

The pain that followed, like an explosion inside his body, eliminated all thought.

"Drink the water!" the voice yelled, as loud and chilling as anything Ethan had heard.

He couldn't breathe, never mind drink. He did his best to calm down.

Slowing his breathing was a monumental task, but it lessened the pain. Water came into his mouth, luscious and as sweet as anything he had ever tasted. It didn't remedy his agony but touched it enough for him to recognize that the pain came from the right side of his lower back, one of his kidneys being the likely target. He sucked on the straw. Without his really knowing it, his mouth filled. He swallowed. He relished the replenishment, his idea to save himself forgotten. It was like discovering a spring of fresh water at the end of a lengthy hike on a hot summer's day. The ache from the kick would not pass soon, but the water at least helped ease it.

"Okay, okay," the voice said as Ethan continued to suck down more water, "take it easy. The water's not going anywhere, but you will be if you don't slow down."

The voice paused. The black boots returned to his field of vision. They stopped again in front of his face, inches behind the bowl. Ethan kept drinking, unable to stop or obey the instructions he'd been given. Like magic, the bowl disappeared, kicked away by one of the black boots. Water splashed onto his face.

"In spite of what we've been through," the voice said, calm and direct, "you're still not learning. Either that, or you're simply as dumb as a stump."

Ethan continued to suck from the straw, unaware that only air was coming into his mouth. His tiny pleasure was over.

"Congratulations," the voice said. "You've now completed your first twenty-four hours in captivity."

The boots shifted. The toes pointed at Ethan's face in front of the wood legs. Beads of water spotted the polished black leather. He watched as the boots rose slightly on the carpet. The voice sat down. The boots were a foot from his face, within easy striking range. In staring at the boots, he noticed something was different below his waist. Without moving his head, not that he would have or even could have, he caught the edge of something round and white midway down his body. It was difficult to tell what it was—maybe he'd been given a pot to piss in and had. It didn't feel as if he'd peed his pants, but the urgency to go was gone. It felt as if his pants were too.

"We have a couple of things to go over," the voice said, "before we begin our lesson today. You will need to listen closely. Learning, if you haven't figured out already, will be key to your longevity here."

The voice paused, as if it were reflecting on what it had just said.

"Come to think of it, that's not much different from life. As I've said, you won't be leaving this room alive. You will come to learn why—ah, that word again—in time, and how well you learn will dictate how long you stay alive."

Unnerved, Ethan had heard what the freakish voice was saying, or some semblance of it, before. He couldn't remember where and wondered if his mind was messing with him. He felt a creepy sense of déjà vu and a distraction from the surreal horror that surrounded him, but it was a distraction he didn't need. He had to pay attention and not move, but the feeling of having been there didn't go away. He kept trying to figure it out, as terrified as he was of missing something that would keep him alive.

"You'll come to know who I am," the synthetic voice said. Ethan was no closer to putting a face to the electric voice than he had been upon first hearing it. "The better you learn, the sooner that will be. I have no intention of keeping my identity secret. You will never leave here, so no one else will ever find out."

The voice stopped. The black boots remained still. Ethan could feel its eyes scrutinizing him. He didn't dare move, but something was different. He heard the music again. It sounded like some Frank Sinatra song his father might have listened to. But it wasn't Frank. As the song played on, he was reminded of summer nights driving back from his nanna's place in the back seat of his father's blue '68 Chevy Impala. They listened to his father's music, and only his music, when traveling in the car. That was just how it was. Most of the time, his father had the dashboard radio tuned in to a crooners' station.

As if in sync with Ethan's thoughts, the voice spoke.

"You probably have no idea why you're here," it said, "but you will. What one is given that another takes away has its consequences." The voice placed emphasis on the last syllables of the word. "We will go through those *con*-sequences over time. You, Ethan, will determine how long those sequences last through your learning and obedience."

There was another pause. Ethan didn't move. His left eye was open, fixed on the bottom of a chair leg. His dried blood and vomit were still on the green carpet in front of him. Due to the position of his head, his right eye was all but in it.

"And so lesson one begins, Ethan," the voice said, "entitled 'The First Hint.' I was given, and you—yes, you—took her away!"

CHAPTER 70

Eyes Stay Open

The suddenness of the voice yelling again caught Ethan off guard. He didn't move but was certain he blinked. The sound carried the surprise of a balloon bursting beside his head. To flinch at such a sound would have been normal, but there was nothing normal about his situation. Although he hadn't noticed the voice moving, he was certain it had leaned closer to emphasize its words. The sound was so loud that he struggled to understand what was even said.

"I'm going to start with a hypothesis today," the voice said, returning to a calm, academic tone. "Everything we do is based, at some level, on the value we give it." The voice paused—the habit of a person who liked to hear himself talk. "And that value is uniquely determined and decided on by the individual."

There was another pause.

"A simple example would be what you've experienced in the last day."

Ethan's heart sped up as the right black boot moved off the carpet. He tried to prepare for another kick. His eye stayed on the wood chair leg. The boot rose out of sight and then came to hang in front of the voice's left boot. The voice had crossed its legs.

"It's very relevant when we look at how we learn. You know, that word just won't go away, will it?"

Ethan relaxed a little, realizing the relaxed position the voice had taken; a kick seemed a little less inevitable.

"Look at you," said the voice, the empathetic tone returning. "You're evaluating pain and its value much differently than you did even, say, a day ago. No?"

Ethan didn't so much as shift his pupil.

"And," the voice added, "I think you learned that moving equals pain. No moving means no hurt. Seems simple enough, but it's taken hours for you to learn. I'll extend moving to a single rule—or governing law, if you prefer. Simply put, do as I say. Remember, I am your hope, your fear, and your truth!" the voice shouted. Then, without pausing, it returned to its normal tone. "That will be more than sufficient for you to live longer."

Ethan doubted he'd ever get used to the suddenness of the voice's loudness. He had no idea whether he'd blinked or not, but the black boots didn't move.

"But don't get your hopes up, Ethan," the voice said. "Your life will come to an end in this room. Your obedience will allow you to live longer, but it won't change the inevitability of your demise. We will find out how much you value a longer life by how well you listen, how well you obey, and how well you learn!"

Ethan wasn't prepared this time for the last word to be shouted. The edge of his eyelid trembled. He didn't know how close the voice would have to be to detect the movement, but the black boots remained in place one above the other.

"There is a bed and a commode. Oh, I like that word. It sounds so—oh, I don't know—much more flowing than *toilet*. The very word constipates me. I do digress, don't I? Behind you, Ethan, are a commode and a bed that you cannot see. Not seeing them won't make them as valuable to you as seeing them—seeing is believing, right? I could be lying. I assure you they will be valuable to you."

The voice stopped. Ethan pictured it holding its chin in one hand between the L formed by its thumb and forefinger while cupping its elbow in its other hand, pensive about what it had said and still needed to say.

"And me—yes, me," the voice said, as if suddenly aware of what it wanted to say. "You will come to value me above all else as you truly begin to understand that I am your hope, your fear, and"—Ethan was ready for the voice to scream this time, but it never came—"your truth."

Ethan continued to stare forward. The voice went silent.

He tried to stay focused on being still, despite his thoughts wanting to take him elsewhere. Shifting his stare fractionally, he looked beyond his dried blood and vomit, the boots, and the wood legs. The room looked to be in the basement of a house. He would have been at the band's house now after the drive back from Bogart's if twenty-four hours had indeed passed, as the voice had said. He pushed the thought away. Good thoughts about being there and being free weren't useful and would only make him feel worse. An image of Greg's Slingerland drum kit replaced the voice's black boots and the wood legs in front of him. He could remember lying on the floor in Greg's parents' basement. Greg had pinched the dime-bag stash of weed hidden between his older brother's box spring and mattress. It had been Ethan's first drug experience, and one of his last, as he preferred the taste and high of alcohol to the vague feelings and musty smell of smoking pot. He had stared at the unfinished ceiling and watched the visible crossbeams change shape to the sounds of Emerson, Lake, and Palmer's *Brain Salad Surgery*. He'd watched as the cross members shifted between grins and frowns as the wood joists stretched and shrank in harmony with Keith Emerson's fingers on the Hammond organ. The grains of wood had seemed to flow like water into the top of the cinder-block wall. He remembered being amazed that he'd never noticed how much wood looked like water. It was odd that he'd never noticed it again or listened to *Brain Salad Surgery* either.

Movement of the right black boot back to the green carpet returned him to the room and his predicament. He watched the boot, fearing the worst.

Had he moved? Was that why the boot had moved? His drifting thoughts had let him down again. Why couldn't he concentrate?

The toe of the boot moved up and down. The Cars' "Let's Go" was playing; the boot moved to the beat.

When the music ended, the boot stopped.

"Bye Bye Blackbird," sung by a female singer Ethan couldn't name, came next—Billie Holiday or Ella Fitzgerald maybe, performers his mother loved. The voice remained quiet. He hadn't thought of his mother until now. He feared that news of these events could kill her. She struggled enough with the chance of him suffering a relapse, but kidnapping? She would go into shock or worse. He could see her collapsing and his father in shambles as to what to do. And Carlyn. *Oh, Carlyn.* It hurt to think of how much grief he'd already brought her. And Mila. *Mila? Not Mila. Christa.* His thoughts were confused. He needed his Orap medication. He was overdue. *Robbie. Why, Robbie?* His roommate had murdered Mila—and was later killed himself in a car accident. Christa would be worried. Those he loved would all be worried, their world turned upside down again. For his mother, losing him again would be unbearable.

Focus, Ethan. He needed his pills.

The voice continued its silence.

The music. Focus on the music. Listen to the music, Ethan.

But it wasn't the music he thought about. It was Syd. What had happened to Syd? She'd been with him. They'd left Gus and Greg to get more beer. He'd heard her voice in the shaking vehicle on the way there, something about a plan. "I'm not part of this," she'd said. What did that mean? Why could she talk? Was she involved? The voice made no effort to hide the fact that it knew him. Ethan didn't know much about her past, as he'd been so enamored with her guitar playing. She didn't talk much about her life in Ottawa.

Ethan couldn't come up with an explanation. If anyone was mixed up with the wrong folks, it was Greg. He was slipping, getting closer to the edge all the time. None of them knew what to do. Gus had come to Ethan. "We have to do something," he'd said with sadness in his eyes. "The road he's on doesn't end with a stop sign. It ends over the side of a cliff."

Even so, Ethan had a hard time believing Greg could be involved. Messed-up people did messed-up things, but Greg couldn't have been part of this hell.

Johnny Paycheck's "Take This Job and Shove It" played. The shiny boots came back into his sight. They'd never left.

The voice still hadn't spoken. The silence was horrifying. He prayed he hadn't moved, certain the voice was watching and waiting like a hawk eying a field mouse. It was dreadful, being coerced to disobey, which would lead to his punishment. Ethan was shocked by his next thought.

Speak, you bastard. Talk to me.

As if cued, the boots sank deeper into the carpet as the voice rose to its feet. Without an electronic word, the wood legs came off the carpet and disappeared with the black boots from Ethan's view. He waited, doing his best to hold his fear in check while readying for the blow that was sure to come—a steel-toed kick to his ribcage, thigh, or worse.

The background music made it difficult to hear any sound the boots made crossing the carpet. The cinder-block walls made him think of the cement underneath him and the basement—a basement suppressed suspicious sounds. Underground was the place to hide. Why did he think that?

He looked at the green carpet and beige block wall. The bastard was going to sit and watch him fail from behind. He had to wait. God help him.

The music played on. He didn't recognize the song that followed Johnny Paycheck's, but he was amazed at how many he did recognize and could name. He knew the music would play until the end, but he didn't know how he knew.

Still, the voice said nothing.

He struggled with the nothingness. How long could he go bound in this position, being watched, hearing music, staring at blankness, and trying not to think about what pain would be inflicted on him next, all while holding his fear and himself in place? It was mind-numbingly exhausting. There was nothing to realize the passage of time, only what the voice told him. The room was lit by lights he couldn't see but knew were above him like the ever-present threat of death that churned his stomach with all that his mind could not let go of. He imagined the horrors young American men must have suffered when dropped into the jungles of Vietnam—hell by a different name. They at least had been mobile.

"So, Ethan!" the voice shouted as if the electronic sound had somehow slithered up beside his ear. Ethan was amazed how attuned his hearing was to the voice even with the music playing. The quieter "So" that preceded his name was loud enough to warn him. He remained still except for his left eyelid, which flicked like a tic.

"You do value living longer," said the voice proudly, like a professor demonstrating proof of his hypothesis to a class of naive students. "You have listened, obeyed, and, to some extent, learned. Congratulations."

Again, the voice went quiet. Ethan wondered how long the silence would last this time. He didn't have to wait long.

"Your reward for completing the first lesson," the electronic voice said, "will be movement."

Ethan's internal warning flags went up. This was a trick.

"Movement, however, will be restricted," the voice said. "Your success with lesson one puts you at the top of the class, Ethan, and gives you the gold star that the child in us secretly craves. Remember sweet Miss Honeysuckle, with her special smile reserved only for those gold-star pupils who answered her questions correctly? Those who wore all the right clothes and said all the right things but were really no different from the rest of us."

Ethan was certain he could hear a sneer in the electronic voice's tone.

"She'd lick the back of that little gold star with the tip of her glistening tongue and place it beside the gold-star name she'd so neatly printed on the card—your name, Ethan. That gold-star pupil would then get to pin the card on the blackboard at the front of the classroom for everyone to see.

"And, Ethan," the voice screamed, unleashing a world of hate, "you!" Another primal scream came before the calm. "You, with your cute little smile and freckly nose, get to pin your gold star up there too."

The voice went quiet before a short burst of witchy titter-cackle.

"Only Ethan," the voice said in its instructive tone, and Ethan pictured the voice's hand coming up over its mouth, as if the voice were feigning embarrassment. "Poor Ethan—you're the only one in the class."

The last words oozed hatred Ethan could feel even through the voice's electronic synthesis.

"But, Ethan," the voice said, losing its menacing tone, "I don't have Miss Honeysuckle's ruby lips or sexy tongue to lick your gold star."

The hair on the back of Ethan's neck prickled. It was coming, and it was not a gold star.

He stared at the beige wall and green carpet with his left eye. He prayed for his life and prayed the pain would be quick.

Skin touched his arm. It took everything he had not to move. He pictured a mangy rat—whiskers twitching on his skin and repugnant, beady eyes waiting—ready to chew into his arm.

"That's right, Ethan," the voice said, a whisper coming through the hum of the electronic gadgetry. "Remember, I am your hope, your fear, and your truth."

The last word was followed by something like a flat piece of cardboard placed on the side of his head. Something hard pressed in behind it.

There was a moment when he thought that was it; something had been added to his restraints, and nothing more was going to happen.

Then the hard thing pressed even harder against his head. *A gun?* A shot went off. The pain was instant in the side of his head.

It's over, he thought, expecting darkness to follow. His eye had closed. He opened it quickly. He could see.

His pain was fading. *Shot?*

"Your first gold star, Ethan," said the voice. "You're my top student. You can stay at the front of the class, stapled gold star and all."

Something was stuck to his head. It hurt, but it wasn't killing him.

"Thus ends lesson one," said the electric voice. A damp cloth that carried the sweet, sick smell of rot covered his face.

This time, the light did go out.

CHAPTER 71

Eyes Open—Fourth Time

He was in the back seat of his father's white Chevrolet. His face was scrunched up against the rear passenger-side window; his hand was on the silver handle used to roll down the window. Carlyn was sitting on the blue vinyl bench seat beside him, curling strands of her strawberry-blonde hair around her index finger.

He was lost in thought, intrigued by how his nose formed to the flatness of the window glass, when a flash of red caught his eye. A lone cardinal, bright fire engine red, hopped out on a guardrail post, yet its surroundings lacked color, like a black-and-white photograph. It seemed strange to see a cardinal at the open roadside, as their song was usually the only thing that gave them away amid the tall conifers of the forest.

As they drove past, the bird turned to Ethan and fluttered its red wings. "Look at me. I'm free," it seemed to say, and then it flitted from the post and flew away.

His face was hard against the glass when he realized it wasn't so smooth and felt scratchy on his cheek.

His eyes opened. He knew where he was at once as the dream vanished. But something was different.

The left side of his face was on the green carpet. He was lying on his left side and could feel his right arm lying along his right side. Now his left shoulder was the uncomfortable one. His left arm, underneath him, now hurt. No doubt it would soon become numb, as his right one had. The weight of his left arm pulled on his right, the reverse of before, his wrists still bound together. His dried vomit and blood were gone.

In front of him was a bed, as the voice had described. He held his right eye steady, although it had surely moved upon opening. A white porcelain toilet sat to the right of the bed—the commode.

Still concentrating on not moving, he heard Elton John's "Saturday Night's All Right for Fighting" playing. It was one of the first songs that had excited him about music. Like before, at the bottom of his peripheral sight, he saw the edge of a large white bowl. He didn't try to look farther. His stomach hurt. He needed to pee. Awake, he could do little to hold back the push. His pants were down, if not off; his lower half was naked, with his penis exposed. The bowl was close enough to pee in. He could feel the side against his thigh. He hoped he wasn't being watched, but he knew better. Hearing the sound of his splashing pee in the bowl was like listening to water from a hose flow into a metal bucket. The relief was marvelous.

The music's tempo changed as the raspy, gurgled voice of Louis Armstrong singing "Mack the Knife" came on. Unexpected emotion overtook him. His stomach tightened as a tear trickled from his open right eye over the bridge of his nose to fall silently to the green carpet. The song brought his mother back to mind, but the tear was for Mila. He couldn't conjure her image—her dark brown eyes, loving smile, and soft skin. Her face was gone. Loneliness fell upon him like the onset of darkness after sunset.

Ethan, this is not a game. Stop playing.

Her voice seemed real, right next to him. Her face felt close to his, near enough to kiss. Hands, impossibly soft, touched his face, comforting in their familiarity. His heart ached at not being with her. He felt her warm skin on his, as if they'd never parted. Fingertips stroked his lips, which were aching to be kissed. Her lips were ready to kiss his, the soft sex of her tongue there and wanting. It was a moment. He moaned.

Just as a single snore could wake him, his moan stopped him. His right eye focused. For an instant, he felt safe. It was still and silent, and for a moment, hopeful, he imagined the sound he'd made had not been audible. But that hope took seconds to extinguish. The soft fingers that had traced his face and lips moments before were wrapped around the baby finger on his right hand. The grip was firm. His right arm stiffened on reflex. A moment later, he realized what was coming—punishment for his indiscretion.

What started slowly went by quickly; time seemed to stretch and contract sharply. He tried to clench his fist in defense, but the effort was futile. The voice had the advantage of two hands and free movement. His finger was forcefully straightened. He imagined the fists that held it. The digit was bent backward. For a moment, long enough for him to hear Duran Duran's

"Hungry like the Wolf" surface in the background, nothing happened. Then, like a dry stick breaking, came the crack. The agony came fast, sharp and hot. His hand went numb.

On the edge of consciousness, he didn't resist. In what seemed like accumulated moments rather than a smooth passage of time, the pain subsided. Remembering Harrison Ford's Deckard from *Blade Runner* moved his mind from the situation. His captor's voice, as if aware of his thoughts, snuffed out the image a second later.

"You messed up, Ethan dear," said the electric voice, modulating between levels of evil screaming. "You will pay for that every time. We'll go lightly this time, as it really wasn't your voluntary self. But you must learn control—if you want to live longer."

There was a lengthy pause before the voice spoke again. At times, the electronic sound made it difficult to believe a human could really be behind it.

"Let's start this over again," said the voice. "I don't like starting a lesson this way."

Ethan still hadn't seen the black boots or any sign of the voice in his new position. His hand throbbed.

A hand moved in front of his face. It poked a straw through the slice in the tape and into his mouth again. Ethan hadn't noticed he was breathing through his mouth until the straw was inserted; his nose was still plugged.

Another bowl of clear liquid was set in front of him.

"Drink, Ethan," the voice demanded. "You must be thirsty. You haven't drunk anything in eight hours."

Again, it used an empathic tone—real or contrived—that was strangely comforting. He was beginning to think of the voice as his, meant only for him, his little piece of evil.

His thirst was enormous. He sucked on the straw without thinking that the fluid would be anything but water. The taste was glorious—what water must have tasted like in heaven, he thought.

"New view today, Ethan," the voice said while Ethan swallowed. "Your reward from yesterday." The voice stopped, seeming to wait for him. "What you see before you will become your goals. Maybe even your friends."

Ethan heard the voice but was rejoicing in the delicious water flowing into his mouth and down his parched throat. It was liquid hope, like sunlight breaking through a cold gray sky. The pain in his hand had become a hard ache. It felt better now that he was lying on his left side.

"If you make it that long."

The voice was behind him. The bowl of water was removed. He sucked air until the straw was pulled away. Worry fell upon him. He wondered what he might have missed the voice say. He was mad at himself for being so easily swayed with the water. He had to stay attentive, no matter how enticing the distraction. He braced himself for what might come: another penalty for what he'd missed. But all that came was fear.

"Lesson two will be it for a while," the voice said, and Ethan was sure he heard a smile. "I have to get you up. It's too much effort to have you on the floor."

Pay attention, Ethan reminded himself as the sense of knowing what was going to happen returned. He had the déjà vu feeling again.

"Your fear and your truth," the voice said, coming back to his ears.

Fuck, he thought, wincing at his own error. *You can't stay focused for even a few seconds.*

Before he thought further about what he'd missed, agony lit up his right calf. Bright light flashed behind his eyes. The pain was so intense he was certain that if he could have looked, he would have seen the blade of an ax stuck in his calf. He waited for the pain to recede, but before it could, more pain struck the front of his shin. The capacity for thought left him. The disturbing image of the bottom of his leg bent unnaturally forward was all that remained.

"We made such progress yesterday!" the voice said, yelling the last word so loudly Ethan thought he could feel it resonate through his damaged leg. "What did I say? You can't move! Move, and I will kill you."

Like the words the voice screamed, pain seemed to shriek through his body. The steel-toed boot drove into his back, surely cracking ribs. Even with the hole sliced in the tape covering his mouth, he couldn't breathe.

"You're going from gold star to dunce in one lesson," the voice growled. "Bravo. I'll be counting the nails for your coffin sooner than I expected."

Ethan was rendered mindless; tangible thought was nearly impossible. Pain had taken over. On the edge of consciousness, he could do little but try to remain still. He stared at the green carpet.

"Remember value, Ethan," the voice said, screaming the word *value*. The voice was so close Ethan was sure he could feel its breath on his face.

"You value living by how well you listen, how well you obey, how well you learn, and, obviously, how well you remember!"

The voice was shouting so loudly Ethan wondered how someone outside of wherever they were didn't hear it. The loudness was painful but minor compared to the terror that accompanied it. He was going to die.

"I'm disappointed in you," the voice said, the electronic fuzz making the situation unreal while taking horrifying chunks out of Ethan's psyche. "I thought you were made of better stuff. No, I'm lying. You're just revealing what I already knew. You didn't deserve her."

The words attached themselves in his head as if he were running through a field overgrown with weeds and a few prickly burs had stuck to his pant leg.

"I have to tell you everything," the voice said, "but that's nothing new, I suppose."

Though the voice was unfamiliar in its distorted form, Ethan registered something recognizable in its words. But the pain didn't allow him to think about it long enough to tell if he was imagining it or if it was real. He hadn't imagined "You didn't deserve her."

Whom hadn't he deserved? Had that statement been a slipup? The voice didn't seem to make mistakes, but the madness in the voice seemed to be growing. Or was he imagining that too? Had the voice gotten lost in its own rant? Ethan struggled with what, if anything, the sentence meant. The pain in his legs and back couldn't find a place to rest and raged on. He tried to think of something else, but the words wouldn't let him. *You didn't deserve her.* There was something about how it had been said, the manner of speaking. He knew it wasn't possible but couldn't help himself. *Robbie.* It was Robbie. But that couldn't be. Robbie was dead. He'd watched him die.

In the park.

The thought chilled him.

For an instant, he forgot the pain but not the thought. The more he tried to rationalize it, the more he realized it couldn't be. His mind was playing games, and then, like an old acquaintance, he felt it—the heavy door. He pushed back, trying desperately to think of something else. He knew what the door offered him, but with it came another fear. Was any of this real? Was he already gone? That made some sense, but if he could think it, he was sure he wasn't gone. He wasn't crazy. But then again, maybe that was the truth.

Syd came to mind. Syd was real. Where was Syd? She'd been there when he woke shaking in the transport. Where was she now? And why had she said, "This wasn't the deal"? Or had even that been a figment of his imagination?

"I would like to put this incident," the voice said, interrupting Ethan's scattering thoughts.

He'd done it again. He'd gotten distracted. What had he done now?

He couldn't see the black boots. Not seeing the boots seemed to allow his thoughts to wander, all but forcing him to do wrong. He stared at the green carpet, aware of holding his eye still.

"Behind us." The voice finished at a higher pitch.

Ethan was like a dog the voice owned. He was expected to obey. That meant one thing: don't move. He was trying to be a good dog.

"And so I will. Lesson two, Ethan," the voice said, again close to Ethan's right ear, "is entitled 'Why Am I Here?' However, lesson one will continue to be important regarding how much you value living longer with the principles of listening, obeying, learning, and remembering!" The voice shouted the last word as if it were the most important. "The intention of lesson two is for you to understand why you're here. It's not by accident. It's not by some random event that had you in the wrong place at the wrong time. No, you are here because of what you did—because of your actions. You have made me," screamed the voice, "have to do this to you!"

Ethan stared at the carpet, focused on a few green fibers. A black boot appeared in the bottom of his peripheral vision. His pupil jittered. He concentrated to steady his stare on the carpet fibers. He prayed his captor hadn't noticed the movement. Ethan pictured the voice straddling him with fists on its hips, in a pose like that of a Nazi SS officer in pantaloons.

"Is that clear, Ethan?" the voice demanded. Ethan's one-eyed stare didn't move. "This is not my fault. This is your fault! Your doing!"

The voice seemed to get closer with each word, as if bending down from its stance.

Ethan was terrified beyond anything he'd known. Pain could come anywhere on his body at any moment—and maybe death. He was helpless to defend or protect himself, vulnerable and reduced to nothing; any second was potentially his last. He didn't know how close he was to the limit of how much he could take, but he could feel its proximity. The heavy door was there. Maybe he was already behind it, inside. He couldn't feel the lock anymore. But wasn't thinking it an indication he wasn't there yet? Maybe reentering the world he'd gone to and long feared was his only way out.

What had triggered his return?

Shit, another distraction. He'd found another temporary refuge from the insanity standing over him. He was still staring at the same spot on the carpet. The black boot hadn't moved.

Why did he come back after performing a song?

He recalled his cousin's diving accident in Cozumel. The story was that his cousin had been unable to write his name in the boat's ledger upon returning to the dive boat and had wound up in a decompression chamber in a Mexican hospital, recovering from what the doctors had referred to as "the bends." There was no explanation for what had happened—they'd followed protocol. His cousin had never dived again.

What the hell am I thinking?

Ethan saw the green carpet again. The fibers pressed into his left cheek. Like his right eye before, his left eye was all but closed. When he opened it, his eyeball nearly touched the carpet.

"She wanted you, Ethan!" the voice said, yelling his name again, the black boot unmoving. "She chose you. But she was mine."

The voice paused long enough for Ethan to again question his present. Whom was the voice talking about? Mila? Christa? Syd? He couldn't ask. Robbie had known Mila, but he'd killed Christa. No, that wasn't right. It wasn't, right?

How long had it been since he'd taken his Orap—the morning of Bogart's? Did it matter? Was he already—

No, Ethan, you can't go there.

"I speak like it's the past, but true love is eternal. She was mine. Still is. You cannot take her away, but you misled her."

The black boot moved. Ethan's eye didn't twitch. The boot disappeared from sight. If he concentrated, he could see the white piss pot in his lower peripheral vision without moving his eye.

"You've wrecked it for all of us, Ethan," the voice said.

Ethan was trying to trace the voice's footfalls but couldn't over the sound of Robert Plant singing, "Going down, going down now, going down."

"Neither of us can have her now."

The voice had moved farther away, down to his feet.

Ethan was having a hard time figuring out who the *her* was. He hadn't been with Christa long enough to know about her previous romantic interests or others vying for her affection; Mila was a closed case. That left Syd. But Syd seemed as much a victim as he was. But remembering again what he'd heard her say confused him: "I'm not part of this." For her to say that was an admission of involvement. *But part of what?* He couldn't figure it out. How could she be part of it but taken with him?

His fading pain kept him thinking. *Why would Syd have anything to do with this thing?* She'd never mentioned anyone. She didn't talk about her relationships.

And the voice?

All along, he'd assumed the voice was male. The electronics could easily fool him with that too.

As thoughts of Syd festered in his head, it was unbelievable to think that any part of this nightmare could be real—but his pain was.

Pain accompanied everything here. He attempted to breathe through his nose again. The tiniest bit of pressure sent tendrils of pain past the backs of his eyeballs, as if to warn him. His right calf felt tight and swollen. His right hand hurt the most. His broken finger throbbed in numbness. He hoped the voice would leave it alone. He knew his fingers were vulnerable and an obvious target to further break him—but break him from what? The polished boots loomed largest in his mind. A kick to his head could bring him to an end.

You can't think that way.

A silent prayer fell on his lips: *"The lord is my shepherd; I shall not want. He maketh me to lie down in green pastures: he leadeth me beside the still waters."*

He recited the prayer in its entirety in his head. He couldn't remember the last time he'd said it, yet he knew it.

Still, the voice didn't speak.

He couldn't believe he was asking it again. *Please say something.*

But the voice's silence continued as Simon and Garfunkel sang about the sound of silence, replacing Led Zeppelin: "Hear my words that I might teach you." That was all he heard.

He was heading back inside his head. His inability to move, with constant scrutiny bearing down on him, was becoming unbearable.

CHAPTER 72

Eyes Still Open

He heard the suck of an airtight door open. A similar sound, followed by a clunk, closed it.

"She's why you're here."

Ethan had no idea of the time or how long the silent wait had lasted. The melodic sounds of Sweet filled the room with their hit "Fox on the Run." If the voice was in the room, the shiny black boots were too, somewhere behind him. It made sense now. Every other time, the voice had knocked him out on departure.

"Drink, Ethan!" the voice yelled above the song.

The shock of the loudness caused him to blink. He knew it. He waited for the blow to come. What would the black boot target next?

But nothing happened—at least nothing he expected.

It started behind his right ear and crossed to his cheek, crawling like a centipede.

Air passed over the hairs on the back of his neck. He felt, rather than heard, the breathing—inhaling and then exhaling—across his face, unseen, again and again.

The breath was harmless enough, but after the third pass, Ethan couldn't stand it. The voice didn't stop. It seemed to get closer with each breath, moving around his earlobe to the top of his ear and back again. The voice breathed down the nape of his neck, below his ear, and under his jaw. Ethan stared at the carpet. He wanted to shrivel up and disappear as the voice's breath passed over his skin.

"Drink, Ethan," whispered the electronic voice as a hand came out in front of him, reinserting the straw that extended into a new bowl of liquid now in front of him. It was the hand of a person whose fingernails and cuticles were chewed to the quick. Ethan tried to suck on the straw but only managed a trickle of water. It was all he could manage with the air blowing on his neck. He wanted to melt into the green carpet. The hand moved away. Then the breathing stopped.

Something wet and alive moved across the soft skin behind his ear. If he'd been on a cliff, he would have jumped off. The heavy door was there again. His balance was precarious. He wanted to reach out and open it; there seemed no other escape.

"Drink some more, Ethan," the whispering electronics repeated beside his right ear.

Whatever had been behind his ear stopped. The heavy door wasn't pressing him. Ethan sucked on the straw, bringing cool water into his mouth. Maybe he would see another hour yet.

"Do you love her, Ethan?" asked the voice, the tone changed.

Ethan didn't move.

"She loves you," the voice said. "She was given to me, but you took her. What one is given, another taketh away; it's in the Bible and how people behave."

There was a brief pause.

"What you must understand," the electronic voice added, steady and serious, "as part of lesson two, is why you're here. You are responsible. You're here because of what you did. If you had just left well enough alone, I wouldn't have to do this. I wouldn't have had to do it to her."

To her? Syd?

The more the voice spoke, the more Ethan figured out what he must have missed; for Syd, the band was not only music but also a way out. It made sense. That was why she'd come to Toronto so quickly—packed her bags and left after only a phone call from a note stuck in a magazine. Music and Ethan were a way to get away from this madman.

The night in the car after Benny's show, she'd wanted to say more. Things had happened between them and effected what they loved. He'd known it would destroy what they were creating, yet he'd still let it happen.

"She wanted you from the first time she met you," the voice said. Ethan was sure he heard something different when the voice shouted the last word. "Crazy how that happens and then turns into such terrible things."

The voice murmured something Ethan couldn't quite make out. It coughed.

"But you can't just take what isn't given to you," the voice said, sounding weak at first but stronger with the last word. "But you did, and you will get what you deserve!"

The yelling caused the speaker to crackle again. There was an unsettling madness in the words.

Ethan had a sense that the voice had moved closer. He couldn't hear any movement, only the gangling voice of Bob Dylan singing "Times They Are A-Changin'."

"And thus concludes lesson two, Ethan," the voice said quietly, speaking just above a whisper. Ethan could again feel the breath of air on his neck. "You're here because of her. Her. Her!"

The voice screamed, hammering Ethan's head yet again with another sonic blow.

"I can't. I can't!" the voice screamed, but the percussive impact wasn't the same, leaving Ethan with the impression that the voice had moved away.

"I won't!" it hollered, stretching the words like the howl of a wolf. "I won't say her name. I can't say her name. She is inert."

For a moment, Ethan didn't know what hit him. It wasn't a physical blow but something he felt inside as soon as he heard it.

It was in the last word the voice said. *Inert.* He knew it—not in the sense of having heard it before or knowing what it meant but in knowing it connected with something in his head that he couldn't quite put his finger on. The heavy door was close again, with its repeating sense of déjà vu blocking him from seeing more.

"She was mine!" the voice screamed. It had now moved a distance behind him. "She was given to me. She was my gift, and you—you, Ethan Jones— took her away!"

The voice was screaming, loud beyond measure, but to Ethan, it didn't seem to be screaming at him. Like someone lost in hysteria, a dog lost in its own barking, the voice seemed to be speaking to something or someone outside the physical dimensions of the room. Ethan could all but see the voice's arms outstretched, as if it were addressing a large audience from a platform instead of the incarcerated captive before it.

Ethan saw Robbie. *It couldn't be.*

Then, in what seemed but an instant, the voice was close behind him again, breathing in and out across the tiny hairs on the back of his neck, disrupting any possibility of thoughts forming in his head—except for Robbie's image.

"You took her away," the voice hissed, close to Ethan's ear. "She didn't even love you."

The next few seconds were stolen from Ethan, confused by the image of Robbie and thoughts of Syd. How could this voice possibly think he'd stolen Syd away? They were part of a band, not a couple. How could Syd possibly have had anything to do with this thing? Worse, the voice spoke of Syd in the past tense.

He couldn't let himself think about that.

The breathing was close to his ear again, and then the slithery wetness was licking behind his ear. It was unbearable.

Had he been knifed in the back, his reaction would not have been different. With what little movement he was allowed by whatever held him to the floor and his limited ability to make any sound, he screamed, jerking his head and body with everything he had. He moved fractionally, hardly enough to matter and not enough to move the voice's tongue from his ear.

"Oh, Ethan," the macabre voice said in a whisper distorted by the electronics, "these are tough lessons for you, aren't they?"

The voice stopped. The tongue returned, tracing the edge of his ear with impossible slowness. The light breath turned him inside out. His right arm pulled on his numb left, the movement causing his broken finger to throb. Something inside said, *Don't*, but it was no use. He either found a way to break loose or opened the heavy door to somewhere else. He could already feel something peeking out from behind it.

Then, as if he were being jerked backward by a force much more powerful than he, it happened.

The pain was excruciating. It was so extreme he forgot where he was. His right arm pulled hard, restricted by his left. He could do nothing but take it. His right ear, only moments before the target of the voice's licking and breathing, was on fire.

The pain began to subside, but his ear was numb. Like a teardrop, warm fluid ran down the back of his neck. The voice was silent until Ethan heard a gurgle and a sputtering spit. Something splashed into the bowl of water in front of him.

Ethan stared straight ahead. His right eye could see the blood dripping from the edge of the bowl onto the carpet. It was only then he connected the terrific pain with what the voice had spit into the water.

"You can only get so far," said the voice, spewing its words, "before things catch up with you. We learn from our mistakes. It just takes some of us longer. Doesn't it, Ethan?"

It asked another question, knowing there would be no response. Ethan's stomach erupted upon his seeing the chunk of ear lying in the bowl of water. He knew now it was blood that ran down his neck.

"The next time you fail to listen, obey, learn, and remember," the voice said without emotion, "it will be more than just a piece of you."

The right polished boot appeared.

"I'm not playing games here, my friend," the voice said, sounding intent on inflicting some other punishment. "Sorry. I misspoke. The expression 'my friend' can be a nice familial expression of endearment, but don't misunderstand it. I am no friend, Ethan. There's no endearment here. This is full-on hate that will not end until you're dead."

The shiny black boot didn't move.

"You must remember. I am your hope, your fear, and your truth. There is nothing else in this room."

The voice went silent above him, replaced by Tom Petty singing the chorus to one of his songs: "Even the losers keep a little bit of pride."

"Things will be different for you the next time. That I can assure you."

A cackle followed the voice's last sentence.

"I want you to remember, Ethan," the voice added, "that you brought all of this upon yourself. There are consequences for our misdeeds. You need to think about this if you want to live past the next lesson."

The voice paused, but the black boot didn't leave its position in front of his face, beside the bowl of bloodied water.

"What was given and taken away is done. There's no taking it back. But you can still listen and obey and remember."

Ethan knew he had paid with his ear for his indiscretion of trying to move; he had stepped way over the line. His loss of control had been a waste of what little energy he had and only amounted to more pain. No one could hear him except the one he didn't want to; his only sounds amounted to little more than muffled grunts.

"I think we're going to get along real fine now, Ethan," the voice said, as if Ethan could have become anything close to a friend in this nightmare of horror. "I know you understand. It's not me but control you're fighting—your self-control. Like I said before, you're responsible for what I do to you. You're the one who makes me do it."

There was another pause. The right boot was joined by the polished left one. The two boots moved back and forth in front of him as if the voice were pacing, thinking of what to do next.

The burn in his ear was fading.

"You know the rules. Now it's a matter of practice and your willingness to follow them. I think you're a good student, Ethan. But thinking and being are not the same. We will discover them together."

The black boots disappeared below what Ethan could see.

"I like that," the voice said, as if responding to something Ethan had said. "Self-inflicted. It describes what's happening to you. You are getting beaten, but it's all self-inflicted. You break the rules; you suffer the consequences."

The right boot came back into Ethan's view as the voice spoke, and before the voice finished saying the word *consequences*, the boot swung into him.

His control was gone. Pain shot through him as if his skin would burst. His body seemed like a mass of exposed nerve endings hit by a dentist's drill. He couldn't see whatever was in front of his eyes, as he was blinded to the edge of consciousness. The agony wouldn't relent and seemed compounded by each beat of his pounding heart. Short of going through him like a cannonball, maiming him for life, the toe of the boot embedded itself in his groin like a stuck piece of pipe.

Unknowingly, he struggled in the restraints; he was nothing.

He gasped for air through the hole in the tape covering his mouth, the straw now gone. Something unstuck in his nasal passage, as if he'd imbibed a stone, but air came into his lungs. As if on cue once his nasal passage had cleared, the pungent smell of sweet rot covered his face again.

Everything went away.

CHAPTER 73

Eyes Open—Fifth Time

"Good morning, Ethan," the now familiar voice said.

He listened, now awake. His back was stiff, his leg was sore, and his ear hurt. He wasn't on his side anymore but sitting in a chair. His head hung down, his chin on his chest. The muscles in the back of his neck stretched. His eyes were closed. He didn't want to open them. It was a conscious thought. It seemed the electronic voice was listening too.

His arms were pulled back behind him. Thick cuffs were fastened to his wrists and cut into his skin. He knew they were steel. They were not comfortable. The cuffs hung from chains attached to something behind him—maybe the beige cinder-block wall he remembered from before. His arms were raised high enough to be even with his shoulders. He couldn't feel his arms.

With his eyes closed, he knew none of this for sure, but it was easier to accept in his mind than to see it for real. He didn't know why he knew all this, only that he did.

His memory then began to serve him quickly. The music came first. Again, he recognized the song. It was fairly new, David Bowie's "Let's Dance." The music never stopped; it wouldn't. He didn't know why he knew it wouldn't. It was part of some plan—a plan that felt increasingly familiar.

The chair he was sitting in was fastened to the cement floor with four-inch lag bolts. He hadn't seen them, but he knew they were there. Carriage bolts and steel brackets finished the job. When he'd first seen the wood legs, they hadn't been bolted to the floor. His ankles were encased in cuffs like those around his wrists but bigger. They were steel too. Each was bolted to the chair leg opposite the bracket. A thick belt of some sort was wrapped around his stomach and fastened to the back of the chair with four more carriage bolts—carriage bolts with round heads, like the ones he'd used on the pool fences while working for Al.

How did he know these things?

He knew that if he opened his eyes and raised his head, the bed and commode—as the voice had explained—would be in front of him.

"Good to see you too, Ethan," said the electronic voice. It sounded a little higher pitched than before. "You gave me a little scare. I was beginning to think you might be dead. What a shame it would be to miss what I have yet to share with you."

There was a brief pause.

"I know you hear me, Ethan. Raise your head."

Ethan didn't move. He was conscious and heard clearly the voice's command, but he didn't move. He remembered how his mother would call him to get up. He wished he were at home now. He would never turn over and cover his head with his pillow again. He wished he'd never done that to his mother.

"It's been almost two days, Ethan," the voice said. "It's time to raise your head. The rules are still active. Raise your head!"

As the voice said the last word, a hard slap hit his face. It shocked him. His head came up. Tape still covered his mouth, but it did nothing to lessen the smarting sting of the slap.

His eyes opened as his head came up to confront the face of platinum-blonde Marilyn Monroe—at least that was who he thought it was. *Surreal* didn't come close to describing how he felt. Mortified, he noticed the position of her famous beauty mark. It wasn't on her cheek but just below her right nostril. Then he knew: it was the popular new face of MTV. The Marilyn Monroe–esque Madonna stared back at him. He couldn't tell who was behind the Material Girl's reproduced rubber face, but he'd known that like the bed and commode, that mask would be in front of him. Again, he didn't understand how he knew. He just did. The mask was disturbing but no more than everything else that surrounded him. He made no indication that anything was out of the ordinary.

"Ethan, you listen to learn," the now masked voice said. The ghoulish face mask tilted sideways like a dog trying to understand what his master was saying. "You learn and obey!" the mask screamed. "And as I told you before, you must remember to do those three things to live here longer."

Ethan stared at the mask, trying to imagine who was behind it. He desperately hoped it wasn't Robbie, yet he could think of no one else. He didn't know anyone connected with Syd, which now seemed odd. Could she really know someone as terrifying and delusional as this rubber-masked thing in front of him? He didn't want to think so, but humans were capable of anything, good, bad, and evil.

"As you listen, learn, and obey," the voice said, "you will be given privileges—privilege to speak, privilege to eat, privilege to drink. That reminds me. You must be thirsty. You've peed enough for two."

Ethan knew without masked Madonna telling him or even looking that not far away was a container for his waste, to be used, if necessary, as a teaching tool. He was to do as he was told, or else. He knew he'd peed but couldn't remember any more. He didn't want to think about it. Instead, he swallowed and found his throat dry enough to hurt. Thirst was again on him, but he was not thirsty enough that drinking his own urine was an option.

He nodded in response to the Madonna's comment.

"Stop moving your head," it said.

Ethan stopped.

"Good, Ethan," the Madonna face said.

Ethan stared forward into the real eyes behind the mask. Already, holding the weight of his head up took effort.

He saw more of the room without moving his eyes. It was about fourteen square feet, maybe longer than it was wide; it seemed about the size of his bedroom at his parents' place, big enough for all he saw to fit comfortably.

Ethan thought of the jail cell his aunt had taken him to as a kid when she worked at a police station; it was a place he'd never cared to visit again. The ghosts of bad things and madness were everywhere: on the walls, on the floor, and on the ceiling. All of it was here too, only covered in green carpeting and a coat of beige paint.

He watched as the Madonna stood up and raised a white water bottle in one hand. It looked like a sports bottle out of a kid's hockey bag. In the other, it held the shiny-bladed knife.

"I had to tape you up again," the Madonna said. Its voice had an encouraging tone, as if it had done Ethan a favor. "The last had become pretty gruesome to look at."

The Madonna chortled the witchy titter-cackle Ethan knew he would never get used to.

"To allow you to drink, Ethan," the Madonna said. The mask's open mouth didn't move. "I have to cut a hole in the duct tape."

The Madonna held the hunter's knife out in front of Ethan as a magician might have shown an audience member a prop.

Ethan knew the glistening blade could easily be the deciding factor in his staying alive.

"As you've already learned," the mask said. Then its electronic voice paused, as if it were remembering something important it needed to say. "And hopefully remembered, you are the one in control of the outcome. You will be the one responsible for making me do something beyond cutting a hole."

The Madonna then held up the white bottle.

"To get this," it said, and it shifted to hold up the knife, "I have to do this."

Ethan's brain began a sort of meltdown as he looked at the water bottle. Thirst, which had found another place to exist for a while, was suddenly upon him like a wave of pressure sucking his breath away. His entire body seemed to salivate for what was in the white bottle. He did everything in his power not to move.

"We need to get on with this, Ethan," the Madonna said. "We have an important lesson to go through today."

The Madonna stared into Ethan's eyes.

Ethan was sure he recognized them. Whether he did or just wanted to, he couldn't tell.

Lower in his peripheral sight, he saw the shiny black boots. They were all he'd known of the Madonna thing prior to now, and they still made him wary. A muscle in his right thigh twitched. It hurt to flex his quad to stop it. He felt tightness in his thigh, as if something were pressed hard into it. He didn't dare look to see what it was. The hunting knife was within striking distance. He doubted the Madonna would hesitate to cut him. But the thought of the black boot coming at his leg or head and the hard pain that would follow caused him the most anxiety. He tried to push the thought away.

The Madonna turned and faced the same direction as Ethan, toward the bed and commode. For the first time, Ethan saw the bedside table.

"You're going to learn this lesson firsthand!" the Madonna said, shouting the last words. "Failure is the best way to learn. Isn't it, Ethan? Remember, you're doing the ultimate learning here, because every failure could be your last or at least a step closer to it. There's not a more effective or efficient way to learn!" electronic Madonna screamed. "Is there, Ethan? How's that for an engineering hypothesis?"

It wasn't the yelling that caught Ethan's attention this time. It was the words it had used: *engineering hypothesis.*

"That got your attention," the Madonna said, seeming to know that it had. "Dinnit?"

Ethan didn't think he'd moved, but he must have revealed something. It seemed to know the words it was using would affect him.

"It's good to see you're following the first rule, Ethan," the mask said as it turned completely around and faced him again. It swung the knife back and forth as if conducting a band behind him. In the background, Chicago was playing their hit song "Saturday in the Park."

"Okay, okay, enough with my chitchat. Lesson three has the working title 'Value-Based Decisions.' No, no, I don't like that at all. Sounds ridiculous. Pretentious. Way too academic. Too 'This is an essay that has no relevance in life.'"

The Madonna then stopped, as if perplexed by what it saw on the floor. Ethan stared at its platinum-blonde hair. It wasn't real. Seconds passed before it raised its head again.

"Goddamn academics," the mask said, shaking its head. "Always messing with words the rest of us can't or don't even want to understand."

The Madonna looked back at Ethan. Ethan hadn't moved as far as he could tell.

"Every decision is based on value," the Madonna said, placing the hand holding the water bottle on its hip. "That's the working title for lesson three. It's not only the third but also the last lesson you will learn in this life."

The Madonna looked back at the floor. "It's very relevant to you, Ethan. It will reflect on how much you really value living a little longer."

Ethan thought he could hear a smile coming from behind the Madonna mask, even in the electronic sound.

"Some might lead you to believe that making decisions based on value is a new thing. That today we better understand how we make decisions. It's a lie! We've been doing it as long as we've been here. Just because we can quantify and measure better, it's as if smarty-pants people like you think they have gained a clearer glimpse into the human mind."

The Madonna again paused.

"They haven't!" the Madonna yelled, as if to emphasize the point to Ethan, but it wasn't looking at him. It was still looking at the floor. It was almost as if the Madonna were talking to someone else. Suddenly, it raised its head, its blonde hair bobbing. "We make decisions, Ethan, because of how they make us feel!"

Ethan couldn't see the face behind the rubber mask, but if he could have, he was certain he would have seen an enraged madman with a pulsing vein down the center of his forehead. Veins and arteries like pull cords would have been protruding from its neck.

"If a decision makes us feel good—and you can be sure we want to feel good—guess what? We make that decision."

The Madonna tilted its head sideways like a chiropractor might have moved it and continued.

"If a decision makes us feel good or better than we would otherwise feel, that's what we'll decide. We'll even make a bad decision because it makes us feel better. Think about it. Ever been depressed? Felt a little down? We'll seek attention by making others feel guilty that they're not paying us enough attention. And guess what? We'll make a bad decision. But it's a decision that we think will make us feel better than we would otherwise feel, even though"—the Madonna screamed the words and leaned forward close to Ethan's face—"we really know the outcome of the decision will not be good for us!"

"No matter how much you math and science guys say about quantifying and measuring and needing more data, it all comes down to making you feel good about your decision. You want to feel you've done enough to make the right decision. It makes you feel good!"

The mask of Madonna took an audible breath. "We make decisions all day long. But we want affirmation that those decisions are right. Take, for instance, a big decision."

The Madonna paused, Ethan thought to scrutinize any movement he might make. Ethan didn't move; inflicted boredom was better than inflicted pain. His fear was exacerbated by his thirst, but he held on.

"What's the first question you're asked after making the big decision?"

The Madonna stopped, appearing expectant that Ethan would answer. Ethan didn't move.

"It's a simple question. Always the same."

The rubber reproduction of the music star's face moved closer and stared at Ethan, seeming to forget its victim's mouth was sealed with tape.

"There I go again, asking you a question you can't answer."

The mask shook its head, its titter-cackle raising the hairs on the back of Ethan's neck.

Ethan didn't notice the changing background music for the most part. Yet the melodic chorus of Toto singing their recent big hit "Africa" made itself heard. "The rains down in Africa" harmony seemed to tease his nearly mad craving for a drink.

"Ethan, my boy," the Madonna face announced, extending its hands and arms in a gesture a performer might have made in front of an audience. The knife was in one hand; the white water bottle was in the other. The Madonna was still conducting. "You're always asked, 'So how do you feel?'"

The Madonna's shout did little to sway Ethan's attention to the water bottle.

"It's like a law," the Madonna said, its voice lowered. "It's like Newton's third law: 'For every action, there is an equal and opposite reaction.' Or your second law of—what is it? Thermo …"

The Madonna seemed to hesitate, as if trying to remember a certain word—a word that Ethan didn't give a shit about.

"Thermodynamics—what a complicated word you guys came up with for heat. Damn, what was I saying? I'm digressing."

For a second, the Madonna's eyes looked into Ethan's.

"Like the second law, things get more complicated over time. Yeah, no kidding, Einstein. You know that better than anyone else right now, don't cha, Ethan? You've got entropy—there's another word—on steroids happening right before your eyes. Remember, you've made me do this to you."

The Madonna stopped as if to catch its breath.

"Like what else is going to happen. Things are going to align and simplify? Are you kidding? Ever been in a forest? The only trees that are lined up are those humans planted. Only our human brain seeks order. We're the ultimate entropy busters, and it's a never-ending effort in futility. Order to disorder over time—really?"

The Madonna mask was on a roll. Ethan watched as it set down the water bottle on the bed. For the first time, he saw how the mask extended down into the mock-neck collar of its black shirt. No human flesh was exposed in the face or neck, only the eyes and hands.

"Think about it, Ethan," the Madonna mask said. "How do you think Truman felt after sending the Enola Gay out with her surprise package for the Japs? How do you feel, Mr. President? He probably didn't say, 'Good,' but I'll bet he said something like 'It's the right decision.' He felt less good about the alternative of losing the war, despite knowing the human devastation that would take place."

Again, the Madonna mask paused and picked up the water bottle.

"As I said, we're going to demonstrate lesson three, Ethan, right before your eyes." The mask turned to face the bed and commode again, like a master of ceremonies announcing the next part of the program. "Here for your enjoyment and education is our first demonstrator—the one, the only, the self-inflicted Ethan Jones. Come on down, Ethan!"

The Madonna mask turned with hands and arms extended, directing the audience—the bed, toilet, and small table—to look at Ethan.

"And look, ladies and gentlemen, he's already here."

The Madonna turned back to Ethan. "Today we're going to find out just how much Ethan values this." The Madonna held up the white water bottle. "We're going to watch how he makes his decision. We'll attempt to prove that we always make decisions based on how they make us feel."

The Madonna screamed the last word, leaning toward Ethan. The rubber mask's open mouth looked as if it were screaming.

"Remember, Ethan," the Madonna snarled, "you've made all of this possible."

CHAPTER 74

Eyes Remain Open

Ethan was terrified beyond his ability to think.

"Let's get back on track," the Madonna face said, looking into Ethan's eyes. Some jazz that Ethan didn't recognize played in the air around them. "Lesson three: every decision we make is based on the value we attribute to what we believe will be the outcome. We measure that value with our emotions. We won't make that decision until we have sufficient information to make us feel good that we're making the right decision. That could require a lot of information gathering or none at all. We—the individual—get to decide. In lesson three, I'll demonstrate it. So, Ethan, let us begin."

The Madonna held up the water bottle. Then it held up the black-handled hunter's knife. "I have to do this," it said, pointing the shiny blade at Ethan. Then it turned its masked head and nodded at the white water bottle. "So you can have this."

Ethan didn't move. He had to remember the rules.

The Madonna mask stepped forward, holding the deadly weapon out in front of Ethan. The point of the knife moved to the duct tape. Ethan could feel the tape pull on his lips as the tip of the blade cut through the tape. He didn't blink or move his eyes. The Madonna's hand moved slowly and steadily, like a surgeon's. The tip of the blade cut into the tape. Ethan did everything he could not to think about what was happening. *The eyes.* There was something in the eyes when they stared into his. It would have taken little effort for the knife to keep moving through the thin layer of tape, through his tongue and the back of his mouth, and into what connected his spine to his brain. Any move he might make to pull away from the plunging knife would make it worse and likely kill him. The Madonna's hand kept moving. Ethan was convinced it wouldn't stop.

"So far, so good, Ethan," the Madonna mask said. "The rules are in check. You've accepted the knife to get what's in the bottle."

The razor-sharp blade remained in Ethan's mouth. He fought his tongue against touching it.

"Under normal circumstances," the Madonna mask said, "you would never accept someone sticking a razor-sharp knife in your mouth in exchange for what might be in the bottle." The Madonna paused and pushed the knife in a little farther. "No matter what is really in the bottle."

Ethan didn't move, trying to show that the presence of the knife didn't have any effect on him. But something else was pushing hard to be let in. He began to doubt there was water in the bottle; a feeling of déjà vu was slipping around his fear.

The knife went farther. The tape pulled his skin. The tip of the knife touched his tongue. It took everything he had to hold his tongue still. His resolve was slipping. The heavy door was back and so close he felt as if he could touch it.

"Now there's a hole you can drink through," the Madonna mask said.

Ethan was sure he could hear the smile in its voice. It was enjoying the terror it was putting its captive through. The knife had stopped moving but was still in his mouth.

"The value equation. *Equation*—now, there's a word you engineers like. Finally, we're getting to that word *formula*. There is a God."

Ethan felt the tip of the blade against his tongue. He was balancing, barely, the door, the déjà vu, and the lethal knife. Again, the Madonna's titter-cackle sounded. It was short-lived but no less dreadful.

"Sorry, Ethan, but this is funny," the Madonna mask said. "The value you have given the knife might just change. What if it's not the means to the end you're thinking but the end itself?"

The Madonna mask had moved in closer to whisper the last words in Ethan's face. Ethan could feel its breath through the mask and whatever it spoke through. For an instant, he thought those would be the last words he heard.

The Madonna pulled the knife from Ethan's mouth, but the blade didn't come out straight. Ethan felt a sting as it nicked his lower lip. His heart pounded its menacing needs in his ears. His tongue went to where the knife had left its mark, but that was all that moved.

"It's funny how our emotions reign supreme over our decisions," the Madonna said, setting the hunter's knife down on the bed. "No matter how hard we try to prove otherwise. We want to make better, right decisions. You guys all want reams of data and information to make better decisions. It doesn't change the fact that your emotions are in charge. Even after all your research and data crunching, it still comes down to how you feel at that moment of truth. It's how we feel!"

The Madonna mask screamed again. Ethan didn't flinch; he didn't blink. Johnny Cash's "Folsom Prison Blues" found its way to his ears.

"What's even funnier is how much you hate that it's true. It's our constant need to be right, to control things. The more right we are, the more power we have. That's how it works, Ethan."

Ethan didn't move. His pupils didn't waver.

"Proud of you, Ethan," the Madonna mask added with the water bottle now in its hand. "You're listening, you're learning, and you're obeying!" it shouted. "You're remembering. You're quite a student when you want to be, you know—and why?"

The Madonna face paused but only for a second. "Because you emotionally measured your decision. Allowing me to cut the hole had more value than the alternative." The Madonna leaned in close to Ethan's face again and hissed, "And you're praying you're right."

The Madonna moved back and straightened up. "What do you think is in this bottle?" it asked, holding the white bottle in front of Ethan. "You can't answer, so I'll help. You want it to be water. You need it to be water. You're at the bottom of Maslow's pyramid—crapping, sleeping, breathing, eating—and you have to drink. It's been more than a day since you last sucked up some water. You're dying of thirst!"

The Madonna's cackle was short again.

"You need water so badly you'll do almost anything for it. Not anything yet but almost." The Madonna nodded. "Now, if this is water, you're all set. You can drink it. Warning: you'll need to drink it slowly, or you'll throw it all back up. Not only will you feel better from the water, but also, the counter will start again. You can go another day or two without more. You'll live longer, and as long as you're living, your game is still on."

The Madonna tittered-cackled, unnerving Ethan with its repetitive horror.

"But, Ethan." The Madonna face bent down closer to his face and whispered. "You're still gonna die in here."

Abruptly, it straightened back up. "But let's get on with this decision. First, do you think this is water? Or is it something else, like vodka or, worse, poison that will kill you in minutes? That's the first decision."

The Madonna mask stopped and moved in close. The real eyes scrutinized Ethan's. Ethan didn't move. It took every bit of willpower he had not to. *Don't think; just do.* It was like confronting a bear in the forest unexpectedly. He had to stop, remain still, and play dead, as he'd read somewhere. Yet he knew that at any moment, the bear could simply turn and tear him apart. What breathed behind the Madonna face seemed to chuff like a bear. Ethan was exposed, vulnerable, and balancing precariously. He felt the heavy door and was nearly ready to risk what was behind it.

The Madonna mask remained close to Ethan's face. The mask was amazing in its detail, with wavy platinum-blonde hair brushed and set perfectly above the clear, perfect skin of its rubber forehead. It looked almost real. Real dark eyes looked out from behind the long-lashed, mascaraed holes. The face was porcelain-doll perfect, with the Material Girl's straight nose and flaring nostrils. Pearl clusters hung from each rubber earlobe and shook with each movement of its Madonna head. Brilliant red lipstick coated the open lips, which surrounded whiter-than-natural teeth. Darkness separated the top teeth from the bottom and emitted the electronic voice. In normal circumstances, Ethan would have screamed. If he got through this, he would never again be able to look without fear at the face that was fast becoming one of the world's most recognizable women.

The heavy door was open.

"This is how it's going to work," the Madonna said, standing up in front of him again. "Hint here, Ethan—the rules are still in place."

The Madonna raised its index finger off the water bottle it was holding and pointed it toward him. "First, there's water in this bottle. That's your decision or the decision you've delegated to me—sound familiar? Now the test."

The Madonna's left hand went into the pocket of its black jeans and pulled out a quarter. "It's a coin toss!" it yelled through the mask's grotesque-sexed mouth. It chortled, causing Ethan to hear the background music of Steve Miller singing "The Joker." He pictured the image of the album cover, with the leather-jacketed figure in a green-and-white mask. The Joker's mouth was open, and his head was back in an apparent state of laughter.

"People laugh at this, Ethan," the Madonna said, settling back into the job at hand. "They say, 'You make your decisions by tossing a coin?'" it said, mimicking some high-pitched voice. "But you know, it works."

The Madonna held up the coin in front of Ethan, holding it between its left thumb and forefinger. "You call it in the air," it said, tossing the coin in the space between them. "Heads, Ethan, because it's your head that's on the line."

It chuckled, caught the coin, and flipped its hand over on its right forearm. The white water bottle was still in its right hand.

"Now, here's where it's not quite what it seems," the Madonna said, bending down so Ethan could see the outcome of the toss. Ethan wasn't sure where the Madonna was going with this display. Another level of fear loomed inside his head at the possibility he wasn't going to get any water after all. The coin toss no longer made death seem extraordinary.

"If it's heads," the Madonna said, "then your decision that there's water in the bottle is right. Now the rub: How do you feel? Emotion, Ethan. Emotion!" The Madonna mask screamed again, all but shaking in its apparent excitement. "See, you get a second chance here. If you feel good, then you know your decision. If you don't, guess what? Then you don't like the decision. You don't feel good. Guaranteed you're gonna reconsider."

The Madonna stood up, appearing satisfied with its demonstration. "Every decision we make, Ethan, instantaneous or long and drawn out, comes down to whether we feel good about it and how we measure its value emotionally. That's it."

Ethan didn't know how he could hold it together much longer. He was going to move. The pressure of fear would find its release somehow. *Fuck this Madonna's feel-good decisions.*

"And so ends lesson three, Ethan. We make decisions based on how they make us feel and what our motivation for that feeling is."

The Madonna then stopped and tilted the white water bottle sideways, dribbling some of its liquid onto the green carpet. Ethan continued to stare ahead. He did not follow the movement of the bottle in the Madonna's hand.

"God, we are so human and not all-powerful," the Madonna mask said, and then it stopped, seemingly for effect. "Except in this room, Ethan, remember, I am your hope, your fear, and your truth. Here, I am all-powerful!"

The Madonna face shouted the last two words as if the loudness made it so.

Ethan was dying for the liquid that dripped onto the carpet—even for a few drops. It looked like water. The Madonna had told him it was water. That was good enough for him. Pain or no pain, he had to drink.

CHAPTER 75

Eyes Still Remain Open

Ethan had made his decision to move and was about to do so when the déjà vu feeling blocked him. It wasn't faint this time. He'd been there before. He knew the lessons, the rules, the cinder-block walls, and even the mask. But the perspective was different. He'd been the one in control. He'd been the one behind the mask. He'd been holding the water bottle. It wasn't water in the bottle. It was vodka, intended to make his victim sick and obedient—and maybe dead.

The Madonna moved the spout of the white bottle toward Ethan's mouth. "Finally," it said, as if it were working in Ethan's best interest, "you're getting a drink."

The Madonna pushed the spout through the slit it had cut in the duct tape.

Ethan prepared. He was fighting himself and the feeling of déjà vu over what was real and what wasn't. *It's not water, you fool. If you drink it, you're gonna die.* The voice was his own yet different—a different him. He didn't understand it. But he held his resolve as the plastic drinking spout touched the tip of his tongue. There was instant recognition in his mouth. The foul taste of alcohol from what remained on the nozzle of the drops that had dribbled onto the carpet.

It's a trick, my boy—sleight of hand. His inner voice spoke again.

Though confused, afraid, and vulnerable, Ethan knew he wouldn't swallow.

The spout rested a moment longer on his lips, and then, suddenly, a gush of burning alcohol exploded in his mouth.

Ethan gagged. He couldn't breathe. He knew what was about to happen and braced himself. The alcohol had to escape. Like an open wound exposed to alcohol, his nasal passages lit up, screaming in agony as the vodka found its path of exit and sprayed out his nose. He was no longer in control. His head rocked backward, and his back slammed against the chair back. His arms yanked at the chains bolted to the wall. The regurgitated alcohol spurted across Madonna's rubber likeness and black shirt.

"You fucker!" the mask yelled, drowning out Kansas playing "Dust in the Wind."

Ethan's eyes closed. The white water bottle was ripped from his mouth, catching on his lower front tooth—a tooth he was sure he would lose. He knew a beating was coming. He'd broken the rules. Despite all his concentration, listening, learning, and remembering, he'd disobeyed. He'd moved.

But he'd done the right thing. The alcohol would have brought him closer to death's door.

He didn't have the strength to lift his head upright; it hung backward over the back of the chair. He prayed the alcohol that burned in his sinuses might be punishment enough for having moved, yet he knew harsher and deeper pain was imminent. His arms extended from his sides, suspended on the chains fastened to the steel bracelets around his wrists. A picture of Christ nailed to the cross rose before his closed eyes. The agony Jesus the man must have gone through, with spikes pounded through his palms and feet, fixing him to the crucifix. Steel cuffs held Ethan to the wall and chair. Jesus had hung in front of the Romans, who'd hated him because of what they thought. The Madonna mask hated Ethan because of what it thought. Ethan knew he was near the edge of his real world becoming what was behind the heavy door.

He opened his eyes to see the flat, drywall-smooth ceiling painted the same beige color as the cinder-block walls. He couldn't remember having seen it before. He'd been unable to. He knew six inches of insulation and soundproofing lay above the painted ceiling surface. No one was about to hear what went on in that enclosed space. They were in the basement of a house that only the Madonna knew about—because the Madonna had built it. Ethan wasn't imagining it either. He knew it. But how he knew it, he still didn't know.

At the bottom of his line of sight, he could see the Madonna wiping its wet shirt with its hand while holding the hunting knife in the other.

"I thought we were there," it said, as if it had just guttered a bowling ball after having knocked most of the pins down with its first shot. "We were close, Ethan—so close."

It held the knife up in front of its mask. "It was a bit of a dirty trick, but it's how the story goes. It is fun to watch you suffer, though."

The electronic titter erupted from behind the Madonna face.

"What's even better is you brought this all upon yourself!" it shouted, and then it tittered and moved toward Ethan.

Ethan caught the flash reflection of the overhead light across the polished knife blade. Then he heard what sounded like the cracking of walnuts, and a wave of agony overcame him as he realized he was hearing his own bones breaking.

The voice, the masked devil incarnate, stood there unmoving, staring down at him, its weight on his foot. Ethan twisted, unable to control himself; an eruption of pain beyond what he'd suffered seemed determined to exit his body.

"You're making it worse, Ethan!" it yelled, shaking its masked head—in rage or laughter, Ethan couldn't tell, nor did he care. He was closing in on the route outside himself and the room.

"You're moving!" the voice shouted, maintaining its weight on Ethan's left foot as he writhed against his restraints. "You know the rule, but even with our best decisions—our best intentions—things turn out differently, and that's when we really learn."

It stepped back; the weight came off Ethan's foot. He had moved. His head was slumped forward, his chained arms holding him from slumping farther. He didn't care.

"It's now time to live, Ethan," the voice said, speaking from somewhere in front of him. Ethan wasn't even trying not to move. "Remember, I am your hope, your fear, and your truth. The length of your stay here depends on me. You forget that, and your life will be shortened just like hers. She was given to me, and you took her away. Sounds a little Shakespearian, don't you think? Kind of 'To be or not to be.'"

Ethan sensed the voice's proximity but paid no attention. He was spent. His foot screamed. It was unbearable not to touch it, hold it, or do anything. His thirst was gone, consumed by his pain.

As he felt the edge of the heavy door come into his hand, his head was jerked up. The jarring pain of a handful of his hair yanked backward muted the numbing pain blaring from his broken foot.

The sweet, sickly aroma of reeking garbage covered his face. Like a rag doll, he was limp to resist.

"Now, let's get on with it," he heard the voice say, and that was all he heard as darkness swept over him.

CHAPTER 76

A Forest

It was unbelievable, yet there she was. The liquid-chocolate eyes that melted him into a stammering adolescent were unmistakable. Gold-hooped rings dangled from her ears like those of an ancient Egyptian goddess on display for all to see yet seemingly for his eyes only. His heart beat to some synchronistic rhythm between them. Her crimson lips parted—full and inviting, meant for his—revealing her perfect white teeth and her endearing smile. It was as if they were meeting again for the first time; his feelings were no less alive and ingenuous. It was like one discovering love for the first time, having never experienced its magnificence before.

Christa was leaning against the trunk of a large tree. He had walked up a dirt road—a path, really—with trees lining both sides in nature's own pattern. Christa's manicured fingers rested on the crevassed gray bark of a huge hemlock, contrasting with the tree's bark, just as she was in contrast to the forest that surrounded her. Diffuse rays of sunlight scattered around them like flashlight beams, teasing them to participate in their orgy of light. If true tranquility existed, he had found it, both in his love for her and in this place.

How he'd come to be there he couldn't remember.

"You have found me, my sweet," Christa whispered, her voice like a light breeze passing through the ferns and foliage around them. "I don't know where you are, but I will find you."

Ethan, unable to speak, stared at her. Instinct told him she would disappear if he turned away, leaving him alone and lost, maybe forever.

He ached for her, longing to hold and kiss her. There was much to explain and understand. But his voice seemed sealed, as his memory was.

"I know," she said.

Just hearing her voice was comforting.

"I found you once," she whispered, her lips barely moving. "I will find you again."

Ethan didn't understand. She would find him? He was right there in front of her. He kept staring, afraid a mere glance away would take her from his sight. Seeing her was a gift to savor. No matter how long she was there, her leaving would come too soon.

"I need you to speak, babe," she whispered.

Ethan shook his head, his eyes not leaving hers. He wanted to point to his mouth; he couldn't speak. Maybe this was heaven; when he was with her, he wanted for nothing.

"I know," she said, as if answering his thoughts. "I will find you and never stop looking until I do."

The beams of light were extinguished above the treetops. White streaks appeared in her hair, as if transferred from the sun.

"Do you like it?" she asked, seemingly in answer to his thoughts again. He didn't need to speak.

Then, with the liquid grace of water poured on the forest floor, she disappeared.

Ethan found himself alone as the forest grew dark. The wind picked up. The lofty trees swayed overhead, gnarling their branches together like cutlery, as if preparing for a feast. The trunks seemed to groan as they rubbed against each other, restrained to the ground. A deer passed close by, seemingly unaware of his presence, moving gracefully. It was gone as quickly as it had appeared. Ethan was soon unable to move, forced to watch as gusts of wind, each more powerful than the last, took down one tree after another. The cracking of the massive trunks was terrifying—an act of God's almighty hand. The ground shook as each tree fell so loudly that he closed his eyes amid nature's grand symphony.

The wind howled through the trees, whipping the tops around like giant dusters. Distracted by the violence above, he didn't see the approach of the collie that appeared out of nowhere. It stopped beside him and barked.

The dog's dark eyes stared into his.

"Don't be afraid."

Ethan heard the words. The dog rotated its head as if trying to comprehend. He reached out to pet the dog. He could move again. The dog's sable coat was soft in his hand.

"Follow me."

He heard the words whispered in his ears, as if the forest were speaking to him through the ferocious wind.

The dog looked at him again. "Don't be afraid," its eyes seemed to repeat. With the powerful storm surrounding them, the collie started away. Reluctant to move, thinking it best to stay put, Ethan decided to follow. Dog was man's best friend; the animal wouldn't intentionally mislead him.

The ground was strewn with the forest's debris. Plants, leaves, twisted limbs, and fallen branches were everywhere. As they moved, more was scattered in their midst. He heard the air-splitting crack of another tree trunk as a pine tree of enormous girth broke in front of him, snapping like a matchstick, falling in slow motion, and crashing to the forest floor with such force that Ethan thought the ground beneath him would split open. The dog ran under the fallen tree, following an unseen line of twists and turns. Ethan could not see a path but followed the collie as he might have followed the red taillights of a car through a winter blizzard.

Ethan fell behind, unable to keep up with the speed of his faster four-legged friend. He tried to call out, but the dog took no notice, no doubt unable to hear his voice, if he even had one. The wind continued its terrifying howl. A whirlwind encircled him in an upheaval of leaves, bark, and snarled branches. His arms rose to protect his head as a thorny vine cut across his face, stinging his skin. The forest was out of control. He had to find cover; otherwise, being lost would cease to matter. It was difficult to see as the forest was hurled around him. At a fallen tree, he crouched and moved to his left. Feeling along the deep crevices in the bark like a blind man, he hoped to guide himself to a safe refuge.

He crept along beside the trunk through the raging wind. As the fallen tree narrowed, a small lean-to came into sight. Something flashed beside it. Relief filled him as he saw his furry friend ahead. Rounding the side of the shelter, he was shocked to see a head of brown hair through the spaces between the branches of the shelter wall. He froze, seeing that it wasn't the dog but another person, and before he could think more, he saw her.

"Hurry!" Christa shouted, the cords in her neck prominent, her face expressing an intensity he hadn't known. He could hear but a whisper.

He looked for an opening and, in the wind's raging torment, lost sight of her. Through an unseen opening, she grabbed his arm and pulled him inside. Inside, Ethan was amazed at how the forest's upheaval vanished. It was warm and cozy, with shadowy light provided by a small lantern that hung from the slanted roof. Christa was sitting on a bed of pine needles with her legs together at her side. The lantern cast shadows across her face, highlighting her gold earrings. Lines on her forehead showed concern.

"Ethan," she whispered, raising her index finger, which was tipped with a golden fingernail, to pursed lips. Her brown eyes, rimmed in black and gold, watched in the light of the lantern's fire. They followed something behind him. He didn't dare speak. Her soft fingers touched his bare arm and pointed. Looking through the branches, he saw a giant black bear lumber past; it was easily the size of a Holstein cow. With each step, the bear's heavy coat shimmered. Ethan was immobilized. Fear and awe held him still. To speak was impossible but unnecessary. The bear continued its course, seemingly unperturbed by the inhabitants of the forest shelter or the tremendous gusts of wind whipping past it. Ethan could feel its shambling presence as the ground shook and the air moved. Unknowingly, Ethan held his breath, anxious for the brazen animal to move on.

"He's here to protect you," Christa whispered. "He won't bother us."

Ethan turned and looked into her brown eyes. She seemed able to read his thoughts and respond in ways that made him want her even more. Her fingertips touched his cheek. He missed her touch and touching her. In the dim light cast by the lantern, he saw her gold eyelids close as he moved to kiss her crimson lips. He moved slowly, savoring the kiss and the warm touch of her skin. She wore a luminescent white gown that flowed like a cascading waterfall to the pine-needle floor. It was open. His hand moved to her warm bare shoulder. She moved with him to his rhythm; he hoped the moment would last but knew the impossibility of such a wish.

"I will find you again," she whispered, turning to him. "Don't lose hope. I will. I promise."

His hand slid down her side. More than anything, he wanted her. His hand moved along the smoothness of her thigh and slid between her legs; his fingertips moved with familiarity, wanting to please her. She acquiesced. His beating heart not only desired her but also craved to give her all he could. His hunger grew, as if charged by the intensity of the tempest that had brought them together. His lips searched hers as if discovering them for the first time. Her hand found him. His fingers found her.

"Please," she whispered, the tip of her tongue slipping along the curve of his earlobe. "Oh, please."

She guided him with the ease of perfect love. With no resistance and no reserve, they moved in unison.

He rolled, his hand on her side, looking at her. He could have looked into her brown eyes and died happy.

Something moved behind her. He heard snorting and a thud on the forest floor beneath them. The bear was back. It would be seconds before it found them and broke their lovers' bond.

The bear was not there to protect him.

The heavy black snout heaved through the branches with the pungent smell of sweet rot. Christa was gone from his arms, replaced by the bear's huge head and gnashing teeth dripping with saliva. The sharp claws were on him, tearing and pulling at his crotch viciously; pain quickly replaced the ecstasy of moments before.

The head of the bear rose enormous above him. In weak defense, he tried to lift his arms to protect his head, a gesture that would be all but futile against such massive power. The bear's jaws opened, revealing colossal yellow teeth ready to crush his skull and sever his head; Ethan's terror resigned to death.

But the bear did not attack his head. Instead, its claws and head pressed painfully into his groin, squashing him and turning his stomach into agony.

"Yes, Ethan!" screamed the voice from the bear's open mouth. "Yeah, baby, come to me."

CHAPTER 77

Eyes Open—Sixth Time—Forest to Doom

He recognized the face with such revulsion that he couldn't hold back his nausea. Acidic bile filled his mouth. Brown liquid squirted from the opening in the tape and dribbled down his chin onto his soiled T-shirt. He could do nothing to control or stop it. The Madonna's rubber face was in his nightmare. It moved back, seeming to pay little attention to the disgusting scene it was in.

"Wow, you're really into this."

The Madonna mask's statement was so matter-of-fact that it made Ethan's disgust even greater.

"I suppose you're gonna crap on the chair too?" its electronic voice added, shifting to its announcer's tone. "Attention, Ethan: what you do on the chair, you're gonna eat. I'm not cleaning up after your doggy doo. But if you're good, maybe I'll let you have mine."

The music seemed louder. Frankie Goes to Hollywood's "Relax" was pounding out its rhythm.

The eyes behind the mask, which he was sure he recognized, gleamed with a mania Ethan could only associate with insanity. His wrists and ankles were still bound. He wore only the soiled T-shirt he'd been wearing since the night he'd been taken. He was still on the chair. The Madonna was on its knees in front of him with a death-grip hold on his genitals, squeezing. His stomach curdled painfully.

"Ain't this what you wanted, big fella?" the voice shouted in his face. "Sure sounded like it."

Ethan screamed.

"Oh, come on!" the voice yelled, its hand moving as if it were squishing a giant turkey baster. "Ya gotta, man. For Mila."

345

Mila?

Hearing Mila's name struck Ethan as if something suddenly broke open in his head. He could feel himself drifting; the heavy door was now open. He'd stepped inside. The immensity of what was before him was no longer coherent. There was no room to pray or do anything else; his brain was bursting with revelation.

"Come on, Ethan," the Madonna pleaded, thrusting its hand at Ethan's chest, insanity on a mission. "I know you have it in you. Do it for Mila, in her memory."

Its manic eyes left Ethan's and looked down at its hands. On the edge, Ethan knew where he was going. He closed his eyes. There was nothing left. He had reached the point where it was unbearable.

"So this is what it was like for Mila," it hissed.

Ethan's stomach cramped and seemed about to split open. His eyes opened. The Madonna mask's eyes looked blank in madness.

"Mila would be proud, Ethan—and jealous."

The titter-cackle fractured the air as his captor stood up.

What he saw eclipsed everything else in his mind. The rape was overwhelming, no matter how powerless he'd been to do anything about it. He asked Mila, and prayed to God, for forgiveness, unable to explain why; his participation had not been voluntary. He was the incarcerated victim of crazy and outside what his mind could comprehend—a grotesque scene of humanity.

With his arms chained to the wall, his head slumped forward, incapable of thought.

"No one will ever know, Ethan," the voice said, chuckling.

Ethan didn't need to see behind the rubber face to know the malevolent smirk that was there. He'd seen it enough in their dorm room. He knew. *Robbie.* He just didn't know how it was possible.

"Our secret is safe with us. I mean me."

Hesitating, the voice paused as if to consider something it was about to say.

"Because you will never see another person," it said, the electronic voice louder, coming closer. "Remember, I am the hope, the fear, and the truth for you, Ethan. That will never change in what's left of your life."

CHAPTER 78

Eyes Open—Again

Ethan woke but didn't open his eyes; he only listened and thought. The number twenty-seven came into his head before anything else. He added one without thinking—twenty-eight. He'd counted the times he'd become conscious. It was his only measure of time passing. He heard Lynyrd Skynyrd's "Sweet Home Alabama" playing and pictured the position he was in, because he still could. His head hung down, his chin nearly on his chest. He imagined what he might see upon opening his eyes. His arms were extended behind him, chained to the wall. Though he couldn't see them, he knew. There was no feeling in his arms; he felt only their weight on his shoulders. He didn't move or do anything that might bring attention to his consciousness. He would be in the wood chair, his ankles still bound by metal cuffs to the chair legs. In front of him were the bed, the toilet, and the night table. He knew from memory. He had no idea how long he'd been out.

He hoped, as he did each time he came back, that none of it was true. Though his hope was close to zero, it was still hope.

Slowly, with what had become practiced care to avoid detection, he opened his eyes. He felt more hope in managing that task.

What he opened his eyes to see was difficult to believe. He saw naked legs. They must have been someone else's. He knew his own legs looked stronger than the ones he now looked at. Practice had taught him not to move when shocked or alarmed, but he felt both as he looked at the thinness of his legs. Nakedness no longer caused him bother, but his weight loss did.

He wondered whether he'd become as emaciated as the starving Jews imprisoned in the notorious Nazi death camps he'd seen in old black-and-white photographs in textbooks.

Shut that thought down.

Would he survive another day, another hour, or even another minute? *Can't think that way, Ethan.*

He thought of Christa and being with her. He could rebuild his body, but death was final.

As far as he could tell, he hadn't moved. He hadn't raised his head, turned his neck, or shifted in the least. But would that be enough for the voice?

Madonna mask?

He blinked. The music playing was Blondie's hit song "One Way or Another."

A thought flashed through his head. Robbie had killed Mila. *Right?* And he'd likely killed Syd. *Right?* How was that possible?

"Good morning, old sport," the Madonna said, touching Ethan's head.

Something was different with his head. He felt the air move before the hand touched him. The tape over his mouth didn't seem wrapped around his head anymore, only across his mouth and cheeks. But there was something else.

"Ah, yes," the voice said in its sick, electronic sweetness.

Ethan didn't move. The black boots that threatened pain moved closer in front of him. They weren't to be trusted; the shiny boots were bad news.

"You've learned well. Better than I would expect of a thief."

The boots moved out of Ethan's sight on one side of the chair and reappeared on the other side.

"Yes, a thief!" it screamed, inches from Ethan's left ear, and then it whispered, "A people thief of the worst order. The kind who steals girlfriends right from under your nose."

The Madonna mask yelled the last two words, as if daring Ethan to move. But moving was a violation, and a violation meant punishment. He did everything he could to deny the voice's apparent need to see pain.

"You look skinny," the voice said, as if telling someone he or she looked tired despite being responsible for causing it. The tone sounded familiar. Ethan remembered the tone Robbie had had as he stood at the door to their apartment. "Trying to cut back?"

Apartment?

The titter-laugh followed. Ethan couldn't remember ever hearing Robbie laugh in such a way. Ethan gave no indication he'd heard anything the voice had said. He had to follow the rules.

Robbie's image returned. *Apartment? No, it was our dorm room. Yes, but …*

Ethan could recall an apartment. *The apartment where Christa—no, the room where Mila lay. No, no. No!*

That wasn't right. He was getting mixed up.

You have to stop this, Ethan.

It was the music. The constant music was intended to confuse. He knew that, didn't he? America's "Horse with No Name" filled the air.

What day was it? He had no idea. It didn't matter. Time was passing, as was evident by his deteriorating body. He'd been conscious and out twenty-eight times, give or take a few he might have missed or forgotten. Going in and out maybe twice a day made fourteen days. *Two weeks?* Was that possible? By the look of his legs, it was. At fifteen, he'd been in the hospital for twenty days and had given up thirty pounds to a burst appendix. It was possible.

"You're still alive, Ethan boy," Madonna-Robbie said, speaking in the electronic tone Ethan had gotten used to. He tried to pick out something of Robbie in the voice. "You have some stamina, man. I'll give you that. More than I would have guessed. Thirsty?"

Just the word made Ethan shiver. He wasn't cold, but the thought of water made him shudder. Dehydration would kill him before the kicks and punches. His captor was somehow giving him just enough to stay alive, but by the look of his thinned legs, that wouldn't be for much longer.

"How can you be cold?" Madonna-Robbie asked, sounding confused, as if it cared. It apparently had noticed his shiver.

A bent white straw appeared. His head was hanging. He didn't move as the straw was inserted into a new hole in the new tape put there while he was out. There was no hesitation this time; instinct did not allow him to hold back. He sucked air until a bowl of clear fluid was held in front of him. Water, alcohol, or poison, it didn't matter.

He drank.

It was water this time.

The liquid was ice cold, jetting into his mouth with its power to sustain life. Down his throat it went with no less pleasure. His ears seemed to take the brunt of the ice-cold liquid. They lit up, burning. Then his throat blew up into his mouth. The three—ears, throat, and mouth—seemed to gang up to blast his head. He imagined his brain crumbling from the force. The pain was unexpected. He shook as the inside of his head throbbed. Bright flares lit up behind his eyes. His arms locked in spasms, and his thighs cramped as if trying to move him off the chair.

He wanted to die.

"I'm sorry," the Madonna thing said, sounding like a person concerned for his welfare even with the electronic distortion. It was speaking close to his right ear, which now seemed filled with something solid that dampened what he heard. "Did you say something?"

Though painful, Ethan did everything he could to bring the muscle spasms in his arms and legs under control. Then he felt something in his hand with the broken finger. Though it was strange, he didn't move to the voice's question, seeing it as another trick of kindness, like proffering poison in a polished red apple.

The straw in his mouth had dropped to the chair. The pain of his thirst for water seemed to have exchanged places with the physical pain of drinking it. Fear accompanied his thirst; if dehydration didn't kill him, he might end up wishing it had. He could remain alive and broken but not without water.

He knew the Madonna thing knew this.

"Could have sworn you were trying to tell me something."

The Madonna face screamed the last word as a panicked mother might have called the name of a child who had run into a busy street. Ethan's numbness kept him still.

"But I've been wrong before," it said, its voice fading as it moved away from Ethan's side.

Don McLean's "American Pie" was taking its turn in the room.

The song seemed to give Madonna-Robbie time to think. It gave Ethan time to think too, even if unclearly. The pause wasn't without intention, Ethan figured. Robbie was smart. But the longer Ethan was conscious, the more he could think too. With no outside stimuli, his mind went inside, searching, made easier by his weakened state. It was harder to try not to think. Worse, Ethan had no control over the duration of the pause. It was all in the Madonna mask's hands. The game was—

Stop it! Stop it! Ethan screamed silently, deafening him inside. *You're not helping.*

If he'd moved, he didn't know it. He could have. He was on the other side of the open heavy door, with the inside begging him to step forward.

"I wanted to do something new today," Madonna-Robbie said, "to reward you for your good behavior."

The straw disappeared from between his legs on the chair. His head remained down, unmoving, like his eyes. If he'd moved, he couldn't remember.

"I don't want to get your hopes up," the electronic voice said, sounding almost apologetic in its tone. "Be assured you won't leave this room alive, but to help speed things up, I thought of this game. I'm calling it Death by a Thousand Cuts."

The Madonna thing could hardly get the words out before its creaky laugh started. The black boots moved into view in front of Ethan.

"We're going to start now," said Madonna-Robbie. An X-Acto knife appeared in front of Ethan's eyes. "The game goes like this."

Without pause, its manly hand grabbed Ethan's right shoulder. Ethan felt his arm move. A sharp twinge of pain followed, as if a vaccination needle had been poked into his arm. The pain burned for an instant and then seemed to dissipate.

"Today"—the Madonna continued flashing the blade, now marked with blood, in front of Ethan's eyes—"we will start with one cut. Each time we play, I will double the number of cuts."

The X-Acto blade smeared with his blood disappeared. Ethan didn't move.

"So," the voice said.

Again, the black boots disappeared from Ethan's right-side view only to reappear a moment later on his left. His captor snickered in the electronics. Ethan wondered what could possibly be funny.

"To move things along, we'll play two rounds today. First round was one cut. This round will be two."

As it spoke, Ethan felt the burning pain of the next stroke into his left shoulder. It seemed deeper than the first. He flinched, but it didn't slow the Madonna. Another slice followed, seemingly just below the second cut. His numb arm jerked the chain that held it.

A drop of blood landed on his bare right thigh from the first cut. He was surprised; the cut hadn't seemed as painful as the last two, yet blood dripped from it. *How deep are the other two?* It wouldn't take a thousand cuts to end him at that rate.

"Now that seems a little unbalanced to me," it said. "A different number of cuts on each arm isn't right."

The voice trailed off, as if again distracted by something. *A different number of cuts on each arm* repeated in his head. He knew those words. Why? Again, he didn't know, but they touched something in his memory, like lines from a movie or something he'd read—real yet not real. *Why those words?* How could they possibly make any difference anyway?

He could feel the heavy door behind him.

This is a mistake, he said to himself. *A fucking mistake.*

The words screamed as if something inside were trying to get out.

Something hit the wall above where he believed the bed, table, and commode to be, though he hadn't seen them during this awake period. The black boots that had been on his left returned to his right side.

The pain in his right arm was instant and stayed longer. He did everything in his power to hold still. The muscles in his arm tightened.

"There. That's much better," the Madonna mask announced. "You're gonna bleed out right here, my man—right here in front of me. I am your hope, your fear, and your truth," the voice behind the mask bellowed.

Ethan didn't look up but was sure if he had, he would have seen the Madonna mask facing the ceiling, yelling the words to some inexplicable deity.

At the same time, the feeling of something in his hand came back. His hands had been numb for he didn't know how long, chained to hang high behind him. The object felt like a book. Surprised by the sensation, he was certain there was nothing there, yet he couldn't deny the feeling. He hadn't moved and was still staring down at his legs, but the feeling of a book in his right hand was there. He could see it in his mind. It wasn't there for him to read; it was there because he needed it. As before, he didn't know why he knew that; he just did. He needed the book's words. His words were in the book. He could see himself holding it, having paid for it with almost all the money he had. The book was important. It represented who he was to become. It was time for Robbie to take off the Madonna mask. Ethan had done it before. It was in the book. It was part of the story. Robbie would reveal himself.

Ethan felt a drip running down his bicep like a bead of sweat, only it wasn't sweat. It was blood—his blood.

What had he heard hit the wall?

Cuts. Bleeding. Slow bleeding. Those were the words in his head.

But what had hit the wall? He wanted to look—needed to look—but looking would have consequences, likely deadly ones. He also knew if he didn't do something, he would die.

The others had died.

If you're not willing to risk it all, you don't want it bad enough.

The line came to Ethan as if he'd just read it. He knew the line. It was his line, a line that had changed his life. Then he saw it. The word was clear.

Act.

The word was in the room behind the heavy door.

He'd written it on the wall. It was time to act.

CHAPTER 79

Eyes Open—Still

Ethan raised his head, knowing it might be for the last time, or at least he imagined doing it.

It was what he had to do.

He was sure of his captor's identity yet in disbelief at how Robbie could have pulled off such an incredible feat in rising from the dead.

It didn't make any sense. *And why Syd?*

But as he said her name in his head, he remembered. This wasn't about Syd. It was about Mila.

But Robbie killed Christa, Ethan. No, Robbie killed Mila.

He was mixed up again. How long had it been since his last Orap pills? Days? A week?

The Madonna-Robbie thing had repeated that Ethan wouldn't leave the room alive. He was there to die. Retribution would be complete when his captor was ready. But there were two people in the room—the Madonna mask and him. Madonna-Robbie had planned what would happen, just like its lecture. Ethan had a stake in that. He had to do something. The Madonna mask's two-minute warning had sounded. Ethan wasn't about to go down without a fight.

He would first raise his head when the black boots moved out of sight. If any luck were on his side, Madonna-masked Robbie would be looking the other way. Ethan knew what he would see: the beige cinder block walls, the wood-framed bed perfectly made up with a sky-blue bedspread and pressed white pillowslip, the night table, and the white-enamel commode beside it. He saw the scene in even more detail than before, as if on a movie set, and he was the camera.

Still he didn't know how he knew that, but he did. There was something on the floor too—something different.

Ethan stopped thinking and raised his head. As he'd thought, he saw the bed, the beige walls, the table, and the toilet—and what he figured he'd heard hit the wall.

On the floor in front of the nightstand, lying open with the dustcover up, was *Browning Station*—his lost hospital copy, protective plastic cover and all.

Staring in disbelief, Ethan was slow to catch Madonna-Robbie's movement.

"Ah," the electronic voice said.

There was a mix of reactions as the two stared at each other. Ethan was incredulous at seeing his lost book splayed out on the floor in front of him. Madonna-Robbie appeared just as surprised at seeing Ethan's head up and facing him. What Madonna-Robbie said next surprised Ethan the most.

"You recognize it?"

Ethan didn't move. He was caught. He would have to deal with what followed. But for the first time, he saw something different in the eyes behind the Madonna mask. They shifted for all of an instant, as if its mind had gone somewhere else, unplanned and unexpected. He'd never seen that in Robbie's eyes. For a moment, he thought someone else might be behind the mask.

"You know," the Madonna mask said, "I first saw *Browning Station* in a bookstore on Rideau Street—with a sign that said, 'Penned by local author.'"

The electronic voice pointed at the book with the X-Acto knife still in its hand. "But then I saw it in your car. I had to have it."

How could Robbie—

The Madonna went over and picked up the book. Without turning around, it seemed to look at the cover, and then it tossed the book onto the blue bedspread.

Queen's "Sheer Heart Attack" was playing.

As if a switch had been activated in its head, the Madonna mask turned around. "You don't know how you came to be here, do you?"

It asked the question in a way that made Ethan recall sitting in front of Dr. Katharine's desk, about to listen to her diagnosis.

"There I go again, asking you a question!" The voice yelled the last word as if speaking in punctuation. Then it calmed. "It was really quite easy. You should be more careful who you pick for friends."

The Madonna face moved closer.

Ethan prepared to be kicked. Greg, Randolph, and Gus came to mind. He stopped at Gus. He'd known Gus for the least amount of time.

"We met at one of your shows a while back," the electronic voice said. "Maybe in London. Maybe Toronto. I've been to a few."

Ethan didn't move. He tried not to listen. He was being set up.

"Sydney seemed down," the voice said. "I bought her a drink. She told me about you. Fucking you. How you were going to leave the band. I told her I might be able to help—scare you a little. Maybe you'd reconsider. She warmed up to the idea. It was easy to arrange in Ottawa. She didn't have to know my real agenda."

Ethan turned his head before he realized what he'd done.

The Madonna changed.

"What are you doing?" it yelled. The hand holding the X-Acto knife turned.

Its arm came up. Ethan knew what would happen before the blade disappeared into his right bicep. He didn't need to see the silver handle sticking out of his arm.

He screamed into the tape. Then the words started in his mind.

You had to let the prisoner drink. Dehydration killed after three days. That wasn't going to happen; they deserved more—much more. But to live, they had to have water. Water would grow their fear.

The hole in the duct tape allowed him to drink but not be heard.

William wanted his prisoner to understand the fear his prisoner's victim had felt—that prolonged, paralyzing, mind-melting fear. This was justice. Call it vigilante. Call it payback. Call it robbing from the rich to give to the deserving. He didn't give a shit what they called it. They could all fuck themselves. This was for those who couldn't fend for themselves.

Ethan knew the Madonna's—no, William's—thoughts. He had read them. No, it was more than that; they had become his thoughts. He saw the Madonna's face and knew Robbie's thoughts. He knew Robbie. He had watched Robbie. *Robbie?* But it wasn't Robbie. *Robbie's dead, Ethan.* He felt as he did when he thought he knew someone in a dream, only to find out it was someone else.

Killing wouldn't be enough for William—no, Robbie. No, it was someone else he saw now; to just let him die wouldn't be enough. It had killed her. Ethan had watched, unable to move. Now it couldn't just let Ethan die. This situation was about control and power—its over Ethan's. It wanted Ethan to know that too. Ethan was to die under its hand, its control—William's control. *No, it isn't William's.* The madman behind the Madonna mask had to kill him, just as he had killed her. *Mila.*

CHAPTER 80

Eyes Open Still—Seeing

The room was the same, just as he'd pictured it—the bed, table, commode, beige walls, and green carpet. Even the chair he was bound to.

The padlock was gone. The heavy door was wide open. Ethan was now inside, behind it.

William Avery. The monster. The same but made up to be different. The identity of the monster was like a faceless hologram in Ethan's mind; one angle showed an image, and a different angle showed another. Her killer couldn't be original even in his killing—but devious and evil? Oh yeah, William Avery had nothing on this thing. Its choreography was impeccable.

But William Avery was a well-meaning, proud family man who was never expected to make a difference. He was Mr. Average in the mediocre world that surrounded him. But William found a way to make a difference. Ethan knew it. He'd lived it. He'd become it. It had made him *famous*?

The title of the book seemed to stare back at him, as if it talked to him. Ethan's world had been *Browning Station*. He'd researched and rehearsed and become William Avery. But his William Avery delivered justice to those who were incapable of getting justice themselves. William delivered justice to those who deserved it. What they had coming to them was in his hands—the child molester; the racist killer; the woman abuser; predators who walked around masked in kindly goodness while preying on the less fortunate, weaker ones.

This imposter masked as Madonna was not William Avery.

Yet everything else in the room reflected William Avery's story. The Madonna hadn't taken Ethan through all of *Browning Station*, but it had made parts of it feel real. The room resembled the set where he'd become William Avery.

Ethan was William Avery.

Ethan screamed into the tape again—no words, only the muffled sounds of terror.

His head shook while he screamed. His arms shook as far as the chains and chair would allow. He bucked in the chair, held back by the strap around his stomach. He rammed his legs up and down against the steel ankle bracelets. The steel cuffs cut into his wrists and ankles as he rocked manically. His broken left foot was in agony with every movement.

Then he heard it again—William Avery's line. But it wasn't William Avery talking. It was Christa.

If you're not willing to risk it all, you don't want it bad enough.

The word again appeared in front of his eyes: *act.*

* * *

It started in his chest. He was screaming and coughed. The cough wasn't real, but Ethan made it real.

He adjusted his scream. His eyes widened. He shook his head as if high-voltage electricity were flowing through him; the fear of God was in his eyes. He glared into the shifting eyes that looked back at him from behind rubber Madonna—mad, blank eyes. He coughed, choking his scream. He contracted his neck muscles, fed by the hot pain of the X-Acto knife in his arm. The knife was erect and obscene like a harpoon stuck in the side of a bleeding whale. Each flex of his thin bicep ignited new fire. He made his fingers and hands shake as if charged by the same high voltage that shook his head and was killing him. His throbbing broken finger egged him on. The toes of his right foot curled while his foot quivered. The pain in his left foot exacerbated the vibration of his right. He'd not seen a convulsive seizure; this was the best of his imagination.

"You're not dying until I say so!" the voice said, exploding its command into Ethan's face.

Foaming saliva bubbled through the hole in the tape, muting his screams.

Every part of his naked body moved or shuddered. Spit sprayed from the hole in the duct tape as he blew out. His eyes rolled back in his head; only the dead-like whites were visible.

"Stop this shit!" the electronic-voiced Madonna yelled, its strong hands on Ethan's head, trying to stop the violent shaking. Ethan knew his head was shaved. William Avery had shaved his prisoners' heads. He could feel the prickliness of the stubble and the sensitivity to the air around his head. Hair would have allowed the Madonna to grab a handful and hold him maybe. The exertion made him sweat, and his head was slippery like greased swine. It was all as real as he could make it—choking convulsions fueled by the evil in the eyes he looked into.

"Stop your monkey shit!" it bellowed.

Ethan did not slow, despite his body's pleading. He became more frantic, his apparent insanity heightened by his refusal to admit his situation, his helplessness, or his vulnerability. He had to be as crazy as his evil captor, the captive no longer on the verge of hell but in the depths of it.

"Fuck! Fuck! Fuck!" hollered the electronic-voiced Madonna mask.

Ethan took his first shot to the head. It hardly registered. If anything, it made real the crushing rage inside him. More spit flew from the hole in the tape and into his face. He pushed his tongue against the tape, trying to push through the hole. His rocking and shaking didn't let up.

The music played constantly. *While the victim was incarcerated, William wanted his soundtrack. It was disrupting, disorienting.* He heard the calm serenity of Andy Williams's "Moon River." *Meant to confuse the victim's emotions around what was taking place.* It now served to drive Ethan on.

The Madonna's open palm slammed hard into the side of his face. Ethan's head whipped sideways, numbing his cheek and tearing some of the tape from his face.

Ethan screamed again. It took his breath. The size of the hole in the tape, compounded by his saliva, made it all but impossible to catch.

He blew out, spraying spittle around like an exhausted athlete.

Then, as suddenly as he'd started, he stopped, as if reaching the eye of his tempest. The calm lasted for all of a second, maybe two, as he played dead, and then the uncontrollable shaking took over. Whether by performance or reaction, his art was now his life.

His plan, like before, was to bleed the victim to death's door and then suffocate them. Stay with the plan, William. Deviations will be punished.

Ethan knew what William was thinking. He knew what masked Robbie would do.

The capture. The room. The wood chair. Ethan knew it was bolted to the floor. It wasn't going anywhere. The brackets were strong, stronger than the wood legs.

As Tylenol was to the medical doctor, duct tape was to the handyman. Shave their heads. Take their clothes. Complete and utter vulnerability. There was to be nothing the captee could attach meaning to, nothing of value. He had to be driven to the lowest level of depravity, Maslow's lowest level of physiological need—air, water, food. The victim must realize he is nothing. Like air, he must believe himself inert.

The words he remembered were his thoughts, William's thoughts, but they didn't still his tirade. Real or not, it was all or nothing. He had to disrupt the plan, the plan he knew—William's plan, his plan, the plan the Madonna mask was carrying out.

It had murdered Mila.

Every decision is an emotional one. Decisions are based on the emotional level one is at, their apparent logic. As if going through a checklist, the brain's living tissue is constantly reconfiguring its input based on emotional state. Excite or depress those emotions changes the checklist and the decisions, creating different actions, first one thing but later another.

Ethan knew this because William knew it. He was the real William Avery; he had become William to perform the role, his role. *William used what his wife, a nurse, brought home or what he picked up from her medical journals to take charge of his victims. Each deserved what he had coming.*

Ethan remained locked to the chair but shook with every fraction of movement he could manage. His broken left foot was on fire but fed the fight still in him. The more he shook his head and twisted his face, the more saliva worked its way out. The tape became less stuck to his skin. The gaps grew, adding loudness to his screaming.

They can't know who you are. Black boots, a mask, and a new voice. Only you know them, a one-way street. Extraordinary circumstances do not mean things go unplanned. All is not spontaneous. We must engineer our success—your success. No mistakes.

Ethan knew the black boot was coming. He anticipated the move as the Madonna's natural defense to something unexpected. What he didn't expect was where it would come from or the agony.

He was shaking and rocking his head back and forth. His numb arms pulled at his shoulders as he jerked himself around. His right shoulder still burned where the X-Acto knife remained stuck in his bicep. Then, on a downward thrust of his head, the black boot slammed into his shin with a force he was sure broke his tibia. The pain brought him to the edge of his consciousness.

The heavy door was behind him. He was inside and not about to leave.

His head flew backward. The top of the chair back caught him just below his shoulder blades. He hardly noticed. His hips thrust forward, forcing him hard against the restraining belt secured to the chair. He didn't have much left. Something had to give soon.

"You will pay with your life!" the electronic-voiced Madonna screamed, its madness extending beyond its mask and into Ethan's craziness.

But something felt different to Ethan, as if the chair had shifted. Somehow, he kept rocking, ignoring the agonizing shrieks of his legs and arms to stop. To stop was to die. Its control was gone. It wanted Ethan dead.

"You bastard!" the Madonna mask screamed above Ethan's yells behind the tape. Ethan heard John Denver's "Rocky Mountain High" between gasps to catch his breath. "You've fucked with the wrong person this time."

Ethan saw Mila, her body limp, in the monster's arms, her shirt unbuttoned.

That monster didn't look like Robbie.

Rage took over.

Ethan turned his head as he rocked hard backward again. Something let go. He couldn't tell whether it was part of him or the chair. His screams were not an act. He thrust his head forward.

The crack was loud. He could feel it in his torso. The pain was exquisite. His shin was broken. He was shrieking.

CHAPTER 81

Eyes Stay Open—Surreal Clarity

Unbearable agony was deteriorating his consciousness, yet he had magnificent clarity. He was sinking like the ground beneath him and the chair was disintegrating.

The tug on his arms came first. As his body continued to shake, no longer in control, his arms took on his weight. Spittle flew from the open gaps in the duct tape across his mouth. His thighs were loaded with weight they could not support. Like a collapsing bridge, the chair he sat on came apart. His legs, clamped to the chair's front legs, pulled back. The back legs of the chair collapsing twisted his arms backward and left him hanging from the chains fastened to the wall. The steel cuffs cut even deeper into his skin.

First, they must not be fed, to slow the body's metabolism. Slow the blood flow and its manufacture. Then let them bleed. Become their hope, their fear, and their truth, their life and death. They're shit. They won't leave the room alive.

Ethan knew what William expected—or had come to expect.

Hanging by his wrists, he couldn't lift himself. His arms, elevated for so long, were of little use, just numb appendages attached to his body. He put everything he had into pushing back with his legs. His right leg exploded in agony, blurring his ability to think. How he supported any weight with his broken left foot, he didn't know; his right leg was all but useless to the fight. The black boots had done their job, but it wasn't only his leg that was broken. The front leg of the chair seemed damaged. He pushed again with his left leg and moved sideways. His right ankle went with it, along with a jolt of pain that went all the way up his leg. He would have grabbed it if he could have. He then realized the black boot had done even more. The front chair leg seemed dislodged from the steel bracket that anchored it to the floor. Hope and idea came together. Normally, such pain would have prevented him from any movement, but his leg was free. Nothing else mattered.

His right leg shot up into something hard and fleshy.

William, how could you let this happen?

They were his words, and it was his scene to make right. He could defeat William because he knew William. He had been William.

As he hung from the chains bolted to the cider-block wall, the masked Madonna's swiping palm connected with his nose, igniting another firestorm inside his head. Ethan found his own madness. He had rocked and shaken before like some kind of convulsing marionette in a forced seizure, but he now was out of control and wild like a rabid animal.

He turned, and as the chair leg fastened to his right foot came away from its mount in the floor, he drove his leg upward. His hips rolled sideways, giving him leverage to drive his limp leg forward. Thought wasn't possible. It was happening. The agony of his broken right leg amplified the intensity of his actions. He burst into a flurry of kicks and thrusts that could only occur when a young man was on the cusp of death and knew it. It was the action that won wars and rewarded average men with medals for their extraordinary courage.

The Madonna was on him, not punching but flailing with the heels of its palms. The eyes behind the mask looked lit up by high-intensity lightbulbs. Madonna-Robbie thrashed its fists into Ethan's body for the kill.

"You've fucked with me for the last time!" the voice hollered, the electronics faltering as it hammered yet another flat palm into Ethan's face. Each hit seemed to add might to Ethan's will to survive. His head fell backward, missing some of the strikes, but he was unable to defend himself with the arms he couldn't feel still chained to the wall.

"This is better than killing her!" it yelled as the side of its fist came down across Ethan's nose. Ethan felt the crunch inside his head as much as he heard the crack.

Her. Her!

The Madonna thing didn't stop; its madness reached new levels of insanity.

"Seeing you, you dumb fuck, screwed up everything!" it shouted, its electronic voice failing and becoming someone else. "It was supposed to be you, you fuck!"

Numbness had taken over Ethan's entire face. The heel of the Madonna's hand connected hard above his right eye.

"I killed her," the Madonna mask seethed into Ethan's face, "and then I fucked her."

It was time. Control was his to take. It was William's turn. It was his room. *Justice must prevail against such evil. No one gets a pass for crimes against the meek and less fortunate.* Not on his watch they didn't.

Ethan knew the scene like the back of his hand. He knew what William was thinking. No one there was going to jail, but somebody was going to die. It wasn't William Avery.

With strength summoned from a place inside reserved only for such atrocities, Ethan planted his bare left foot on the carpet. With an instant of balance, the short muscles in his legs firing at once, his right knee shot upward. His legs were so weak that the force with which his leg came up flipped the lower part of his leg below the knee forward. The wood chair leg still fastened to the steel bracelet around his ankle turned. The leg of the chair swung sideways and connected. Ethan not only heard it but felt it. The Madonna's swinging palm dropped, falling short of Ethan's face.

Blood poured onto Ethan from whatever gash the chair leg had ripped into its head. The Madonna slipped sideways like a heavy bag of wet cement, all but immovable.

Ethan hung from the chains in the wall. The Madonna's masked head settled against his arm, its right eye no longer visible; blood was consuming its rubber whiteness. Ethan couldn't move away from the blood that poured on him. He had nothing left.

He closed his eyes.

B. J. Thomas was singing "Raindrops Keep Falling on My Head" from the *Butch Cassidy and the Sundance Kid* soundtrack.

Didn't that beat all, as if the tune were making fun of him?

* * *

Ethan didn't know how long he'd been out.

Again, he awoke without opening his eyes and thought. *Twenty-nine.* It was the twenty-ninth time he'd awakened. He was still alive and still thinking. But something was different this time. He hurt everywhere.

Something heavy lay across him. He wasn't sitting on a chair. He was hanging by his arms. He tried to move. The pain nearly tipped him out again.

His head was back against a hard surface. Barbra Streisand was singing "On a Clear Day You Can See Forever."

His mind started to race, suddenly remembering, chased by pain that seemed to come from everywhere and nowhere. It surpassed anything he'd ever known, yet he could still think. He opened his eyes, or thought he did. He could see slits of light from the overhead lights, but it took him a minute to focus. He'd not seen much of the ceiling before, as he'd almost always been facing the floor. His face felt huge and tight, balloon-like. He didn't move, not that he could have from the position he was in.

The rules remained present in his head. There was no moving. But that was before.

He pulled his head forward with everything he had.

He started to shake.

The Madonna mask had shifted on its owner's face. He recognized the face.

It wasn't Robbie. It couldn't have been. Robbie was dead.

Sean Wayland lay on top of him.

Sean beside Mila. Sean at Charly's. Sean Mila's killer. The monster. Get him off! Get him off!

Ethan tried to scream, but his mouth was still covered with the duct tape. The little he could see didn't matter. It was enough. His body shook.

He remembered Sean at *Another Color Blue*—Sean at the show after killing Mila.

His leg shrieked. Pain had replaced his blood.

Like a claustrophobic man caught in an underground drainpipe, Ethan shook, trying to rid himself of the dead monster that lay atop his withered and raw body.

Sean at the gravesite. Sean.

He could not lift his head again. It was as if the mad creature had somehow attached itself to his body like a giant leech sucking what remaining life he had left.

He had no strength in his arms to lift himself. His left foot was still held to the floor, bolted to whatever was left of the chair.

He shook. He didn't try. His body had taken over.

Through the thin slits his swollen face allowed, he could see blond hair. The last of the Madonna mask was almost off. The monster's weight seemed all but immovable. Still, Ethan shook. As if hyperthermia had set in, he shivered uncontrollably. His body needed to rid itself of the virus that lay on top of him.

The longer he shook, the more violent his shivering became. Sean's head—repulsive enough to make him dry heave—slid off his shoulder. The top part of the torso slid with it to the floor. But it wasn't far enough.

The rest of the corpse remained slung over Ethan's upper left thigh and stomach, its legs on one side and its body and head on the other.

Ethan continued to shiver until his adrenaline was spent. Exhaustion took him by force while pain held the upper hand.

It brought him to a throbbing stillness—and a new realization.

The monster had been right. He'd known what he was doing all along.

Sean would have his way again.

Nobody knew where he was.

He was not going to leave the room alive after all. His eyes rolled up into the top of his sockets. It felt better.

Aerosmith's "Dream On" began to play.

Mila's killer had won.

CHAPTER 82

Tuesday, February 19, 1985
Eyes Open—The Nightmare is Real

Ethan would never be able to explain what followed, as he would never be able to separate fully what had been real and what hadn't been.

Hearing Christa's voice and seeing her face made him think he could tell the difference.

"Ethan?" Christa asked.

He could feel her fingers through the thick white gauze bandages around his arm. His face hurt and felt bigger with the hardness of the bruised and swollen tissue. With only slits for sight, he could barely see her. Tears stung his cheeks.

"Yes," he answered, unable to manage anything more than a low whisper. The stiffness of his face made opening his mouth difficult and clear speech impossible.

"Sorry, ma'am," he heard someone say in an efficient, professional-sounding voice he didn't recognize. "I'll need you to step away."

"It's okay; I'm a nurse," Christa replied, her fingers leaving his bandaged arm. He watched her bite her lip and then her knuckle. Her cheeks were wet.

"We have to get him to the hospital," another voice said, an urgent speed in his words.

Ethan heard a number of things; most were indecipherable as he tried to keep the thin spaces he looked through open. He was tired. Christa disappeared from view. It was a dream. Strong hands grabbed his arms as he tried to move. He couldn't let her go again, dream or no dream. He could utter little more than anxious grunts.

"Whoa, cowboy," said the first unfamiliar voice he'd heard. "You're not going anywhere. Ya gotta take it slow."

Ethan shook, trying to move his arm, his hand reaching to find his beloved Christa's hand.

That was when he noticed. He heard sirens, moving feet, and voices, but the music was gone.

EPILOGUE

"But man is not made for defeat," he said. "A
man can be destroyed but not defeated."
                                            —*Ernest Hemingway,*
                                            The Old Man and the Sea

Thursday, February 21, 1985

"Good morning," Christa said as she walked into the room Ethan had occupied for a day and a half and would get to know well over the coming weeks.

"Good morning yourself," Ethan replied to the smile that always made him feel better. It still hurt to move his mouth.

He knew before she spoke—there'd not been much improvement in his swollen face. Something in her face revealed it—a slight furrow of her brow or a minute narrowing of her brown eyes. It was only an instant, a flicker, but it was enough. He doubted she was even aware of it. He refused to look in a mirror, scared of what he would see. He wondered whether getting old brought a similar feeling.

"How's Syd?" he asked. He'd asked about her before, and hesitation had followed, with Christa skirting anything more than a vague answer. "I still don't know."

He watched as Christa shifted her weight from her left leg to her right. In a fraction of a second, her expression turned from dark to light.

"Sydney's why you're alive," she said, her voice quivering, tears on her cheeks. "We would never have found you in time."

Christa grabbed his left hand and squeezed. "She's pretty heavily sedated down the hall," she said. "She's banged up and bruised and who knows what else."

She turned and sat on the edge of his bed. "Seems whoever was holding her took off. Maybe after—" Christa stopped and brushed her cheeks. "She somehow got out and brought the police to you."

Ethan didn't say anything, relieved that Syd was okay.

He stared into the brown eyes he'd thought he'd never see again. It seemed hard to believe he was looking into them now. When he thought about what had happened, it seemed more like a nightmare than anything that could possibly be true.

The never-ending questions from doctors and the police had already started. Most of the story seemed to be coming together but not all of it. He was relieved to be in Ottawa General and not in psychiatric care at the Royal. Not being at the Royal at least made all that had happened a possibility. He didn't think he'd gone away, as he could remember things, including much that he didn't want to.

A detective, Sergeant Derek Scott, had been there earlier, before Christa had walked in. He'd left Ethan struggling with more questions than answers. Parts of what had happened were clear in his mind. Some he remembered, some he didn't, and some he just left out. He shook his head anytime Syd was mentioned. Syd was the hero. He was okay with that. Syd had saved his life. That she'd had anything to do with their abduction and their capture would remain with him for now.

Christa was still sitting on his bed, holding his hand, when Carlyn and his parents knocked on the open door. Christa stood up and stepped out without a word.

His mother, with his father by her side, was in immediate tears.

"Oh, Ethan," she sobbed, "you have no idea. I'm so sorry."

He'd seen little of them since their Christmas fiasco. His mother held and squeezed his bare hand. That was enough. Carlyn stood at the foot of his bed. Her eyes were bloodshot. His father put his arm around his mother's shoulders.

"I don't think Ottawa's your town, Son," he said, shaking his head, his face trying a smile that his eyes weren't up to.

"I hate it here," Carlyn said, shaking her head. "Ya gotta get outta here, Ethan. It's creepy."

They stayed until Greg and Gus came to the open door. They were all staying at the same hotel and had had breakfast together. Greg and Gus hadn't left Ottawa since Ethan and Syd had disappeared.

"We'll be back later," said his mother, holding his left hand in both of hers.

He winced as she raised his arm. The image of a stuck X-Acto knife surfaced.

"Oh, Ethan, I'm sorry." Tears filled her eyes. She let go of his hand and turned away. She headed to the door without saying another word. He knew she couldn't.

"Like your mother said," his father added, as if he could think of nothing else to say, "we'll see you later on."

Greg and Gus closed around his bed as his parents left. Carlyn stayed a little longer, as if she wanted to say something, but then she just waved and left.

"Have you seen Syd?" Ethan asked. As he asked the question, he remembered hearing Syd's voice in the shaking vehicle, which now felt more dreamlike than real.

"Syd's not saying much," Greg said, his eyes as bloodshot as Carlyn's. Ethan wondered if it was for the same reason. "Unbelievable, Eth. She's messed up."

"How you doin'?" Gus asked.

Ethan thought for a moment. Both his legs were in casts on the bed in front of him. The doctor—Dr. Ramey maybe—seemed most concerned about getting fluids into his body. An intravenous was stuck in each arm. He had cracked ribs and a broken nose. His face, especially around his eyes, was badly bruised and swollen, but it had no fractures. His right leg would require more surgery and was pinned with a rod and plate for now. It would be weeks, if not months, before he could put weight on it. Two bones were broken in his left foot, which doctors had set the night before. He had ligament damage in his right knee but didn't yet know how severe it was. Repairing his broken bones and getting him hydrated were the first priorities. He had a splint on his broken baby finger. Plastic surgery would fix his ear, but there'd always be a chunk missing from it. He had deep cuts on both upper arms that required stitches. It all hurt. The painkillers took the edge off but did little for the hurt.

That was the stuff that could be seen.

"Pretty good, I think," Ethan said, "short of what's coming."

Gus nodded. "Good to have you back, buddy."

"Ya got that right," Greg said, appearing to pick at something on the bed's blanket.

No sooner had Greg spoken than Randolph stuck his head in the doorway. His girlfriend, Rachel, was beside him.

"Man, oh man, Ethan Jones in the flesh," Randolph said, all but ignoring Greg and Gus. "You're a sight for sore eyes."

"Randolph," Ethan said, his face suddenly hurting under the bandages around his face. He'd smiled.

"Still Randolph," Randolph replied, seeming noticeably pleased to see him. He was dressed in a brown suit and white cotton shirt. An open camel-hair overcoat revealed a brown plaid scarf. It was the first time Ethan had thought of the cold outside, even though everyone was dressed for the wintery weather. "Haven't left Ottawa since I heard. I needed someone to call me Randolph."

Randolph was grinning, but his face wasn't smiling, as his eyes seemed to take in the extent of Ethan's injuries. He turned to Rachel but didn't say anything.

"I brought along something I thought you'd like," he said. His right hand slipped inside his jacket. His eyes shifted toward Greg and Gus. "And you won't be the only one."

For an instant, Ethan was scared, unsure what Randolph was reaching for. The beeping heart-rate monitor sped up. Black boots flashed in Ethan's head.

Randolph pulled a small cassette tape out of his jacket pocket and held it out in front of him. "In my hand, I hold the official recorded songs of the Release," he said.

Ethan slowly turned his head. His neck hurt.

"No way," Greg said, nearly stretching the two words into one in expressing his disbelief.

"Yes, my friends," Randolph said, "you are now immortalized on tape for the world to hear."

He placed the tape on the bed beside Ethan, but Ethan didn't move. He remembered the tape he'd given Carlyn.

"I'll bring you a player later," Gus said.

"I've a couple more tapes in the car," Randolph said, putting his arm around Rachel. "I didn't know I'd see you guys here."

He introduced Rachel to Greg and Gus.

Ethan closed his eyes. He'd done nothing yet was exhausted. It seemed easier to listen with his eyes closed. He heard a few words exchanged between Gus and Randolph—something about a song. He didn't catch which one.

The song he heard changed. He didn't know what it was. He was in the wood chair, facing a calendar hanging on a blank wall. The calendar had the title *Browning Station*. *X*'s marked off days in the first two rows of the month, followed by a row of blank squares. In the middle of the bottom row was a square with something handwritten inside. He couldn't read it from where he sat. He went to reach for the calendar, but his arms were strapped to the chair. He stopped. He mustn't move. He knew the rules. There were consequences in breaking them. His eyes went back to the calendar. The words were now visible: "Last day to live. Love, Sean."

The scream was his. He heard it before he knew it.

"Ethan," said the sweetest voice he knew.

Someone touched his chest and then his arm.

"Ethan?"

The slits of his swollen eyes opened to the most beautiful face in the world. Christa was leaning over him.

"It's okay, Ethan," she said. "I'm here."

Christa was alone.

His hand rose to touch the gauze bandages on his face. He could feel his hand on the bandages. In some places, he could feel his touch; other places he couldn't feel at all. "Damaged nerves," the doctor had explained. "Give it time." He ached but couldn't tell where—everywhere. He was hungry but didn't want food. His weight was down. They fed his arms. He was alive.

The door opened. Someone looked in.

Ethan saw who it was.

Christa's hand moved from his arm.

He reached out for it.

"I saw the book," he said as she turned and looked at him.

"The book?" Christa asked, her left eyebrow rising. "What book?"

Jonah Vetch entered the room. He didn't say anything.

"*Browning Station*," Ethan whispered, as if Christa should know. "I brought it with me when leaving Ottawa but could never find it when we got home."

Christa tilted her head and squinted, as if asking him to go on.

He didn't. Instead, he looked at Jonah.

"Good to see you awake," Jonah said, sounding hesitant.

"Just."

"I'll only stay a minute," he said. "I flew up as soon as I heard."

"Thanks," Ethan replied.

"How are you?" Jonah asked, moving to the bed opposite Christa and standing on the other side.

"Can't really tell yet," Ethan said, "but I'm alive. Christa, this is Jonah Vetch. Jonah, this is Christa White."

They shook hands over Ethan's legs.

"I know I interrupted," Jonah said quickly, "but I had to see you for myself."

"Thanks," Ethan said again. Something about seeing Jonah pleased him. He didn't know why. Though Jonah's overcoat was buttoned, instead of looking orderly, as he normally did, his longish brown hair was messy.

"I'll drop by for a few minutes in the morning," Jonah added, already backing toward the door. "Lots to talk about. Nice to meet you, Christa." He turned to Ethan. "See you tomorrow."

He waved and left.

Christa looked at Ethan. "That was quick," she said, sitting down beside him.

"Sean stole it," Ethan said.

"What?"

"The book—*Browning Station*. Randolph said I carried it everywhere in the hospital. I thought you'd remember it."

Christa nodded.

"He killed her," Ethan said as if reading a passage from the book.

"What?" Christa said.

"Sean killed Mila," Ethan said. He was staring at the ceiling tiles. "It wasn't Robbie."

Christa looked at him. Her eyes widened. He hadn't told anyone.

"He was using the book to kill me," he said. "William Avery saved me."

"Did he now?" Christa's eyes shifted from Ethan's to the sheets on his bed. "You know, I do kind of remember seeing the book around."

"I can't believe you don't remember."

"I do, Ethan," Christa said, looking back at him with a tear on her cheek. "*Browning Station,* huh? Kind of an odd title for a book, don't you think?"

The End

CPSIA information can be obtained
at www.ICGtesting.com
Printed in the USA
LVHW041531180419
614686LV00002B/341